NEMESIS

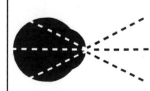

This Large Print Book carries the
Seal of Approval of N.A.V.H.

NEMESIS

THE FINAL CASE OF ELIOT NESS

WILLIAM BERNHARDT

THORNDIKE PRESS

A part of Gale, Cengage Learning

GALE
CENGAGE Learning·

Detroit • New York • San Francisco • New Haven, Conn • Waterville, Maine • London

GALE
CENGAGE Learning™

LIBRARY OF CONGRESS CATALOGING-IN-PUBLICATION DATA

Bernhardt, William, 1960–
  Nemesis : the final case of Eliot Ness / by William Bernhardt.
    p. cm. — (Thorndike Press large print thriller)
  ISBN-13: 978-1-4104-1502-8 (alk. paper)
  ISBN-10: 1-4104-1502-3 (alk. paper)
  1. Ness, Eliot—Fiction. 2. Serial
murders—Ohio—Cleveland—Fiction. 3. Murder—
Investigation—Fiction. 4. Large type books. I. Title.
PS3552.E73147N46 2009b
813'.54—dc22   2008054779

Published in 2009 by arrangement with The Ballantine Publishing
Group, a division of Random House, Inc.

Printed in the United States of America
1 2 3 4 5 6 7 13 12 11 10 09

FOR JOHN WOOLEY
I couldn't have a better friend.
Kachow!

Things fall apart; the centre cannot hold;

Mere anarchy is loosed upon the world,

The blood-dimmed tide is loosed, and
everywhere

The ceremony of innocence is drowned.

— "The Second Coming,"
William Butler Yeats (1920)

PROLOGUE

February 16, 1957

The days were all the same now.

The best part of Eliot Ness's day was breakfast with Bobby. His marriage with Betty had its ups and downs, as had his previous two marriages. She was an artist, a sculptor. He had no idea whether she was talented but ohe certainly had an artist's temperament. Her suggestion that they adopt a child, however, had been a brilliant stroke that had transformed their lives, only for the better. All his life he had been awkward around children. Now he was a doting father who never missed an opportunity to spend time with his only son.

Most people expected a corporate president to be a busy man. Instead, Ness found himself getting more idle by the day. The North Ridge Alliance Corporation had been in trouble for a long time now, almost from the start. It had started with such a brilliant idea. Using a special watermarking technique, they would produce checks that could not be forged. He would be providing a useful service — and still stopping crime, in a new way.

But the truth was, he had no head for business. One of his partners had run off with the corporate secrets and started his own corporation. Then they were denied a patent because there were other preexisting watermarking firms. They had moved their offices from Cleveland to Coudersport, Pennsylvania, a small town near the New York border, to reduce expenses. But it wasn't enough. They were holding on by their fingertips and the money coming in wasn't nearly enough to pay the bills.

And that was how the great hero of the Prohibition era ended up in a backwater burg in Pennsylvania without a penny in savings and exceedingly poor prospects. Who would blame him if he took lunch at the same bar and grill every day, a pastrami sandwich with a whiskey chaser? Maybe two. A quick stop at the store and he was home with far too little to do until Betty and Bobby got home. He would pour a drink, sit in his favorite easy chair, and remember when every day had been packed with more excitement and activity than most people could handle . . .

The doorbell rang.

"Hey, Oscar. You're early."

"That okay?"

"Sure. I'm not doing anything."

"I just wanted to get some work done before you were . . . you know. Before you got too tired. It's hard, trying to remember stuff that happened so long ago."

"Yeah."

Ness let Oscar Fraley into his home. He liked Fraley. He was a good listener. He was a friend of Ness's partner, Joe Phelps. A sportswriter, by trade. They'd met in a bar where Ness was telling his stories, as usual. But unlike most, Fraley seemed genuinely interested. He believed what Ness told him, or at least acted as if he did. And unlike most of the young punks at the Bar and Grill these days, Fraley remembered who Al Capone was.

"Like a drink?" Ness asked, hiccuping.

"No thanks," Fraley said. "Not while I'm working. But you go on ahead."

"Don't mind if I do," Ness replied, refilling his glass. "Helps me remember."

"Can we pick up where we left off last time? You and your people had finally put away Al Capone. For tax evasion."

"Yeah. People made fun of us for putting

away a killer on such lame grounds. But it worked. Me and my boys kept him busy, preoccupied, a constant thorn in his side, while Frank Wilson slowly put together a case proving Capone wasn't paying his taxes. We got him off the street, out of Chicago. He wasted away in prison — he had syphilis, you know. He got out, but my buddies tell me he was a broken man, barely able to dress himself or go to the toilet without help. Finally died about ten years ago. The tax charge did what we wanted. It put an end to the bloody reign of Al Capone."

"I gather you feel no shame about the way you did it."

"None at all. To the contrary, we were proud of ourselves for using our brains for once. Being creative. That's what the times were like back then. Learning something different every day. New scientific discoveries. Forensic labs solving crimes detectives couldn't. How long could criminals survive in this brave new scientific world? We thought we'd found the cure for crime. We thought we could end it for all time."

His eyes darkened. "But it turns out, crime is more resilient than we realized. It's — what's that term scientists are using now? It's a mutating organism. It adapts to new environments. Builds up resistance to the vaccine. We may have figured out how to deal with people like Capone — but something new, something different came along to take their place. Something we had no idea how to handle."

"Are you talking about Cleveland? The Torso Murderer?"

Ness took a long draw from his drink. "I don't want to talk about that."

"Why not? It's a great story. Scary, suspenseful, and filled with —"

"I don't want to talk about it. I don't want anything about it in this book you're writing. You understand me? Nothing!"

Oscar held up his hands. "All right, Eliot, stay calm. Don't work yourself up. We'll stick with the Capone saga."

"Good." There was no reason to get into the rest of it. No reason at all. So few knew anything about it these days, outside of Cleveland. Better to keep it that way.

If only there was some way he could make himself forget . . .

1

September 13, 1935

It was just after three in the morning and the glint of moonlight off the metal barrel of Michael Frescone's tommy gun told Eliot Ness he was exactly where he wanted to be.

"Let's get back to the car and radio for backup."

Ness's eyes remained glued to the binoculars. "We don't have time, Sheriff."

"We don't have a choice. Those mob guys are serious trouble."

"They always are."

"They got guns."

"They always do."

"They ain't afraid to use 'em, neither!"

"That remains to be seen."

"Some of Frescone's men are crack shots. Like to brag about how they can hit a Nehi bottle from fifty paces."

Ness pushed a loose strand of hair back into place, slicked-back and parted in the center. "Well, I'm not so sorry with a pistol myself, Sheriff. Won a marksmanship award at the U.S. Coast Guard range."

Cuyahoga County sheriff Ray Potts looked as though he were about to internally combust. "Do you understand what we're talking about here? There's two of us and a dozen of them. They're heavily armed and they're killers! Frescone has been blamed for at least ten gangland murders. They're transporting illegal hooch worth thousands of dollars and they'll do anything to defend it. These are impossible odds, Ness. Impossible!"

Ness glanced at his colleague. In the moonlight, his eyes seemed to twinkle. "Sounds like fun. Ready?"

Ness climbed out of the ditch they were using for cover and headed toward the dock. While he crept forward, he put away his binoculars and unholstered his pistol. He was always more comfortable with a handgun than those bulky machine guns. He'd learned to shoot with accuracy, even from a distance, and he preferred that to the spray-everything-in-sight technique of the tommy gun.

The slope was steep. He had to be careful — and quiet. If the smugglers heard him coming, he'd be a goner. His only chance was to catch them by surprise.

The wind coming off the river chilled him, sending shivers coursing up and down his spine. Seemed no matter how many times he did this, the gnawing in the pit of his stomach, the strange combination of exhilaration and terror, never entirely subsided. Probably just as well. If he ever lost that edge, he might get sloppy. The rest of the world thought he was fearless — well, that was fine. Only he need know better. Only he needed to know that he got scared every time. And it supercharged him like nothing else could.

He chose each step cautiously, testing it before he put his weight down, careful to move as silently as possible . . .

"Stay down!" Potts hissed. "If they see you they'll blow you from here to perdition! Let me tell you — there ain't nothing scarier than staring down the wrong end of a gangster's gat."

"When I worked in Kentucky as a revenue agent, I got shot at six different times," Ness whispered back. "Those hillbillies holed up in the Moonshine Mountains with their squirrel guns gave me more close calls than Capone's whole gang put together."

Ness never wanted to leave Chicago, his hometown, but he was in government service so he had followed orders. After Prohibition ended, he spent about a year working in Ohio, Tennessee, and Kentucky for the Alcohol Tax Unit within the Bureau of Internal Revenue, chasing down backwoods rumrunners. It was tough work. Things had been simpler in Chicago, when the Volstead Act was still in place. Booze was illegal, period. You saw it, you seized it. And you took the criminals to jail. But Prohibition had been repealed in 1933. Ness didn't object on principle; he enjoyed a drink every now and then. But the new liquor laws complicated his work. He arrested moonshiners, not because they had booze, but because the rotgut they distilled from heaven-knows-what could be dangerous, tainted with leads and sometimes lethal. More important, at least from the standpoint of the federal government, they didn't pay liquor taxes or import duties.

Frescone got his illegal hooch someplace in the blue hills of Kentucky and smuggled it upriver into Chicago. The mob controlled the flow of corn syrup, the easiest and cheapest way to make moonshine liquor, which allowed them to control distribution as soon as the hooch was hatched. He'd been waiting for more than an hour, watching the men unloading casks from the boat and carrying them into a dockside warehouse not far from the Detroit-Superior High Level Bridge. Just a few minutes before, a truck had pulled up, probably to transport the goods to their final destination, one of the Irish gambling parlors that sprang up during Prohibition and remained illegal.

Ness stopped his slow descent. There was no chance of moving any closer without being detected.

"Do we have a plan?" Sheriff Potts asked. They were only about twenty feet from the warehouse. Ness could see two men in white undershirts loading the truck. " 'Cause I would feel a lot better if we had a plan."

"I do my planning before I leave the office." Ness watched as the docked boat pushed off, back onto the river, taking six of the men with it. That left four men inside, two loading. They would never have a better opportunity.

The dockside double doors were closed and, judging from the sound, bolted with a wooden crossbar. A few more minutes and the truck would be loaded and the hooch would be gone. "Still got that long axe?"

Potts passed him the sharp implement. "I

don't think running in there with an axe is the same as having a plan."

"Worked well enough in Chicago."

"This ain't Chicago."

"You're right about that. Let's go."

"Wait just a —"

Too late. Ness was already running down the wooden planked bridge that led to the dock. Sheriff Potts swore silently and followed. Ness stopped in front of the warehouse doors and, without hesitating a second, swung the axe.

The crash of metal against the doors was like a crack of thunder splitting the silence of the night. The wet and weathered wood splintered easily. Potts looked frantically all about them. So far as he could tell, no one was coming this way and no one was shooting at them. Yet.

Ness turned just in time to see the two men previously loading the truck leap into the front seat and speed away. Cut and run at the first sign of trouble — that must have been their working orders. Which was just fine with him. Now the enemy's numbers were down to four.

With the second swing of the axe, Ness severed the crossbar holding the doors closed, but a lock still held them together. With the third swing, he tore open a passage wide enough to step through.

He dropped the axe and grabbed his pistol. "Best hurry," he told Potts. "I imagine they know we're here." He winked, then pushed through the opening.

"Freeze! Federal agent!"

Four men in gray pinstriped suits and white hats stared back at him.

"Hands in the air!"

They complied. They seemed neither threatened not threatening.

Come to think of it, Ness thought, this really *isn't* the same as Chicago.

"Something I can do for you, sir?"

Ness recognized Michael Frescone. The droopy left eye he'd picked up in his boxing days and his acne-scarred skin were unmistakable. Plug-ugly — and dangerous. Not just because he was a killer — they all were. But Frescone had the added threat of being smart.

The warehouse was almost completely filled with wooden barrel casks. The kind moonshiners favored.

Ness approached slowly, winding his way through the barrels, his pistol poised, keeping his eye on the four men. "I'm holding you under suspicion of violating the federal tax laws by illegal importation. I have a warrant to search this warehouse. You have the right to examine it."

Frescone remained calm. "Not necessary. Search all you like."

"You're very obliging."

"Least I can do to show my respect to a duly appointed officer of the law."

The three goons with Frescone exchanged confused glances. Ness knew they were wondering if their boss wanted them to take him on, and if so, whether they could do it. And who would make the first move.

"Don't try anything foolish, gentlemen," Frescone said calmly.

More furtive glances. No one spoke.

"Good." Ness tugged at the lid of the nearest cask. It didn't budge. He turned slightly to face his companion. "Potts, get —"

Ness only looked away for a moment, but it was long enough. The goon nearest him lunged forward, swinging. Ness blocked the punch and delivered one of his own to the stomach. The attacker lashed out again, but Ness ducked and the only thing the thug punched was air. Angry, the man rushed forward, arms outstretched. Ness whirled around and reached back over his shoulder, grabbing the man's left hand. With one fluid motion, he pulled the man over and, thrusting upward with his back, flipped him into the air. The man fell in a heap among the casks.

Ness leveled his gun again. "Anyone else?"

Frescone's lips parted. "What — was that?"

Ness smiled, a guileless grin that lifted years off his already boyish face. "Jujitsu."

"What?"

"Something I learned in college."

Frescone twisted his neck. "Swell way to keep the flies off. Maybe I should learn it."

"Requires discipline. You couldn't do it." Ness glanced over his shoulder. "Potts, get the axe."

The sheriff scrambled back outside, then returned.

Ness pointed to the nearest cask. "Get the lid off this thing."

It took the sheriff eight tries, but he finally managed to pry off the lid, expecting to see a dark, potently pungent liquid.

Instead, Ness found a white gelatinous substance. He put his hand in and rubbed a little of it between his fingers.

"Thing is," Frescone said, his eyebrows dancing, "I didn't realize the government was taxing cold cream."

Ness looked up. "Cold cream? You're smuggling cold cream?"

" 'Smuggling' is such a dirty word. Try

'importing.' Turns out there's a big demand for this stuff here in Cleveland. Your wife probably uses it to take off her makeup at night, when you two get done cutting the rug at those downtown jazz clubs. Edna, right?"

Ness glared at him with narrowed eyes.

"So I'm having this stuff sent down to my factory on the wharf and they'll bottle it and we'll get it into the stores for Christmas. Should make a killing. If you know what I mean."

"You went to all this trouble to import cold cream? In the dead of the night?"

"Just a simple business transaction. I work long hours. It's the secret of my success."

"Or a diversion. The real hooch is coming in somewhere else. Probably the Ohio River. South side." Ness paused. "Someone tipped you off."

"I receive information from many sources. Nothing illegal about that."

"No, but it's illegal to be the rat-fink turncoat traitor."

"Such language. You're not yourself. I'm afraid this evening has been something of an embarrassment for you, Mr. Ness. The great all-American hero is looking fairly stupid this time."

Ness smiled. "That's where you're wrong,

Frescone. I got exactly what I wanted."

"You think shipping cold cream is a crime?"

"I learned a long time ago that you can't catch crooks if you can't trust your own men. You've got to root out the dirty ones and work with what's left. The untouchables. The point of this operation wasn't to seize your booze. Though I will, in time. The point was to find out who the stoolie was. Now it's clear. It has to be someone inside the county sheriff's office."

Potts stepped forward. "What? Are you slandering my department?"

"With the truth."

Potts pounded his fists together and swore. "I guess you figure someone back at the office tipped off Frescone."

"I think I can narrow the field more than that."

"But you told the whole office we were making this raid."

"True. But I told everyone else we were going after the gambling parlor in the basement of Hannigan's Hardware."

"You're saying — you lied?"

"I still plan to raid the hardware store. The night is young."

"But then — what was the point —"

"Here's the thing — I only told one

25

person I traced a load of illegal hooch to the Cuyahoga and I was coming out tonight to raid the warehouse before the stuff slipped into the city." Ness pressed his finger into Potts's lapel. "You."

The expressions on the faces of Frescone and his men were nothing short of astonished.

Sheriff Potts took a step back, slapping away Ness's hand. "What are you playing at, Ness? They're the criminals!"

"There are many different kinds of criminals, unfortunately, Sheriff."

"If you think for one minute that I'm involved in this lowlife moonshine operation —"

"Oh, you're a lot more than involved. You and five of your men, including your deputy, John Lavery, have built up a little bootlegging empire over the last five years, haven't you? It started with holding up moonshiners coming in from Steubenville and demanding payoffs. Pretty soon, you wanted more than a piece of the action. You wanted to run the show."

"That's a filthy lie."

Ness didn't blink. "Your bank records show you've been making real estate investments far beyond anything you could afford on your sheriff's salary."

"I came into an inheritance."

"I've found payoff records that an expert will testify are in your handwriting. But I didn't have any conclusive proof, and I didn't think your buddies on either side of the river were likely to help. So I told you about this little raid tonight and waited to see if you'd tell your friends. You did. Now I have my evidence."

Frescone spoke hesitantly. "You knew he'd tip us off? You knew —"

"Yes, I knew you'd send the booze somewhere else."

"And you're not taking us in?"

"Not tonight. But I will." Ness slid the cuffs over Potts's wrists. "Come along, Sheriff. You've just been voted out of office."

2

"So you'll come back to my place?"

"Sure, mister. I don't mind."

"That's very obliging of you."

"The customer is always right."

"A noble attitude."

"It works."

"And you don't mind if things get . . . a trifle unusual?"

"Believe me, mister. I've seen it all before."

He smiled. "You never know."

Perfection itself. Why kidnap someone when you could persuade them to come with you voluntarily? That made it ever so much simpler to travel through Kingsbury Run unnoticed, to bring her back to the brewery. To do what he wanted to do to her.

"No one works here?" she asked, as she walked around the abandoned building.

"Not anymore. Prohibition put it out of business."

"Shame. I like a beer every so often. How

'bout you?"

"I prefer something stronger."

"I pegged you for a drinker."

"Now and again."

"Pardon me for sayin' so, but you seem a little too classy to be hangin' out in Kingsbury Run."

"Appearances can be deceiving. Have you seen the Sailors' Home?"

"Sure. Oh — I get it. You really do like a drink now and again."

"Just as I said."

He removed the plank in the floor, took out the ropes, and tied her to the chair.

"Hey, what's that about?"

"Just a harmless ritual. I'm . . . complicated."

"I get it. You like a girl to seem helpless. Like you're in control."

"Something like that."

"Hey, can you loosen them knots a little? I'm not sure I can move."

"I'm not sure I want you to move."

He shoved her and her chair forward across the table. Her hands were tied behind her back; her legs were tied together. Her torso was flattened across the length of the table while her head dangled off the edge.

"Hey, this is gettin' weird." For the first time, her voice contained a trace of apprehension.

"You said you were ready for anything."

"Look, you want to take me that way, just do it."

"That isn't what I had in mind."

"You're not trying to get some action?"

"Not in the way that you mean."

"You're some kinda customer."

"I'm a man of science."

" 'Zat so? What's this, an experiment?"

"You could say that."

"Hey — what's with the axe?" Her voice had passed well beyond the point of apprehension. She was scared.

He took careful aim. If he judged it correctly, one slice would be sufficient to sever the head at the level of the third intervertebral disk . . .

He swung. It worked. Severed in a single slice. Superb.

But what is the point if no one knows? How could there be any pleasure in that?

He liked swinging the axe. It was a good feeling. He liked using his physical strength. They let him use knives at the hospital, scalpels, but never anything like this. This was better. From now on, he would devote his energies to the endeavors that truly mattered. Not the coddling of the sick and infirm. Something on a grander scale.

The blood rolled down the slanted floor and into the drainage tunnel. So much could be discarded that way. She had told him she loved the waters. Perhaps she would have chosen it for her final resting place. Perhaps he would choose it for her.

She had not screamed when the axe touched her neck. That was a disappointment. It happened all too swiftly. There was no time to react, no chance to savor the moment.

He would learn from his mistakes.

He pushed open the sliding door and stepped outside, brushing the blood from his apron as he walked. Across the river, the smoke and dirt hovering over the city made a visible cloud that never cleared. He preferred it here, away from the mad traffic, the insane hustling back and forth, the people who thought they were so modern but in fact had no idea what modern was.

He would show them.

Something new had come to town.

3

December 1, 1935

Cleveland's city hall was one of the older sandstone buildings in a metropolis where even the newer buildings didn't look good anymore. There was no money for improvements, not in the middle of the Depression and the most sluggish economy in history. Nonetheless, Mayor Harold Burton reflected, gazing out his office's wide double window, it wouldn't matter what they did to the buildings, not so long as that perpetual dark cloud hung over the city, day and night, regardless of the weather. He should be able to see the Terminal Tower rising above the other buildings like an arm stretched to heaven. Not anymore. The Tower was still there. But the dark cloud rendered it invisible.

He pressed a hand against his back. It still ached. Why had he agreed to those dancing lessons? Of course, he wanted to please his wife. He needed her on his team, especially during the campaign. But that music — what they were now calling "swing"? Hideous. And the rumba. Who thought they needed a new way of dancing? Give him a waltz any day.

"Mr. Mayor?"

Burton slowly turned about in his swivel chair. He still hadn't gotten used to it. Had they stolen this from a barber shop? As soon as he thought no one would notice, he was bringing in a chair from home. A good steady chair that kept four feet on the floor and didn't move.

"Wes. Please come in."

Wes Lawrence had earned his right to the mayor's ear. He had been one of Burton's leading supporters, contributing both finances and wisdom to the campaign. Burton would've listened to Lawrence, though, even if he hadn't played a role in the campaign. The man was street smart. Savvy, particularly about politics.

Burton gestured toward the chair on the opposite side of his desk. "What brings you to my office, Wes?"

Lawrence tugged at his pleated pants before taking the chair. "I wondered if you've given any thought to what you're going to do?"

"Can you be a little more precise?"

"You were elected as a Reform mayor, Harold. On a Reform ticket." His eyebrows rose. "So what are you going to reform first?"

"Honestly, Wes? I don't know how much a mayor really can do. Only the legislature —"

"That kind of thinking will not go down well with the press."

"Wes, I handled the Huns during the Great War. I think I can handle a few scribblers."

"Unfortunately, being a war hero won't get you reelected. Only the people can do that."

"Isn't it too early to be thinking about reelection? I just won the first one."

"It's never too early to think about reelection."

"Relax already." He pulled a sizable humidor out of his bottom desk drawer. "Have a cigar. They're from Havana. Best in the world."

"I'm not interested in tobacco. I'm interested in knowing what return I'm getting for my investment. We've spent too much time and money to end up with a one-term mayor."

Burton folded his hands flat and sighed.

"Fine, fine. What societal ill would you like me to tackle first?"

"You know what's wrong with this city as well as I do. You talked about it enough during your campaign. The mob is taking over. We may not have an Al Capone but we have a lot of little terrors who might add up to something worse. Racketeers control the unions. Our traffic system is chaotic. The economy stinks. We've got a shantytown filled with poor and itinerant unemployed, people who can't afford to live in anything better than a shed or a cardboard box. Women, children, living in conditions like that, searching through garbage cans for something to eat."

"So many choices. Where shall I begin?"

Lawrence continued. "The police department is thoroughly corrupt. Gambling parlors thrive. Juvenile crime is at an all-time high. Prostitution —"

"All right, I get the message. But I'm still just the mayor."

"You have to do something."

"Look, pick the issue you think will play best and I'll propose a municipal directive —"

Lawrence shook his head. "You can't get personally involved."

"Excuse me? You just said —"

"Do you really think you can solve any of those problems? Because I don't. I don't think anyone can. If you get personally involved, you'll sink like you were in quicksand."

"So if I understand you, Lawrence, you want me to appear to be working on the city's problems without actually working on the city's problems because any effort to solve the city's problems is doomed to failure. Is that about right?"

"I knew you'd come to understand politics one day, Harold."

Burton leaned forward across his desk. "Then what is it you want me to do?"

Lawrence paused a few moments before answering. "The position of Safety Director remains vacant."

Burton blew air through his teeth. "Lavelle turned that job into a joke."

"It doesn't have to be. The right man, with ample authority, could restore credibility. You need someone with a higher profile." He opened his briefcase and pulled out a copy of the *Plain Dealer.* "Read the paper this morning?"

Burton grimaced. "I saw the piece about the disembodied torso. Think that was a mob rubout?"

"Probably. But the article I'm interested

in is on page three." Lawrence spread the paper across Burton's desk and pointed.

G-MAN NESS CLEANS UP LIQUOR RING.

Burton shrugged. "So? The city's got a lot worse problems than illegal booze."

"I agree. Almost trivial compared to police corruption and deadly traffic. But —" He stopped, then leaned back into his chair. "How much do you know about Eliot Ness?"

"Who?"

"You're kidding me. You don't know who Eliot Ness is?"

"Not that I recall."

"Treasury agent. Formerly in Chicago. Provided the testimony that got Capone indicted on Volstead and conspiracy allegations."

Burton thought for a moment. "Didn't they put Capone away for income tax evasion?"

"Yes. They could never make the other charges stick. But Ness and his so-called Untouchables hounded him for years. And Ness got a lot of favorable coverage in the process. The press loves this man. That baby face and unassuming modesty make for a very appealing image. He can afford to be modest — his accomplishments speak for themselves. Dwight Green, one of the

37

prosecutors in the Capone case, gave him a ringing endorsement. William Clegg, foreman on the Capone grand jury, was also a big booster. I've talked to them both. They tell me you couldn't find a straighter arrow if you searched the world over. They call him an American hero — maybe the last of his kind. Hardworking, honest to a fault. He's been offered all kinds of bribes and payoffs. Turned them all down."

"And you want me to bring him to Cleveland?"

"Read the article, Harold. He's already here. Has been for months. The Alcohol Tax Unit posted him here as a special-investigator-in-charge."

"Why here?"

"Because according to the Feds, we have more bootleg liquor passing through our town than anyplace else in the country. And from here it flows into all the major eastern cities."

"Then maybe we should let Mr. Ness do the work he's been assigned."

"I hear he's frustrated. Thinks he can do more. Applied for the FBI. Got turned down."

"If your man is so amazing, why would the FBI turn him down?"

Lawrence inched forward. "This is just

between you and me. But what my sources tell me is that J. Edgar Hoover doesn't like agents who attract more publicity than he does. While Hoover's made a name for himself catching hick bank robbers, Ness went after organized crime, which according to Hoover doesn't exist."

Burton snipped off the end of a cigar and lit it, puffing till it caught. "I'm not so fond of people who attract better publicity than I do, either."

"No need to worry. He may be good with the press, but he's politically inexperienced. Doesn't understand the machinery."

"And I do."

"You have me to advise you."

"Still sounds like a potential scene-stealer."

"But don't you see, Harold? If you appoint him, anything good he does is a feather in your cap. You benefit even more than he does. And if he fails, well, it wasn't your fault. You did everything you could."

Burton puffed on his large, long stogie. "I like that part." He thought a moment. "But I think Safety Director is too high profile. I'd rather have someone safer. Maybe Robert Turkel."

"Turkel is a desk man. You need someone more visible. Ness hates to be deskbound.

Always goes out on the raids with his men. Been shot at more than half a dozen times."

Burton mulled it over, rolling the cigar between his fingers. "Maybe I could just put him in the police department. Make him some kind of special investigator."

Lawrence shook his head vigorously. "How can he clean up the police department if they can fire him? Plus, he would be limited to police duties, and they can't improve the traffic fatalities or the congestion or the exhaust fumes so thick you can't step outside without getting nauseated. No, he needs to be completely independent. And he needs all the executive authority you can give him. All the powers and support of the mayor's office."

Burton blew a cloud of smoke into the air. "That's a lot of power to give an unknown variable."

"It takes a lot of power to accomplish a big job. And right now, Cleveland is a big job."

Burton leaned across his desk. "Now you're sounding like you really think this Buster Brown can clean up Cleveland."

"Sometimes underdogs prevail."

"I don't see it happening here."

"No one thought Braddock could take down Baer, either. But he did."

"On points."

"No one thought Omaha would win the Triple Crown."

"This isn't sports, Wes, and I'd like a straight answer. Do you think Ness can clean up this town?"

Lawrence waited a long time before answering. "I think it is important to your political future, Harold, that you be perceived as doing everything you can to clean up Cleveland. That's what Reform candidates do. Hiring a hero to tidy up the joint can only make you look good. Even if it turns out that taking on a big city hurting bad is a little tougher than putting away Sicilian rumrunners. With him on your team, you can't be faulted for not trying to make a difference." He reached down for his briefcase. "He's your ticket to reelection, Harold."

Burton contemplated a moment, then spread his hands expansively across his desk. "All right, then, Wes. You win. Have the junior g-man come and see me."

4

"Can't you throw any harder than that?"

"I could, but you couldn't catch it."

"Aw, baloney. You throw like a girl."

"No, you catch like a girl."

"I ain't had any trouble catchin' anythin' you've thrown."

"I been holdin' back. I don't wanna scare you." Jimmy Wagner and Peter Kostura had been playing catch for the better part of an hour. Jimmy was glad to have the company, though he would never admit it. Peter was four years younger than he was, a mere twelve, and he knew he'd get ribbed by some of the kids on the street if they knew he was messing around with such a punk. But where were they now? Truth to tell, there wasn't much to do this time of year in Cleveland. Especially on Kingsbury Run. So they played catch on Jackass Hill. What else was there?

"All right," Peter screeched. His voice still

hadn't changed, and it tended to break when he got loud. "You asked for it." He reared back his arm and tossed the baseball with all his might.

Jimmy caught it without trouble. "Oooh. My hand is stingin'." He laughed. "The Bambino probably couldn't hit that one."

"He's a goner."

"He's retired. He ain't never gonna be a goner." Jimmy grinned. "But you are."

"Yeah? Let's see what you can do."

"Happy to oblige." With the advantage of four more years of muscles, well-honed by the menial jobs he worked to keep himself fed, Jimmy hurled the ball back.

Peter caught it. "Hah! See, you ain't exactly Lou Gehrig yourself."

Jimmy grinned. He hadn't thrown the ball half as hard as he could.

He liked Peter. Kids were everywhere these days: no work, no one watching the schools, lucky if they even had parents. But friends — not just street trash but actual friends — were hard to come by on Kingsbury Run.

His father had told him — the last time he saw the man before he disappeared — that there had been a time when Kingsbury Run was a nice neighborhood. The wide, deep gorge stretched all the way from

Cleveland's industrial area, the Flats, to East 90th Street. Once upon a time, according to his father, people had come here for picnics because the green seemed to stretch forever, and there was a brook and trees that provided shade. Even wildflowers. Folks used to come on dates, his dad had said. It's where I took your momma, first time we stepped out together.

Jimmy had to wonder if his father had made the whole thing up, if it was just as false as a lot of the other stuff he said. Ever since the Crash, as long as Jimmy could remember, Kingsbury Run had been dirt and weeds and trash and bums. Over thirty different railroad tracks crisscrossed the Run, feeding supplies to the factories in the Flats and bringing in trash from all over the country. Hobo Jungle, some folks called it. They built the shantytown that housed the poorest and most desperate of the aimless wanderers who came to town looking for work, looking for a better life, and finding nothing.

Jimmy's family came from the north side of the Run, where most of the colored families congregated, near Woodland Avenue. The working-class white folk lived on the south side of the Run, most of them with funny names he couldn't pronounce.

His father had said those names could give you a clue to what part of Europe or Asia they came from, but he'd never managed to figure it out. He didn't spend that much time on the south side of the Run. He knew he wasn't welcome. Things were more comfortable here, in no-man's-land — at least during the day, when the bums were either scrounging for work or sleeping it off.

"Are we playin' catch or countin' sheep?"

"Sorry," Jimmy mumbled. He lobbed the ball back toward his pal, who caught it with ease. Peter was actually a pretty salty ballplayer, not that he would ever tell the kid that. Course, Peter still saw his dad every now and again. His dad took him to a real-live Indians game at Municipal Stadium. And his mom had a radio, so they could listen to the games and Walter Winchell and *The Shadow* and all the other swell stuff that came over the airwaves.

"Are you ready for my fastball?" Peter shouted.

"I can handle it."

"I'm gonna burn a hole right through your hand."

"Gosh willikers. I'm a-tremblin'."

"You sure you're ready?"

Jimmy cracked a smile. "Give me everythin' you got, champ."

Peter did. He threw the baseball as hard as he could — right over Jimmy's head.

"Aw geez."

He knew they shouldn't have been playing on Jackass Hill. It was great for sledding, when there was snow, but a stupid place to play catch. The ball sailed over the crest of the hill down a sixty-foot slope and into a gully.

"No way I'm goin' down there," Jimmy said.

"Well, I'm not goin'."

"You threw it."

"You missed it!"

Jimmy sighed. This was a bum deal, but it was his only baseball and he didn't want to lose it.

"All right," Jimmy shouted. "You're probably too puny to make it down there and back up again."

"Am not!"

"Prove it."

"Why should both of us go?"

"Because it's a race. Whoever's toughest gets the ball first. Go!"

Both boys tore into action, barreling down the hill as if their shoes were on fire. Jimmy was closest, so he took an early lead, which only got wider as the race proceeded. He still had the advantage of age, not to mention at least fifteen pounds. Despite the fact that it was a cold day, sweat dripped down the side of his face as he ran at his very best speed. He was panting and short of breath, but that didn't matter. His manhood was at stake. He couldn't be beaten by a kid four years younger. Couldn't even let him come close.

Jimmy blazed his way through the bushes and tall grass and weeds till he hit the gully, well ahead of Peter.

"No fair!" Peter cried. "You had a head start!"

Jimmy cackled. "Wimpy!" He adopted a fake, high-pitched British voice. "I'd gladly pay you Tuesday for a hamburger today!"

He scanned the gully, searching for the baseball. The weeds and bushes were mostly stomped down, but it could still be a chore to find something as small as a baseball, particularly one that had already lost most of its cover and was more brown than white.

He started toward the north, tracing the length of the gully, hoping that no matter where the ball went it would eventually roll back to the lowest point. He pushed aside some weeds and something caught his eye —

Jimmy froze, chilled to the bone. His lips parted, but no words came out. He wanted to make a noise, a really loud noise, but he couldn't do it.

Couldn't move, either. And he really truly desperately wanted to move.

Finally, a toe at a time, he managed to get his body working again. He raced back up the hill, twice as fast as he had come down, his eyes wide and his face wild.

He practically collided with Peter. "Don't go down there!"

Peter stared at him, confused. "What? Did you find the ball?"

Jimmy slowly shook his head. "Something else."

"Like what?"

Jimmy grabbed Peter's arm. His hands were ice cold. "Like, a man."

"A man? What kinda man?"

Jimmy could barely form the words. "A man with no head."

5

From the front page of the December 12, 1935, Cleveland *Plain Dealer:*

". . . when this reporter learned that Eliot Ness, formerly an agent for the Treasury Department, has been appointed by Mayor Burton to be the new Safety Director, filling the position vacated by the unpopular Martin J. Lavelle. Apparently Ness had a brief meeting with the mayor yesterday morning, then less than an hour later was sworn in to office. Ness will receive an annual salary of seven thousand five hundred dollars and will have authority over the entire police, fire and traffic control departments . . ."

Ness stepped outside the Central Police Station at 21st and Payne on Cleveland's East side, a four-story sandstone edifice with an imposing façade. He was carrying a large stack of files.

Six reporters were waiting for him on the front steps.

With his free hand, he buttoned his tan camel-hair topcoat, bracing himself against the December chill.

One of the reporters stepped forward. "I'm Jim Crawford of the *Courier.* Are you Eliot Ness?"

Ness nodded. "Guess I'm not as famous as some of the people inside seem to think."

"We heard you were here. It's just — well, you don't look much like a copper."

"Why not?"

" 'Cause you're . . ." He hemmed and hawed, searching for the word.

"Good lookin'?" one of reporters suggested. "Not just another mug?"

"Well, yeah. I mean, not that I care what men look like —"

"Of course not," Ness said.

"But you're dressed nice and you got a soft voice and you look . . ." He scratched his head. "Exactly how old are you?"

"Older than I look."

"And that is?"

Ness grinned. "You members of the fourth estate are relentless. I'm a little past thirty."

The reporter whistled. "Youngest safety

director this city has ever had."

"Sometimes youth can be a good thing."

"Is it true you brought down Al Capone?"

Ness shrugged. "My department did its part, sure. But the tax investigators were the ones who put Capone in prison. My work just got more press, that's all. A midnight raid is a good deal more sensational than an accounting ledger."

"Are you going to start an Untouchables squad here in Cleveland?"

Another big grin. "We'll see."

"What was the first thing you did after the mayor appointed you safety director?"

"I told my wife, naturally."

"What was her reaction?"

For the first time, Ness hesitated before answering. "Edna has always been very supportive of me and my career. She's a fine woman."

Another reporter, with a press pass stuck in the band of his boater and a Brownie camera dangling from his neck, thrust himself forward. "Bill Dowling of the *Cleveland News.* Can you tell us what you were doing here at the police station?"

"Getting to know the people I'm going to be working with. I met the chief of police, George Matowitz."

"What did you think of him?"

51

"I thought he was tall." The reporters laughed. True, Matowitz was six feet, but then, so was Ness.

What Ness really thought was that Matowitz was lazy and uninspired. He might not be corrupt himself, but he was negligent enough to allow corruption to fester. He would never be of any real use, but Ness was careful not to make an enemy. He would need the support of the chief once he started demanding resignations.

"Do you anticipate any problems working with Chief Matowitz?"

"Of course not. Why would there be? We both want the same thing. A clean police department and a safe city."

"The previous safety director never stepped out of his office. Some people see it as a political appointment that never does anyone any good."

"Those days are over," Ness said firmly, his jaw set. "I'm not the supervisor type. I'll be right on the front lines. But first I need to become a little more familiar with the police force and the local crime scene. I need to know this city, inside out." He glanced at the materials he was carrying. "That's what all this is. Homework. City charter. Crime statistics. Maps. You name it."

"That's a lot to bite off."

"I've always been a good student. I'll know more tomorrow and a lot more than that the next day. Goodbye, gentlemen."

Ness started down the stone steps toward his black Ford, but the reporter held out a hand to stop him.

"Here's the thing I don't get, Mr. Ness. Why would a Fed like you want to get involved in a city's dirty problems? Mobsters, murder, prostitution — seems like it never ends. You can't win. This city never runs out of criminals."

"I think you're wrong about that." He moved on down the steps and tossed his study materials into the backseat of his car. "This is the best time ever to be in law enforcement. Science is on our side. The FBI has developed the greatest crime lab in the world, and they're showing the rest of us how it can be done. Cleveland has a first-rate Bertillon department. Top-notch forensic coroner. We're learning more every day about blood types and fingerprints and bodily fluids. It won't be long until we see an end to these problems that have plagued society since its inception. I think it will happen in our lifetime. Crime will become a thing of the past."

6

First night on the job, and Ness was already enjoying the luxuries of his new position. He'd been appointed a driver! He didn't have to motor himself, not even to take his wife out to dinner. Not that he minded driving — in fact, he rather enjoyed it. But that beat-up Ford, though it might be all he could afford on a Treasury agent's salary, was starting to look a little shabby. Didn't really fit the image of the dynamic new safety director.

When they'd arrived at one of Cleveland's swankiest downtown restaurants, the maître d' recognized Ness and gave him the best seat in the joint. This was a great job. Absolutely great.

"I tell you, Edna — they were eating out of my hands."

"I'm sure they were."

"This safety director business could be something terrific. Might lead to something really special."

"I would've thought it was already something special."

"You know what I mean, Edna. The FBI."

"Eliot — why would you want to be some podunk FBI agent, working under Hoover's thumb, watching him take all the glory?"

"It's what I've always wanted, Edna. You know that. Ever since I was a kid."

"I think you've done all right for yourself without J. Edgar Hoover's help."

He leaned a little closer to her. "So you're happy for me? For us? Doesn't this job sound terrific?"

Her lips pursed. "I think it sounds like a good excuse to stay away from home all day long."

Ness stopped. The smile faded from his face. "Can't you be happy for me?"

"I can't change how I feel, Eliot. I would've told you that when the job was offered. If you'd asked me. Before you accepted." She made a minute adjustment to the lie of her hat, a black felt pillbox pinned to her brunette hair. "You did it anyway."

"It's a great job."

"It's a loser. For losers."

"What?"

"I've asked around. No one who ever held this job came out looking good. No matter what you do, there will always be people complaining that you haven't done enough."

"Just give me a chance."

"Isn't that what I've been doing? All these years?" Edna's voice was thin and strained. She was a pretty woman, had been, since they'd first met as children. They'd gone to the same elementary school, though they didn't see each other for many years afterward, until Ness spotted her working as a secretary for Alexander Jamie. He thought she was beautiful, with her dark hair cut short in the current fashion, light blue eyes, delicate heart-shaped face. Somehow he had summoned up the courage to ask her out to dinner, something that turned out to be harder than facing down Capone. But it was worth the effort. They'd been together ever since. "And what has it gotten me? A lonely lake house and an absentee husband."

"I put a lot of money into that house. Money I couldn't really afford to spend. Because I wanted to make you happy."

"Or was it because you wanted to hide me away, far from everyone and everything?"

"That's nonsense. You're just trying to spoil my —"

"Are you listening to me at all, Eliot? I'm lonely!" Her blue eyes fairly bulged and her voice hit such a volume that she instinctively looked around to see if any of the diners at other tables had noticed. "I'm stuck out there all day with no one to talk to. Nothing to do. A husband who comes home around midnight — if I'm lucky. If he comes home at all."

Ness twisted his neck, trying to work out the kinks. He hated these conversations. Spats. And they seemed to be coming more frequently. "I don't know why you have to be so harsh." He paused, fidgeting with his napkin. "I can't — I can't help but think things would be different if — you know. If we had children."

"But we don't," Edna said, with a finality that terrified him. "We can't."

"Honey." He stretched his hand out toward hers, but she did not reciprocate. "We don't know that."

"I know I can't do it alone."

The waiter brought their food: a beefsteak with hash brown potatoes for him, and grilled salmon for her. It was good — Mayor Burton's recommendation was dead on target. Perhaps the food would brighten her spirits, Ness mused. But he saw no indication. They ate in silence.

"I — I could try . . . to come home earlier," he said, so quietly even he could barely hear it.

"I'd like that." She looked down at her food. "But I've heard it before."

"This time will be different."

"I've heard that before, too."

"Seriously, Edna, it will be. Good grief — all I'm supposed to do is clean up the city. It's not like they're asking me to bring in Capone."

She laid down her fork. "I think the only time you're truly happy is when you're working. That's why you do it so much."

"That's ridiculous."

"And that's why you'll never change."

"I will. You'll see. Starting tonight."

"Tonight?" She arched an eyebrow. "I thought you had homework."

"Maybe . . . that could wait." He reached out again with his hand, and this time she let him take hers. "Maybe tonight we could spend a little private time, just you and me."

"Sounds good."

"Maybe you could get out that little number you bought for our honeymoon — you remember? The red silk one."

She lowered her head, smiling and blushing at the same time. "It isn't really silk."

"I don't care. It feels good, whatever it is. Maybe we could put some music on the radio. Is Rudy Vallee on tonight? You wear that sweet little nothing and —"

He heard a throat clearing just above them. "Sir?"

It was Alphonse Carrelli, his new driver.

"Sorry, but we're not ready to leave yet."

"No, sir. I just thought you might like to know, given your reputation and what you said earlier today . . ." He cleared his throat again.

"What is it, Alphonse?"

"I was in the car, sir, listening to the radio."

"More news from Germany?"

"No, sir. Local news. Seems there's been a robbery. The police think they've got the two felons trapped."

"Why are you telling me this? Can't you see my wife and I are having a meal?"

Alphonse cleared his throat again. "Sir — it's just two blocks from here. At the City Savings and Loan Company."

Ness's eyes lit up. His back arched. "Two blocks?"

"That's correct, sir." As he spoke, through the front window of the restaurant, Ness saw and heard a police car racing by. The red light of the siren momentarily flooded the restaurant, then faded into nothingness.

Ness's hands twitched on the tabletop.

"Sir, I've got the car waiting just outside

the front door."

Ness looked into Edna's eyes. She stared back at him, stony and expressionless.

"No," he said.

Edna's shoulders rose. The corners of her lips turned upward.

"No, if it's only two blocks, I'll walk." He pushed himself to his feet, reached into his pocket and tossed a wad of bills onto the tabletop. "You stay here and take Mrs. Ness home. When she's ready."

Edna did not speak.

"As you wish, sir. Sorry for the intrusion."

"You did the right thing." He grabbed his coat. "Edna — see you at home."

She remained silent. But her eyes said quite a bit.

"Point me in the right direction, Alphonse." He did. And Eliot Ness went roaring out into the cold Cleveland night, buttoning his topcoat to protect himself from the December wind blowing off Lake Erie.

7

Peter Merylo had been on the Cleveland police force for more than fifteen years, most of that time as a homicide detective. But he had never seen anything like this. Never.

"You say two boys turned this in?"

Lieutenant Zalewski nodded. "Found it this morning. Ran for the first adult they could find. He called it in. Before we had a chance to get anyone out here, two white kids found the same thing."

"Kids play out here a lot?"

Zalewski shrugged. "Guess so."

"Four kids find the same corpse the same day. That suggests there's enough traffic to find it anytime. So the corpse must not have been out here long."

"Possible somebody found it but didn't say anything."

Merylo stared down at the corpse in question. "Somebody stumbled across this mess and kept it to themselves? I don't think so."

The corpse was male, although that was not immediately apparent because he had been thoroughly emasculated. He was stripped naked, all except for a pair of dirty cotton socks on his feet. And his head had been severed — head and neck actually — cut clean across the shoulders.

"Think he kept the head for a souvenir?" Zalewski asked.

"How should I know?"

"Kind of person who could do something like this, I think he kept it for a souvenir."

Merylo's bushy eyebrows knitted together. "How long have you been at this work, Lieutenant?"

"Almost two years now. Sir."

Merylo nodded. "I thought as much."

Merylo was a short man, stocky, muscular, with large eyes highlighted by dark circles earned over the course of fifteen years courting the worst element of society. He had a bulldog reputation. Maybe he wasn't the brightest man on the force, but he was a hard worker, tireless. His wife and daughter would be the first to say so. And the fact that his mug could scare the truth out of Satan himself gave him a great edge in the interrogation room.

Like most of the Cleveland police force,

Merylo had no education past high school, but contrary to what most people assumed, he was no dummy. He took pains to keep himself educated. He read the slicks every week, high-quality magazines, so he knew what was going on in the world. He even read the made-up stuff, like the stories in *Argosy* and *The Saturday Evening Post.* He loved *Scientific American* and he genuinely believed science was going to change the world for the better. Any day they'd be driving flying cars and using sunlight to power engines. The world was changing, and he was not going to be left behind.

"A more logical reason for keeping the head," Merylo suggested, "would be to make it difficult to identify the victim. 'Cause if we can't figure out who the chump was, figuring out who had a motive to kill him is pretty tough."

Zalewski pondered. "Huh. Hadn't thought about that."

"Still got the men searching?"

"Oh yeah. Every available member of the No. 6 Police Emergency."

"I count four men."

"Well, you know, the Emergency's never had much of a budget. I hear that Eliot Ness guy wants to change that. Get us the money we need. Think he will?"

Merylo grunted. "If there's a photographer nearby."

"Lieutenant!"

Zalewski and Merylo both swung their heads around. A uniformed officer raced down Jackass Hill at a speed that outpaced his coordination. He tumbled face first to the ground, then rolled for at least ten feet.

There was a brief pause as the officer pulled himself together. He patted himself over from head to toe, as if checking to make sure everything was still connected. Then he pulled himself to his feet, obviously mortified, and brushed dirt and grass from his uniform.

"Something to report?" Merylo said, trying to keep a straight face.

"Yes, sir. They — they found it, sir."

"Could you be a little more specific?"

The officer was having trouble getting the information out. He stuttered several times before anything emerged. When at last it did, he spoke in a whisper. "The head."

Without another word, Merylo made his way up the hill.

"Well, this blows my theory, doesn't it?"

Lieutenant Zalewski wasn't sure what he meant. "Your theory, sir?"

"That the killer cut off the head to disguise

64

the identity of the victim. Can't expect it to stay a secret long if you leave the head twenty feet away from the body on the same side of the hill."

"He did bury it."

"But left hair sticking out. Enough for your man to find it. If the killer really wanted it hidden, I imagine he could've dug a little deeper."

"Then why did he do it, sir?"

"Do I look like Dick Tracy?"

"No, sir. Haven't got the chin for it."

Merylo gave Zalewski a long look. If he didn't know better, he might suspect that this naïve, witless man wasn't quite as much of either as he first thought. "Maybe he's trying to send a message."

"So it's a mob thing. Lots of mobsters in town these days. Eliot Ness said so."

Merylo took a deep breath. "Then it must be true. Look, kid, I don't know what the reason is, but I know there is one. A logical explanation. We need more evidence before we start running around guessing why anyone would do something like . . . this."

The head had deteriorated considerably, but Merylo could still make out the essential features. He was a fairly young man, Caucasian, dark hair parted on the left side. But the face seemed strikingly different from the many faces of the dead into which Merylo had peered over the years. His skin seemed unaccountably reddish, tough, leathery.

He'd seen a lot of mob rubout victims, too. But none of them ever looked like this.

Something was wrong here.

"You still got those kids nearby, Zalewski? The second pair who reported finding the body?"

"Sure. They're brothers. Steve and Leonard Jeziorski. They're in a car on the other side of the Hill. Why?"

"I want to talk to them." He paused. "Something here doesn't add up."

Zalewski pulled a face. "You think they're lying?"

"No." He stood up and granted himself the temporary mercy of looking away from the severed head. "No, I don't. But there's still something wrong here."

"I'm afraid I don't follow, sir."

"Didn't those boys you've got describe the corpse as fat?"

"I think the word they used was 'stocky.' "

"Yeah, that's the word people always use when they're describing fat to someone who's fat. Problem is — our corpse isn't fat."

"Well, they're just boys, sir. I doubt if they

66

spent very long looking."

"Said he was on the short side, too, didn't they?"

"Ye-es . . ."

"Our corpse is tall. Almost six foot, I make him. Adding in a head, of course."

"What do boys know? Everyone looks tall when you're their age."

"But they said he was short."

"Well, everyone looks short when they're lying on the ground. With no head."

"Have you given this head a good long look?"

Zalewski's voice dropped a notch. "Not any longer than I had to."

"He's young. Barely more than a boy. Skinny."

"Like I said —"

"This is not the head of a fat man. For that matter, the neck isn't the right size."

"The neck — ?"

Merylo removed his hat and wiped his brow. "What I'm trying to tell you, Zalewski, is that this head doesn't match that torso."

"But — it has to. I — I don't understand how —"

"You don't have to. Just get your men back into the field. And call headquarters. I want more officers out here. I don't care if you have to pull boys in from other precincts. I want two dozen police officers scouring this hill. Fanning out all across the Run if necessary."

"They won't like it, sir."

"As if I care. Get the men out here. Your boys in the car didn't find the same corpse as the kids this morning. They found another one."

8

From the December 13, 1935, Cleveland *Plain Dealer:*

". . . and this reporter was not the only one impressed by the tireless energy and enthusiasm shown by Ness on what was only his second day on the job. Although the two burglars escaped pursuit by jumping to another rooftop, Ness accepted an invitation to join the officers on their nocturnal patrol of the crime-ridden Roaring Third, with its rampant vice, gambling, and illegal liquor. Ness then accompanied them as they responded to a five-alarm fire at a nearby warehouse, and in the small hours of the morning participated in a raid of a local house of prostitution. Unfortunately, when the police entered, they found the building had been vacated.

" 'Obviously,' Ness announced, 'someone in the department tipped them off. I will find out who it was,' he added, making it sound less like a prediction than a promise. 'I will demand their badges.'

"It is still early days for our new safety director. But already he is forming an excellent reputation with the people in government and law enforcement — everyone but those who know their days on the force may be numbered, because this is a man who means what he says. Six feet and 172 pounds of fight and vigor, an expert criminologist who looks like a collegian but can battle vice with the best of them, Eliot Ness is dedicated to his job of ensuring law and order in the city of Cleveland. Mayor Burton should be complimented for hiring a safety director without political ties or aspirations who has a spotless record of battling corruption . . ."

Ness squeezed the paper in his fist and slapped it against his desk. "Did you read this, Robert? Did you read it?"

Robert Chamberlin, the man temporarily assigned by Chief Matowitz to help Ness get situated, nodded. "Indeed I did. Great press. The papers love you."

"That doesn't matter."

Chamberlin blinked. "Well, now. That's the first time since I entered government service that I've heard that."

Ness bounced out of his desk chair and paced around the office. He had always had a hard time sitting still. "What matters is whether I have the clout to clean up the city. These newspapers are helping me get it."

"You're the safety director, whether they like you or not."

"Yes, but for how long? And what exactly are my powers? Do I take orders from the mayor or am I independent? No one seems to know. I can't do anything without funding, and the city council controls that. No, I need popular support if I'm going to accomplish my goals. That's why I play along with those newsboys."

Chamberlin fingered his wire-rimmed glasses. "Is that why?"

"Yes. Means to an end, that's all."

"I see."

"You have any idea how much five hundred traffic lights cost?"

"I don't even know what a traffic light is."

Ness laughed. "You will. And then there's the cost of motorcycles, ambulances. Two-way radios. All the latest scientific innovations. Everything this city needs to relieve congestion and make driving safer. But all of it has a price tag."

"I'm sure the city council will give you whatever you need."

"As long as supporting me looks like the popular thing to do. Any news on the brothel raid?"

"I think it's a lost cause, Eliot."

"No such thing, Robert. Our only problem has been that we move too slowly. The word gets out to the crooks. Gosh, even when it doesn't, these mobsters can usually get everything and everyone hidden away between the time our officers knock and the time we get in. We have to move faster. And we have to plug up the leaks."

"Easy to say, Eliot. Hard to do. There are too many suspects, too many police officers who knew about the raid."

"And it could have been any of them?"

"It could have been all of them."

"Get me names, Robert."

"I can't be sure, Eliot. I have suspects. But nothing certain."

"Then I'll put them on suspension. Then we'll try the raid again and see what happens."

"You can't do that." Chamberlin was a tall, lanky man, experienced in dealing with bureaucrats and politicians — which had not fully prepared him for working for someone like Eliot Ness. Ness liked that. He knew Chamberlin was more political than he, and that was fine. He could use help in that particular arena. "You can't take away a man's job without proof."

"Not talking about firing them. Suspension with pay."

"I don't know . . ."

"I have to know who I can trust, Robert." Outside his office door, a man was painting his name, just above the words SAFETY DIRECTOR. He liked the way it looked. "I have to find my Untouchables."

"We will, sir. But you must be patient."

Ness chuckled. "Not my best virtue." His eyes were fixed on the letters on the door. FBI agents got their names on the doors, at least the top ones. He wondered if they looked the same.

"By the way, Eliot — your wife called."

Ness looked up abruptly, breaking out of his reverie. "Edna?"

"She wanted to know if you'll be home tonight."

"Well — of course I'll be home." He paused. "I'm not exactly sure when." The light flickered back into his eyes. "Chief Matowitz and I have made special plans."

73

"Anything you'd care to tell me about?"

Ness winked, then he grabbed his hat and headed toward the door that now bore his name. "You can read about it in tomorrow's papers."

9

Merylo hated visiting the coroner's office. Hated it worse than he hated wide ties, Joan Crawford, and that jazzy music. "It Ain't Necessarily So" — what kind of song was that? Bad grammar excusing bad scansion. But at least he could turn off the radio. Visiting the coroner was part of the job, more and more so with every passing year. When he had started with the force, fifteen years ago, there hadn't been all that much a coroner could do, other than pronounce a corpse officially dead, fill out the death certificate, and make a semi-educated guess as to the cause of death. Today, modern science had given them the ability to do much more; the coroner had become an integral part of the crime-solving team. So here he was.

But Merylo still didn't like it.

Fortunately, the new coroner in Cleveland, Arthur J. Pearce, was one of the best in the country. Merylo knew he had written scientific articles for the top forensic journals. Merylo had even read some of them, though he usually got lost in the scientific gibberish. The man had a national reputation. He could be helpful.

Pearce hunched over his examining table, a sharp instrument in one hand and a blunt one in the other, doing something to one of the corpses.

Merylo cleared his throat, but the doctor proceeded with his business as if he hadn't heard. Maybe he hadn't — he seemed very focused.

"Got anything new for me?"

No answer.

"Any tips at all? Cause of death? Time of death? Weapon?"

No reaction. Pearce was scraping at a wound. Extracting something. Merylo didn't really want to know.

"Have you at least matched up the right head to the right body?"

Pearce stopped. His head tilted to one side. He slowly drew himself erect.

"You had done that before the bodies arrived in my office." He spoke with a clipped, East Coast accent. Merylo wished he could learn how to talk like that. It made the man sound smart. Or maybe that was because he was smart.

"You never know. I might've gotten it wrong. Or you might not have caught up with me yet."

Pearce arched an eyebrow.

"You'd tell me, wouldn't you? If I got it wrong?"

"Of that you may be certain."

Pearce turned as if to resume his work, but Merylo stepped forward. "So what have you learned so far?"

Pearce sighed, then laid down his dissecting instruments. "What would you like to know?"

"Cause of death?"

"As you might suspect. Decapitation. With a sharp instrument. Single blow. The killer severed the head in the midcervical region which concomitantly instigated a fracture of the vertebrae."

Merylo felt something roiling in his stomach. "I was kinda hoping maybe he killed the guys first."

Pearce shook his head. "When the decapitation occurred, they were very much alive. Given the rope burns around his wrists and ankles, he was probably physically restrained. Tied up."

"Must take a lot of strength to hack off a man's head in one whack."

"Indeed."

"So we're looking for someone strong. Someone male."

"You're assuming too much." Pearce removed his protective gloves. "In the case of Victim Number Two, the killer took several — how did you say it? — whacks. There are telltale signs."

"Hesitation marks?"

"I'm not sure I see any evidence of hesitation. Or regret, or any other human emotion. The skin edges were clear-cut. But he didn't get the head off in one blow. Neck bones are tough — they're designed that way. Do you know how many times the executioner had to chop at Mary, Queen of Scots, before he got her head all the way off?"

He did not. Nor did he care to. "What kind of weapon did the killer use?"

"Impossible to say. But there's no reason to suppose it was anything other than your common axe. Such as you might find in most of the homes in Cleveland. Even a strong knife would do the job, given enough power behind it. Possibly a sword."

"So he hacked off their heads, then hauled the body parts to Jackass Hill?"

"Not quite so quickly as that summation supposes." Pearce took a cigarette out of his

78

lab coat pocket and lit it. Smoking, of course, was all the rage — it looked so glamorous when Bette Davis did it. But Merylo hated the smell. Made him cough and sputter. Didn't Pearce realize his operating room was nauseating enough already? "First he hacked off the heads. Then he drained all the blood out of the bodies."

Merylo winced. "How do you know?"

"Did you see dried blood where you found the bodies? Or anywhere nearby?"

"No. And we searched the whole Run."

"And there was almost no blood in either body. Ergo, they had been drained."

"Why would anyone want to do that?"

Pearce gave him a withering look. "Why would anyone want to hack off a man's head and then deposit the pieces on Jackass Hill?"

"Good point." Merylo turned, took a deep breath and tried to clear his head. "Did you do anything with the clothes we found? Or the other stuff?" After the second corpse and body were discovered, the men searching the surrounding area also found several pieces of rope, a blue coat, a white shirt and trousers, a checkered cap, and a tin bucket filled with engine oil laced with blood and black hair.

"The clothes belonged to the second victim. Some of it bears his blood. Presumably he was wearing them when he was decapitated. The killer removed them later."

"Why?"

"Detective Merylo, would you please stop asking me that?" He blew cigarette smoke into the air. "My job is to provide data. Your job is to provide the why." He took another drag, then continued. "The rope may have been used to restrain the victims, or to bind their bodies to ease transportation, but I have no means of confirming either theory. And as for the bucket of oil . . . well, I simply have no idea. Can't even . . . imagine." He looked away. "Don't particularly want to."

"Could he be . . . making something? What do you get when you mix engine oil and blood?"

"A huge reeking mess."

How scientific. "What about their skin? I've seen corpses before, Doc. Even some long-dead ones. But I've never seen anything like that before. There's something wrong with the color. The texture of the skin."

Pearce nodded. "I agree. I can't prove this, but I believe some kind of chemical was used. Perhaps a preservative."

"Like — like he wanted to keep the bodies from decaying? So he could keep them around and admire them?"

"You're asking me 'Why?' again, Detective." He ground out his cigarette in a nearby ashtray. "I can't be certain it was a preservative. It wasn't formaldehyde — I'm certain of that. But whatever it was — it does seem to have had some sort of sustaining effect."

Merylo's head reeled. What was the killer up to? Was this a mob hit? Were they preserving the corpses so they could be put out on display? As a scare tactic? To discourage others from defying them?

He decided to give his stomach a break and change the subject. "What about the time of death?"

"Given that a preservative may have been used, that becomes extremely difficult to determine. All I can say with certainty is — it wasn't anytime recent. The killer must've kept them in a safe place for a good long time — perhaps weeks — before finally disposing of them."

And why dispose of them at all? Anyone this cruel must've been able to make a body disappear. Why dispose of them on Jackass Hill, a place where they were almost certain to be found?

"Did Joe come by? I asked him to."

Pearce nodded. "Your friend from Bertillon was here. He took many pictures.

And prints."

"Did he see anything of interest?"

"I wouldn't know. He didn't speak. Most unfriendly." Pearce picked up a scalpel, still red at the tip, and held it up to the light. "He seems uncomfortable around me. I don't know why that would be."

Can't imagine. "Thanks for your help, Doc." Not that any of it was actually helpful. "If you reach any conclusions, be sure to let me know."

"As it happens, I'm about to reach a conclusion right now. Would you like to stay and witness it?"

"Of course I would. What've you got?"

Pearce picked up a green rectangular sheet of paper — a death certificate. He scribbled his name across the bottom of it. "I hereby declare these two unknown persons as being officially — dead. Would you like a copy?"

Merylo smashed his hat back on his head. "That's all right, Doc. Thanks for the insight."

10

Ness couldn't help but smile as he watched Chief Matowitz rubbing his hands together, trying to fight off the bitter chill of a cold Cleveland night. Matowitz was not accustomed to being away from his desk, much less at two in the morning. Ness had asked Matowitz to join him and his men on the auspicious occasion of his first nocturnal raid since his appointment as safety director. Chamberlin had helped him understand the value of including the chief in his activities, especially when he was simultaneously asking for the suspension of dozens of police officers. But he also had to admit that he derived a certain amount of pleasure from showing the man who previously had been so ineffectual at stopping the mob in Cleveland how he used to do things back in Chi-Town.

"Are we ready to start?" Matowitz asked, jumping up and down to stave off the cold.

Too many years of paperwork had made him soft, Ness thought. And he needed a better coat. He had no sense of style — though perhaps, if he wasn't on the take, he might not be able to afford better than the threadbare cloth overcoat he was wearing.

Ness checked his watch. "Not quite yet."

"I don't understand what we're waiting for."

"Be patient. We need all the elements in place before we go storming in."

"I don't know what the point is. Frescone probably knew about this raid before we left the station house."

Ness mulled that ominous thought. "It's always possible. But I think I know who he was getting his info from, and those men have been at home cooling their heels for the past week. I doubt he's had time to bribe anyone new."

"Then he'll find another way to wriggle through your fingers. You think you have all the exits covered, but there's always an escape hatch somewhere. A tunnel, a hidden door. Frescone didn't get where he is today by being stupid."

"I agree with you about that. I've been careful not to underestimate him." Ness knew he shouldn't say it, but he couldn't resist. "Capone wasn't stupid, either."

They were huddled beside a warehouse on the south side of Lake Erie, a district once populated by breweries but now largely disused. A chill wind whistled through the birch trees, making it colder, but also creating a constant background noise that would shield their movements from the people he hoped were still inside. It had taken him days of pounding the street and forcing people to talk, but he'd finally persuaded a stoolie to tell him about this vital link in Frescone's operation.

Assuming the informant had been telling the truth. There was never any way to know, except to burst in and find out — so that was what they were going to do. It had worked for him in the past.

Ness gazed at the south side warehouse. It was in bad repair. The wood was worn and several windows were broken. The lights were dark. It had once been used by one of the local businesses, but it had been abandoned since the Prohibition days. Perhaps a place for storing hooch till it could be smuggled out safely.

Robert Chamberlin emerged from the shadows on the south side of the building, fingering his glasses. "We're ready," he said quietly.

"Gentlemen," Ness said to the four officers on temporary assignment to the safety director, "it's time."

"Wait a minute," Matowitz said, grabbing Ness's arm. "What happened to the other officers? Shouldn't we wait for them?"

"No."

"But they're missing!"

Ness grinned. "You'll see."

Ness reached inside his coat and retrieved a sizable metal whistle. He glanced at his watch and softly counted down the seconds. "Five . . . four . . . three . . . two . . ."

He blew the whistle. It was ear-piercingly loud. Anyone who might be inside the warehouse would have heard it. Probably all the people sleeping within a square mile radius heard it.

Ness grabbed the door handle and found it locked. He was not surprised.

"Gentlemen?"

Two of the special agents stepped forward carrying a large sawed-off pole with handles screwed into the sides. A homemade battering ram. They punched it forward, hammering away at the worn wooden doors. On the second thrust, the doors separated enough to reveal a set of chains holding the doors shut. Another officer stepped forward with bulky metal cutters.

The chains fell and the men surged inside.

It had taken fewer than fifteen seconds.

Ness had barely taken two steps forward when he heard gunfire. A bullet whizzed by him only a few inches from his head.

"Look for cover!" he instructed his men. He grabbed Matowitz and ducked behind a barrel. The gun fired repeatedly.

"You see what I tried to tell you?" Matowitz cried. "The gunman holds you back while the others escape. If you catch the gunman, he won't know anything. This raid is a wash."

"Maybe not," Ness said, as the bullets ricocheted all around him. "Look to the skies."

Above them, a single skylight permitted the weak moonlight to stream into the warehouse. Seconds later, the sky burst into a thousand pieces.

"Duck!" Ness shouted, pulling his overcoat over his head, as glass rained down all around them.

A second later, four bright lights were visible above the skylight, and a second after that men descended on ropes faster than the confused gunman could track.

"The absent agents," Ness said quietly, telling Matowitz what he had already deduced.

"What are they doing up there?"

"Making sure no one escapes."

As later reports would explain in great detail, the four men hit the ground and immediately spread out, covering the expanse of the warehouse and looking for anyone who might be beating a hasty retreat or trying to destroy evidence. The sniper continued to fire wildly, moving from one target to the next, not connecting with anyone.

"You've got him in a tailspin," Chamberlin said, running up behind Ness.

"For the moment. But he'll get lucky eventually, and our men are exposed. Can you tell where he is?"

Chamberlin pointed his flashlight toward the north corner, illuminating a large cache of barrels.

"He's on top," Chamberlin said. "See?"

"Well enough." He turned to Matowitz. "Can you cover me?"

Matowitz didn't even have his gun out. He slowly unholstered it. "Where are you going?"

"Closer." Ness pulled a half-dollar out of his pocket and tossed it to the other side of the warehouse. It clinked and clattered when it landed.

The sniper pivoted and fired in the direction of the half-dollar.

"Now." Ness raced out. Matowitz leaned

over the top of the barrels and let loose, one shot after another, forcing the sniper to keep his head down. Ness ran fifty feet as fast as he could manage, throwing himself down behind a long-disused crate.

Chamberlin still had the sniper's nest spotlighted. Ness took careful aim and fired.

The sniper went down with the first shot.

Once the firing stopped, Ness's men gathered around him.

"Did you kill him?" Matowitz asked.

"Gosh, no," Ness replied. "Just took out the arm holding the gun. Robert, see if he needs first aid."

While Chamberlin ran his errand, Ness used his crowbar to pry open the lid of one of the barrels. This time, it wasn't cold cream.

Ness leaned down and inhaled deeply. Too deeply — he gagged on the strong alcoholic aroma. "It's the real deal," Ness said. "We got it."

A cheer went up from the ranks. Ness grinned. "Good work, men. Good work."

"It gets better," Chamberlin said, once again pointing with his flashlight. In the rear, Ness saw the men who had entered from the skylight.

They had four captives.

"That's how you prevent them from getting away," Ness said, beaming proudly. "A quick, coordinated attack. Kept secret until executed."

"I have to admit it," Matowitz said, clearing his throat. "That was . . . not unimpressive."

"Couldn't have done it without your help, Chief," Ness said. "That's what I'll be telling the newspapers, too."

Ness strode forward to meet the oncoming captured. He saw a familiar face.

"Well, now," Ness said to the man on the far left, who was wearing a pinstriped suit and a much too familiar white hat. "You're one of Frescone's lieutenants, aren't you? You were out at the dock the other night shipping cold cream." He glanced back at Chamberlin. "And Frescone?"

Chamberlin shook his head. "He wasn't here."

"It's probably past his bedtime. What's your name, mister?"

The thug stiffened. "I'm not sayin' nothin' to nobody. I wanna lawyer."

"Of course you do. And we can play it that way, if you want. That is, if you want to do twenty years in the state penitentiary. Or you can give us the goods on your boss and maybe we can make a private arrangement."

"I'm not sayin' nothin' to nobody."

"Right, I heard that. Let's put him away for a few days and see if he changes his mind. We've got four potential squealers here. Five, once the sniper with the lousy aim gets out of the hospital. There must be someone in such a large and distinguished group who doesn't want to spend the rest of his life in prison."

"You'd think," Chamberlin remarked.

"You would indeed. Can you take it from here, Robert?"

"Sure. We'll get these boys downtown. And we'll call the ATU and have them confiscate all this illegal hooch."

"Good. Give all these agents the day off. They've earned it."

Faces all around him suddenly brightened.

"Will do. Best to Edna."

"Actually, I think I'll head downtown myself. I want to be there for the interrogations. I might be able to help."

Chamberlin nodded. "Of course. See you there."

Ness turned back to Matowitz. "Not a bad night's work, I think, Chief. Can I give you a lift home?"

"You sure can," Matowitz replied. "Could I talk you into a cheesesteak? I know a great place that's open all night. All this running around and shooting has left me famished."

Ness clapped a hand on Matowitz's shoulder. "Hard to turn down an offer like that, Chief. Lead the way."

11

"Pass the ketchup, would you?"

"Certainly. Want some mayo?"

"Nah. Sissy stuff."

"Pickles acceptably manly?"

"Sure. Onions, too."

"Glad to hear it. I love onions. Don't care what they do to my breath. Have some more."

"Don't mind if I do."

"Care for some chopped torso?" Merylo closed his eyes. "I mean, tomato."

Lieutenant Zalewski grimaced. "You sure know how to blow the fun out of a picnic."

"You're not the first one to tell me." He took a bite of his Coney. "You sure you want this job?"

"You talkin' about the picnic? Or workin' with you?"

"Take your pick."

"I'm sure I want to be your partner. I'd be crazy to say no. You're the top homicide detective on the force. I figure this jumps me up five, maybe eight years ahead in my career."

Merylo didn't argue. "And the picnic?"

Zalewski shrugged. "I was told I'd have to make sacrifices for my career."

Merylo smiled. This must take some getting used to for Zalewski, especially given Merylo's bulldog reputation with the rest of the boys on the force. All work and no play. Nose to the grindstone. Never give a sucker a break. And here they were, on the highest point of Jackass Hill, sitting on a red-and-white-checked tablecloth, having a picnic. On a cold day, no less. Yes, the rest of the boys would think they were insane. Or something worse.

"I noticed you didn't use mustard," Merylo commented.

"Never cared for the stuff. Hard on my stomach."

"It's not a Coney without mustard."

"I'm doin' okay."

"And sauerkraut — that's the key to the whole thing. You didn't take any sauerkraut."

"What kind of red-blooded American puts sauerkraut on somethin' as American as a Coney?"

"The ones who like good food."

"Hmph. Sounds like a Kraut thing to me. You got a thing for the kaiser? Or that new kid?"

"Adolf Hitler?"

"Yeah, him. I hear he's really whipping that country into shape."

"Is that what you hear?"

"Yeah. He got that Saarland back, didn't he? Made military service mandatory. Got rid of the Versailles Treaty that was slowing him down."

"And you see that as a good thing?"

"Personally, I think we went too easy on the Krauts after we beat them down in the Great War."

"The War to End All Wars."

"Yeah. But with this Hitler guy in charge, maybe they'll get civilized. Join the rest of the world."

Merylo addressed his attention to his perfectly constructed Coney. "I hear he burns books."

"Yeah, well, tell you the truth, I was never that crazy about books myself. So," Zalewski added, obviously choosing his words carefully, "mind if I ask why we're out here in the middle of winter having a picnic?"

"I think you're entitled. Seem strange?"

"Well . . . it doesn't match up with the standard Merylo image."

"When you're on a case, working the streets, working over some thug, you need a certain authority."

"I can see that."

"But I can still appreciate a picnic. And I thought it might give us a chance to get to know each other. Since we're going to be working together. Right?"

"Right. Right."

"So what else is bothering you?"

"Who said — ?"

"You haven't taken a bite out of your Coney."

"Oh! Well . . ." He picked it up and crammed half of it into his mouth. "Mmm. Good."

"Glad you approve. There is fancier fare. But it's hard to beat a good Coney. I practically survive on 'em. Which may explain why I look the way I do," he added, patting his firm but substantial belly.

"So, okay, we're having a picnic," Zalewski said, wiping his mouth, "we're getting to know each other. But why here? In Kingsbury Run. On a cold day."

"Now that's the question. Glad you finally got there, Lieutenant." Merylo put down his dog and gestured expansively. "Look around you. What do you see?"

Zalewski took in a panoramic view of the

countryside. From here on the apex of the Hill, you could see for miles around. "Lotsa scrub. Brush. Dirt. Some kids playing. More kids running all over the gully, probably hopin' they might find another corpse. Industrial complex to the northeast, pumpin' more soot and smoke into the air."

"Keep going."

"Two trains headed toward the factory. Some decent houses off to the south, some wretched ones off to the north. And Shantytown, of course."

"Exactly. Spent much time in Shantytown?"

Even as he asked the question, Merylo already knew the answer: Why would he? Why would anyone? A miserable assortment of derelicts and destitutes living in packing boxes or, at best, makeshift sheds. It was the embarrassment of the city.

"Tried my best to avoid it, tell the truth," Zalewski said, a trifle shamefaced.

"Nothing to be embarrassed about. Perfectly understandable. If a crime hasn't brought you out there, what would? Got any notion who's living there?"

Zalewski shrugged. "Bums. Vagrants. Hoboes."

"That's true. We get a lot of those. They ride in on the rails and stay, least till they get in some kind of trouble and have to move on. Most cases, there's no record they were ever there. No one remembers."

"Sounds like bad news for crime solving."

"Exactly. Thing is — it's not just bums."

"It isn't?"

Merylo shook his head. "Sure you won't try some sauerkraut?" Zalewski declined. "There's some good folk out there, entire families even. Poor joes who lost their jobs when the stock market crashed and work got scarce and haven't been able to get back on their feet since. Migrants escaping the Dust Bowl. There's even some poor boys who've found some kind of job or other, but it doesn't pay well enough for them to live anywhere else."

"Really?"

Merylo nodded while he smeared mustard on a second dog. "Imagine that. You work all day in some damn factory or slaughter-house, and still your family's living in a shack. During a Cleveland winter. That," he said, giving a decisive twist to the lid of the mustard jar, "might drive a guy to do any-thing."

Zalewski swallowed. "You mean — even cutting off two men's heads?"

"That's not the act of a desperate man. But I think desperation might cause a man to do things he ought not be doing. Ever wonder why the corpses were left here?"

"Seems like a lot of work."

"Exactly. You can't drive a car down that gully. They weren't rolled down the hill — that would've left marks. The killer had to carry them a long way."

"Maybe that's why he drained the blood. To lighten the load."

Merylo avoided rolling his eyes. "Don't think that would make much difference. Especially to this killer. He had to be strong to get those corpses out here. I don't think I could do it."

"Maybe he had help."

"That's possible. Especially if the mob's involved."

Zalewski gave him a narrowed eye. "You know something, don't you?"

"In fact, I do." Merylo pulled a folded report out of his coat pocket. "Know much about the Bertillon department?"

"That's, uh, French, isn't it?"

"Well, it's named for a French guy. Invented what we call anthropometry. A way of taking precise measurements of a criminal's features, so they can be used later to identify him. He came up with a lot of other stuff we use every day — like the mug shot. Using plaster to preserve footprints. Ballistics. Showed us how science could be used to solve crimes."

"Sounds like a smart guy. For a frog."

"He got the Dreyfus case totally wrong, but who hasn't made a mistake at one time or other?"

Zalewski looked puzzled. "But how's this help us? We haven't got a footprint. Or a bullet."

"True. But we do have hands. And the hands have fingerprints. You know what they are, right?"

"Course I do. Did that Bertillon guy discover those, too?"

"No, but he showed us how to use them. Our Bertillon department has a pretty substantial collection of them. Including one for a Hungarian mug named Edward W. Andrassy." Merylo paused. "Also known to you as the first victim."

Zalewski's eyes bugged. "What? How'd you figure that out?"

"Andrassy was picked up in 1931 for carrying a concealed. They printed him. Took a mug shot, too. Course, his face is pretty messed up now. But it's definitely him."

"Was he in the mob?"

"Nah. Strictly small potatoes. Long record of petty offenses. Gambler. Drunk. Good-looking — people say he was popular with the ladies, go figure. I never could understand what dames go for. He liked to hang out in some of those sleazy joints on Rowdy Row. Third District. No indication that he ever did anything big time."

"Then why would anyone want to kill him? Like that."

"I'm just guessing, but the mob boys have been known to go crazy violent when they want to send a message. We know Andrassy gambled, and we know that every gambler eventually has some bad luck. Maybe he needed money. Maybe he made the mistake of borrowing from the mob. Maybe he couldn't pay it back."

"So they whacked off his head?"

"Or maybe this big lover boy got involved with some dame he shouldn't. Maybe some hood's moll. Might explain why we have two victims. Maybe there was a love triangle."

"So they whacked off his head."

Merylo swallowed the last of his third dog. "It's not impossible. I went out to his wife's place last night. She said there were some suspicious characters hanging around about two weeks ago. She didn't know who they were and her loving hubby wouldn't tell her."

"Mobsters."

"We shouldn't jump to any conclusions.

But it's possible. Wife told me something else. She said she'd seen one of her neighbors in the window several times with a pair of binoculars. Pointed toward Jackass Hill."

"The killer!"

"I hoped. I went over and talked to the guy." He sighed. "Turned out he's got a thing going with a married dame on the other side of the Run. Whenever her husband leaves, she waves this white handkerchief. Lover boy sees it in his binos and skedaddles across the Run to give her a good one."

"Ouch. Not the killer."

"Don't think so. More like a homicide victim in waiting."

Zalewski's eyes lit up. "What about the other corpse? The big guy. Did you print him?"

"Couldn't. Body has decomposed too severely. Apparently he's been dead a lot longer than Andrassy."

"I bet he was a punk thug, too."

"Maybe. It's something to check out."

Zalewski sat up, his eyes bright. "You've done a lot of work. I hadn't heard any of this."

"No one has. No point."

"But you've got a real lead!"

"Did you see the papers after the news of

the murders broke? They went gaga with this stuff. The *Plain Dealer* called it 'the most bizarre double murder in Cleveland history.' The *Press* ran front-page pictures of the boys and the *News* said it was 'vengeance for a frustrated love affair' — even though they had no evidence at all to back up their glamorous story. The newsboys are going to be all over this any day Eliot Ness isn't smiling for the cameras. If we announce that we have leads, they'll expect us to have a killer by Tuesday. I'm going to lay low. Not a good idea to stir things up till you've got something solid."

"I guess not."

Merylo began packing away the picnic. "I asked if you were sure you wanted to be my partner. For a reason. There's tons of work to be done, and whether I like it or not, I know I can't do it all. We've got to blanket the area, the homes, the factories, the shanties. Everything you see around you now. Talk to everyone. Especially in Andrassy's neighborhood. Cleveland's got the largest Hungarian population outside of Budapest — did you know that? We're gonna talk to every one of them. Maybe someone saw something suspicious. Maybe someone carrying a large heavy bundle. Who knows what it might be? But this guy lugged two corpses

— and their heads — all the way out here and down the gully. Surely someone saw something." He paused, giving Zalewski a steely eye. "We're going to find that someone."

"Understood." Zalewski helped him put away the condiments. "You know . . . I think I'm going to like working for you."

Merylo grunted his reply.

Zalewski couldn't let it go. "We're gonna catch this guy, aren't we?"

Merylo looked right into his eyes. "You bet we are. You and me, buddy. He's as good as nailed."

12

Ness stared at the barnlike structure known to the underworld as The Thomas Club. Most of the building still looked like a warehouse, and a dilapidated one at that, but the front façade had been redressed in a swingtown New Orleans style. Still looked tacky to Ness, especially with all the windows draped to ensure that no one could see inside. But whether it appealed to him or not, he knew it was one of the most notorious gambling dens in the county.

On the surface, The Thomas Club appeared to be an ordinary nightspot for drinking and dancing. But everyone for miles around knew it was also one of the largest gambling parlors in the city, replete with table games and slot machines and horse rooms — off-track betting arenas. The Club was conveniently located in Newburgh Heights, which was just outside the city limits and thus beyond the jurisdiction of city police officers. Given that Matowitz couldn't touch it — and the corrupt county sheriff Potts, recently removed from office thanks to Ness, wouldn't — it had thrived for more than five years. Some of Cleveland's most prominent citizens frequented the place. They felt safe here, because the law couldn't touch them.

That would end tonight.

Over his shoulder, Ness eyed Chief Matowitz, huddled behind him. He seemed a good deal more comfortable than he had been the last time they went out on a raid. Perhaps it was because, on Ness's advice, he'd bought himself a better coat. But Ness suspected it had more to do with the lead story on the front page of the *Plain Dealer* the night after the raid, a story that prominently featured Matowitz's "pivotal" role. Overnight, George Matowitz had been transformed from uninspiring civil servant limping toward retirement to a local celebrity.

"Appreciate your presence here tonight," Ness whispered. "Especially since we're outside your jurisdiction."

They were huddled on the opposite side of a dirt road, Ness, Matowitz, and Chamberlin, sheltered from the prying eyes of the arriving clientele by deep shadows and thick bramble. "Always willing to loan some of my boys out to the city's safety director. You'll have to make the arrests, though."

"With pleasure."

" 'Bout time to go?"

Ness shook his head. "Few more minutes. Waiting for those men you loaned me to get into position."

"Right. I remember." Matowitz checked his watch. "Nice article in the paper."

"That it was."

"Haven't seen such favorable press in twenty-one years on the job."

"Well, the newspaper boys have to be courted a little. Like a reluctant spinster at a church social."

Matowitz pursed his lips. "You're pretty good at that sort of thing."

"It's part of my job."

"Is that why you keep going out on these late-night raids? Because just between you and me, I think illegal hooch and gambling are probably the least of Cleveland's problems right now."

"I treat all parts of my job equally," Ness said, bristling only slightly. "But the truth is those newspapers are never going to get very worked up about traffic safety. Can you imagine tomorrow's headlines being SAFETY DIRECTOR BUYS 500 TRAFFIC LIGHTS? Not likely. But midnight raids capture the public's imagination. And the support of the public is key to capturing the support of the city council. They control my funding, as my associate continually reminds me."

Chamberlin doffed an imaginary hat in Ness's direction.

"So," Ness concluded, "think of the midnight hooch and horse raids as the part of my job that pays for the rest of it."

They watched as a man in a full tuxedo and top hat stepped out of a limousine. He was a prominent local banker and his date, whom Ness knew for a fact was not his wife, wore a red beaded gown and a near endless strand of pearls.

"Is that who I think it is?" Matowitz said, blinking.

"It is," Ness replied.

Matowitz twisted his neck from side to side. "I hope your tip is correct, Ness. 'Cause if you're wrong, we're gonna be in a big mess of trouble."

"I'm not wrong."

"He has half the politicians in Ohio in his hip pocket."

"That's the rumor."

"And he gambles?"

"High-roller gambling."

"This joint owned by Frescone?"

"He's one of several co-owners, along with Shimmy Patton and some of the other big-shots in the Mayfield Road Mob. They control the flow of illegal liquor in these parts."

Matowitz whistled. "Ness — you ever consider maybe starting with the little fish and working your way up?"

The boyish grin crept across Ness's face. "You cut off the head, the serpent dies." He turned toward Chamberlin. "We sure Frescone's inside?"

"Absolutely," his lanky assistant replied, adjusting the lay of his wire-rims. "Saw him go in myself about an hour ago. We've got all the exits — all the sides of the building — covered."

"Maybe he's got a secret exit," Matowitz suggested. "A tunnel or something."

"This club's built on solid bedrock," Chamberlin informed him. "You'd need dynamite to dig a hole in it. And you'd take down the building in the process."

"Still —"

Chamberlin shook his head. "He's inside. Guarantee it."

"Well then," Ness said, rubbing his hands together with relish. "What are we waiting for?"

He lifted his metal whistle to his lips and

blew as hard as he could. The shrill alarm permeated the night air.

Ness and his men raced across the street. The three plainclothes officers Matowitz had contributed brought out their battering rams and started working on the front door.

It didn't break. Didn't even budge.

"Toughest wood in the history of creation," Ness murmured. "Try it again, boys."

The three men battered away at the door. They made no progress.

Ness waved them aside and took a closer look. The battering ram had cracked through the exterior wooden doors — but they were reinforced by two solid steel doors.

"That's disappointing," Ness said, with the same inflection other people might give a swear word.

Matowitz's brow creased. "What's going to happen when my men go in through that skylight?"

"They'll be on their own." Ness snapped his fingers. "Men, keep pounding at that door. Bob?"

"Yes, sir?" Chamberlin answered.

"Tell the men on the roof not to go in till they hear me whistle again. From the inside."

110

"Got it." Chamberlin sprinted around the corner of the building until he reached the ladder.

He returned less than a minute later.

"Not to worry," he said, panting and frowning at the same time. "They can't get in, either."

"What?"

"Seems the skylight has been reinforced. They can't make any more progress than we have."

Ness bit his bottom lip and stared at three men still futilely pounding away at a steel surface that would never give in. At least not unless they used something a great deal stronger than what they had.

"You want them to keep poundin'?" Matowitz asked. "The people inside must've heard it, unless they're all stone deaf."

"Which they're not." Ness glanced at his watch. Four minutes since they started the assault. More than enough time to hide anything.

The men were still beating away at the steel doors when a sliding panel at eye level suddenly opened, revealing a pair of eyes on the other side.

"You knocked?"

Ness stepped forward, showing his badge. "I'm Eliot Ness, safety director. I want this door open. Now."

The eyes disappeared for a moment. Ness heard a soft-spoken word of assent in a voice he thought he recognized. A moment later, he saw one of the heavy metal doors swing open on creaking hinges.

A butler in full evening dress stood on the other side. "You may enter."

The Thomas Club was packed with even more people than Ness had imagined. For the most part, they were well dressed and obviously affluent. The dance floor was filled and a small jazz quartet was playing "Begin the Beguine." The clientele appeared absorbed in themselves and barely noticed the arrival of the newly appointed safety director. Liquor was everywhere, but Ness knew the club had a license and occasionally bought some legal liquor so he would never be able to prove these particular drinks were rotten.

There was not the slightest trace of any gambling or gambling equipment. No sign that it had ever been here at any time.

"Bob, check the kitchen."

Chamberlin pushed his way through the crowd.

Ness carved a path through a wall of people in the opposite direction. He knew there were probably a dozen guns trained on him. He tried not to let it bother him.

At least they'd been right about one thing. Frescone was here. He stood by the band wearing another of his tailored pinstriped suits that probably cost more than Ness made in three months.

"Mr. Ness. So good to see you again."

"Can't say the same. Where'd you stash the gambling equipment?"

"Gambling?" He frowned. "Mr. Ness, are you not aware that gambling is illegal here?"

"Everyone in town knows this is the premiere gambling parlor."

"Would your informants be the same ones who told you I was smuggling alcohol last September?" He turned, addressing the audience. "Instead, our distinguished safety director managed to seize a lifetime supply of cold cream."

A few titters rapidly developed into full-out boisterous laughter that filled the room. People shook their heads in disdain and elbowed one another in delight.

Ness did not like being laughed at. Never had, not even when he was a child and the other kids called him "Elegant Mess" because of his unique combination of snazzy attire and social awkwardness. He was always careful not to make too much of himself; he knew immodesty could blow up in his face. But he still wanted people to take him seriously. He needed that.

"This isn't the end," Ness said. His voice was soft-spoken, as always, and just this once he wished it had a little more grit in it.

"Yes, you've said that before, haven't you? Your predictions aren't worth very much."

"You lost a big stash of liquor last week."

"Who did? Certainly you're not claiming you've been able to link that contraband to me?"

Frescone obviously knew Ness had not. Who told him? "You're smart, Frescone. I'll give you that. You learned from your previous mistakes. Reinforced the door. Barricaded the skylight. Figured out a way to hide all the gambling jiggery, fast. But I will get you."

"Mr. Ness, I am a private citizen and I am entitled to the same rights as other private citizens. This continual harassment is unacceptable. I will be calling the district attorney, who you may know is my personal friend. I will proffer charges against you, Mr. Ness. And that goes for your little lapdog, Chief Matowitz, too."

Every head in the room turned. Standing by the door, Matowitz looked as if he wished he could crawl into a hole and die.

"You know," Frescone continued, lowering his voice a notch, "I could find a place for you in my business organization, Ness. You don't have to be saddled with these —" He glanced contemptuously at Matowitz. "— civil servants."

Well, Ness thought, Frescone was a snappier dresser. And quite possibly more intelligent. But no. "I don't think so."

"Why be a patsy? This safety director routine is for losers. Give it up now and save yourself a lot of anguish."

"Thank you for your sage advice," Ness replied. "But I like my job just fine. And I will be back. Mark my words."

"As you wish, Mr. Ness. You'll be just as successful as you were tonight. But next time, I'll have my attorney waiting."

Ness turned silently and headed toward the door. He felt as if he were passing through a gauntlet, brushing against the shoulders of privileged and wealthy patrons who either sneered at him or ignored him altogether. They were no better in his mind than the criminals who ran the place. Maybe worse, since they didn't need this to make a living. They thought breaking the law was fun.

As he passed, the Banker subtly slipped a business card into Ness's pocket. He was looking away as he did it. He obviously didn't want Ness to make contact. Now.

"Will I be reading about this raid in the newspapers tomorrow?" Frescone shouted after him. "Or will this story be . . . untouchable?"

"I don't know," Ness said, just before he reached the door. "Can you read?"

He tipped his hat slightly and left The Thomas Club, feeling much more like The Elegant Mess than a renowned crimefighter. He would have to reverse this setback, as soon as possible.

He had to. So much depended upon it.

13

"You must be kiddin' me. Fifty dollars?"

"Swear to God."

"I could live two years offa fifty dollars."

"I know you could."

"And all I gotta do is come back to your place?"

"That's all."

"There must be some catch."

"Not at all. These are hard times. We have to help one another whatever way we can."

"That's good of you. But you know — a lady's got to be careful. There's been creepy stuff goin' on around here."

"I know that, too."

"How do I know this won't turn into something weird?"

"Do I look weird?"

"Nah. You're not from around here, are you?"

"Not originally."

"Let's just do it. I could really use that dough."

"Follow me."

It was so easy here. Almost too easy. Kingsbury Run teemed with the disaffected, the lost, the penniless. It was not a challenge at all. There had to be something more . . .

That was what his wife had said. That was what she always said. Always pushing him. Do this, do that, do more. A staff position at the hospital wasn't enough for her. Start your own practice. See patients of your own. Why? What was the challenge? How would that give him what he needed?

Curse the woman. He was better off without her.

This one was so stupid she wasn't suspicious until he had her tied to the chair.

"Hey, I said I'd let you have a little fun. I never said I'd let you tie me up!"

"Perhaps there was some miscommunication."

"Get me outta this. Now!"

"I believe you have misunderstood the nature of this visit."

"I know I don't want to be tied up. Have you heard about those people! Those corpses?"

"A little bit."

"So you see what I'm sayin'. Let me loose."

"I'm sorry. I can't. Not now."

"Then when?"

Hesitation. "When you least expect it." He shoved her forward onto the table. Her head dangled off the edge.

"Hey, what's this? What are you, some kinda pervert?"

"Some kind."

That was what his wife had said when she walked out on him. Of course she was bitter. She had not gotten what she'd bargained for. She wanted an uptown respectable citizen, and she got someone who would . . . never be that. Never wanted to be that.

Fine. But notifying the authorities — that was too much. Why had he endured all those twisted inquisitioners, would-be Freuds, trying to pry inside his head? They reached their verdict — but what did they know about it? He didn't need that job; he knew he would be provided for. Ignorant panel of so-called experts. Did they know what he knew? Had they glimpsed his destiny? The thought of so many unworthy people casting their aspersions on him — it made him angry. It made him want to hurt someone.

"Cut me loose and I'll give you something you'll like."

"I'll just use my imagination."

"Let me go!"

"When the time comes."

"What does that mean?"

"It means — hold still. If my aim is off, it will hurt a great deal more."

Back in school, they had told him that pain was to be avoided at all costs. Modern science had given them a solution. Anesthesia. We could numb the pain. Eliminate the suffering. People could undergo all kinds of mutilation and dismemberment and never feel the agony. This was a great advance for medical science, they had told him. But even while they were saying it, he felt a loss deep within the core of his being. Science had taken so much from him. Science needed to be put back in its place.

"Hurt? What are you talking about?"

"Let's hope nothing. I'm a lot better at it than I used to be. And more careful."

"What are you talking about?"

"Good night, Sleeping Beauty."

He swung the axe. It cut clean. He was definitely getting better at this.

And then it was over. So soon. Much too soon. It had barely begun to move him. There would have to be more cutting. Much more cutting.

He couldn't wait until the next time. And all the other times thereafter.

14

January 26, 1936

Whose idea had it been to move to Cleveland?

Angela Felice rolled over in her bed. Her hands and feet felt like ice. No quantity of blankets — not that they had that many — would be sufficient for a night such as this. It had been years since they could afford heating, and never once in Cleveland. She was grateful that Johnny had found work, such as it was, but she would never be accustomed to these unbearably freezing nights, so harsh she could hear water crackling into icicles and could feel every year of her life aching in the marrow of her bones.

She had not slept all night. Bad enough that Johnny snored louder than thunder. No matter how many times she kicked him and shoved him and pushed him onto his stomach, he always rolled back over and started snoring again. And then there was the dog. She belonged to that boy, Nick, over on Charity Avenue. Why wasn't he caring for her on this terrible night? She had been howling mournfully, uninterrupted, as if she desperately wanted to get someone's attention. And then, bizarrely enough, just as the sun was beginning to rise, Angela heard footsteps, loud footsteps, and a pounding, as if someone was beating on a nearby door. She thought she heard voices — or was it a single voice? She couldn't make out many of the words; her English was still so imperfect.

"Johnny? My Johnny?"

It was useless. He would wake when it was time to go to work and not a moment before. He had always been the soundest sleeper — and snorer — she had ever known. Nothing could rouse him before his time.

Enough. She rolled out of bed and gathered her tattered bathrobe. She was not going back to sleep. Perhaps she could at least chase that dog away. Even if she was not destined for slumber, she could do something to assist the sleep of others.

Her neighbors had told her that this neighborhood, surrounding East 20th and Central Avenue, near Charity Hospital, had once been quite respectable, even prestigious. No longer. The buildings had decayed and so had the people living and working within them. The streets were lined with a ramshackle collection of shops and manufacturers. Every other building was closed. The homes were weathered and the apartment complexes housed the worst possible neighbors, far too many children crowded into too little space, families with both parents and sometimes children working and still only a step away from Shantytown. They had prostitutes now! Women of ill fame and their filthy brothels, rubbing shoulders with family dwellings.

But it was all she and Johnny could afford and the sad fact was, she knew they were fortunate to have it.

She started coffee, then slid into her boots and her only overcoat, the fraying tan one with patches over the elbows. When she opened the door, a burst of frigid air slapped her like a fist across the face.

She stopped in her tracks, trying to catch her breath. She had forgotten how cold Cleveland could be in the early morning. And she had complained about how cold it was when she was in bed!

Angela steeled herself and stepped out into the street. Her body tensed. She imagined she could feel her blood turning to ice within her veins. Snow had fallen during the night and the bleak whiteness of the landscape made it seem even frostier than it was.

"Lady! Lady!"

She was trying not to shout. It would do little good to shoo away the dog if she woke all her neighbors in the process. She followed the sound of the barking until she found herself in the yard behind the Hart Building. She shopped at the White Front Meat Market on those rare occasions when she could afford such luxuries as meat.

"Lady! Go home. Go home now!"

The terrier made a whimpering noise but did not move. Angela noticed that there were two large half-bushel baskets beside the dog.

There was something inside the baskets.

She stepped closer. The dog barked louder.

She nudged the burlap bag covering of one of the baskets and saw the contents were wrapped in newspaper. The *Plain Dealer* — she recognized its distinctive typeface.

Her mother had always told her that curiosity would be her undoing. That might be extreme, but she found she couldn't stop herself from unwrapping the careful folds of the newspaper.

Lady barked as if her tail were on fire.

At first, Angela thought they must be hams. The market must've had some leftovers, or tainted meat, something they put away that naturally attracted the attention of a hungry dog.

Then she looked closer.

She felt her knees buckle. She fell forward, first against the wall, then down into the snow. She knew the wet snow would chill her skin, but she could not feel it. She could not feel anything except a sickness that started in the pit of her stomach and radiated throughout her entire body. She was glad she had not eaten, because she was certain that if she had she would have lost it. She was desperate to move away from the baskets, but found that her body would not respond. She could not move a muscle. She was forced to remain there, staring at the hideous contents of those baskets.

Mother of God! What has come to our neighborhood now?

15

Given that it was just after three in the morning, Ness tiptoed as quietly as possible through the front door of his Bay Village home — but he was not quiet enough.

Edna was waiting for him, sitting upright in an easy chair in the living room. All the lights in the house were off. He knew Edna was there because he could see the disembodied flare of a cigarette tip hovering in the air.

"Surprise, surprise. My hero husband home. And it isn't even dawn."

Ness walked toward the light. "Edna, what are you doing up?"

"Waiting for you."

"You should be in bed. What if I hadn't been able to come home tonight?"

She blew smoke coolly through pursed lips. "Then what difference would it make?"

He crouched down before her and laid his hands gently on her knees. "Honey, what's

127

wrong? What's bothering you?"

"You know what's bothering me." She wasn't even wearing nightclothes. She was wearing the same dress she'd had on the last time he'd seen her. Which, now that he thought about it, had been several days ago. Had she been wearing it continuously? Or had it cycled back around? "This is Chicago all over again."

"That's not fair."

"It's the truth."

"And to tell you the truth, I'm getting a little tired of having people throw Chicago in my face."

"The truth can be painful."

"We did good work in Chicago. We put away Capone. And over a hundred other mobsters."

"At what cost?" Her words had an edge so sharp Ness felt it cutting through his flesh, straight to his heart.

"Honey," he said quietly, "it won't be like this forever. I just started a new job. Of course it takes a while to get everything into place. But all this work will calm down in time and —"

"And you'll start making your raids during business hours?"

"Well . . . no."

"Do you ever think of me, when you're

off at work, doing brilliant important things, saving the world from evildoers?"

He tried to reach for her free hand, but she snatched it away before he could. "Of course I do, sweetheart. I bought you this house."

"I hate it."

"This is a very desirable neighborhood."

"I'm isolated. The buses don't come here. It takes forever to get to the city."

"You have neighbors."

"Not many. And they're all much older than I am."

"It wouldn't hurt you to get to know some of the people who have homes out here. Some of them are very influential —"

"That's your game, Eliot," she said, with as much disdain as she could muster. "Not mine."

Ness sighed. "I bought you furniture. Best we could afford. Clothes."

"I don't care about clothes. You're the clotheshorse."

"Well then, what do you want?"

"Are you entirely deaf, dumb, and blind?" She ground her cigarette bitterly into an ashtray. "I want a husband."

"You have a husband."

"No, I don't!" she screamed, so loudly Ness wondered if any of their few neighbors could hear.

"I took you out to dinner just . . . a few weeks ago."

"I can't believe you have the gall to even mention that. What a humiliation that was."

"I enjoyed it."

"Of course you did. You ate, enjoyed my company for a few seconds, then ran off to play Jack Armstrong, the All-American Boy."

"You're not —"

"Do you have any idea how humiliating that was for me? Left alone — dumped — while my dinner date runs off to play cops and robbers?"

"It was an opportunity I couldn't pass up."

"That's the truest thing you've said all night. You can't stop yourself. You're just like the drunkards and gamblers and drug addicts you put away. You have a constant craving for adventure you have to satisfy. Except it's never satisfied, never for long."

"Edna . . ."

"Another man might be interested in finding a little adventure at home with his wife. In the bedroom."

"Edna!"

"But not you. Never you. At least — not with me."

Ness held his head in his hands. How had

he let this happen? How was it possible to be so successful in the world — and such a disaster at home?

It occurred to him that the best course might be to simply put her in bed. But he hated for them to go to sleep mad, especially when they saw so little of each other during the day. He had never been a quitter. He tried again.

"I realize I can't be with you as often as I should. I have to show Cleveland I can do this job. But I will commit to spending as much time with you as is humanly possible. And I will promise you that as soon as I have shown Cleveland that I *can* do this job, everything will change. I will delegate the midnight raids to others. And anything else that's delegable. I will become a regular working stiff, keeping regular hours, home every night by six just as you're putting dinner on the table."

"I've heard this so many times . . ."

"I mean it."

"I know you do." For a moment, even in the darkness, he saw the faintest traces of a smile play on her lips. "That's what's so sad about you, Eliot. So tragic. You do mean well. But you'll forget everything you've said tonight the first time you get a tip about some third-rate moonshiner. A mere woman

131

can never compete with tomorrow's headlines."

Ness tried to think of something he could say, something that would save the night, save them. But nothing came. For all his education, it was amazing how quickly words deserted him when he needed them most.

"The mayor has invited us to dinner," he offered feebly.

"I don't want to go."

"Did you hear what I said? The mayor!"

"No."

"You said you wanted us to spend more time together."

"That won't be us spending time together. That will be you social climbing, trying to impress the mayor and the mayor's wife. I'm not interested."

Ness pushed himself to his feet. He felt wrung out, exhausted, much too tired to think clearly. He started toward the bedroom.

"Will I be reading about you in the papers tomorrow?"

Ness stopped. "I sincerely hope not."

"That's not the Eliot Ness I know."

"The raid tonight — didn't go so well."

"Eliot." For the first time all night, her voice softened a bit. "No one wins every time. Not even the great Eliot Ness."

"No," he replied quietly. "I suppose not." As he shuffled into the bedroom, he added, just under his breath: "But I can sure as heck try."

16

Using a pencil to avoid leaving fingerprints or other trace evidence, Merylo carefully unwrapped the last of the newspaper-wrapped bundles they had found in the two half-bushel baskets behind the White Front Meat Market at 2002 Central. They had expected to find meat in them. They had been right.

And terribly terribly wrong.

"You ever seen anything like this before?" Lieutenant Zalewski said in a hushed voice. His face was an ashen white.

"No," Merylo had to admit, "I have not. Not in fifteen years. This is . . . bizarre."

"You ever hear of the mob doing anything like this?"

"No." Merylo bristled slightly. "But that doesn't mean they didn't. Those boys can be downright inventive sometimes."

Zalewski stretched, glad to pull away from those revolting baskets. "Uniforms find the rest yet?"

"No. Nothing. Not even —"

Merylo didn't want to finish, and he didn't need to finish. They both knew what they were thinking.

No one had found the head.

Once the papers were unwrapped, it became all too clear that they contained the severed pieces of a human body. Tidily wrapped and stored in those two baskets, they found the lower half of a female torso, both thighs, and a right arm.

"Have them fan out," Merylo said. "Widen the search. Get as many men on it as possible."

Zalewski dutifully passed along the commands while Merylo tried to make some sense out of what they had discovered.

Was it the same killer? He wasn't sure what was worse — to imagine that the previous killer had descended to this level, or to imagine that there might be more than one hood capable of doing something like this.

He wondered what this would do to the *Cleveland News* theory that the first two victims had been the product of a sordid love triangle. They had no evidence in support but lots of glamour, and thus it captured the largest share of the public's imagination. He didn't see how this third victim, a female, fit in. If she was the third side of the triangle, who was doing the killing? A third lover? A morally indignant neighbor? It just didn't make any sense.

Zalewski returned to his side. "I got them on it, sir. There are actually some men volunteering to help. Even as disturbing as it is."

"They're scared," Merylo said quietly. "They want this killer caught. Before he gets to their neighborhood. Their families."

"Anything else I can do?"

"Call Pearce and get him down here as soon as possible. Wrap up that arm and get it to the Bertillon boys."

"But Pearce can be awfully —"

"Zalewski, do you have any idea how important the first forty-eight hours can be? That's when most crimes are solved — if they are solved. After that the trail goes cold. Right now we've got a lot of men — volunteers even — scouring this area. The more information they have, the better. So if Bertillon can identify this corpse, we're going to let them."

"Yes, sir. Of course, sir."

"If you learn anything from working with me, son — and I hope you do — you should learn this. A cop has to keep his nose clean. Stay off the take. Follow the rules." He

136

paused. "Except those rules that sometimes have to be broken to keep some butcher like this one from hacking another innocent person to bits. Do you understand me?"

Zalewski swallowed. "Yes, sir. Perfectly."

"Good. Now where is this woman who found the baskets? Angela Felice."

"They took her to the hospital, sir. She went into shock. Might even have some frostbite. After she found the baskets, she passed out. Collapsed in the snow, and she wasn't wearing much. She was discovered some time later by a drunk looking for shelter."

"Did he revive her?"

"No. He shook her, but it didn't work. He was pretty impaired."

"Gotcha."

"He ran into the Meat Market and got help. He was slurring badly so it took them awhile to figure out what he was saying. Finally the owner, Charles Page, came out and found the body parts. He called the police."

"Good thing someone got involved who had the wherewithal to get the word to us. Might've been spring thaw before we were on the scene." He frowned. "You think there's any chance at all this woman —"

"I don't think so, sir. Mrs. Felice was

really shaken up. If she was behind the killing, they oughta give her an Academy
Award, 'cause she would be the best darn
actress in the world."

Of course that was right. Didn't make any
sense that she would be involved. Merylo
was embarrassed at himself for asking.
Showed just how desperate he was for a
clue, for any workable theory.

"Look, Zalewski, you go check on her at
the hospital, then let's meet back at the office at five and see if any reports have come
in from the men working the streets. If we
—"

" 'Scuse me. You in charge?"

Merylo looked down at the scrawny man
with the camera that was wider then he was.
Didn't recognize him, but the brownie said
it all. Press.

"I guess I'm in charge, but I don't have
anything —"

"My name's O'Rourke. I'm with the
Cleveland News. Can you confirm that this
is the work of the same killer who left the
corpses on Kingsbury Run?"

"I'm not prepared to give interviews at
this time."

"Does that mean you affirm or deny?"

"Neither. I —"

"Is there a police cover-up? Are you hiding something?"

"Don't be absurd. It's just —"

"So this is the work of the same killer?"

Merylo cleared his throat. "It's too early to draw any conclusions. In time —"

"Do you think there's one killer, or a gang of them?"

"A gang? Look, this kind of yellow journalism isn't going to help anyone. Let us do our job and if we learn anything —"

"I think you do know something. You're just not telling."

"Listen here, O'Rourke." Merylo could feel his temperature rising. He quickly checked it. Chief Matowitz would not be pleased if he told this man what he thought of him. Of his whole profession. How did Eliot Ness do it? How did he come off so calm, so charming in all those press conferences? He made it look easy and he came off a hero. Merylo always came out looking like a grunting pig. "If we have anything we'll notify the press. We may need your help disseminating pictures or descriptions. Like we did with Andrassy."

"What effect do you think this will have on tourism?"

"None, I hope."

"We've got the Expo coming up. The American Legion convention. Is anyone going to want to come to Cleveland after this gets out?"

Merylo wiped his brow. "Honestly, man, have some sense. More people died last week in traffic accidents than this killer has taken."

"Then you do think this is the work of the same killer?"

Merylo's eyes darkened. "This conversation is over. I'm leaving. If you have any further questions —"

"Do you think these murders are connected to the Lady in the Lake?"

Merylo stopped in his tracks. "What are you talking about?"

"You remember that one, don't you? The Lady in the Lake?"

"You're not talking about King Arthur . . ."

"I'm talking about September of '35. Guy named LaGassie was walking along the shore of Lake Erie, just east of Bratenahl near Euclid Beach Park. Sees something in the water. Turns out to be the lower half of a woman's torso, legs cut off at the knees. A couple weeks earlier and about thirty miles east, a handyman found vertebrae and ribs with some rotting flesh attached. People assumed they went together, but I don't think anyone was ever really sure."

"When was this?"

O'Rourke checked his notepad. "September 5. Last year." He beamed. "My paper came up with the name, Lady of the Lake. At the time, people were saying the frail musta gotten caught in a boat propeller, some kinda weird accident. But now . . ."

Merylo looked at him sternly. "Are you sure about this?"

"Course I'm sure. You don't believe me, ask your coroner. Pearce was on duty. He must know all about it."

Merylo felt his chest heaving. That insufferable, uncooperative son-of—

"So what do you think? Did the killer start all this more than a year ago?"

Merylo wrapped his coat tightly around himself. "Of course not. That's absurd. It's just a twisted coincidence."

"Can I quote you on that?"

"Absolutely. The first victims were the ones we found on Kingsbury Run. Now if you'll excuse me, man, I've got some work to do."

Merylo strode away before O'Rourke could protest. He didn't have time to go on jabbering with this flunky. He had too many places to go, people to interview.

Starting with Dr. Arthur Pearce, county coroner.

17

Robert Chamberlin hunched over Ness's desk, feeling as tired and frustrated as he ever had in his entire life. He had been an athlete in his younger days, and he still considered himself to be in excellent shape. So he shouldn't be completely tuckered out by forty-five minutes of talking. But he was.

"Sir, are you sure about this? You've got almost three hundred names here. That's a third of the force."

"What surprises you? That there aren't more? We both know the Cleveland police department is rotten to the core."

"But that doesn't mean you can start firing everyone."

"I'm not firing them. Not all of them." Ness pointed to the explanatory lines on the chart. "Most are just suspended, like before. Some are being transferred."

"But — so many!"

"Bob, you know as well as I do that I'll

never be able to go after the mob effectively, or the labor racketeers, or anyone else, if there are spies in the department informing them of every move I make."

"But sir — you must see that cutting so many people will stir up animosity in the police department."

Ness leaned back in his chair and put his feet up on the desk. "Well, Bob, my general impression is that they're not all that crazy about me over there as it is."

Chamberlin burst out laughing. "You may be right about that."

"I know I am. And I don't blame them. Now, Matowitz is okay — even after that fiasco at The Thomas Club, he's getting better press than he has in his entire career. But the rest of the men, the rank and file. Working hard, day in, day out, walking the beat, paid too little and appreciated even less. And then some out-of-town hotshot sails in and starts stealing all the headlines. No, they have every right to their resentment." He paused. "And I have the right to clean out the dirty ones. Fair's fair."

"Sounds like you've got it figured out."

"Well, I am a college man, you know."

"I believe I've heard the police officers mention that once or twice. And the way you dress. And the way you talk."

"I can't help it if my voice is somewhat high-pitched."

"It isn't that."

"Then what?"

"You really want to know?"

"If I didn't, why would I ask?"

Chamberlin pushed his wire-rims up his nose. "It's the things you say. Gosh. Gee whiz. Holy moley."

"And what's wrong with that?"

"Let's just say that most of the men on the force go in for more colorful expressions."

"That kind of talk is for people who haven't had the education to express themselves more intelligently."

"Be that as it may, it perpetuates your Boy Scout image."

"And what's wrong with being a Boy Scout? Anyway, I want this list of suspended officers on Matowitz's desk before close of business."

"It's your funeral."

"Why did you agree to work with me, Bob? You could've stayed with Chief Matowitz."

"They weren't using me, sir. Not like they should."

"And how should they use you?"

"I'm smart, sir. Not to toot my own horn —"

"I think you already did."

"Well — I don't care. It's true."

"And Chief Matowitz didn't appreciate you?"

"Mostly had me making coffee. Running errands at the five-and-dime." He lowered his head. "Walking his wife's dog."

Ouch. "And you thought you could do more?"

"I —" He swallowed, then started again. "I know why your raid on The Thomas Club failed, sir."

"I know why it failed, too, kid. Frescone and his men had time to hide the gambling paraphernalia."

"It's more than that. From what I've heard, The Thomas Club is very elaborate. They have table games — blackjack and poker and stuff. They have off-track betting. Run a policy game. Roulette. They didn't have time to stash so much stuff, even if they were using lightweight tables with breakaway legs, like some of the parlors do." He paused. "They did, however, have time to move the people."

Ness looked at him levelly. "Huh?"

"The people. Patrons. Much easier to move people than all that equipment."

"Move them from where?"

Chamberlin grabbed a rolled up paper from his briefcase. "May I?"

Ness nodded. Chamberlin spread it across Ness's desk.

"This is an architectural plan of The Thomas Club. At least as it was constructed, thirty years ago, to serve as a warehouse."

"Where in the world did you get this?"

"City Hall. They have to be filed to get a building permit."

Ness rubbed his forehead. "I didn't know that."

"Don't feel bad, sir. Most people don't. But I did. Because —"

"Because you're smart."

Chamberlin averted his eyes. "Yes, sir." He removed two photographs from his briefcase. "These pics were taken by the press about a month ago, inside The Thomas Club."

"That's just like what I saw."

"But compare it to the blueprint, sir. Notice anything strange?"

It only took Ness a moment. "The building is bigger than it looks. Or was."

"That's right. To be specific, what looks like the rear wall, isn't. There must be a passageway somewhere. A hidden door."

Ness immediately grasped what Chamberlin was saying. "There's another room in the back. A hidden room. That's where they do the gambling."

"I — I think so, sir, yes."

Fire lit in Ness's eyes. "So next time, we raid the rear."

"I don't believe it's quite that simple. They reinforced the front door and the skylight. Even if you find the hidden door or doors, I think you have to assume it's reinforced as well."

"Probably doubly reinforced. All right, Bob, this is your operation. How do we get in? Fast enough to catch these crooks in action."

"I have some thoughts on that, sir."

"I figured you did."

"But before I share them, um — could you talk to Chief Matowitz about a full-time appointment? Not just a loan arrangement. I want to work for you."

Ness looked at him sharply. "Have any idea how much work, how many hours, that might involve?"

"Haven't I been out with you every night?"

"Good point. Can you keep your nose clean?"

"Absolutely."

"Got any objection to working days at a time?"

"Not the least."

"Got a wife?"

"Nope."

"Probably better that way. You sure you want to do this?"

"I am, sir. My mother says you're doing God's own work, right here in Cleveland. I want to be a part of that. I want to help you any way I can."

Ness grinned, then slapped Chamberlin on the shoulder. "Then you're on the team, pal. Now tell me how we get into that club."

18

"Why didn't you tell me about this?"

"There was nothing to tell."

"You're saying another woman bein' butchered is nothing?"

"It happened some time ago. I had no reason to believe there was any connection. Still don't."

"You should've said something."

"You should've known."

Merylo bit down on his lower lip, which prevented him from saying what he was thinking. Pearce had always been an arrogant so-and-so, but now he was interfering with Merylo's ability to do his job, and that was unacceptable. The coroner was supposed to help the team, not hinder it.

"That woman's torso must've been brought to you. How could you forget something like that?"

"I didn't. I simply didn't see a connection. And excuse me, but weren't you on the homicide squad? Why didn't you re-member?"

"Because it wasn't reported as a homi-cide." It was a mistake, meeting Pearce here, in his own inner sanctum. It gave him an edge. A home-team advantage. Should've thought of an excuse to make the good doc-tor come to him. "They had the idea that it was an accidental death. Boating accident."

"It might have been. The body was too decomposed by the time I got it to draw any definitive conclusions."

"Whether it was or wasn't, that shrimp from the *News* is going to tell people it was. He's going to say this Torso Killer has been running around Cleveland for more than a year and we haven't done anything to stop him."

"I don't see that this is my problem, much less my fault."

Lieutenant Zalewski took a tiny step forward, clearing his throat. Pretty pathetic when your greenhorn assistant has to play peacemaker. "I read your report on the first case, Doctor. The Lady in the Lake. Despite the state of decomposition, you wrote that there was something unusual about the texture of the skin."

"I recall that," Pearce said, fingering his glasses.

"In fact, you wrote that it was possible the body had been exposed to some sort of preservative."

"And your point is?"

"His point is obvious," Merylo barked. "It's the same thing you said about the Kingsbury Run corpses. It makes a strong case for a connection between the murders."

Pearce took a cigarette out of his pocket case and lit it. "Perhaps." He inhaled deeply, then waved it about in the air. Merylo wondered if he used cigarettes as a shield, something to create a barrier between them. "There are other possible explanations. A corpse floating in Lake Erie could be exposed to many corrosive chemicals."

"No one at the *News* is going to report that. They'll go with the obvious. Reporters always do. Nothing can stop them."

"Of course something can stop them. Catch the killer. That will stop them cold."

"Do you think I'm not trying?" Merylo could feel his frustration mounting. Soon he wouldn't be able to suppress the anger. He needed to get himself out of here. He probably wasn't doing any good, and he risked alienating someone who, like it or not, he needed on his side. "It took two days, but my men found the rest of the last corpse on Orange Avenue, just a few blocks south of where we found the baskets. Everything except the head. Have you examined it?"

Pearce shrugged. "They recovered the upper half of a female torso, minus the right arm, which we already had, and the head. Both lower legs. Mixed with extraneous substances that have been positively identified as charcoal, chicken feathers, and hay."

"So . . . our killer is a farmer?"

"I would not jump to any conclusions. None of those substances are difficult to find in the city."

"Is there anything useful you can tell me?"

Pearce glanced at his report. "The torso was bisected at the second lumbar vertebra. A vertical incision runs the full length of the bottom half. The thighs were significantly obese and severed at the hip. The right arm was severed at the shoulder joint. It evidences signs of rigor mortis. Also" — he drew in his breath — "her complete reproductive system was removed. The whole thing. And half the appendix. And as before, the killer left smooth edges, neat incisions. He is good with a knife."

"Like — some kind of professional? A doctor?"

"There are any number of people accustomed to dissection or cutting flesh. I personally find the suggestion that the crime might have been committed by someone trained and educated in the medical arts abhorrent and . . . unlikely in the extreme."

"Then who was it?"

"I couldn't possibly say."

"Look, Doc," Merylo said, "we're desperate here. We've been combing the countryside for miles around Kingsbury Run, and Andrassy's home neighborhood, and now the Charity Hospital area."

"With no leads?"

"We get leads. But none of them go anywhere. Trouble is, the papers and radio are getting people so worked up, they're just not rational anymore. They're scared, and scared people do stupid stuff. Every time they hear a footstep or a barking dog or see a picnic basket, they go into a panic. They suspect every stranger, every neighbor with a pair of binoculars, everyone with a funny accent. The leads don't lead anywhere because they're based on irrational fear, not information."

"Your killer has twice left corpses in very public places. Eventually you're bound to find someone who caught him in the act."

"You'd think, wouldn't you? But so far not. So far no one saw him do anything."

"Or at least," Zalewski added quietly, "no

one who saw him do anything lived to talk about it."

Another disturbing possibility, and one that Merylo had to admit had crossed his mind.

"We've been trying everything we know. We've questioned Andrassy's relatives, everyone who knew him. We got nothing. Interviewed all the women associated with him — and there were many. Learned nothing."

"Except," Zalewski said, interrupting again, "whatever it was that man had, I wish I could get some."

"Yeah, the ladies loved him, but someone else didn't. Some folks say Andrassy carried an ice pick with him for protection — but that didn't save him from the man who cut off his head. My men canvassed the neighborhood at the summit of Jackass Hill, showing the Andrassy mug shot around. No one knew anything."

"What about his work history?" Pearce inquired. "Have you investigated that?"

"Of course I have. What do you take me for, an amateur? Problem is, he rarely had anything you could call a real job. Your typical con man. Grifter. Had a job at City Hospital that he worked off and on over eight years. Probably came back whenever he needed some cash, left as soon as he didn't."

Pearce tapped the tip of his cigarette against the ashtray, his eyebrows knitted. "Where did he work in the hospital?"

"The loony bin. Why?"

Pearce laid down his cigarette. "You're sure about that?"

"Yeah, I'm sure. What's your point?"

"I don't have a point," Pearce said, turning his eyes away and staring at a fixed point on the wall. "But it would not surprise me to learn that this killer had spent time in a psychiatric ward."

"You suspect some freak who can't even think straight could pull off these crimes and get away with it? I'm not even sure the mob's top man could commit these crimes and get away with it!"

Pearce sighed heavily, then retook his cigarette and inhaled deeply. "Detective Merylo. Have you ever heard of a man known as Jack the Ripper?"

Merylo searched his mind. "Think so. Some kind of murderer, right? In England?"

"What do you know about him?"

"I — don't really remember."

"Jack the Ripper stalked the streets of London in the 1880s," Pearce explained, "in Whitechapel, one of the poorest and most decadent parts of the city — not unlike Kingsbury Run. Took at least five victims. Taunted the police with cryptic messages. Used a knife. But he wasn't content to simply kill his victims. He destroyed them. With such anatomical accuracy that some people suspected he might be a doctor. Or a butcher. He seemed particularly interested in destroying female reproductive systems. Ripped them to shreds. Hence the name."

"Was he ever caught?"

"Never."

Merylo squinted. "And you're saying this . . . Jack the Ripper might be the one who's killing people in Cleveland?"

Pearce's eyes drifted heavenward. "No, that is not what I'm saying. Detective, have you considered the possibility of consulting an alienist?"

Merylo blinked twice. "A what?"

"A doctor of the mind."

"How's he supposed to catch a killer?"

"By understanding how he thinks."

"How's that going to help?"

"If the killer is not behaving rationally, traditional methods of crime solving will be of no avail. You must develop new approaches."

"Sounds like a load of hogwash to me."

"If you understand how the killer thinks, you might be able to anticipate his next move."

"I don't want a next move! I want to catch him before he strikes again."

Pearce blew a dense cloud of smoke into the air. "Have either of you gentlemen heard of a Viennese doctor called Sigmund Freud?"

"No," Merylo said gruffly. "We haven't."

"Um, actually . . ." Zalewski shuffled his feet. "I have."

Merylo stared at him as if he were some kind of bug.

"What do you know about him?"

Zalewski's face flushed. "A few years ago, I was having these really bad dreams. Nightmares, you know? I'd dream I woke up in the morning and parts of my body were missing. Or I'd be coming to work, except with no clothes on."

"That's just weird," Merylo grumbled.

"Not really," Pearce said. "Those are universal fears. Haven't you ever had dreams like that?"

Merylo's face hardened. "No. Never."

"Anyway," Zalewski continued, "my ma was worried about me. So she got me this book by that guy you were talking about, that Freud. *The Interpretation of Dreams.*

Turns out this guy thinks your dreams are like symbols, and by examining your dreams you can learn about yourself."

"What did you learn about yourself from the book?" Pearce asked.

Zalewski stared at the floor. "Tell you the truth — I thought it was kinda tough goin'."

Pearce smiled slightly, possibly for the first time Merylo had ever seen. "You're not the first to think so. Doctor Freud is perhaps a greater doctor than a writer. And there have been questions about the accuracy of his English translator." Pearce paused, taking another drag on his cigarette. "If you're interested, I could put you in touch with an alienist of my acquaintance. He lives in New York but for a case of this significance, I'm sure —"

"Thanks very much, Doctor," Merylo said abruptly, "but I don't think we need any newfangled college-boy nonsense. We'll solve this case the old-fashioned way. By beating the streets and doing good solid detective work."

"As you wish. But if you change your mind —"

"Thanks, Doc, but I won't. Andrassy may have been a punk, but he was still a criminal and he hung with criminals. If we sniff around long enough, we'll find out who wanted him dead bad enough to —"

All at once, the door to the coroner's office flew open. "Detective Merylo!"

Merylo recognized the kid as one of the boys from Bertillon, but he couldn't remember his name. "Yeah?"

"We've identified the new corpse."

Merylo's eyes ballooned. "Yeah?"

"Took awhile — the fingers were in such poor condition. But we managed it. Turns out we have her prints on file."

A smile spread from one end of Merylo's face to the other. "Because she has a criminal record?"

"Exactly."

"Swell." Merylo gave Zalewski a little shove toward the door. "We've identified two victims now. All we have to do now is figure out what — or who — they have in common."

He waved at Dr. Pearce as he passed through the door. "Thanks for nothing, Doctor. Turns out we don't need you after all."

19

Ness had been to The Thomas Club before. And he'd been thinking about it ever since.

Predictably, his failed raid had been all over the papers. He knew he couldn't afford another flop, not if he wanted to get the funding he needed for all his plans to make the city safer.

Chief Matowitz had opted not to join him tonight. Funny how quickly a man could go from camera-ready to camera-shy. He had at least loaned Ness some of his men. Ness would need them.

Chamberlin came to the front of the building after making his final inspection tour. He was efficient as ever, perhaps even more so now that he had a permanent assignment to the Office of the Safety Director.

"Everything in order?"

"Yes, everyone is where they should be. But I still don't understand —"

"Humor me."

If Ness weren't mistaken, the front façade of The Thomas Club had been gussied up in the short time since his last raid. It was looking not so much New Orleans as bordello. Was the gambling business that profitable? Or was this simply Frescone's way of thumbing his nose at the cops, and Ness in particular? You can't touch me, he was saying. I'll build an opulent, garish, neon-lit pleasure palace right under your nose, and there's nothing you can do about it.

Ness felt his jaw setting together. We'll see.

"Watches synchronized, sir."

"Excellent."

"Perhaps we should give them three more minutes. Just to be sure."

"Two will be enough."

"Sometimes people don't move too fast when they've been drinking."

"They moved pretty fast the other night."

Chamberlin almost smiled. "Threat of imprisonment is probably a decent motivator."

"Exactly. About time?"

"It is."

Ness knew Chamberlin hated being kept in the dark. Regrettable, but unavoidable.

"I'm moving to the east side of the building," Ness announced, buttoning up his camel-hair overcoat. It was still bitterly cold outside. "I want to be able to watch both sides of the operation."

Precisely two minutes later, every car parked in the lot facing The Thomas Club — all of them owned by police officers — turned on its headlights. The tacky gambling den was bathed in white.

"And as if that weren't enough . . ." Ness muttered quietly to himself.

The horns blared in every car, creating a fearful din. Ness reluctantly covered his ears with his hands. The combined trumpet of all those horns was head-splitting, even worse than he had imagined.

Ness could hear the migration begin. Someone opened the front door, peeked out, saw the array of cars, and slammed the door shut again.

Two minutes was too long, Ness thought. Next time go with one, unless they're moving from another city.

He waved his left arm, signaling Chamberlin to proceed. An instant later, another row of vehicles turned on their lights. These were trucks, heavy-duty freight vehicles. And in the bright, almost blinding light, it was clear that each had been fitted with a metal battering ram attached to the front grill. Chamberlin had gotten the idea from observing the cowcatcher on a train passing through Kingsbury Run.

An instant later, the trucks roared into action. They raced their engines for a few moments — a warning to anyone who hadn't already moved to the front lobby. Then the trucks lurched into action. They rushed forward, tires squealing, moving so fast Ness could feel the wind rush against his face. All pointed toward the rear of the building. The secret annex Chamberlin discovered on the blueprints.

They had pinpointed the room as best they could, but it was impossible to be one hundred percent accurate. The trucks that hit a steel-reinforced door didn't get as far. One truck had to back up and ram the plate three times before it broke through. The two on the ends sailed through the wooden frame like it was papier-mâché.

Ness closed his eyes. Please, let them find something. A poker chip. A playing card. Something.

As soon as the engines were shut off, twelve of Matowitz's men rushed into the now exposed rear room of The Thomas Club.

The boys laid off their horns, and for the first time, Ness could hear the cries of the patrons huddled at the front of the building, the distressed tumult of too many people crowded into too little space, the usual protestations and complaints encountered when the wealthy and privileged were inconvenienced. But this must have sounded as if an earthquake had hit Cleveland.

What he would do for a picture of that.

Ness headed toward the building. As he walked, he noticed a group of boys watching. They looked dirty and badly dressed, their clothes torn and ragged. They were obviously poor. He knew from the reports he'd read that they were probably living with one parent or had no parents at all. Living off scraps they could find in trash cans behind Automats and cafeterias. Street toughs, the kind that made Cleveland the worst city in the country for juvenile crime. Some of the reports he'd read talked about kids becoming hardened criminals before they hit puberty.

He waved. One of the boys shouted back at him. "Are you really *the* Eliot Ness?"

"I suppose," he shouted back.

The boys whooped and shouted and cheered, throwing their hands up into the air. Interesting reaction, Ness mused, coming from hardened criminals.

He wished he could stop and talk to them.

There were some details you just couldn't learn from reading reports. But that would have to wait for another time.

As Ness neared the building, he saw Chamberlin restraining someone by the shoulders. Frescone. He watched as Chamberlin slipped handcuffs over his wrists.

"He was trying to escape," Chamberlin said. This time his excitement had overcome his reserve. "It worked!"

"It wouldn't have worked without your investigative work."

"It wouldn't have worked if you hadn't gotten the rats off the force."

Ness tilted his head to one side. "Teamwork."

"Yeah."

"I haven't done anything," Frescone growled. "You've got nothing on me."

"He was carrying a concealed weapon," Chamberlin offered.

Ness nodded. "That's good enough for now. It'll get better."

"You won't get away with this!" Frescone bellowed.

Ness stopped, looking at the mobster calmly. "I already did." He took a step closer, then whispered. "You should've shut down when you had the chance. I told you I'd be back."

"I don't care what some stinking cop says."

"You should. I always keep my word."

Ness started to walk away, but Frescone jerked forward. Chamberlin pulled him back.

"You'll be sorry, Ness. Don't you know what this means? Me and my friends — we're declaring war on you."

"You're too late. I declared war on you the day I took the oath of my office. This was all inevitable." He winked at Chamberlin. "You were just too stupid to realize it."

By this time, he mused, the men inside should have things well under control. "Bob, you go in the rear, see what the boys have found."

"And you?"

"I'm going to the front door and knocking. Polite, like my sainted mother taught me. I'll meet you somewhere in the middle."

Ness passed through the line of officers, then knocked on the front door.

It was opened by Shimmy Patton, one of Frescone's co-owners.

"I'm Eliot Ness, Safety Director. I have a warrant to search the premises."

"We ain't doin' nothin' wrong."

"Then you have nothing to worry about."

"You can't come in and start bustin' up

the place. It ain't legal."

"That's for the judges to decide. In the meantime, I have a warrant to search. I believe my colleagues have already begun the process. You may have heard them entering your secret gambling parlor."

Over Patton's shoulder, Ness saw Chamberlin waving at him, holding something up in the air.

A roulette wheel.

"May I come in?" Ness said, smiling.

Patton couldn't manage an answer.

"Are you feeling all right, Shimmy?" He grinned. "You look all shook up."

20

Merylo had never eaten in Pierre's. In fact, he'd never been inside the place before and he didn't expect he ever would again. But it was a tenet of his profession that police work sometimes led one to unsavory locales. And that included this swanky eatery and nightclub, where in the midst of the darkest days of the Depression the fortunate few men who could afford to do so sat in tuxedos, sipped ten-buck bottles of champagne, and danced the night away.

"Excuse me," Merylo said, trying to use his most soothing voice, which still wasn't all that soothing, "are you Arthur Dollarhyde?"

The man with the snowy white mustache barely looked up at him. "And you are?"

"Peter Merylo. Homicide Division."

"What can you possibly want with me?"

"Just a little talk. It's part of an investigation."

Dollarhyde looked at him with a withering expression. "I'll send my assistant around tomorrow morning."

Merylo saw this was going to be more difficult than he had imagined. The police force was still a relatively recent addition to city government, mostly staffed by lower- and middle-class immigrants, and some people didn't give them much respect. Especially the very rich, who considered talking to police officers beneath them and felt that as pillars of Cleveland society, they ought to be permitted to do anything they wanted to do, regardless of the law.

"No, sir. I'm afraid I need to speak with you now. If you'd like, you may excuse your wife. In fact . . ." He hesitated just a moment, hoping his message would come across. "I think it advisable."

"Nonsense. Margaret and I have been together for thirty-one years. We have no secrets."

"Everyone has secrets."

"And let me tell you something else." Dollarhyde drew up his shoulders and leaned forward, obviously putting on a show for his wife. "You'd best be careful what you say. I have a reputation in this town and I will defend it."

Merylo pulled out an available chair and

seated himself, even though he knew this would irritate Dollarhyde. Actually, that was pretty much why he did it. How his plain brown suit must stick out in this sea of penguin getups, he thought, taking a little pleasure in that, too.

"Last chance, sir. You really should excuse your wife."

"I will not!"

Merylo sighed. "As you wish." He withdrew a black-and-white mug shot from his jacket pocket. "Have you ever seen this woman before?"

Dollarhyde barely glanced at it. "Of course not. She looks like the lowest class of woman."

"Pretty much was."

"Then I am offended that you would ask if I knew her." He gestured at a waiter who promptly appeared at the table. "Bring my wife and I another bottle of champagne. And get this odious man out of here."

Merylo waited patiently.

The waiter was obviously conflicted, caught between two worlds. "I am so sorry, monsieur," he said, in an accent so thickly French that Merylo wondered if it could possibly be real. "The gentleman is a gendarme. That is, he is with the police. We cannot prevent him from speaking to our

170

customers. Much as we might like to do so."

"I'm outraged!" Dollarhyde bellowed. "If you don't evict him immediately, I will not come here again!"

"If you do try to evict me," Merylo said quietly, "our exalted safety director might be here tomorrow evening with a big axe."

The waiter shrugged. "You see, monsieur? There is nothing I can do. I will bring the champagne." He disappeared, and Merylo suspected he was glad to be gone.

Merylo tapped on the photo, redirecting Dollarhyde's attention. "Name's Florence Polillo. Friends called her Flo. She was an occasional waitress, an occasional barmaid, and by all accounts, a full-time drunk."

"A perfectly hideous woman."

"I won't argue the point." Merylo leaned in closer. "But I will tell you that I have three reliable witnesses who tell me they saw you employ her services on the night of September 26 of last year."

"Preposterous. I can assure you I would never eat or drink in any establishment that would employ her."

"That I don't doubt. But waiting tables and slinging drinks were her day jobs. By night —" He paused, glancing again at the man's poor, probably entirely innocent, wife. Well, he had twice told him to excuse

171

her. "By night, she worked as a prostitute."

Dollarhyde gasped. A bit too much, Merylo thought.

His wife turned slowly to face him.

Dollarhyde spoke in low guttural tones. "My lawyer will be at your office tomorrow morning."

"I'll send my assistant over to talk to him."

"What's your game, copper? Hoping to get your name in the paper? Thinking you'll find your way out of the vice squad by fingering a person who has contributed more to this city in a day than you will in your entire life?"

"You are confused," Merylo said, maintaining the same even tone. "This is not a vice investigation."

"But you said the woman was a — a —"

"Yes, she was. But according to the fingerprints on her right hand, she was also the last victim of the Torso Murderer."

Dollarhyde's wife's eyes ballooned. She pressed one hand against her beaded chest.

"Are you suggesting that I —"

"The only thing I'm suggesting, sir, is that you knew her."

"I deny it."

"I don't blame you. But you did, and I'm hoping you can give me an idea why someone might want to kill her. And hack her into pieces."

Dollarhyde stared at Merylo for a long time, his chest heaving. His hands were visibly shaking. He tossed down an entire glass of champagne. "Margaret. Leave us alone for a few minutes."

"I'd rather stay."

"Margaret. Go!"

She glared for a moment, then obediently left the table.

"Wonderful woman," he muttered. "In many respects. But not in one very important one. The one that makes a man a man. You know what I mean?"

"I think I do."

"She's had back problems for years. She can't . . . support my weight. So what else could I do?"

Merylo could think of several alternatives, but he kept his mouth shut.

"I tried to be discreet. Limited myself to women of the lower orders so word would never travel back to my wife or any of her friends."

"That makes sense." Merylo was a patient man, but not really interested in the great titan of industry's true confessions. He needed to get back to the crime. "Do you know any of Flo's friends? Acquaintances?"

"Absolutely not. Only person I ever met

in connection with her was that disgusting Chink Adler. At The Harvard Club. Do you know it?"

"I've read about it in the papers."

"He knew Flo. He introduced us."

"Do you think he might . . . hold any hostility toward her?"

"I never saw the two of them together when they weren't fighting. He was always threatening her, and then she'd threaten back. Saw him whack her more than once, too."

"Not a very nice way to treat a friend."

"Friend?" He made a small snorting sound. "Hardly that. He was her business manager."

"Her — excuse me?"

Dollarhyde mouthed the word. *Pimp.*

Merylo felt sweat racing down the sides of his face as he leaped the fence and raced across the open yard onto Euclid Avenue. Why did the jerk have to run? He was too old for this kind of chasing around. Actually, even ten years ago, he hadn't been that good at it. Short legs and twenty unnecessary pounds were not the ideal attributes for a sprint.

"I just wanna talk to you!" Merylo shouted, but the man did not stop, did not even slow. He had been ten feet ahead when this chase started and he was at least thirty feet now. Merylo had a hunch this was not going to end well.

"Police! I order you to stop!"

As if that were going to do any good. The twerp must've had a reason for running and that reason wasn't going to be assuaged by the knowledge he was being chased by a police officer. Skinny little runt, who knew what he had done?

Sure could run, though.

He headed toward another fence and Merylo hoped that might slow him down, but the kid vaulted over as if he were walking on air. Merylo knew that if he tried that, he'd fall flat on his face. It was hopeless. This chase was over. He'd have to try another —

"You wanna talk to this guy?"

Merylo stopped short, leaning breathlessly against the fence, panting for air.

Zalewski was holding the punk by the collar, his service revolver pressed into the kid's side.

"Where'd you come from?"

Zalewski shoved his captive up against the fence. "When he took off running, you took off after him. But I knew that alley emptied out onto Euclid and I knew the fences and hills would slow him down. I grew up around here. So while you did the line drive I circled around to where I knew he'd have to come out."

Merylo nodded, slowly regaining enough breath to speak. "Next time I'll circle around. You do the chasing." He grabbed the breathless punk by the collar and shook him. "I already know you were Flo Polillo's pimp, Adler, so don't bother lying about it. We're not from vice, and I'm sure you'll say you were only trying to protect her."

The skinny man in the oversize sport coat jumped on that opening like a cat on tuna. "It's not just about the protectin'. It's about the huntin'."

At least the man was talking. Now if he could only say something that made sense. "Hunting?"

"For clients," he explained slowly, as if he were teaching ABCs to a toddler. "Paying clients."

"Like Arthur Dollarhyde?"

He didn't deny it. "That was brilliant. Great stroke of luck. I knew Flo could charge a man like him three times what she normally got. She had something that Dollarhyde dude really liked."

"A strong back."

"What?"

"Never mind. If Flo was making so much money, why did she have to work days?"

"Well, she had a bad habit, if you know what I mean." He made the gesture of drinking from a bottle. "Most of my girls do. Don't know why."

"If I had to work for you, I'd be a drunk, too," Merylo said, tightening his grip. "Who were her other clients?"

"Not sure they'd appreciate my sayin'."

"You think I care what that dirt wants? Talk!"

Adler held up his hands. "Keep your shirt on, mister. I'll give you names."

"Was one of them a guy called Andrassy?"

Adler thought for a moment. "Don't recall that I ever heard that name."

"Be sure!" Zalewski showed him the picture. "Ever seen him around?"

"No. Never. I'm sure."

Merylo swore beneath his breath. "Know of anyone who might want to kill Flo?"

"Nah. Everyone loved Flo. She was cheap."

"See any suspicious characters hanging around her?"

"Have you been to that bar where she worked? Everyone there is a suspicious character."

"Have any idea how this might've happened? How she got tangled up with a violent murderer who'd want to hack up her body? That's a pretty tough way to go."

"Way Flo lived, there was no other way to go but bad. Didn't expect her to get hacked to bits. But she couldn't go on long the way she was."

Merylo sighed, then threw the man back against the brick wall of the alleyway. This was getting him nowhere. Like every other one of the hundreds of interviews he'd conducted since this case began. "Don't suppose you ever thought about helping her? Trying to get her straight?"

"Hey, she chose her life."

"And you wrung it dry."

"I didn't do nothin' I didn't have the right to do!" Adler protested. "She was mine, man! I owned her!"

Merylo and Zalewski both stared back at him. "Case you haven't heard, punk, slavery has been abolished. People can't own other people. It ain't legal."

"That's a load of bull."

"It's true."

"You sayin' a wife ain't supposed to do what her husband tells her? That the man ain't the boss of the family?"

Merylo wagged his head. "That's different, and besides, you're not her husband."

"No, but I met the man. And he sold her to me, for twenty-two dollars, cash. I owned her. And I had a right to recoup my investment."

Merylo and Zalewski were shoulder to shoulder as they entered the downtown post office.

"Did you know about this guy?" Zalewski asked.

"Honest?"

"If you're in the mood."

Merylo frowned. "I didn't even know Flo was married. I thought Polillo was her maiden name."

"Thanks for being honest."

"There's no shame in it, though it isn't exactly a source of pride, either. I've talked to dozens of people who knew Flo. None of them knew she was married."

"How could that be?"

"We're about to find out." Merylo spotted the man he sought behind the counter. He'd made sure in advance he'd be on duty.

He flashed his badge. "Peter Merylo, Homicide Department. Are you Andrew Polillo?"

The mail clerk's shoulders sagged. "Wondered how long it'd be before you boys came round."

Merylo nodded. "So I guess you're not denying that you were married to Florence Polillo?"

"Don't 'spect there'd be much point in it." His face was pocked and he looked undernourished. He was one of the lucky few who still had a job, but Merylo got the impression that his life had not been easy and probably never would be.

"Care to explain why you left your wife?"

"Left her? We're divorced. Her idea. Didn't you know?"

Merylo and Zalewski exchanged a glance. "Just checking. How long have you been divorced?"

Polillo thought a moment. "Must be almost three years."

"Since you . . . sold her to a man named Chink Adler?"

Polillo did not deny. He did not even seem particularly perturbed. "She was already hookin'. What difference did it make? Seemed like I was entitled to get a little somethin' out of the marriage. It cost me enough."

"So you sold her to a pimp."

"What I hear, workin' with a pimp is a lot safer than workin' on your own. Women in that line get roughed up when they don't have someone lookin' out for them."

Merylo didn't argue the point. "Bitter about it?"

"Not bitter enough to kill her, if that's what you're gettin' at."

"Someone did."

"It wasn't me."

"Why'd you dump her?" Zalewski asked, injecting himself into the conversation.

Polillo fidgeted with his date-stamp. "I loved Flo. I really did. Loved her like I've never loved anyone. Took care of her. But she was always a hard drinker. Didn't leave much room for me — she was in love with the bottle. I told her I'd had enough. She was going to have to give up the drinking, or give up me."

"And that was the end of it?"

"Not quite. She was sympathetic at first. Cried and everything. Showed me a side I'd never seen before. Said she was going to go visit her mother for two weeks to get herself straight. I said fine. So she went away for two weeks — and didn't come back. Few days later I saw her go into a restaurant right here in town with another man, some big husky guy who had his hands all over her."

Polillo stared down at his desk. "Few days later, I asked her for a divorce. She said, *Sure, why not?* That was the end of it. Adler gave me some cash, said he'd look after her." Merylo was amazed to see Polillo's eyes were misting. "All I wanted was the best for her. That's all I ever wanted."

Merylo's teeth clenched together. What a stupid job this was.

"You have any idea who might want to kill her?"

"No."

"You ever see her with any suspicious characters?"

"Haven't seen her at all for three years."

"Ever hear of a guy named Andrassy?"

"Saw his picture in the paper. Never saw him or heard of him before that."

Merylo folded up his notepad. "Thank you for your time. Zalewski?"

The two men made their way out of the post office.

"You think he was lying?" Zalewski asked.

"No."

"You think Adler was lying?"

"No. I don't think either of them knows a damn thing about it. Or Dollarhyde. Nobody we've talked to." He shook his head. "I thought identifying a second victim would be the key to solving this whole case. Seems I may have miscalculated."

Zalewski looked at him anxiously. "So then . . . where does that leave us?"

"Exactly where we've been all along." He opened his car door and slid behind the steering wheel. "Nowhere."

"You don't think we'll crack this case?"

"We'll crack it. Just not as soon as I'd hoped. But we'll catch this guy, you wait and see. 'Cause I won't stop trying until we do."

21

Ness was astounded when he saw how many people were waiting to hear him talk. He had readily agreed to speak to the Cleveland Advertising Club, one of the leading professional organizations in the city. Never hurt to brush shoulders with the folks who made the greatest contributions to the city coffers. This meeting was in the downtown hotel's largest ballroom and it was packed. He didn't see an empty seat anywhere. Surely these people couldn't all be advertising men!

No, he realized, as he scanned the room. Some of the attendees were women — wives, probably. Or secretaries. He even spotted some youngsters. One was wearing a button on his lapel with a picture of Ness cut out of the newspaper.

He wasn't just the safety director anymore. He was a teen idol. Right up there with Charles Lindbergh. A hero.

Come to think of it, hero status hadn't worked so well for Lindbergh, had it? Last Ness heard, he was still in Europe, dodging all the ugly publicity stemming from the kidnapping. Hauptmann was in jail awaiting trial.

Ness would have to be very careful.

"In any city where corruption exists, it follows that some officials are playing ball with the underworld. The dishonest public servant hiding behind a badge is more detestable than any street criminal or mob boss. If officials are committed to a program of protection, police work becomes exceedingly difficult, and the officer on the beat, discouraged from his duty, decides it is best to see as little crime as possible."

Ness gazed out at the crowd of stony faces. He didn't know what was going wrong, but this presentation was clearly not what most of the audience was expecting. It wasn't that they disagreed so much as they were . . . well, bored. He knew he wasn't a flashy speaker. Never had been. Could get his message across, but he lacked a certain pizzazz. That's why he had resisted all offers to run for public office. Mayor Burton might have a silver tongue, but he did not. Edna had suggested that he start with a joke, but his attempts at humor always flopped. Any time he tried to tell a joke he ended up being sorry he had started.

Ness outlined the evidence he had found that many police officers were taking bribes, tipping off mobsters, drinking on duty — or any combination of the above. He also explained what he had done to stop it.

"A public official always puts himself in danger when he threatens someone's livelihood. There are ripples throughout the community. Even if the cop is crooked, is his wife? Are his children? Should they be punished for what he has done? These are difficult questions. But I could not possibly accomplish the job I was sworn to do until these leaks were plugged. And so I suspended over three hundred officers. Most of them will never return to the force. And a strong message will be sent to those who remain."

That at least got a few heads nodding. Or were they just nodding off?

"Political favoritism can also bring a city down. I plan to submit a procedure to institute a system of merit-based promotion, with scientific civil-service testing, to determine who is promoted and who is not. As businessmen, you must understand the harm a city suffers when its economic resources are drained off to underworld mobsters who don't pay taxes. In the short time since I took office, our midnight raids have confiscated almost two million dollars in illegal booze. Ironically, even after the repeal of Prohibition, bootlegging is still the most profitable mob enterprise, smuggling Canadian hooch across Lake Erie. But they are also killing the city with gambling parlors. I don't know if gambling is morally wrong, but I know it turns criminals into financial tycoons. Do we really want the city run by men who won't obey the law? I think not."

Ness thought that was a pretty good argument, a clever way of converting even those men who liked a little drink and a poker game every now again — and he suspected there were several in the room — to his side. But he still wasn't reaching them. How could he strike home?

"How many of you drove to this meeting today?" Most of the men in the audience raised their hands. "Then you're lucky to be alive. As you must know, the traffic situation in Cleveland is horrendous. We've been voted the most dangerous city in America several years running. Did you know there were over four hundred traffic fatalities last year? Well, we're going to fix that, with something called a traffic light — something that ironically was invented in Cleveland but never used here. I've asked the city council to support an ambulance corps to get the wounded to the hospital faster, and a roving patrol of motorcycle officers who will be able to weave in and out of congested traffic. If all my plans are implemented, I believe we will see traffic deaths drop dramatically."

Enough. He'd tortured himself with this much longer than necessary. He'd wrap it up and let the good citizens get back to their homes and offices.

"Am I finished? Have I done all that needs to be done? Of course not. There are still problems to be confronted — perhaps the greatest of them being our out-of-control juvenile crime problem. So long as there remains a way to make our city safer, my job will never —"

"Mr. Ness!"

He looked up from his notes. A man in the third row had his hand in the air.

Ness had not planned to take questions. But what could be the harm? Maybe it would liven up this dour proceeding.

"Yes?"

"Mr. Ness, what are you going to do about this monster?"

"Um . . . could you be more specific?"

"This butcher. The Torso Killer."

An audible rumble rose from the audience. People leaned forward, shifted in their seats. For perhaps the first time since Ness had begun talking, they were interested.

"Well . . . you know . . ." Ness cleared his throat. "I'm not a homicide detective. I'm the safety director."

"How can anyone be safe while this man runs around killing people and cutting them up?"

"Well . . . I know it is distressing . . . but —"

Another man rose, a portly gentleman with pomaded hair who was dressed in an immaculately tailored three-piece suit. "Mr. Ness, I'm Congressman Sweeney. I'd like to know what exactly you plan to do to stop these killings."

"Well, again, that isn't really my job, and to tell you the truth, I don't know that much about it. But I believe that all crimes will cease to flourish if we continue to apply scientific methods to eliminating the elements that corrupt our society. We have an unprecedented ability to fight crime with forensic science. We can apply new technology to our traffic problem. We can employ sociological knowledge to combat juvenile delinquency. Despite the poor economy, this is a great time to be alive." He smiled, and the twinkle returned to his eye. "I pledge that I will use all these tools and more to make this city a safe place for you and your children. That's what a safety director does."

The audience responded with an enthusiastic round of applause.

22

June 5, 1936

Gomez Ivey tried to see how far he could travel on one rail of the train tracks without falling off. As it turned out, he could go a good long way, especially if he used his fishing pole to keep himself balanced.

"Look at me!" Gomez hollered. "I'm the New York Central train!"

"You ain't no train," Louis Cheeley shouted back. Louis was two years younger than Gomez — only eleven — but even Gomez knew he was far more sensible. He would never pull the same crazy stunts. Come to think of it, he normally wouldn't ditch school to go fishing, either. But he'd warmed to the idea pretty fast when Gomez suggested it. "You may be black, but you ain't no train."

"You think they'll miss us back at Outhwaite?" Gomez asked, referring to the school they both attended — or were supposed to attend.

"They might miss us, but what they gonna do about it?"

Gomez kept moving. "Serves them right. Who ever heard of having school this late in the year? When it's crazy hot outside. And the fish are bitin'."

"What's gonna happen if we get caught?"

"We ain't gonna get caught."

"Yeah, but —"

"Look, if you're so worried about it, you can just go home now."

"I'm not goin' home," Louis said, suddenly defensive. "I may never go home."

"Yeah, right."

"If my papa finds out I played hooky, I won't be able to sit down for a week."

"Aw, don't be such a baby."

"Easy for you to say. You ain't got no papa."

Gomez fell silent a moment, his lips pressed tightly together. "I've got a papa. Everybody's got a papa. He's just off gettin' work."

"Uh-huh."

"He's gonna be an engineer someday and he's gonna ride the rails just like we're doin', 'cept he's gonna be inside the train lookin' down at boys like us and pulling the whistle and givin' us the big smile."

"You be sure and let me know when that happens, Gomez."

"I will."

"I wanna be there on the tracks, wavin' back."

"You just do that."

Gomez was relieved when the kid decided to change the subject. "You got any change?"

"Not since I was born. Why?"

Louis wiped the sweat off his brow. "I was just imaginin' how good an ice-cold Nehi might taste right about now."

"Man, don't get me thinkin' about that."

"How can you not be thinkin' about that?"

"There's no point in —"

Gomez fell silent. He glanced down at a point between the train tracks and the rapid transit line, just beneath a willow tree.

"You see that? Over there." Gomez pointed. "Beneath the tree. Look like a pair of pants."

Louis squinted into the sun. "I think they're tweed."

Gomez jumped down off the tracks. "Let's check it out."

"What for?" Louis trailed a few feet behind. "You can't wear tweed this time of year, you fool. You'll melt!"

"Who's a fool? If there's a pair of pants

that only some white boy would be wearin',
there might be some change in the pocket.
Aren't you the one who was wantin' some
scratch?"

That changed everything. "Lead the way."

They walked over to the tree, wishing that
a willow provided more shade.

The trousers were rolled up neatly and
evenly, just at the base of the tree, where
thousands of people passed every day.

Gomez tilted his head. There was something strange about all this. He wasn't quite
sure what it was, but something was . . . not
right. Off-kilter. Wrong.

He tentatively poked at the bundle with
his fishing pole.

Slowly, one of the pant legs began to
unfold.

A human head rolled out. Dirty, blood-
soaked, severed at the top of the neck.

The boys didn't stop running until they
reached home.

23

Ness closed the shutters on Chief Matowitz's office windows. He didn't want anyone
observing, not even reading lips or taking
cues from facial expressions. This was a
private conversation. It had to be. This time,
his concern was not that snitches in the
police department might convey information to the mob. He was concerned that
they might convey information to the press.

"There must be something more you can
give me," Ness said, hovering over Matowitz's desk. "Toss me a bone. Something I
can tell the newsboys."

"There isn't."

"There's always something."

"Not this time." Matowitz pushed away
from his desk, creating more space between
himself and his interrogator. "We got nothing."

"You told me you thought this was over."

"I said I hoped it was over. It's been —

what? Three months since the last one?"

"Ought to be long enough for you to catch one killer."

"Maybe for the man who brought down Al Capone."

Was it Ness's imagination, or was Matowitz enjoying this subtle shift in their relationship? In the past, Ness had always held the dominant hand. Ness might come to him for help, for manpower, but given that he was the mayor's specially deputized agent with an increasingly high profile, Matowitz didn't have much choice in the matter. The midnight raids were in Ness's jurisdiction, totally foreign to what Matowitz normally did. But this was different. Ness was entering Matowitz's playground, the world of homicide detection. And Matowitz was distressingly nonforthcoming.

"Who have you got working on it?"

"Peter Merylo. Best damn detective on the force. Locked up more men than you can count. We're not just talking about rumrunners. We're talking seriously dangerous killers."

Ness wasn't nearly dumb enough to miss that jab. "Then why hasn't he locked up this one?"

"Because we have no clues."

"You've identified two victims."

"And that's a miracle." Matowitz reached into his top desk drawer and withdrew a brown file. "These victims have been transients, lowlifes. Scum of the earth. Not folks with a lot of friends or family. No one keeping an eye on them. We think maybe it was some kinda mobland rubout."

Ness shook his head. "I've been up against the mob for a long time. And I've seen the remains of some grisly executions. But I've never seen them hack a body to bits. That's too violent, even for the mob. Might violate their twisted sense of honor."

"Then what's your theory?"

Was this man still bitter that the first raid on The Thomas Club went bad? Or that he wasn't there for the one that succeeded? "There must be some connection among the victims. Maybe they all knew something that someone didn't want to get out. Maybe it was a revenge killing. Someone was sure as heck mad about something."

"Revenge for what?"

"I can't know that till I know what they all had in common. Maybe they all knew the thief. Andrassy."

"Possible that Flo Polillo did. She seems to have gotten around. If you know what I mean."

"Maybe it was some kind of sordid love

triangle that went bad." His voice dropped. "Seriously bad." Problem was, even as Ness said it, he didn't believe it. Just didn't sound right. There had been jilted and betrayed lovers since the dawn of time. But he'd never heard of one responding by hacking up bodies. He'd never heard of anyone doing anything like this in his entire life. No matter how he tried to think it through, it just didn't make any sense. "With all the science we have at our disposal, surely we can come up with some kind of useful lead."

"Not so far. And we've got a pretty smart coroner. He's a college man." Matowitz made a sniffing noise. "Like you. You're welcome to talk to him. He'll be back in his office this afternoon."

Ness checked his watch. "Not possible. I've got about two hundred traffic lights to get up and running. And a training session for the Accident Prevention Squad that starts at —"

There was a knocking at the door. He hoped it wasn't a reporter. He wasn't in the mood.

The door opened and Chamberlin poked his head through. "Boss?"

Ness held up his hand. "Can it wait? I'm busy."

"It's about last night's raid. I wanted to

tell you what happened."

"Another midnight raid?" Matowitz looked at Ness. "And you didn't go yourself? What has the world come to?"

Ness frowned. "I had an . . . engagement. With my wife."

Matowitz's thin lips spread. "I understand. There are bosses, and then there are bosses."

Ness did his best to hide what he was feeling.

Chamberlin cut through the silence, alleviating the tension, at least temporarily. "Can I tell you about The Harvard Club?"

Matowitz's eyebrows rose. The Harvard Club was a notorious gambling and booze joint in Mayfield Heights run by one of the top men in the Mayfield Road Mob, "Gameboy" Miller. Now that The Thomas Club was closed, it was probably the top joint in the city.

"Did they know you were coming?" Ness asked.

"No. But they were ready, just the same. Bouncers met us at the door, armed with submachine guns. Refused to honor the warrant. Then Miller himself came to the door and said, and I quote, 'Anybody comes in gets their — um — their head knocked off.' Deleting the colorful adjective."

"And you showed him the warrant?"

"Twice. I didn't want a bloodbath. I decided to retreat."

Ness laid his hand on his shoulder. "You did the right thing. You didn't have enough men. We'll go back tonight."

Matowitz rose. "I can't order my men to get mowed down by those tommy-gun-toting thugs."

"Then I'll ask for volunteers. There are still some officers who don't like seeing duly appointed officers of the law get pushed around by mob punks."

"I don't know if I can allow that."

"Are you kidding?" Ness gripped the edges of the man's desk. "This is the most brazen defiance of the law I've ever seen. If you let something like this go unchecked, soon there won't be any law at all. We have to show them we mean business. We have to show them there's still law in this town." He turned back to his assistant. "You understand what I'm saying?"

A boyish grin spread across Chamberlin's face. "I'll begin rounding up volunteers immediately."

"Good man. We'll go tonight." Ness followed him to the door.

Matowitz did not appear particularly sorry to see him go. "And the Torso Murderer?"

200

"Get your men out there pounding the streets for clues. Let me know if they find anything." Ness grabbed his fedora. "I've got a job to do."

24

Merylo stared down at the filthy head protruding from the right trouser leg. It was lying on its left side, lips parted, as if the victim died in a moment of surprise — or terror. Its eyes were closed, and he silently thanked God for that small favor.

He had really hoped it was over. He would rather have caught the filthy killer, but he was willing to settle for having the murders come to an end. The papers had ceased running their lurid panic-inducing stories filled with more speculation than fact. Cleveland was gearing up for the convention season, the Great Lakes Exposition, the American Legion, and all the others. Some people had forgotten about the murders.

But not Merylo. He had never forgotten, and he had never stopped tracking down any lead he thought might possibly pay off. Yes, he had hoped that the killer had given it up, or moved on, or been rubbed out.

But he doubted it. No matter how hard he tried to convince himself, he had never been able to make himself believe it. His gut told him this butcher would kill again. And his gut had been right.

His reverie was interrupted when he heard a sentence that had become all too familiar since this case began.

"We found the rest of him."

Zalewski beamed as if he had won a Kewpie doll at the county fair. "It's not far. And it's intact."

"Show me." They began to walk north of the willow tree, in the general direction of Jackass Hill. "Have the men found anything else?"

"Two shirts, both bloody, one torn at the shoulder."

"Two?"

"Right."

"Like . . . the victim might've been wearing two shirts at once?"

"Not really, no. One's casual, one's a dress shirt."

"Oh." Merylo didn't need a detailed explanation to tell him what that implied. "What else?"

"Pair of men's shorts. Oxford shoes, size seven and a half, laces tied together and a pair of socks stuffed inside, striped and orange at the top."

"Orange?"

"It's fashionable these days, sir."

"Maybe in your neighborhood. Anything else?"

"A leather belt. A dirty cap. Seems like it's been soaked in something oily."

"Like maybe the motor oil we found with the other corpse?"

"Maybe, yeah."

"Anything that might lead us to the killer?"

"Well, the Bertillon boys want to run tests, but . . ."

Merylo gave him a look. Zalewski had been working with him long enough now to have a sense of when they had something and when they didn't.

"No," Zalewski said quietly. "Probably not. But the corpse is interesting."

"In what way?"

They reached a spot perhaps a thousand feet from where the head had been discovered, just east of the 55th Street Bridge. Merylo could see part of the body lying on its side, partially obscured by twigs. "It's illustrated."

"Excuse me?"

"You know. Tattooed."

Merylo took a step closer, even thought

the stench made him want to move in the opposite direction. "How many?"

"We found six."

Sure enough, Merylo spotted two flags tattooed on the left arm, not far from a heart, an anchor, and perhaps more interestingly, the letters. W.C.G. On the left shoulder, he discovered a full-color butterfly, wings unfurled.

"Nice," Merylo muttered. "But I only count five."

"You missed Jiggs."

"Would you please speak English?"

"Jiggs. You know, from the comics. *Bringing Up Father.*"

"Never read it."

"You don't read the comics?"

"I don't read newspapers at all. They depress me. Especially when I notice how much they get wrong. So show me this . . . what was it?"

"Jiggs. And it's not an it. It's a he." Zalewski used a twig to subtly move the lie of the corpse's leg to reveal the final tattoo, on the left calf. It was a cartoon drawing of a middle-aged man wearing a checkered vest and tie, his hair sticking up and a cigar in his mouth.

"That's Jiggs?"

"Yup."

"Why would anyone want Jiggs tattooed on their calf?"

"Beats me. Guess they like him. Maybe they . . . you know, sympathize with him. He brought himself up from nothing to something, you know."

"It's a Horatio Alger story."

"Uh . . . yeah. I guess. Jiggs was an Irish immigrant, a bricklayer, till he wins a fortune in a sweepstakes. His snob wife and daughter keep trying to 'bring him up,' you know, teach him how to live the good life. Be rich. Socialize with the swells."

Merylo squinted. "But Jiggs just wants to live like he did back in simpler times. Eat the food his Irish mama cooked. Run around with the lads."

"Exactly! So you have read it."

"No. But I've seen the musical, *The Rising Generation*. And I'm betting the guy who writes *Bringing Up Father* has, too."

"What d'ya mean?"

"Never mind. The question is, why would anyone tattoo this character on his leg?" He paused. "Or perhaps a better question is, why would this make anyone want to kill him?"

"You think he was killed because of his tattoo?"

"Probably not." Merylo hesitated again.

"Still . . . is this comic derogatory of the Irish?"

"Not really."

"Anybody else? Italians? Mobsters? Rich people?"

"Not so much."

Merylo sighed heavily. "Then maybe we should focus on the letters. They could be initials."

"For who?"

"For about a million people, I suspect. But it's something. I want you to start running those initials through every list we've got. Criminal records. The phone book. Public agencies."

"But that could take —"

"Then you'd better get started, hadn't you?"

"Yes, sir." Zalewski made a small salute, then skittered off.

"One other thing."

Zalewski stopped. "Yes?"

"Tell Pearce I want him to clean that head up real nice — then put it on display."

"What?"

"You heard me. In the morgue. Front office."

"But — isn't that kind of —"

"Yes, it is. But we can't solve this case unless we identify more of these victims. You run with the letters. We'll tell the papers the head is on display and people are welcome to take a look."

"Who would want to do that?"

"You might be surprised. People are attracted to the grotesque."

"What if Pearce says no?"

"He won't. He'll love the idea. All those people coming to his office, like he's the center of the investigation. Sherlock Holmes with a medical degree. He'll probably sit out front and sign autographs."

"If you say so."

"I do. So get to it, Zalewski. I want that head out as soon as possible. Drive as fast as you can." He held up a finger. "But of course, pay close attention to our safety director's traffic lights. We don't want anything dangerous to happen."

Zalewski departed. Merylo turned back to the headless corpse lying among the weeds and sticks. Something about this bothered him, and it wasn't just that cigar-chomping cartoon character, either. The head had been neatly wrapped in the trousers and carefully — almost tenderly — placed under the willow tree, just as Flo Polillo's body parts had been wrapped in newspaper and burlap bags, then placed in baskets. At the same time, the body, only a short walk away

— assuming this was the body that went with the head — had been carelessly, almost disdainfully dumped among the tallgrass weeds and bramble. Two entirely differently methods.

Could there be two different killers? Or more? That would explain a lot, but Merylo didn't believe it. His gut told him that was wrong — and his brain did as well. If there had been more than one person involved, by this time, someone would have talked. No, they were looking for one man.

One man — with two completely different personalities. Was such a thing possible? He remembered what Pearce had said, back when he was talking about that British nut and his friend the alienist, the guy who could explain crazy behavior. There was definitely something weird about this case . . .

No, he told himself, rising, there was an explanation for all this. A logical explanation. He might not have the slightest idea what that explanation was. But he knew it existed. And given enough time, he would figure it out.

25

Ness wrapped his overcoat tightly around himself and strode toward the front door of The Harvard Club. The men watching could only marvel at his bravado. After what had happened the night before, it would take extreme courage for any law enforcement officer to make his way to that door. And Ness was particularly recognizable, with his camel-hair coat, fedora, and Scandinavian good looks.

He held up his badge and knocked. "Eliot Ness. Safety Director."

The door slot flew open. A beefy scarred face appeared on the other end. "Blow off, copper. Anyone comes in here gets their f—"

"Yes, I've heard. But I've got a warrant, and I'm coming in."

The man sneered. "I got three men with heaters trained on your head."

Ness smiled pleasantly. "I've got forty-two

armed men positioned all around the building. We've got four trucks ready to carve out a new doorway, if we can't use the one you're currently blocking. Plus there are about a dozen reporters with cameras standing behind my officers, and something like a hundred or so spectators behind them." Ness took a deep breath. "You can't escape. You're spending the night in jail."

The man's bushy eyebrows knitted. Ness got the impression that thinking was not his forte.

"Ask your boss what he wants to be charged with. Operating a gambling parlor, ten years with a chance of parole — or killing a police officer, mandatory death penalty."

The beefy head began to flush. Anger or indecision? Ness couldn't be sure. But he got the distinct impression the man wished he'd let someone else get the door.

"Step aside, Manny."

Ness knew the voice. A moment later, Shimmy Patton appeared in the slot.

"Whatsa problem, Mr. Safety Director? This is private property."

The man was already free on bail, awaiting trial. Sometimes the law made Ness crazy. "I have a warrant to search for evidence of illegal activities."

"Hey, maybe you haven't heard. That Prohibition thing — it's over. We can drink now."

"That depends on where you get your hooch. And gambling is still illegal."

Patton pressed a hand against his chest. "Gambling? Who — me? I wouldn't dream of it. I've learned my lesson."

"Then you have no reason not to let me in, do you?"

Patton glanced over his shoulder. At first, Ness had thought Patton's appearance at the door was a sign of his enormous over-confidence. Now he realized it was just a stalling tactic. He was buying time for his assistants to hide all the gambling parapher-nalia.

Ness heard sounds of scuffling and move-ment in the background. After a few more moments, Patton answered. "Well, geez, Mr. Safety Director. Since you put it like that. Come on in."

He closed the slot. A moment later, the door opened.

Ness stepped inside. The front room was jam-packed with patrons, mostly well dressed, mostly swilling drinks, pretending he didn't exist. The servers were dressed in low-cut outfits that bordered on public indecency, and the bouncers looked nearly naked themselves now that they'd stashed their weapons.

"As you can see, Mr. Safety Director, we're clean as a whistle."

"Are you now?" There was no trace of gambling apparatus. These men were good. And fast.

Patton waved expansively. "No gambling in here. No sirree."

"Not now."

"Don't be a sore loser."

"The only loser is you, Patton." Ness leaned out the door. "Chamberlin! Bring in the men."

"Hey, hey, hey!" Patton jumped into the doorway. "That ain't right. You ain't got nothing' on me! Look around, blind boy. There's no gambling."

"There was."

"You can't prove it."

"I think I can."

"You search all you want, you won't —"

"I don't have to search."

Chamberlin rushed through the door with five other men. "Search these clowns for weapons. We're going to make some arrests."

Patton jumped in front of him. "I'm callin' my lawyer, right now, see? You got nothin' on me. He'll get you so tied up in lawsuits you won't be able to move. You got no proof, no witnesses —"

"I've got better than witnesses. I've got pictures."

"What?"

"Little movie camera, latest scientific gadget."

"I've been here for the last hour. No one's come through that door."

"True enough. But you ought to be careful about leaving a window open upstairs." He smiled. "Especially when the safety director comes calling. With a ladder."

Ness waited outside The Harvard Club as his officers systematically loaded the operators and patrons into paddy wagons. This was the second shift of prisoners making their way downtown. Most of the patrons would probably be released after the officers scared them a little and lectured them on the evils of gambling. Locking away prosperous citizens wasn't their goal here. Putting away the Mayfield Mob was.

"Matowitz is going to be sorry he didn't make this one," Ness said. "Bound to be the headline story in all the papers."

Chamberlin nodded. "Unless another torso turns up."

Ness grunted. "Even if. This is big news. Shutting down The Harvard Club. You know how many people told me it couldn't be done? Lots."

He waved to the spectators, many of whom were calling out his name. Good thing he'd tipped off the papers.

He waved again. He was greeted with a chorus of enthusiastic cries and shouts.

Ness smiled.

Out the corner of his eye, he saw several young boys drifting by. If he wasn't mistaken, it was the same group he'd seen outside The Thomas Club the night they shut that one down.

"Excuse me a minute, Bob."

Ness trotted toward the crowd. He smiled cordially, but passed through quickly, heading for the youngsters. When they realized he was coming for them, they began to scatter.

"Wait a second," he shouted. "I just want to talk."

They slowed but did not stop.

"Seriously. I need your help. I want to deputize you."

That did the trick. The three boys slowly turned around.

"That's more like it. You have me at a disadvantage. You know my name, but I don't know yours. How about it?"

The tallest of the three, who wore a felt

crown-shaped cap, kicked at the dirt. "My name's James. But people call me Bud."

"Nice to meet you, Bud."

The boy to his right, the blond kid in the dirty torn shirt, waved. "Joe."

Ness shook his hand.

The smallest of them, who couldn't have been more than ten, looked uneasy about the whole situation. But he answered. "I'm Billy."

"Good to meet you all."

Bud cleared his throat. "Are you — are you really . . . Eliot Ness?"

"The one and only. Far as I know."

"You're the guy who beat up Al Capone?"

Ness laughed. "Well, not with my fists. But we got him locked up. He's still behind bars."

"My dad said you were a real honest-to-goodness American hero."

"Do you live with your father, son?"

Bud kicked at the dirt again. "Not anymore. He's dead. Tuberculosis."

"Your mom?"

"She's dead, too."

"Where do you live?"

"Wherever I can. Shantytown. Under a bridge. Maybe a flophouse, when I've got a little money. But that isn't often. Most people won't hire me 'cause I'm too young.

216

Even the ones who will hire me don't pay much."

"Any of you have homes?"

"Billy does." Billy nodded his agreement. "But his mom doesn't like him bein' around nights. She works nights. Men come back to her place."

"What do you eat?"

Bud shrugged. "Whatever we can. There's a restaurant downtown that lets us go through their garbage and eat whatever we find."

Ness winced. "What about you, Joe? Where do you live?"

"My dad's got a one-room on Third Street. But he ain't home much and sometimes he forgets to pay the rent. He travels. Rides the rails. Says he doesn't have enough money to leave me any."

"When was the last time any of you had baths?"

No answer.

"Any of you ever play a game of baseball?"

Joe frowned. "I saw one once."

"Any of you have any male relatives or . . . any kind of person to keep an eye on you?"

No answer.

"Well . . . that's fine," Ness said. He placed his hand firmly on Bud's and Billy's shoulders. "Now you do."

26

"Two thousand people?"

"That's what his secretary says."

"That's not possible."

"Apparently it is."

"In two days?"

"What have I told you, Zalewski? Nothing attracts people quite as much as something that should repel them."

Merylo couldn't help feeling a certain amount of pride. Although Pearce hadn't resisted his plan to put the latest head on display in the morgue, he had expressed doubts that anyone would come to look at it. So had Zalewski and everyone else in the department — including Chief Matowitz. Fortunately, he was so busy rounding up poker players with the safety director that he was pretty much letting Merylo do whatever he wanted these days. Which was exactly how Merylo liked it.

There was only one problem — one tiny

matter that prevented him from finding complete joy in this victory. Although approximately two thousand people had come by to look at the head — no one had recognized it. Not even a possible identification. Nothing. And this head was in the best condition of any they had found yet.

"Why do you think no one recognized him, sir?"

Merylo shrugged. "People look different after they're dead. Haven't you ever been to an open-casket funeral?"

"No."

"Well, if you can avoid it, you should."

"You think maybe he's a transient? Vagrant? He was found near Shantytown."

"Possible."

"But then how does it tie into your theory that these are all organized crime rubouts? That it all ties back to Andrassy?"

"I never said it all tied back to Andrassy. I said they all must've been involved in something with Andrassy." And he only said that because Andrassy and Flo Polillo were the only two corpses they had managed to identify.

"Still — the more bodies we get, the harder it's going to be to make a connection."

"Not once we know what the connection

is. Once we figure that out, it will all make sense. Mark my words."

"Of course." Zalewski shifted uncomfortably in his suit. "See the paper this morning?"

"I told you, I don't read the papers."

"This unidentified head bumped the Republican National Convention right off the front page."

Merylo sighed. "Well, I'm not that fond of Alf Landon. Reminds me of some of the guys I used to put away for running penny-ante gin joints. Any luck on the finger-prints?"

"Sorry. We got good prints, but no one has them on file. He's got no record."

"And the initials tattooed on his arm?"

"Nothing."

Merylo swore. He'd had two good leads, two solid chances to identify the victim. And neither had produced anything.

From the rear office, Arthur Pearce emerged, pulling off his gloves and adjusting his horn-rimmed glasses. "Any luck, gentlemen?"

"No ID."

"Well, it was a valiant effort."

"Maybe in time —"

"Merylo — I can't leave a dismembered head on display any longer. It's going to deteriorate. Then it will be useless."

"Just give me another day."

"Sorry, can't." He removed his surgical apron and hung it on a coat hook. "But I can do this. The head is in good enough condition to make a plaster cast — a death mask. You can put that up anywhere you like. Perhaps someplace that gets more traffic than my office."

Merylo pondered a moment. "Got any suggestions?"

"Well, I doubt if the Republican National Convention would have it. But I read in the paper today that attendance at the Great Lakes Exposition is waning. They're afraid they may have to close early."

Zalewski frowned. "Why is that good? Don't we want to put it somewhere there's lots of people?"

Merylo smiled patiently. "Yes, we do. I think what the good doctor is suggesting is that if the Exposition needs to boost attendance, what could be better than an exhibit that brought two thousand people to a coroner's office in the seedy side of downtown?"

"You — you really think they'd want it?"

"I think they might be willing to lower their standards a bit. As a public service." He smirked. "And to keep the backers from taking a bath on this stupid Exposition." He tipped his fedora. "Nice going, Doctor."

"Always like to help out when I can." He patted his pockets, searching for a cigarette.

"What else have you got?"

"Nothing much, unfortunately. This is the freshest corpse we've discovered. He was killed less than forty-eight hours before you found him. Age around twenty, twenty-five. Reddish hair, brown eyes, five missing teeth."

"A fighter."

"Or a malnourished vagrant. His head was severed just at the axis between the chin and the body. Oh — here's something different. This time, there were several hesitation marks."

"Sign of a conscience developing?"

"Or a struggle. Maybe the victim wasn't well-secured. Maybe he tried to resist. Escape."

"You're giving me too many maybes, Doctor. Not enough answers."

"I don't give answers, Detective. I give information. Answers are your department."

The front door to the morgue swung open. Merylo expected to see more gawkers, but instead, it was Officer Cromsky from the Fifth. He was breathless.

"Detective Merylo!" He was unable to

catch his breath, practically hyperventilating. "We've — we've —"

Merylo laid a hand on his shoulder. "Calm down, man. What is it?"

Cromsky inhaled deeply, then tried again. "We've — we've found something. This guy — guy at a bar. John Moessner. On Fulton Road. Tall guy, photographer, likes to give discounts to women who —"

"Get to the point, man!"

"He saw the picture in the *Courier*. Of the head. He thinks he recognizes him. And he thinks the guy knew Andrassy."

"Why didn't you say so?" Merylo grabbed his hat, his teeth clenched tightly together. At long last, the break he had been waiting for. "Let's go, Zalewski. And this time, you can ignore the blasted traffic lights!"

"You've got pictures of Andrassy!"

Despite being a tall man talking to someone almost a foot shorter, John Moessner was not the dominant player in the conversation. He clung to the bar between them, using it as a barricade.

"They were just for fun."

"Why him?"

"Because he said yes. Along with dozens of other people."

"So you've been fooling around taking

pictures of lowlifes just because it amuses you! Like, it's your hobby?"

Moessner's head twitched. "It is my avocation. And it's not just fooling around. It's an art form."

"Taking pictures of lowlifes?"

"Photography. Notice how I've artfully arranged the scene, the placement of the chair, the head. I've observed the rule of threes —"

"Don't give me that college crap. Have you been to art school?"

Moessner sniffed. "I took a correspondence course." He was a lean man with a weak, indecisive face. His mustache was wispy, barely there, as if the entire project had been an afterthought.

"Why didn't you tell the police about this sooner?"

"I didn't see how I could help. They're just pictures."

In truth, Merylo didn't see how he could help, either. But Moessner still should've reported the potential evidence.

"And you think you've seen this new victim before?"

"I think so. I mean, I can't be sure. He was alive then. But he had that same prominent forehead, broad nose."

"And you saw this guy with Andrassy?"

"Yes. At least once. They talked for a long time."

"About what?"

"Sorry. I've tried to remember — but I just don't. Don't have any idea."

"And you don't know his name?"

"Do you have any idea how many people come through here?" He shrugged. "Andrassy was a regular. This other guy, he came in once, maybe twice, tops." His head turned slightly, as if trying to recall something. "You know — I think he was a sailor."

Merylo recalled the anchor tattoo on the man's arm. "Why?"

"Said something about catching his boat or . . . something."

"What else?"

He shook his head. "That's all I remember."

"The initials W.C.G. mean anything to you?"

"Sorry."

"Could this guy have been called William? Or Walter?"

"I'm sorry. I would help you if I could. I want this butcher stopped just as much as anybody. But I don't remember anything else. I don't think I ever really knew anything to remember."

Merylo pressed his fists against the bar.

"Listen to me, mister. You remember any-thing else about this man, or Andrassy, or Flo Polillo, you call me immediately. Got it?"

"Got it."

"You know how quickly I could shut you down?"

"Yes."

"I could search your place. I bet I might find some photos the police would be real interested in."

Moessner held up his hands. "No — I —"

"So if you hear anything — anything at all — you let me know."

"I will. I swear to God. I will."

Merylo stomped out of the bar. Had he done any good? Impossible to know. But this was a killer he was looking for, not the Invisible Man. Someone out there must've seen him. Must've seen something.

He just had to find that someone. And he would. Even if he had to harass everyone in Cleveland in the process.

27

July 22, 1936

Marie Barkley loved her new dress. It was stylish, fashionable, and most important: She looked good in it. She wasn't being immodest, just realistic. She'd had enough experience to make a fair appraisal of when she looked good and when she didn't. And right now, walking south down West 73rd in a black-and-white print with brand-new silk stockings, she looked like a million bucks.

Her mother would never approve of this purchase. It wasn't the cost, though that wasn't inconsiderable, especially in these times, with her poor father working two jobs to make ends meet. No, her mother would be worried by the same thing that delighted Marie — she looked good in it. Men are wolves, she had told Marie, time and again. Don't let yourself be fooled. They're only after one thing. And if they get it, you'll never see them again.

Marie couldn't help but wonder how much her mother's personal history shaped her opinions about men. She would never know. Her mother never talked about her past and she probably never would. Didn't matter. Marie was smart enough to calculate her own age versus the date on her parents' marriage license and draw her own conclusions.

Marie's mother hated her new young man, Barry Trussell. He was much too sharp-looking for her. Pity that a man's good looks could be held against him. But her mother was afraid she would run off with him and get married, now, when she was only seventeen. Or worse, that she would *have* to run off and get married to him, now, when she was only seventeen. She might be able to stretch her father's income to a new dress every now and again, but a Mexican abortion? That was just not going to happen.

Marie had offered on more than one occasion to go to work. Her mother, predictably, was appalled by the idea. *But Mother,* she insisted, *a lot of the girls are working these days. The world has changed.* Not enough for her mother, though. Marie saw nothing wrong with working a few hours a week in a shop, but her mother wouldn't hear of it. You'll be tarnished for life, she said. Apparently she equated the shop girl with another working girl of a more intimate nature. It was crazy. Like it or not, the world had changed, and you didn't have to be Susan B. Anthony to realize there were worse things than working in a shop.

It's not as if she were a suffragette, not by a long shot. She had read about those women over in England, arrested because they had the audacity to seek the vote, force-fed and sometimes killed in the process. They'd done their job — women in England had finally gotten the vote, a year before American women did. So in four years, Marie would be able to vote — but she still couldn't work in a shop. It was absurd, simply absurd. She was pretty enough to get a job at a time when a lot of able-bodied men were going hungry. What could possibly be wrong with that?

She crossed Denison, then the Baltimore & Ohio railroad track, making her way toward Brooklyn. She couldn't wait to show the new dress to Millie. It would make her insane, which of course was the whole pleasure of the thing. This dress was the cat's meow; she looked so good it in you could eat her with a fork. If she did think so herself.

Marie saw some charcoal kindling on the

ground and gave it a wide berth. Hobo campfires. She knew a lot of tramps and out-of-work transients camped in this field at night. Maybe she should've gone another way, but this was the quickest route to Millie's place, and she was sure she would be all right as long as the sun was out and she didn't do anything stupid. Still, it might not hurt to walk a little faster. So she did.

Until something stopped her dead in her tracks.

What on earth was that hideous smell?

The stench was so strong and pervasive she felt herself getting woozy, like she'd inhaled a bad perfume at Woolworth's, only a thousand times worse.

It was coming from the brush to her right, just off the path.

Skunk? she wondered. Because she certainly didn't want to get to Millie's smelling of skunk.

So why did she keep walking closer?

The odor grew more intense with every step. She felt her head spinning and her knees getting a little unsteady. Perhaps she should not have worn heels.

She stepped into the brush and the stink was so strong it slammed against her head like a brick wall. What on earth could it be?

She pushed aside a tall bush and that was

when she saw it, so black and gray that at first she did not recognize it for what it was. A human body. Or the remains of one.

She covered her mouth with her hand. Why had it taken her so long to realize this was a corpse?

The answer came quickly: Because in addition to being black and leathery, it was missing one of the most readily identifiable aspects of a human body. The head.

Marie made her way out of the brush just as quickly as her heels would allow her. Maybe she didn't need to see Millie after all, not right away. Maybe she needed to get out of here, fast, before she ran into whoever — or whatever — had done this. Could it be that monster she had read about in the *News*? That Torso Killer?

A chill shot down her spine. Her pace quickened. She broke both heels before she made it to police headquarters, but that was the absolute last thing on her mind.

28

Chamberlin ran into Ness's office.

"Here are the papers, sir. All the major dailies."

Ness glanced up from his report. "And?"

Chamberlin sighed. "You're going to be disappointed."

"What?" Ness snatched the top paper from the stack. It was *The Courier.* Above the fold, where he had expected to see one of the many photographs taken by reporters at The Harvard Club raid, there was instead a line drawing of a hideous ghoulish creature, a slavering bald-headed monster with clawlike fingernails and a leering expression.

The headline read: TORSO KILLER STRIKES AGAIN.

The smaller subheadline read: WHO WILL BE THE NEXT VICTIM?

"Blast!" Ness said, throwing the paper down. "Of all the luck."

"It gets worse, sir." He opened the paper to the op-ed page, then pointed to the top letter to the editor. "It's from Congressman Sweeney, the man who questioned you at the Cleveland Advertising Club meeting. Basically, he's demanding that you stop all other — he calls them, 'less important activities' — and start working the torso case."

"What does he expect me to do?"

"Apparently he expects you to catch the killer. He's pretty hot about it."

"It's absurd. I'm not a homicide detective."

"He says, 'Surely the man who caught Capone will have no trouble catching one sadistic killer.' "

"But — that's not my job. It's not what I was hired to do."

"I don't think he cares, sir. And if I may say so — I don't think anyone else does, either. The whole town's in a panic. Scared to death. They won't feel safe until this man is caught."

"Swell." Ness wadded up the paper and threw it into the trash. "Are the reporters here yet?"

"Sir . . ." Ness could tell Chamberlin didn't want to say whatever was coming next. "Do you really think that's wise?

Given what's in the paper?"

"I've got no choice. I can't start my Boys Clubs without funding from the city council. And I won't get that without public support."

"I'm just thinking maybe the time isn't right . . ."

"You must be kidding. Juvenile crime is out of control in this town."

"That's not what I meant."

"These reporters aren't idiots. At least not all of them. They'll come around. Once I explain how important this is. And they'll take the message to the people."

"I don't know . . ."

"I have a good track record, don't I?"

"Of course you do. But this — this is something totally different. You've never been up against anything like this before."

Ness rose from his desk and grabbed his suit jacket. "Surely I've earned a vote of confidence on my plan to combat juvenile crime."

"I'm just concerned that —"

"They'll come around, Bob. You'll see. I've handled the press before and I'll handle them again." He grabbed his hat and headed out the door. "I know people are upset about the murders. But that doesn't mean they can't see sense."

Ness hated flashbulbs. Those reporters didn't mind getting right up in your face with them. They flashed at the least opportune, least flattering moments, and left him literally blinded for a good ten or fifteen seconds. He understood they were just doing their job, and he sometimes liked the result. A flattering photo on the front page of tomorrow's papers might guarantee the funding he needed. But it was still annoying. Broke his concentration. Made him squint. His eyes were already a little smaller than he might like, a little too beady. He didn't want to look untrustworthy.

"Thank you for coming out today," Ness said to the throng of reporters and photographers gathered on the steps of Cleveland City Hall. He tried to amplify his usual soft voice; he needed to sound firm and confident. In control. Funny how he always felt insecure when he gave a speech, but felt entirely comfortable giving a press conference. "I'm here to formally present my plan to deal with the juvenile crime problem that has plagued this city for many years. My problem has been that I couldn't figure out why Cleveland should have so much more juvenile crime than other cities of similar size. So I did what I always do when I'm trying to tackle a big problem. I investigated."

Ness saw a hand shoot up from one of the reporters in the rear, but he ignored it and proceeded with his prepared remarks. "I walked the streets at night and talked to many of the young men who have formed gangs, who are committing the petty and increasingly serious crimes that put a dent in this city's economy. And having talked to them, all I can say is — I'm surprised it isn't worse. You would be astonished to learn how many young men are out there with no place to live, no regular source of support, poor, poorly educated, one parent or no parent or no employed parent, ravaged by this Depression, no healthy environment. No role model. It's truly shocking. Many are living in cardboard boxes, under bridges, in Shantytown, where they're exposed to the worst possible element. The fact is, my friends, we have a juvenile crime problem because we have not been taking care of our children. We have not protected and nourished the next generation."

Two more hands shot up. For the most part, however, the assembled reporters remained stoic. Their pencils were moving,

but he sensed it was more a matter of polite-
ness and patience than any genuine interest. Was he losing his knack for this sort of
thing? He was tempted to take a question,
but his better judgment told him to go on
saying what he had to say.

"To that end, ladies and gentlemen, I am
presenting to the city council this day a plan
to institute a series of Boys Clubs throughout the city. To reduce costs, I have scouted
out buildings still in good condition but
abandoned due to our current economic
crisis. The city can acquire them at a reasonable price and adapt them to our needs. The
youth of this city will have a safe, whole-
some place to play and to learn. These Boys
Clubs will keep them off the streets, teach
them useful skills, and instill values that in
some cases are sadly lacking."

This was not like the other press conferences Ness had conducted. He was giving
them good ideas — grand ideas. And for
the most part they were sitting like statues,
phlegmatic, increasingly impatient. Chamberlin had warned him that this might not
be the best time for the conference. But
surely, when they heard about everything he
had been doing, working days and nights
for weeks on end . . .

"In addition, I have been in contact with

the leaders of the Cleveland chapter of the Boy Scouts of America. They too are concerned about the rise in juvenile crime, but have been hampered by a lack of volunteers. They'd like to start many more scout troops but can't find men to act as troop leaders." Ness paused dramatically. "Well, in that respect, I can help." He reached into his pocket. "I have here a list of fifty police officers who have volunteered to give up ten hours a week to help set our youth on the right path." His eyes twinkled. "I'm going to lead one of the scout troops myself."

He paused, and it seemed as if a thousand hands shot into the air. The short hairs on the back of Ness's neck bristled. He had the distinct impression that none of these questions were going to be about Boys Clubs or Boy Scouts.

"One more thing I'd like to add," Ness said. His voice squeaked; the pitch rose ever so slightly. "And, uh, I — then — I can entertain questions. I have just received word of an amazing event that should make all the citizens of this city proud. You may recall that before I got here, a national survey determined that Cleveland was the most dangerous city in America. I have just received word from the National Safety Council that Cleveland will soon receive a safety *award.* Due to the dramatic decrease in organized crime and traffic fatalities, our mayor will soon travel to Washington to receive a national commendation honoring Cleveland for its dramatic transformation from one of America's most dangerous cities to one of the safest —"

"For God's sake," one of the reporters in the back said, throwing down his hat. "When are you going to talk about the Torso Killer?"

Ness took a deep breath. "I know many people in this city are concerned about these murders. Understandably so. The loss of life is always deplorable. But these other gains —"

"What have you got to say about this latest murder? The body that poor girl found? On the west side."

"The west side?"

"Right. Where respectable people live, not just bums. That makes five — possibly six — victims," said a female reporter with bobbed black hair, the one the mayor always called His Girl Friday. Ness couldn't even remember her real name. "Only two of them have even been identified."

"Yes, but we've decreased traffic fatalities from over four hundred to less than forty so far this year. That's more than three hundred lives saved and —"

"By all that's holy, man, will you stop?"

The portly man in the three-piece suit was unmistakable. Congressman Sweeney.

"I'm — sorry, I don't quite follow —"

"Do you not understand? We have a butcher loose in this city. A cold-blooded killer. Hacking up people like so much meat. And you stand there babbling about traffic lights and . . . Boy Scouts!"

"Sir, the traffic problem and the rise in juvenile crime are two of the matters I was specifically told to address when I was appointed Safety Director."

"Times have changed, Ness." Sweeney was grandstanding, and Ness couldn't help but notice how fast the reporters' pencils were moving now that they sniffed a little conflict in the air. "You have a new assignment."

"Only the mayor's office can —"

"Are you saying you refuse to get involved? Our vaunted safety director has no interest in the safety of our citizens?"

"Of course not." Ness felt as if he were treading invisible water. "If we could all just . . . remain calm. Working the public into a frenzy accomplishes nothing."

"I demand action!" Sweeney bellowed, and he was met with an audible chorus of assents. "This should be our Golden Age. We're hosting the Republican National Convention. We're hosting the Great Lakes Exposition to celebrate the centennial of this fine city. The American Legion is having their national convention here in September. So is The Townsend Club. This could create the economic ripple we need to get back on our feet. But not if nobody comes! And who would be foolish enough to come here when we have a crazed killer chopping people into bits!"

Ness held up his hands, trying to hold him at bay. "I assure you, the Cleveland homicide department — the people who have the job of trying to catch this killer — are on the case. I personally met with Chief of Police Matowitz recently and he told me he has assigned his top men to it. They're doing everything they know —"

"Apparently it isn't enough," remarked the reporter in the rear.

"Maybe they don't have enough manpower," His Girl Friday remarked, her voice dripping. "Since you fired half the police officers."

Ness pursed his lips. "I most certainly did not fire half the police officers."

"How many replacements have been hired for the men you let go?"

"We're trying to be careful," Ness explained. "To screen more carefully and to require more rigorous training. I have a plan to develop a formal police academy."

"How does that help us now?"

"It would be pointless to release men who are corrupt or useless and then replace them with others just like them."

"But who's going to catch this killer?"

"You're so concerned about the youth of this city." This came from another woman, a blonde. Ness didn't think she was a reporter. She didn't have a notepad. He was almost certain he'd seen her enter with Congressman Sweeney. "I have an eleven-year-old girl and I can't even get her to go play outside because she's afraid to leave the house. She's not sure she's safe in the house. She's afraid that monster will get her."

"Surely you can explain that there is no monster, only one ruthless lawbreaker who is being aggressively hunted by skilled and capable detectives with —"

"Do you have any children?" the woman shot back.

Ness's neck stiffened. "Well — no."

"I didn't think so. If you did, you wouldn't be worrying about booze and blackjack players. You'd be hunting this madman!"

A rousing cry followed, and after that there were so many people talking at once Ness couldn't even make out what they were saying. The press conference had descended into chaos. He wanted to blame the reporters; they were being blatantly unfair. But when he looked into their eyes, he didn't see spite or anger. He saw fear. And Congressman Sweeney was effectively exploiting that fear.

Ness might never come near the Torso Killer, but at this rate, there was a good chance he could become the killer's next victim.

"Please," Ness said, trying to quell the outrage. Out the corner of his eye, he saw Chamberlin hovering at the fringe, wondering if he should intervene and make some excuse to get Ness out of this mess. The press would see through that, though. They would perceive it as cowardice. And they would be right. He had to do something to turn the tide.

"Please. If I could just say a few words." In this rare instance, Ness raised his voice several notches. *"Please!"*

Eventually, the noise of the crowd diminished to a degree that would permit him to speak. "I understand your concern. I truly do. But these other problems have been plaguing Cleveland for a long time, and they will continue to do so unless we adopt the vigorous plans I have outlined. We must build on the progress we have already made."

He drew in his breath and proceeded quickly, before the mob had a chance to start bellowing again. "But I also understand that fear can be a dangerous thing. Whether rational or not. And as safety director, it is my sworn duty to tackle the dangers in our city and to try to eradicate them."

He laid his hands flat on the lectern. "Therefore, as of this moment, I hereby announce that I am personally taking charge of the torso murder investigation."

The reporters cheered. They actually cheered. The faces in the crowd smiled. The pencils flew.

Only Congressman Sweeney's face seemed inscrutable. "With the mayor's permission, and the cooperation of the police department, I will make this case my number one priority. I will become personally involved in this investigation. I will make sure every child can walk to school without fearing for their safety. I will put an end to these murders once and for all."

He leaned back, finally feeling his heartbeat subsiding. "And then we can all relax and go back to tackling the fundamental problems preventing this city from reaching its fullest potential."

There was a spattering of applause, none of it from Sweeney or the blond woman who Ness was certain was aligned with him. Ness thanked them all and raced back up the steps as quickly as he could — without making it obvious that he wanted to get far away as fast as possible.

He removed the handkerchief from his lapel pocket. He was dripping with perspiration. He had walked up to the door of The Harvard Club alone and not even felt his heart race. He had faced down a clan of moonshiners and never blinked. But these reporters and one congressman had made him sweat like a dog in the desert.

"Don't say it," Ness said as Chamberlin joined him on the front steps.

"Wouldn't dream of it," he replied, pushing his glasses up his nose. "Too obvious. Besides, I like my job."

"Do you think I saved it? At the end?"

Chamberlin didn't answer.

"They cheered? Did you hear that? They cheered. So that means I saved it. Right?"

Chamberlin took so long to respond it made Ness's skin crawl. "That depends upon whether you catch the murderer."

"Surely it's just a matter of time. But if they'd hammered me in the press, I'd never get the funding I need for the Boys Clubs. Or the police academy. It was all going down the tubes. So I saved myself. Right?"

Chamberlin tilted his head to one side. "You either saved yourself," he said quietly, "or crucified yourself."

29

At last. A challenger.

The famed Eliot Ness was coming after him. It was flattering, really. A compliment. Cleveland was sending the best it had to offer.

A voice came to him through the bedroom door. "Sir? We have breakfast ready."

"Thank you, ma'am. I believe I will be going out this morning."

There was a brief silence. Her disapproval was impossible to miss. "Will you be gone long?"

"I really don't know."

"You know, I'm charged with the responsibility of keeping an eye on you. Making sure you don't have any . . . bad actions."

"I assure you I will do nothing to bring shame on this lovely home, Mrs. McGovern."

"And the drinking . . . ?"

"I will avoid strong spirits. I have work to do."

"Sir, I know you still drink."

"Not to excess."

"I've seen it in your room."

"Why have you been in my room?"

"It is my charge here, sir."

"Just a little sip now and again. Just enough to get me through the night."

"But if you leave —"

"I will behave myself."

A longer pause ensued. "Just as you say, sir."

"Thank you, ma'am. You are a kind and generous woman."

The radio report had ended, but the words still lingered in his brain even as he walked outside and headed toward Shanty-town. He would have to show them that he was unafraid. And after only a few minutes in Shantytown, he believed he had spotted someone who could help him do that.

"I just thought you might need a place to spend the night, my dear."

"Harvey said —"

"Do you want to sleep in a cardboard box?"

"No, but the choices —"

"That man will be pawing at you. Trying to compromise your virtue."

Her head hung low. "I know."

"I'm offering you something better."

"Why?"

"Because I care about you."

She laughed, much too loudly. Too boisterously. "You don't even know me."

"I know more than you can imagine. I think I know everything that matters. Did you know my girl Flo?"

"Flo Polillo? Course I did. Everyone knew Flo."

"She was a friend."

"Did you hear what happened to her?"

"Yes."

"Horrible."

"Indeed."

"Being all cut up like that."

"Disgraceful. Now come along, dear. I'll take you somewhere safe."

How much time before he would be missed? How much time to indulge himself? Was it possible to give too much time to his soul?

She was so numbed by the cold and the booze that she barely even noticed when he tied her up. She had not felt anything — until he swung the axe.

It left him feeling strangely unsatisfied.

He definitely needed a new challenge. A

challenger. And now he knew who that would be.

30

Merylo slammed the man in the sailor's cap up against the wall, hard enough to rattle the hanging pictures and knock two of them to the ground. "Do you know who I am?" he bellowed.

The sailor was taller than Merylo, bulkier, and by all appearances, stronger. And he was terrified. "Sure, mac, sure. I know who you are. Everybody knows you."

"Who am I?"

"You're the man. The Bulldog. The guy everybody's talkin' about."

"Yeah?" Merylo tightened his grip on the man's lapel. "And what are they saying?"

"They're sayin' you're like a crazy man. Like you're plowin' through the docks, knockin' heads together, mowin' down everyone in your way."

"They're right," Merylo growled. He leaned in close enough to smell the onions on the sailor's breath. "And you're going to be next, unless you start talking."

"But I don't know anything!"

Merylo slammed him against the wall again. "That's not good enough!"

"But I don't!"

"Who was he?"

"Who? The guy they got at the Exposition? Or the new one?"

The new one. The words echoed in Merylo's brain so painfully he thought it might explode. "I'm talking about the head."

"I didn't know him."

"Maybe you've seen him around?"

"No. Never."

"Was he a sailor?"

"No. I mean, I don't know. I don't know him!"

Merylo twisted his fists under the man's chin. "Then how do you know he's not a sailor?"

"I'm just sayin' I've never seen him before!"

"But you knew Andrassy!"

"I knew who he was. I didn't know him personally, but I've seen him in some of the joints. Dance halls and stuff."

"You like dance halls?"

"Sometimes. When I got shore leave."

"The ladies like you?"

"Not like they liked Andrassy."

"Well, this new corpse was a friend of Andrassy's," Merylo barked, not really knowing if it were true. "So how can you know Andrassy if you don't know this guy?"

"I just don't remember seein' him, that's all. I don't get into Cleveland that often."

"I got a witness says he was a sailor. He had an anchor tattooed on his arm."

The sailor blew air through his teeth. "That don't mean anythin'. My aunt Matilda's got a tattoo on her arm. She's never even been out on the lake."

Merylo tightened his grip as much as was possible without strangling the man. "If you're lying to me —"

"I'm not!" he insisted, his eyes wide. "I just don't know nothin'!"

Merylo released him and he fell to the floor in a crumpled heap. "You hear anything, you call me, understand? Right away. You call me!"

"I will. I promise. I will!"

Merylo didn't doubt it, as he watched the man scramble away on all fours. Nobody could be that good an actor. The man was scared witless. If he had known anything, he'd have spilled it.

Like everyone else Merylo had talked to since the tattooed man had been discovered.

And now they had a new corpse, the one

found by Marie Barkley. The first one found on the west side. All the previous remains had been found on the east side, most of them on Kingsbury Run near Shantytown, so he had concentrated his search on vagrants and hoboes. Andrassy and Polillo had both frequented cheap gin joints and dance halls that were little more than meeting places for shady ladies and their clients, so he'd spent weeks searching there. He'd had a lead suggesting the last one might be a sailor, so he'd spent the last three weeks pounding the docks along Lake Erie, trying to turn up someone, anyone who might know something about these crimes.

And still he had nothing. No more information than he'd had before.

And to make matters worse, the killer had moved to the nice part of town.

All the previous victims, so far as they knew, had been scum of the earth, and Merylo knew that had been to his advantage, because even though people wanted the murders stopped, no one could get that worked up about losers like Andrassy and Polillo. But if this killer started going after decent folk, prominent citizens . . .

There would be hell to pay. And he'd be the one footing the bill.

He unfolded the *Cleveland News* tucked

inside his suit coat. He hadn't lied when he told Zalewski he didn't read the papers. He hadn't — in the past. But he'd had to start. He had no choice.

After the corpse had been found on the west side, the so-called Torso Killer was in the headlines again:

"Is there somewhere in Cuyahoga County a madman whose god is the guillotine?

Or is he a cool and calculating killer who decapitates his victims with the skill of a physician?

Does he dissect his victims in some grisly workshop, carrying them to the isolated sections of the county where they are found?

Or does he lure them to the outdoor scene of the execution, acting with a deceptive charm and style?"

Merylo wadded the paper up in his hands. The fearmongering speculation went on for pages, doing its best to work readers up into a state of panic. The reasons were not hard to comprehend. They sold a lot more papers to the upscale folks on the west side than the folks on the east side who were barely scraping by. Before, this story was someone else's problem. Now it was closer to home, potentially affecting every rich daddy whose son or daughter might be walking home late one night . . .

Merylo had been criticized for continuing to follow the trail of the tattooed man after the corpse was found on the west side — but there was a reason. They kept calling the west side corpse the latest victim — but he wasn't. Dr. Pearce's tests showed that that man had been dead for at least two months — meaning that the tattooed man was the more recent victim. Merylo hoped that the foray into the west side had been a onetime accident, perhaps something compelled by circumstances he couldn't understand but that were unlikely to be repeated. There was no way of knowing.

Other than a particularly vague time of death, mandated by the state of decay before the corpse was discovered, Pearce had been able to tell him precious little about this so-called latest victim. He had been five foot five, around 145 pounds, with long brown hair, approximately forty years old. The skin was hardened and brown from exposure. He had been decapitated, obviously, between the third and fourth cervical vertebrae, but there were no signs of any other mutilation by the killer. Nature had not been as kind to the body, however. His chest had been chewed open by rats and insects, and the entire abdominal cavity was infected with worms. The body was far too decomposed to provide usable fingerprints and there were no useful clues in his clothes or on his body — not even a tattoo. Nothing that might provide any indication who this man had been or why anyone would want to kill him. Zalewski had scoured the missing person reports but come up with nothing helpful; there was no one fitting the description Pearce had provided.

He heard Zalewski huffing and puffing behind him even before he heard his voice.

"Sir! Sir!"

Merylo turned slowly, casually hiding the newspaper beneath his suit coat.

"Sir! Have you heard the news?"

"Should I have?"

"It's big, sir. Really big. About this case."

"You've caught the killer single-handedly."

Zalewski stopped short. "Huh? Me?" He stopped to catch his breath. "No, it's not about me. It's about the safety director. Eliot Ness."

Merylo felt a tingle that began at the tips of his toes and worked its way upward. A wave of nausea, and it wasn't because of those four Coneys with sauerkraut he had for lunch, either.

"What about him?"

"He gave a press conference today."

"As if that's news. He talked about the torso murders?"

"Well, it wasn't why he called the conference. It was supposed to be about his Boys Clubs. But Congressman Sweeney was there and he kept changing the subject."

That was predictable enough. Sweeney's biggest financial support came from the west end business community. Plus, as a Democrat, he would undoubtedly love to embarrass the appointee of the Republican mayor. "So what did the distinguished Mr. Ness have to say?"

"You really haven't heard? It's been all over the radio."

"I've been busy."

"He says he's going to end the killing!"

"How? Ask the killer pretty please?"

"Criminy, sir, I don't know what he plans to do. But he's going to be working on this case. Our case. Isn't that great news?"

Merylo remained silent. The nausea intensified.

"Maybe we'll get to be Untouchables! Can you imagine? We're going to be working with Eliot Ness!"

Merylo shook his head, lips pursed. "We're

not going to be working *with* him, son. We're going to be working *for* him."

31

Ness tiptoed as he stepped through the front door of their bungalow. It was late — it always was — and he didn't want to wake Edna if he could avoid it. Unfortunately, he was so loaded down with files and paperwork it was difficult to walk, much less creep.

A light came on. Edna was sitting in an armchair in the living room, wide awake. She was wearing her best dress, a lovely red satin number that he thought made her look like Claudette Colbert in *It Happened One Night.*

"Honey." He dropped the paperwork on the nearest coffee table and moved toward her. "What are you doing up?"

She glared at him, her eyes colder than steel. "Waiting for you."

"You shouldn't stay up so late. I told Bob to call and tell you I'd be late. Didn't he call?"

"Indeed he did," she said, not blinking, expressionless.

"Honestly, honey, do we have to repeat this same discussion every time I come home late? You know how demanding my job is. I've had to deal with the press all day —"

"As if that's a great burden to you."

"— and I'm launching this brand-new project, the Boys Clubs. It's going to be something really special, Edna. I've got funding from the city council, plus I've managed to raise contributions from private donors. I'm going to get all those stray kids off the streets and teach them how to be —"

"Do I look like a reporter?"

The volume of her voice rose so sharply and so suddenly that Ness literally reared back. "I — don't —"

"If I wanted to hear this, I'd ask for a copy of your press release."

"That's not fair."

"What's fair? I never wanted to be married to a hero." Her voice grew quiet. "All I ever wanted was a husband."

Ness took a deep breath, then laid his hand on her wrist. She immediately withdrew it, recoiling from his touch. "I know I said I'd try to be home earlier, but —"

"We missed the Petersons' party."

The words hung in the air like a dirigible, suspended between them but going nowhere.

Ness racked his brain but he couldn't think of anything to say, nothing intelligent, nothing witty, certainly nothing conciliatory. "Was that tonight?"

"Yes of course it was. Why do you think I'm dressed this way? Just so you could indulge your Claudette Colbert fantasy when you finally stumbled through the door?"

"Honey . . . I don't know what to say. I'm sorry."

"You're not."

"I am, darling. I sincerely regret that I —"

"No, you're not!" she shouted. She stood up and walked to the fireplace, turning her back on him. "You want to placate me, but you're not remotely sorry. You think you are absolutely justified in doing everything you do. Your work comes first."

"That isn't so."

"Don't kid a kidder, Eliot. I've been with you too many years. I know the score. You love your work." She braced herself against the mantel. "Much more than you ever loved me."

"Don't sell yourself short."

"I don't think you could ever love any woman the way you love catching bad guys. And nothing can compare with the thrill you get from playing for the reporters, getting your picture taken, receiving the praise of strangers." She pressed her hand against her forehead. "Pity it's not possible to make love to a camera. Then you might actually have children."

Ness's lips parted. "Sweetheart — how can you — what are you —"

"I think you know exactly what I'm saying."

"All this because I missed some party?"

"It wasn't just some party. It was the Petersons."

Ness shrugged. "They're nice people, but they're hardly —"

She whirled on him. "They're the only friends I have in this godforsaken town!"

She covered her face with her hand, and Ness noticed for the first time that her fingernails were painted red, perfectly matching her dress. "You have coworkers, underlings. People at your beck and call. Reporters. What do I have? A little house a million miles from the heart of the city, hardly any neighbors, and one friend. And we missed her party."

"You should've gone alone."

"I couldn't go alone. Do you have any idea what people would say? What they already say?" She paused. "That would only give them proof."

Ness took a step closer to her. She arched her back, twisting away. It was a chilling move, one that stopped him dead in his tracks.

"Let me make it up to you."

"I don't think that's possible."

"I think it is. The mayor is throwing a huge bash. Fancy dress, all the most important people in the city. And we're invited. You'll meet all kinds of people. Won't that be fun?"

When she finally spoke, her voice was so low and dark it chilled him. "No, you stupid fool. It won't be fun at all. For me. You'll love it. You'll be the toast of the town. The famous Eliot Ness. I'll be lucky if I see you all night long."

"No, sweetie, I promise. I'll show you off, introduce you to some of the other society wives —"

"I am not a society wife! I don't want to be a society wife!"

"It'll be a good time."

"No, it'll be you advancing your career, making connections, shaking hands. And me being miserable."

"Well . . . there's the police cotillion —"

"Oh, that sounds like fun."

"Look, Edna, I'm sorry I've been so busy. But I'm making a commitment to you, right here and now. I'm going to spend more time at home — lots more time. I'm going to be here every night for supper. I'm going to be home so much you'll be sick to death of me. I give you my Boy Scout promise."

"Really?" she said coldly. "And how are you going to do that when you're busy catching the Torso Killer?"

Ness sighed. Guess she'd been listening to the radio.

"I don't know how I'm going to do it, Edna, but I will. I'll do whatever makes you happy. I'm pretty tight with Mayor Burton. I'll ask what he and his wife do, where they go —"

"Eliot, are you even listening to me? I want to be with regular people. I want to do regular things. Go out to dinner. Play canasta. Do what normal couples do after the husband comes home at a normal hour."

He averted his eyes. "I — don't really know how."

She laughed, a sharp, bitter laugh. "That's the truest thing you've said all night."

Ness dared a tentative step toward her. "I don't know what you want. If you'll just tell me . . ."

She whirled around, grabbing his hand with a fierce intensity and pressing it against her bosom. "I want you to want me!"

"I do, darling. Honest."

"Do you? Do you really? Does this do anything for you at all?"

"Well, of course . . ."

She flung his hand away. "Bull. If it did — we wouldn't be standing here talking." Her mascara streaked down her face. "I'm going to bed. Alone. You can sleep out here." She paused. "I think you're more comfortable that way anyhow."

"Edna —" He held out his hand, but it was no use. The bedroom door slammed in his face.

He fell down onto the sofa, his eyes tightly closed. He just didn't understand what was wrong with her. Sure, he knew she was mad about the party, but what could he do? After that press conference, he'd had no choice but to get up to speed on the Torso Killer case as quickly as possible. What did she expect?

He took a deep breath and opened his eyes. Like it or not, he had a lot of reading to do before he went to sleep.

He reached toward the top file he had gotten from Chief Matowitz, then stopped. The mail was lying on the coffee table, still wrapped in a rubber band. Apparently Edna hadn't done any more than bring it into the house.

He thumbed through the envelopes, only marginally paying attention. Bills, bills, more bills. More than he could afford on his salary. For all the media attention he got, he still wasn't paid better than most police officers with his experience. Gas, water, coal —

He froze. His fingers stiffened. His eyes strained to read the scrawled handwriting.

It was a postcard.

He brought it closer to the lamp to examine it more carefully. The letters were all in capitals, but uneven, of varying shape, like something a child might do. But they didn't look childlike.

HOW DO YOU PLAN ON KEEPING YOUR PROMISE?

The only signature, if that's what it was, was a letter S. The bottom of the card was filled with strange circles and lines and shapes. There was no return address.

Ness stared at the postcard, turning it back and forth, over and over again in his hands. There was something strange about it, even beyond the words. As if it gave off an . . . aura. A personality. A very disturbing one.

It seemed Edna wasn't the only one who listened to the radio.

The killer knew Ness was coming after him. And he wasn't worried. Wasn't scared. He was taunting him. Just like the boys in school had taunted him, all those years ago.

Ness walked to the cabinet and took out a bottle of whiskey he kept for special occasions, company and such. He poured himself a shot. Then he poured another one. Then he read the postcard again.

HOW DO YOU PLAN ON KEEPING YOUR PROMISE?

32

Despite his numerous years on the police force, including his later years as a detective, Peter Merylo had never before been inside the city hall building. Never had any reason to. He reported to his immediate superior, and these days, to Chief Matowitz. He had nothing to do with the mayor and he didn't get invited to the mayor's parties. Which suited him fine. In fact, he preferred it that way and never expected it to change.

Until this morning when, before he could even get himself a cup of joe, Matowitz informed him that he was to report to City Hall immediately.

The safety director wanted to speak to him.

He wasn't surprised.

Merylo had grabbed his hat, grabbed Zalewski, and made his way downtown. He'd known it would only be a matter of time, ever since he'd learned that Eliot Ness had promised to bring in the Torso Killer. Hard thing to do, unless you talked to someone who actually knew something about the case. In fact, hard thing to do even if you did.

Ness's secretary kept them waiting for ten minutes in the lobby outside his office. Merylo admired the lobby, which was itself larger than any office in the police precinct building. But through the window in the door, he could see the vast expanse that was the office of Eliot Ness. Could anyone but the mayor have a larger office? It was hard to imagine. All the furnishings looked new, plush, comfy. Merylo couldn't help but think about the furniture in his own shabby apartment, the rented stuff his wife had lived with since they'd been married. The only time they ever bought new furniture, if you could call it that, was when he bought a crib for Margaret. Plush sofas and chairs weren't in the budget of a police detective.

Eventually the door to the office opened and a tall man wearing wire-rimmed spectacles stepped out. Merylo recognized him from the papers — the ones he never read — as being Robert Chamberlin, Ness's personal assistant.

"The safety director will see you now."

Merylo nudged Zalewski. They followed Chamberlin into the spacious office.

Ness was sitting at his desk, working furiously on some sort of report. There were no chairs outside the desk. They stood for almost a minute before Ness spoke.

"You favor a straw hat."

Merylo blinked. He had been prepared to be pumped for information, criticized for a lack of results, even castigated for poor spelling. But he hadn't seen this coming.

Perhaps that was the point.

"In warm weather," Merylo said dryly. "When Cleveland turns cold, I switch to my felt hat."

Ness nodded. "Prefer a fedora, myself."

"Not in my budget."

At last, Ness looked up. His face was soft, but he was handsome. Merylo could see why the papers liked him so much. "Not in mine, either, to tell the truth. But appearances are important."

Merylo looked at him squarely. "I'm more interested in results."

"In my experience, appearances can lead to results."

"In my experience, the only thing that leads to results is hard work."

Out the corner of his eye, Merylo saw Zalewski staring at him wild-eyed, as if he'd lost his mind.

"You have a reputation for being a bull-dog, Detective Merylo."

He was amazed at how soft-spoken the famed crimefighter was. Didn't sound like a tough guy at all. More like someone you'd expect to meet out on the tennis court. "I guess I do."

"Which can be a tribute to your tenacity." He paused; Merylo suspected Ness was wondering if he knew what the word meant. "Or your stubbornness. Which is it?"

Merylo didn't blink. "Both."

"I admire tenacity. But I can't work with people who can't take instructions. You get my drift?"

"Yup."

"And I can't have loose cannons bringing my department into disrepute."

"You're afraid I might sully your squeaky-clean image?"

"I have been told that you have a fondness for offensive language. That even when you play a critical role in an investigation, prosecutors hesitate to put you on the witness stand because they fear you will appall the jury."

"I guess I'm a bad boy, then."

Ness continued. "Do you consider yourself a religious man?"

"I consider myself a cop. And you don't get where I am — as a cop — by being religious. Or by talking like a Sunday school teacher."

"I can comprehend that. But what I'm trying to discern is how much is image and how much is the real you. I have to know who you are before I can know whether I can work with you."

"What do you need to know? I'm the lead detective on the torso case."

"That could change."

Merylo drew in his breath, then slowly released it. "I'm a simple man, Mr. Ness. What you see is what I am."

Ness rose, then opened a file on his desk. "I think not. You haven't always wanted to be a cop, have you?"

"Well . . ."

"In fact, at one time, you considered the priesthood."

Zalewski's eyes ballooned.

"You spent a good while at a monastery and —"

"That was a long time ago."

"Maybe. But men don't change so much, not in my experience. You may not have become a priest — probably because you couldn't afford the education — but I wonder if you're still trying to save souls."

"Look, could we talk about —"

"You're the force's reigning pistol champ." Ness looked up. "I'm not too bad with a pistol, either. Know jujitsu?"

"Uh, no."

"Maybe I could teach you. I've been thinking about starting a class." He returned to his notes. "You're fiercely protective of your family. I admire that in a man."

"Could we talk about the case?"

"You love violin music."

"How did you —"

"You speak several eastern European languages fluently, which makes you the perfect person to be conducting interviews with the immigrants living in the Kingsbury Run area."

"Lots of the men on the force —"

"I know you're well-read. You're an auto-didact."

Merylo blinked twice. This time, he really didn't know what the word meant, blast it all. It infuriated him.

"You're self-educated. It shows, in your language, when you're not playing the tough cop. It shows in your work, too. I've re-viewed your files. You have an impressive record. Chief Matowitz tells me you're his best detective."

"Look, are we going to talk about me or

are we going to talk about the Torso Murderer?"

"Both." Ness walked around the desk and leaned back against it, just a few feet away from the two men. "I guess you boys know that I've committed to getting involved in this case."

Zalewski jumped in. "I heard your press conference on the radio, sir. I thought you really told off that Congressman Sweeney. He was totally out of line."

Ness shrugged. "He's a Democrat. He wants to use the murders to attack the Republican administration."

"But you did promise to get involved," Merylo said. "You promised to bring the killer to justice."

Ness frowned. "Yes, I did, didn't I? And you know where that leaves me?"

"You've made an impossible promise." Merylo waited a beat. "And you want us to deliver on it."

Ness ignored the barb. "The problem with these newspapers is, they get people so worked up they can't see straight. They think this killer is the only danger the city faces. And now he's on the west side and there's a thousand-dollar reward for information leading to an arrest. The city's going to get even crazier. Good grief — even

Happy Hitler took time out from his Four-Year Plan to declare these murders proof of Western decadence. They've been de-nounced in fascist Italy, too. You can imag-ine how that plays with elected officials. The political pressure to find the killer is fierce."

"And you put yourself in the middle of it."

"I didn't have much choice. I never in-tended to get personally involved — only to take a more supervisory role. But all that's changed now. I got the word from Mayor Burton. He wants me to take over."

"Have you talked to Chief Matowitz about that?"

"I don't work for Chief Matowitz," Ness said crisply.

"Look," Merylo said, "I don't know any-thing about politics. All I know is how to be a cop. So tell me — now that you're taking over — are you going to fire me?"

Ness grinned. "Detective Merylo — that's what we're currently in the process of deter-mining."

Ness had eyed Merylo carefully from the moment he had arrived, while he waited in the lobby, and even later, while they thought he had his head buried in paperwork. He found he could learn most about a man when he didn't know he was being observed, just as he gained most from an interview when the subject didn't realize he was being interviewed. Zalewski didn't matter — as long as he wasn't on the take, Merylo could pick his own assistant. But if Merylo was going to be the main man on the street, he mattered. Ness had read Merylo's file and he looked good on paper. But if Ness had learned anything from his time in Chi-Town, it was that what was most important when you were assembling your team was a man's character — and that was something you couldn't get from a report.

"What do you know about the killer so far?" Ness asked.

Merylo apparently decided honesty was the best policy. "Not much."

"With all due respect, Detective, that's not good enough."

"We know he's good with a knife. That leads the coroner to believe he might be a butcher. Or a doctor, but Pearce thinks that's unlikely."

"Because doctors are too socially respectable to be killers?"

"And they aren't usually messed up with lowlife criminals like Andrassy and Polillo."

"What else do you know?"

"He's strong. Strong enough to decapitate

a man with one blow. Strong enough to lug a corpse out to Jackass Hill."

"What else?"

"He may be smart. Educated. He uses a chemical preservative, at least some of the time."

"And he's managed to kill at least five people without getting caught."

"Another good point."

"What's his motive?"

Ness eyed Merylo carefully, and for the first time the detective hesitated before answering. Ness suspected he was considering whether it would be better to say he didn't know, and risk looking stupid, or to speculate, and risk being found wrong. "I used to think he was with the mob. But now I think it may be some kinda . . . sex thing."

"Because one of the victims had his genitalia removed."

"Yes."

"But the others did not."

"True, but he still might —"

"And there's no sign that any of the corpses were sexually molested or penetrated, correct?"

"How'd you know that?"

"Because I stayed up late reading the files. Haven't slept in more days than I care to remember. But I don't think this is a sex crime."

"The killer totally emasculated —"

"Some of the victims. Not all. And we have victims of both genders. So I have to ask, Detective Merylo — is this conclusion of yours really based on the evidence? Or have your many years working on the vice squad preconditioned you to find sexual perversion even where it may not exist?"

Merylo's neck stiffened. "You asked me what I thought, sir. I told you."

"So you did."

Zalewski chipped in. "Doctor Pearce thinks we should talk to an alienist."

Ness turned his head slightly. This was this first thing he'd heard in the entire conversation that he didn't already know. "Really?"

"Yeah. That's some kinda doctor that reads minds or —"

"I know what an alienist is. I studied psychoanalysis in college. How long ago did he make this recommendation?"

Merylo and Zalewski exchanged a glance. "Several murders back," Zalewski answered.

Ness pursed his lips. "Tell the doctor we want to talk to his alienist. As soon as possible. Did you know Pearce is planning a seminar?"

"About what?"

"About the murders. He's bringing some of the best forensic scientists in the country in to examine the evidence and see if they can tell us anything we don't already know. I plan to attend." He paused. "I think it might be a good idea if you boys did, too."

"Does that mean we're still on the case?"

Ness ignored the question. "You mentioned Andrassy and Polillo. What about the other victims? Have you ID'd them yet?"

"No."

"Do you think you can?"

"Probably not. But I haven't stopped trying. And I never will."

Ness laid a hand on each of the men's shoulders. "That's what I wanted to hear. Now listen to me, boys. I'm not an easy man to work for. I know that. I demand long hours. Hard work. I demand that you keep your nose clean."

"We're clean," Merylo grunted.

"I know that," Ness interrupted. "If you weren't, you wouldn't still be on the force. But things change sometimes, when the going gets tough. I need your word that you won't bring disrespect to my office."

Ness turned his eyes upon both men. They looked back at him.

"You have our word," Merylo said quietly.

"Good. There's just one other thing I demand from my people. Results."

Merylo held up his hands. "Look, we've been killing ourselves on this case, chasing our tails, doing everything possible. But I can't make any guarantees."

"I heard the same thing about Capone, back in Chicago. He's too big. You can't bring him down. But we did. And we'll get this monster too, understand?"

"Yes, sir!" Zalewski said enthusiastically. Merylo said nothing.

"Good. Then I would be very much honored if you two gentlemen would become my primary field lieutenants on this case. You will work directly for me. I'll arrange everything with Chief Matowitz. You report to me, or if I'm unavailable, to my assistant. And no one else. Not even your buddies on the force. Not even the press."

"I thought you liked the press," Merylo said.

"No, my friend, I use the press. Those are two totally different things. At any rate, that's my job, not yours. I want no leaks."

Zalewski appeared flush with excitement. "Does this mean we're going to be Untouchables?"

Ness thought for a moment. That was almost a good idea. But Merylo was too

281

well-known, too high-profile. All he could perform were official duties. What if he had a group of people out of the spotlight? People who could go beyond official duties . . .

Ness smiled. "You're already untouchable, officers, as far as I'm concerned. Now we've got to be unbeatable."

"Yes, sir!" Zalewski actually saluted.

"All right then. Get to work. I'll expect a report at eight o'clock tomorrow morning. And every morning thereafter until this murderer is caught. I'll be formulating a plan, and as soon as I complete it, I'll give you specific instructions. I will expect to see them implemented expediently and effectively. So you'd best get started."

He watched as the two men left the office. He hoped he wasn't making a mistake. In the past, he'd always obtained the best results by creating his own team, rather than adopting the men already in place. But he needed men with police experience, real crime-solving skills. With Capone, they already knew who was behind the crimes; they just needed the evidence to bring him down. In this case, they had no idea who — or what — they were fighting.

He had spoken rashly to the press. If he didn't deliver, they would eat him alive like the piranhas they were. And there were other considerations . . .

Involuntarily, his mind returned to the postcard he had received. He had not turned it in to the police, nor had he given it to the Bertillon department for analysis.

It was possible it was a fake. One of the nuts all this press coverage was sure to shake off the tree.

But what if it wasn't? What if the killer saw this as a personal grudge match? A battle between him and the Fed who supposedly brought down Capone?

The man who wrote that postcard knew where he lived. And Edna.

He returned to his desk. He had implemented the first part of his assault on the so-called Torso Murderer. Now it was time to implement Phase Two.

33

It occurred to Merylo, once again, that he should have requested that this meeting take place somewhere other than the coroner's office. The front lobby was too busy and Dr. Pearce's office was too small, so the only logical place to have the meeting was in the autopsy room. And the fact that Merylo had been here more than a dozen times on various cases had not in the slightest altered the fact that the place gave him the heebie-jeebies. Happily, there were no corpses currently on display, but there had been before, and there would be again. He couldn't help but look at each of the compartment doors that lined the south wall and wonder whether there was a headless body hidden behind it.

Merylo had pushed the operating table to one side and arranged some folding chairs in the center of the room. Zalewski was seated beside him. "Sir?"

"Yeah?"

"Do you think they're coming?"

"Yeah."

"They're late."

"Well, they're important people."

"Which ones? The doctors, or the safety director?"

"All of them."

"In that order?"

Merylo allowed himself a thin smile. "No comment."

Through the glass-windowed door Merylo saw the good doctor Arthur Pearce enter the room with another man of the same height but considerably slimmer build. He wore glasses, thick ones, and he was clutching a black leather bag. He was wearing a checked suit, too big for him, and even more notably, no hat.

"Kraut," Zalewski whispered under his breath. "Probably a hebe, too."

"What difference does it make?"

"I'm just sayin' —"

"I haven't heard any characters named 'Zalewski' on *Jack Armstrong* lately."

"I'm just sayin'. I never cared much for Krauts."

The two men entered the room. Eliot Ness was just a few steps behind them.

"Detectives," Dr. Pearce began, "let me

introduce you to my colleague, Dr. Ernst Hunstein."

The two detectives rose, but the new doctor did not extend a hand. "I believe you've already met the safety director."

Merylo tipped his hat slightly. "We've had the pleasure, yes."

"We are most fortunate to have the opportunity to consult with Dr. Hunstein. He has only in the past year emigrated from Germany."

Zalewski gave Merylo a decided "told-you-so" look.

"I'm surprised you could leave the Fatherland," Zalewski said. "I hear most of you people like to stay home."

"I love my home," Hunstein said. His voice was quiet, and between that and the thick accent, he was difficult to understand. "But I now reside in New York. Given the changes of late, the Nuremberg Laws against my people, I thought it best to leave as have so many others."

"You talking about Happy Hitler?"

Hunstein's eyes narrowed. "That is not how we refer to him in Germany. Are you familiar with the actions of the Führer?"

Zalewski hedged. "I saw him in a newsreel once. This summer, at the Berlin Olympics."

"Ah. Of course. Your Jesse Owens performed very well. He won four gold medals, I believe. Hitler was not happy about that."

"He probably didn't like seein' his medals leave Germany."

Hunstein fingered his glasses. "I do not believe that was the problem."

"Didn't Hitler get ninety-nine percent of the vote in the elections?"

Hunstein sighed. "That is what they say."

Merylo figured this was a good time to intervene. "Dr. Pearce says you're some kind of head doctor."

"I am an alienist, yes. I studied under Dr. Freud himself."

"And he thinks you might be able to help us on this case."

"And you are skeptical of this, no?"

Merylo's head pulled back. How had he known that? "Well . . . it isn't how we usually go about our police work."

"Perhaps it should be."

"The tried-and-true methods —"

"Have not caught this criminal. Possibly if you had brought me in sooner, the killer would not have remained at large for so long."

Merylo did his best to hide his irritation. "Yeah, and possibly if the moon were made of green cheese we'd all be fat and happy, but who's to say?"

Dr. Hunstein bowed his head. "Indeed. It is all a matter of speculation."

"I don't mean to be rude," Merylo said, "but we've got a lot of work to do, plus reporters checking up on every move we make, so if you don't have anything for us —"

"I have taken the liberty of reviewing the police documents my colleague Dr. Pearce was able to obtain from Chief Matowitz and the safety director. I have spent the past three days doing so."

Three days? That slowed Merylo down. "Then you know that we've done a lot of work, but haven't found information that would tell us anything useful about this killer."

"I disagree entirely. I was able to discern a great deal from reading your files. Most interesting."

Merylo's eyebrows crinkled. "You're going to stand there and tell me you know who the killer is?"

"No. I cannot tell you *who* the killer is. But I can tell you *what* he is."

"With respect, Doc," Zalewski interjected, "we know what he is. A cold-blooded killer."

"No, sir. You do not know what he is. And that is why you have not caught him." He paused. "Have either of you any familiarity with the work being done in Vienna on the psychosexual aspects of crime?"

Merylo thought back to his experience on the vice squad. "Are you saying these are sex crimes? 'Cause I also —"

"Not exactly. I see no evidence of a sexual motivation. But an investigation into the likely sexual history of the killer yields much information about his psyche."

"And why is that useful?"

Dr. Pearce answered for him. "This is what I was trying to explain to you before. If you know what he is, and why he does what he does, then you can anticipate what he might do next. And if you can do that, you just might be able to catch him."

"Ask yourself," Hunstein continued, "what could produce such hostility, such anger, as to make a man capable of committing the atrocities that have been perpetrated on these victims?"

"Merylo thinks they all worked together on some scam," Zalewski volunteered, to Merylo's dismay. "Or maybe they were all involved with the same woman."

"I think that unlikely," Hunstein replied. "I think it much more plausible that the killer's psyche was scarred by a traumatic incident, or a series of incidents, in his childhood."

"Now I have a real problem with that," Ness said, scooting forward in his chair. For the first time, he seemed interested in the conversation. Merylo couldn't help but wonder why. "Lots of people have bad child-hoods. Doesn't make them repeat killers."

Hunstein lifted an eyebrow. "Indeed?"

"Gosh, I work almost every day with troubled boys, in my new Boys Clubs, or in my Boy Scout troop. Many of them have come from seriously troubled homes. But they're not crazy. They just need a good role model. Someone to show them the way."

"I think perhaps," Hunstein suggested gently, "that you do not understand the magnitude of the childhood trauma I am describing."

"Like you think the killer witnessed a murder or something?"

"Perhaps. But in our experience, it is more likely something of a sexual nature. It is most probable that your killer was abused as a child."

"Abused?" Zalewski screwed up his face. "You mean, like slapped around? 'Cause my ma used to —"

"I mean sexually abused. Repeatedly."

"Oh." He fell silent. "By who?"

"In most cases, a close friend or relative. Probably a male, since most of his victims have been male. A father. Grandfather. Friendly uncle or neighbor. It doesn't matter. But this killer exhibits all the pathology of a mind twisted by sexual abuse, deranged by the conflicted feelings arising from being abused by people he adored."

"Does that happen? To boys?"

"I'm afraid that it does. And it can work devastating effects on the personality. Particularly when coupled with other elements of instability — broken homes, single parents, alcoholism, drug abuse. He was probably isolated as an adolescent, or even earlier. Lonely, withdrawn, always suppressing feelings of great rage. He probably engaged in fantasies in which he was a person of great power. An *über*-man. Interpersonal relationships would have been difficult, so he probably did not play sports or join clubs. He may have indulged in pornography, if he could find it, as a way of redirecting his interest in sex, since he would be unlikely to sustain a healthy relationship with a female of his own age. He might turn to drugs or alcohol for relief. Eventually, he found the means and ability to carry out his power fantasies. On other people."

Merylo couldn't remain silent any longer. "This is all well and good, hearing about the killer's tragic childhood. But who is he?

You haven't actually given us any information about the murderer himself."

"My dear detective, have you not been listening? The information is all around you. I can tell you much. He is almost certainly male, probably between the ages of twenty and forty, probably white."

"How can you —"

"He is smart, well-read, familiar with chemistry. Strong."

"This is old hat."

"He may very likely have a physical deformity."

Merylo fell silent.

"He was probably raised in Cleveland. He knows it well. He has some kind of income flow, some means to support himself while he plans and executes his crimes. Given the unlikelihood that he is able to maintain a job of any substance, he may come from a wealthy family."

"Come on!"

"I will go further. He may not only be connected to money — it is very possible that the other members of his family know, or at least suspect, that he is a dangerous man. They, perhaps, may even suspect that he is the notorious Torso Killer."

"Then why wouldn't they say anything?"

"Would you want it known that the Torso

Killer was your son? Or nephew? Or husband?"

Merylo did not reply.

"At best, you might try to hide him away, or somehow remove his ability to kill. But you would not turn him in, especially if you were well connected. Prominent. To do so would be to destroy yourself."

"If this guy's so rich," Zalewski asked, "why's he hanging out in Kingsbury Run all the time?"

"Where better to find easy prey? People no one will miss. He has killed five, perhaps six times. And you have identified two of his victims. Kingsbury Run will provide him an endless supply of unknown or little-known victims."

Merylo scratched his head. "I don't know. This all seems pretty far-fetched."

"I assure you, it is not."

"But if the guy is just some loony rich kid preying on vagrants for no reason other than that he got hurt when he was a kid, how are we ever going to catch him?"

Pearce leaned forward. "Dr. Hunstein is an alienist, not a detective."

Hunstein held up a hand. "That is true. And I would not presume to interfere in your work. But if I were to be allowed to make one small suggestion . . ."

"Yes?"

Hunstein paused. "I believe that in the past you have interviewed people in Kingsbury Run looking for connections. Associations. But this killer is much more likely to select victims with whom he has *no* association — so they can never be traced back to him after the bodies are found."

"I'm not sure, Merylo," Zalewski said quietly, "but I think he's sayin' we're barkin' up the wrong tree."

"I'm sure," Merylo grunted back. "So you think we got it all wrong, huh, Doc?"

Hunstein considered. "I think you are looking in the right place for the wrong person. Instead of looking for connections, I would look for someone who has no connections. I would go to Kingsbury Run and look for the man who does not belong, but still does not attract attention. The man who is not a vagrant, or hobo, or small-time criminal, even though he might pretend to be. Look for the man who is there solely for the same reason that you might go to a well-stocked trout pond." He drew in his breath. "Look for the man who is stalking his prey."

Merylo considered. He still didn't buy into all this childhood trauma huggermugger. And the killer being well connected? Preposterous. But the idea of looking for the man who did not belong . . .

It was almost worth considering. He had to try something new. What he had done so far hadn't produced any results.

"Thank you for your time, Dr. Hunstein," Ness said, rising. "We appreciate your contributions. I'm sure there's much to what you said. I'm all for using science whenever possible. Though I prefer the sciences that are . . . you know. More certain."

Hunstein seemed to hesitate. "Ye-es . . ."

"Was there something else?"

Hunstein obviously thought carefully before he spoke again. "There is one aspect to this case that . . . troubles me. That does not fit the usual pattern."

"And that is?"

"As I told you, the killer is likely in the thrall of a massive empowerment fantasy. Delusions of grandeur, we call it. Something he has nurtured since he was a small boy. I would expect such an individual to be self-absorbed. Narcissistic. To believe himself superior to all others. Unbeatable. Untouchable."

Ness bit down on his lower lip. "And you don't think he is?"

Hunstein batted his lips with his finger. "I would expect such a man to be playing games with the police. To be taunting them.

Perhaps even to be sending them messages."

Out of the corner of his eye, Merylo saw a change in the expression on Ness's face. It was small and subtle. But he was almost certain it was there.

"Really?" Ness replied. "That seems risky."

"Jack the Ripper did it. Repeatedly. And of course he was never caught. Why does this killer not do the same? It is the one element that does not fit."

"Well," Ness said, smiling, "I'm sure every case can't be exactly alike."

"No," Hunstein said somberly. "Not precisely. But —"

The door to the room opened and Pearce's secretary stepped through. "Mr. Safety Director? I — I have a message for you."

Merylo rose to his feet. He didn't need to hear what it was. He could tell just from the expression on her face.

"Yes? What is it?"

"It's — it's from Kingsbury Run. A stagnant pool near East Thirty-seventh. A huge crowd has gathered."

Ness's face sobered. "Why?"

"Sir — they've found another body. Or to be more accurate — pieces of one."

34

September 10, 1936

"How many of them do you think there are?"

Merylo gazed across the small creek to the shore. "Hundreds. No, thousands. Thousands since we got here."

"What are they waiting for?"

"The head. Or better yet, the killer."

"So they think he's just going to show up and make a guest appearance? Return to the scene of the crime?"

"He has before. About five times."

"Not while anyone was looking."

"As far as we know."

The crowd on the shore was so thick that the fire rescue squad had a difficult time getting through, and an even worse time getting their pumps into position. Merylo had called for more men, just to control the crowd. But he knew that would take time — and they might not come at all.

Zalewski pulled on the oars, propelling the small boat they were in just the tiniest bit forward. "Jeez — some of those people even brought their kids! Why do they come?"

"Who the hell knows? Bored. Unemployed. Most of the people living in Shantytown don't have a lot to do during the day."

"That don't cover it all. Look at some of those guys. Suits. Fancy hats. Better than mine. They aren't unemployed. They're first-class citizens."

"I guess everyone's interested in this case now," Merylo mumbled, but he knew there was more to it than that. Some came, looked awhile, and moved on. Others had been here all day and showed no inclination to leave anytime in the near future. More people than attended the Great Lakes Expo in the course of a day. More than came to town for the Republican National Convention or the American Legion Convention, or any of the others.

The Torso Killer was now Cleveland's number one attraction. Or detraction. It had become the thing most famous about Cleveland, its national calling card.

The murderer had killed six people, possibly more, in gruesome, horrifying ways. And he would kill again. All the spectators crowded on the bank of this foul-smelling, stagnant pond that they euphemistically called a creek knew that.

"You quizzed the guy? Harris?"

Zalewski nodded, still straining against the current. "Colored guy. Vagrant. Around twenty-five or so. Hails from St. Louis, came in on a train. Was looking for a ride out when he saw two halves of the torso floating in the water. Called the police."

Merylo nodded. For once, the response of the police department had been speedy and deliberate, not that it made any difference. They got the two portions of the decapitated torso out of the water and sent them down to Pearce's office, then began looking for the rest of the victim. The fire rescue squad searched the pond with grappling hooks. When that produced nothing, they switched to ceiling hooks, larger and heavier. They discovered the lower halves of both legs and they were still looking, hampered by the crowd that only increased as word spread through the town and went into a near frenzy every time a new body part was discovered. Merylo and Zalewski borrowed a boat from the Coast Guard and rowed into the center of the pond with the grappling hooks, hoping they might find something that had drifted from the shore. With no arms and no head, they had virtually no chance of discovering the identity of the victim.

"Clothes?"

"Oh yeah," Zalewski said, puffing out his cheeks as he strained against the oars. With the hooks down, the boat was tough to move. "The guy always leaves us clothes, doesn't he?" He brought the oars around again. "Blue workshirt, gray felt hat, dingy green underwear. Shirt and underwear have bloodstains. Probably knife marks. So where does that get us?"

"Nowhere. As usual." Merylo sighed. "Want me to take a turn at the oars?"

"Nah. I got it."

Merylo nodded. Even if Zalewski was his assistant, he didn't want the man to think that meant he had to do all the rowing. Then again, it was pretty hot outside . . .

"Mind if I ask you a question?"

Merylo thought a moment. "I suppose that depends on the question."

"What d'ya think of that Ness guy?"

"I think he's our superior."

"He isn't even on the police force."

"Nonetheless."

"But what do you think of him? What do you think of him taking over our case?"

"It's not like he wanted it."

"I don't know," Zalewski said, bringing the oars around again. "My Myrtle says she thinks he's a glory hound. He knows the torso case is where the headlines are."

Merylo shook his head. "Whatever else he may be, Ness is smart. Very smart. He knows this case is quicksand. Great exposure if we catch the killer, but who knows how long that may take? No, he was much happier dealing with traffic lights and gin joints. Things he could control."

"You think he really wants to work with us? 'Cause my Myrtle thinks he's just using us. For if we don't catch the killer. He's gonna use us as . . . as . . . what was her word?"

"A scapegoat?"

"Yeah. That was it. What d'ya think?"

"I think if we don't catch the killer — soon — it's not going to be pretty for anyone."

"But we got no clues! How can anyone expect us to catch a killer when we got no clues?"

"People aren't interested in excuses. They want to stop being scared. Even though there are a thousand other things out there to be scared of, what with what's going on in Europe and all. But right now the Torso Killer has their attention. They want him stopped."

"Even if we do stop him, I bet Ness takes all the credit."

"Is that what Myrtle thinks?"

"Yeah. How'd you know?"

Merylo smiled. "I'm sure Ness would acknowledge our valuable contribution."

"Yeah?"

"Sure. Haven't you noticed? Whenever someone brings up Capone, he always reminds them that a lot of people worked on that case. It was a team effort." He gazed across the pond. "But how many of those people does he mention by name? How many have you seen in the papers? His apparent modesty just makes him seem all the more important."

"Maybe we should catch the killer and not tell him."

"Maybe Ness will catch him and not tell us."

"Really? You think so?"

"Anything's possible. The only thing that really bothers me is — Ness has no background in police work. He may know how to bust up mobsters — known entities who aren't hiding. But he has no experience with detective work. And he's running the show."

"So what are you gonna do about that?"

"I'm going to do whatever the safety director tells me to do," Merylo said. "But I have a few plans of my own."

"Like what?"

Merylo didn't answer. He turned his attention to the near shore, where thousands of people were still watching the show. "We need to fan out. Search the area. Talk to people."

"How we gonna do that? We can't even get enough men to keep the crowd in line."

Merylo slowly turned to look at his assistant, drenched in sweat from rowing the boat. "Zalewski — you're brilliant."

"I am?"

"I think you've just answered your own question."

"I have?"

"We need more able-bodied men. And I see about a zillion of them on that shore."

"You're not thinking —"

"I am."

"That's crazy!"

"Maybe."

"You can't pay them."

"I won't have to."

"It'll be chaos."

"It already is. But I can tolerate some chaos. If it gets us our killer."

"Listen to me!" Merylo bellowed, trying to be heard above the roaring crowd. "I need your help!"

"You sure do!" someone shouted back. Half the crowd laughed in response. The noise was thunderous.

Merylo began to wonder if this had been a very bad idea. He was perched on a wooden ledge on the edge of the pond, atop a dumping platform, to increase his visibility to the crowd.

"Listen to me. Please!"

Eventually, the tumult subsided. "We need to search the area. The whole Run. Look for clues. A head, for instance. Maybe a witness who saw the body get dumped."

"Isn't that what the police are for?"

"The police are stretched to the outer limits. We got all these conventions in town, plus these murders and a lot of other crime. It would take days for my men to search the area, and by that time the trail might be cold."

"What's in it for us?" someone shouted. "We need cash."

"I can't pay you."

"If you don't pay, we don't work."

"Why? You got something better to do?" That got a large laugh. Merylo liked it better when they were laughing with him, not at him. There were a lot more of them than there were of him. "Listen, some of you people live out here. Do you like having this killer running around slaughtering people? Do you feel safe?"

"No!" came a chorus of replies.

"Then help me stop him. Be my foot soldiers. I'll be here all night long. If any of you find something, you report back to me. Let me split you up into groups so you can canvass the area. Systematically. There's enough of you to cover the whole Run before nightfall. What do you say?"

As Merylo expected, he received a mixed response. That was okay. He didn't need all of them.

"All right then. If you're willing to help, line up over here. Let's send a message to this monster. Let's tell him that if he goes after the Run — we'll go after him!"

Another enthusiastic response. Merylo felt like Henry the Fifth on the eve of battle. These people would probably encounter less danger. But they were no less important to the cause.

He gazed out into the crowd. What a motley, ragtag assortment of humanity. He saw men in tattered clothes; he saw men in three-piece suits. He saw sunbaked faces and calloused hands; he saw men who obviously had never done a day's labor in their life. He saw some who had already ruined their lives with booze or drugs; he saw some whose lives were just beginning. The employer and the unemployed. The book-educated and the street smart. And a few who appeared to have no smarts at all. Didn't matter. He could use them all.

"All right, you four, take the east side of Thirty-seventh and walk due north until you reach the tracks . . ."

35

The last guest arrived just after midnight. Ness intentionally kept the lights dim in the apartment, ostensibly because he didn't want to attract attention, but more importantly because he wanted to strike the proper mood, one of mystery and intrigue. He had to ignite these men's sense of adventure for his plan to succeed. He knew many of them read the pulp magazines that were so popular these days — even if they would never admit it; he'd seen one in The Banker's briefcase. *The Shadow, The Spider, Doc Savage, Weird Tales.* Ness had read one or two himself, when he had time and he was sure no one was watching. They seemed to thrive on exotic wonders, on the premise that the reader was being inducted into a secret society known only to a chosen few. That was exactly the kind of atmosphere he wanted to create tonight.

The Banker offered Ness his hand.

Ness shook it firmly. "Thanks again for coming, Lou."

"Well, I owed you for that business at The Thomas —"

"I remember."

"I appreciate your keeping my name out of your reports."

"You weren't who I was after."

"Appreciated, just the same. So I came and I brought some friends, just as you asked. What's this all about?"

"I'll tell you in just a moment."

"When did you get this Clifton Boulevard apartment? I thought you and the missus had a nice place out by the lake."

"We . . . do," Ness said, clearing his throat. "I just use this when I have to stay out late." He smiled a little. "In my line of work, I often have to work nights."

"I can imagine. Gotta catch the wolves while they're on the prowl."

"Exactly." Ness entered the main living room where he joined The Steel Magnate, The Meat Packer, The Uptown Physician, The Councilman, The Prosecutor, The Railroad Tycoon, The Oil Baron, The Architect, and The Radio Magnate. All the captains of industry were gathered together in one room. "I suppose you're wondering why I've invited you here. I'm hoping you can help me solve a problem. And I suspect that you already know what that might be."

"Well, I'm guessing you aren't going to ask us to buy more traffic lights," The Oil Baron said.

"No, I'm not. Although I would like to see more of you involved with my Boys Clubs. Those lads need strong role models — like every one of you. Men who have worked hard and made something of themselves. Men who can show these boys that even if they've got nothing to their name, fortitude and determination —"

Ness stopped and smiled. "Now see what you've done, Paul. You got me totally off track."

"Didn't take much," The Oil Baron commented.

"No, I'll admit, I'm passionate about the Boys Clubs. I wish the press were as interested as I am. Unfortunately, these days they only seem to be interested in one thing."

"Here it comes," The Railroad Tycoon said, his bushy gray eyebrows dancing up and down.

"I'm sure you saw this coming. Gentlemen, I need your help catching this cold-blooded killer who walks among us. The Torso Murderer."

Someone in the rear of the room whistled. "Tall order."

"Yes, it is. That's why I asked Lou to only invite tall men, people who aren't afraid to reach for difficult goals others might find unattainable. I know we can catch this murderer. If we work together."

"But haven't you already got a team working on this case?" The Uptown Physician asked. "He's in the paper almost every day. That stout fellow — what's his name? Murrow . . ."

"Merylo. Yes, he's the chief detective, leading the police department's investigation. And he's a fine man — intelligent, skilled, experienced. Tenacious. Pugnacious. He has a fine track record." Ness spread his hands. "And you see what his efforts have produced. Absolutely nothing."

"Maybe you need to replace him."

"I've considered it, believe me. But I genuinely believe that he is the best, most qualified man for the job. And I trust him, which counts for a lot. No, my friends, I don't want to replace him. I want to supplement him."

The Meat Packer ground out his cigar in an ashtray. "I don't see what we could do to help. I certainly don't know my way around Kingsbury Run, and I doubt if anyone else in this room does."

Ness dropped his voice a notch. "What you need to understand, gentlemen, is that although Peter Merylo is a fine detective, he has two major handicaps. First, he is absolutely dogged by the press. They watch every move he makes. Consequently, the killer can watch him, too. And second . . ." Ness's voice fell even lower. "The second handicap is that Detective Merylo is absolutely dogged by the law."

He paused a few moments, letting the words sink in before he continued.

"You may have noticed that I did not invite any newspapermen here tonight, even though several of them are among the richest and most prominent men in our society. There's a reason for that. I suppose the fourth estate plays an important role in our democracy — although sometimes I wonder — and I know that many of you have occasionally had cause to wonder yourselves."

A chorus of vaguely assenting grunts passed through the room.

"I need men who can move without being watched. I need men who can get close to this killer without having a photographer following in their footsteps. We'll never catch this butcher so long as he knows everything we're doing."

311

"Makes sense," The Meat Packer said, as he snipped his next cigar. "Perfect sense."

"And," Ness added, "we don't want the press watching our every move if our men are engaging in . . . unorthodox procedures."

The Banker chuckled. "Now we're getting to the heart of it."

"That's right," Ness agreed. "We are. Some of you who are familiar with my activities in Chicago" — he knew that would be all of them — "will recall that I occasionally was forced to . . . stretch the law here and there to get the job done. And I took some flack for it now and again. But I closed the case." He looked out into the crowd, letting the overhead light strike his eyes. "I think we need that sort of approach here."

"What exactly are you proposing?" The Banker asked.

"I want to appoint an independent team of investigators. Men outside the control of the police force."

"Where will you find them?"

"Leave that to me. I know who I want. After chasing Capone in Chicago and moonshiners in Tennessee and everything I did in Cleveland before I was safety director, I know a lot of people. Good people. Strong men."

"What do you want them to do?"

"Whatever they need to do, without having to worry every second about whether they're violating someone's constitutional rights. I want them to go where they need to go and talk to whoever they need to talk to."

"All for the greater good?" The Uptown Physician said. "Forgive me, Eliot, but you're sounding a bit like that fellow over in Italy."

"I don't think so. I'm not trying to take over. I just want this killer caught."

"In a bit of a sticky situation, aren't you?" The Banker asked. "You made big promises to the reporters. Now they're expecting you to deliver."

"And you want us to help you do it," The Meat Packer added.

"Perhaps," The Architect interjected, "you should have consulted us before you made the big promises."

Ness could feel the tide turning against him. He knew he had to move quickly. "I can't change what's already done. I probably did speak imprudently, in the heat of the moment. But that's not what matters. The only important question is this: Do you want this killer caught? Many of you talk about philanthropy, and noblesse oblige and the responsibilities of the very wealthy. Well, here's a chance to really do something. Here's a chance to eliminate a dire threat to this community." He stopped for a moment and made eye contact with each of the assembled men. "And let me remind you, gentlemen, that the killer has recently made inroads into the west side. Who knows where he might strike next?"

Silence blanketed the room. Whatever growing dissent there might have been before had been stifled.

"What is it you want us to do, Eliot?" The Railroad Tycoon asked. "Surely you don't want us to be your elite team of lawless investigators?"

Ness disregarded the dubious phrasing. "No. I'll find the men. But good men must be paid. And that's what I need from you. Financing. Financing that must be kept completely off any official books or records."

"And how do you expect us to accomplish that?"

"I don't know," Ness said, and for the first time that evening, his eyes showed a bit of their characteristic twinkle. "But having worked in the Treasury Department for many years, I have a suspicion that many of you *do* know how to do it."

More harrumphing, followed by a few winks and eyes averted toward the rug.

"I have a question," The Meat Packer said.

"What would that be?"

"If we sign on for this — does that make us Untouchables?"

Ness sighed. "I get that a lot."

"I might fancy that," The Uptown Physician said. "Imagine telling the little woman I've become an Untouchable."

"Which of your little women would that be?" The Architect asked, followed by the loudest round of laughter yet.

"Stop right there," Ness said. "If you sign on for this — for that matter, even if you don't — you can tell no one. Absolutely no one. I've learned how quickly an operation can be compromised by leaks. You can't tell your friends, your wives, your mistresses. No one."

He took a deep breath, then opted to answer the question. "No, I don't think you'll become the Untouchables. I think you'll become . . . the Unknowns. My problem here isn't that I think the killer is buying people off. My problems are the press and the law. I need people who can work under the cover of darkness, in the shadows. People only accountable to me. And unknown to everyone else."

The Meat Packer nodded approvingly and ground out his cigar. "The Unknowns. I like that. Sounds like something out of a Charlie Chan picture."

"Charlie Chan never faced any criminal like this, gentlemen. But I don't need him, or any of his many sons. All I need is your help. Your support. Can I count you in?"

To his dismay, there was no immediate response, no reaction of any kind. At first, the men appeared to be looking from one to another, checking faces, wondering who would go first. If anyone.

"Supposing you catch this maniac," The Oil Baron said. "Will you acknowledge our help then?"

"Probably not," Ness answered. "That might get us all thrown in jail. Or spoil a prosecutor's case."

"Not much of an investment if there's no chance of a return," The Banker sniffed.

"No argument," Ness replied. "There's nothing in this for you at all. It's just the right thing to do."

"Can't even use it to impress women," The Uptown Physician groused.

"Gentlemen, please." Ness tried not to let his voice sound pleading. He knew that would not be effective with men such as these. "Think of the safety of the city. The people. Those victims."

"I'll tell you what I'm thinking about,"

said The Councilman, speaking for the first time this evening. "My daughter Joan walks home sometimes, even though I tell her not to. Won't take a cab, says she likes to stretch her legs. She walks almost the same way that Barkley woman did. The one who found the corpse on the west side."

He looked Ness straight in the eye and held out his hand. "I'm in, Eliot. For whatever you need."

"Thank you, Jim."

"And me," said The Architect.

"And me."

And then they all followed, one after the other, every single one of them, giving Ness an even better showing than he had hoped for. He would have more than enough money now. He would be able to finance six, maybe even eight operatives.

He would contact them immediately and put them to work. There was no time to waste.

This evening, he had received another postcard. At his newly rented apartment.

36

Merylo stared down at the dry creek. Debris littered the surface — discarded metalworks, train tracks, paper, clothes, refuse of all kinds. But no body parts. Not a one.

"How long did it take them to drain the creek?" Merylo asked quietly.

"Three days. Cost a fortune, too."

"And nothing to show for it." Merylo smashed his hat between his hands. First they had brought in a high-pressure pump to stir up the water. Then they sent in divers. Then they tried ceiling hooks again. They managed to snag the right thigh, but no head. They built makeshift bridges from wooden planks to extend the reach of the hooks, without avail. Another diving operation produced nothing. Even the volunteer foot soldiers Merylo sent out produced no results.

All within view of the teeming spectators. According to the *Cleveland News,* over one hundred thousand people had come to watch the operation at some point. To watch the police fail. Again.

"The chief won't be happy about this," Zalewski said. "Especially getting civilians involved. And since it was done on your order . . ."

"Ness told me to do everything I could think of to catch this killer," Merylo replied. "So I did. If we'd found a head, and could identify it, we'd be a lot closer to catching our murderer."

"Pearce says by this time, even if you found a head, it would be so decomposed —"

"Never mind what Pearce says." Merylo clenched his teeth together, trying to suppress his anger. "No, I take that back. What does the good doctor say? About the victim, I mean. Based on the parts we've been able to locate."

Zalewski took out his notebook and flipped it open. "Vic weighed about 145 pounds and was something like five feet ten. Maybe thirty years old. Brown hair. Head was cut severed from the body between the third and fourth cervical vertebrae, in two cuts."

"Not his best job," Merylo grunted, "but still admirable."

"The torso was cut between the third and fourth lumbar vertebrae. Cut the stomach and kidney. Vic was emasculated." Zablewski paused. "That means his, er, things were, you know, cut off and —"

"I know what it means. Go on."

"No hesitation marks. Examination of the heart shows that it was still beating when the dismemberment began. Final conclusion: 'Probable murder by decapitation and subsequent sectioning of body.' "

"Probable? Did he imagine we thought the guy might've committed suicide? By cutting himself into bits? While he was still alive?"

"Hey, I'm just reporting what the doctor said. Don't kill the messenger."

"Right. Sorry."

Zalewski turned away from the pond. "Did you see the *News* this morning?"

There was a slight twitch in Merylo's eye as he responded. "Of course not."

Zalewski pulled it out of his pocket and read. "The killer is probably a muscular man. He has expert knowledge of human anatomy. The incisions of his knife were clean and were made in each case without guesswork. He may have gathered his knowledge of anatomy as a medical student. Or it is possible that he is a butcher."

"Like that's news." Merylo rubbed his chin. "Bad time to be a Cleveland medical student. Particularly if you're a little odd-looking."

"Yeah. I like the way they conclude that the killer is either a medical student or a butcher. As if they were basically the same thing."

"But never a doctor," Merylo said, holding up a finger. "Never a surgeon. Even though that would be the obvious conclusion to draw from the killer's anatomical knowledge. Even the *News* would not dare say that a highly educated respectable member of society might be a cold-blooded killer."

Merylo was not so limited. During the past few days, he had visited both medical schools in town and talked to several doctors, looking for leads. He didn't find any. No practicing physician was willing to acknowledge the possibility that the killer might come from their ranks.

For that matter, Merylo followed up dozens of other leads — an Oriental who was reportedly fond of knives. A scrap dealer who said he saw two men carrying a coffin. Railroad police. A man living under the Lorain-Carnegie Bridge with four hundred pairs of women's shoes. A voodoo practitioner on East 40th. An escapee from the Athens State hospital. No lead was too small or too unlikely for Merylo. And no lead so far had produced anything positive.

"I gotta tell you, sir," Zalewski said hesitantly. "Some of the boys back at the station are talking."

"If you hear anyone criticizing our work, assign them to the case," Merylo grunted. "That'll teach them."

"No. Not about that. I mean about — you know." He rubbed his chin.

Merylo was letting his beard grow. It was a slow process — he had a light beard — but it was beginning to show. "Tell them I'm so busy I don't have time to shave."

"Whatever you say. But — I think the safety director might not like it. He's so goody-two-shoes clean-cut and all."

"He won't mind. It's not like he wants *my* picture in the paper."

"You got some kind of plan?"

"I do. But if my idea is going to work — I want as little attention as possible. From the papers or anyone else."

37

"The Unknowns?"

Ness grinned a little. "Yeah. What do you think?"

"Doesn't have as much zing as the Untouchables."

"Doesn't matter. No one who isn't a member is ever going to hear about it."

"And this worked?"

"Like you wouldn't believe. We've got enough cash to hire eight operatives — plus you — long-term. Freedom to do whatever you think necessary. Without being watched. Without being hampered by government restrictions."

David Cowles paused. Ness could see the wheels turning in the man's bald head. He had known Cowles, a member of the Cleveland Scientific Investigation Bureau, for some time now, and he trusted him. Cowles had been the genius behind several of the most successful cases the police department took credit for solving.

"What do you want me to do?"

"Enlist men. Send them out. Penetrate the underworld. The two victims who have been identified were both criminal types. Probably they all were. If you send your men around, quietly asking questions, not acting like cops, they're bound to find something. And if they have to use somewhat illegal means . . . well, they're not police officers, are they? They're just private citizens working for you."

"Sounds risky. What if someone finds out? What if the whole thing blows up? You don't need that kind of publicity."

"Me?" Ness said, pressing his hands against his chest. "I didn't have anything to do with it. I'm only the safety director."

Cowles fingered his dark, round owl-like glasses. "I'm beginning to see the way this thing works. The trail ends with me."

"You ever read Sherlock Holmes?"

Cowles opened the small box on Ness's coffee table and took out a cigarette. "Can't say that I have. Though I hear the man was very scientific."

"He was. And he also had a group of private operatives. The Baker Street Irregulars, he called them. They were just kids. But they could fan out through all of

London and learn anything Holmes needed to know without attracting attention. That's what we need here. Put your men out into the city. Find the killer."

Ness leaned in closer. "But here's the most important part, David. They report to you. You and only you. No one else. They don't even know I'm involved. Understand?"

"Perfectly."

"Think you'll have any trouble finding men?"

"Nope. Already got one in mind."

"Tell me."

"Sure you want to know?"

Ness smiled. "I'll forget the name as soon as I hear it."

"Fellow named Joe Teran."

"Mexican?"

Cowles nodded. "Marijuana dealer. My evidence put him away a few years ago. He's free now."

"An ex-con? Is that wise?"

"He's a smart man, Eliot. Tells me he's reformed. But he still has lots of contacts in the underworld. Not the kind of underworld you're used to dealing with, the highfalutin' mobsters and such. His people are the lowest level of filth the city has to offer. But I believe those are the contacts that could prove most useful in this case."

"I'll trust your judgment."

"And Joe knows lots of other useful people. Heaven knows it isn't hard to find good men who need work these days. I'll have your Unknowns out on the street before the end of the week."

"Appreciate it."

"My pleasure. I want this creep caught as much as you do. This might just work."

"Let's hope so. The people are demanding an arrest."

"And the press, huh?"

Ness looked at him sharply, then, after a moment, his face relaxed. "Yes, the newspaper boys, too."

"I know you want to keep this secret, Eliot, and I understand why. But the press are expecting you to do something. Something they can report."

"Don't worry. I've got a plan. Meanwhile, you get to work. Check in with me as often as possible. Let me know if you have any leads. Or if you need more assistance. Anything. Whatever it takes. Bring me this monster."

"You going to tell Chief Matowitz about this?"

"Not a chance. Let them follow their path, and I'll follow mine. They can be the decoy.

Deflect the attention of the press. While we catch the killer. Because we've got to catch him, David. The headlines in the papers get larger every day. They've totally forgotten about everything else I've done for this city. All anyone cares about is this Torso Killer. So let's give him to them. So I can get on with my work. And my life."

38

"Mr. Ness! Mr. Ness!"

"Can't stop, boys. I'm working."

"Just a short interview."

"Can't do it."

"The people want to know —"

"Sorry, must keep moving."

"Not even a picture?"

Ness slowed. "Well . . . make it quick."

The photograph revealed Cleveland's esteemed Safety Director, Eliot Ness, and a substantial number of police officers, standing in the very heart of Shantytown. All around him were low-level homes — if they could be called that. They would be more accurately described as shacks, cardboard boxes, piano crates. Tents, in a few instances. Squalor was everywhere. The few people visible were dirty, tired, malnourished. It was like a snapshot from hell.

Ness continued moving.

"What are you doing out here?" one of

the reporters, the one from the *Courier,* asked as he chased after him, running at his heels.

"Trying to catch a killer. Most of the victims have been deposited in this area. Stands to reason that the killer lives here, or at the very least is a frequent visitor. Someone must have seen him. Might not have known they did. But they did."

"Do you think the killer is a transient?"

"I think many of the victims were. That's what makes them so hard to identify. Even that fellow who's on display at the Exposition. No one recognizes them because they weren't here long, didn't make friends. What friends or family they may have had didn't know they were here."

"What do you think of Shantytown?"

Ness hesitated. He had to be careful. "I think President Roosevelt is doing everything he can to improve the economy. But when men are out of work, crime is a natural consequence. Who knows what forces may have driven this killer to murder? All I know is this is a good place to look for information, whether this is the killer's headquarters or his favorite hunting ground. So I'm going to talk to these people. And we are going to catch this killer, my friends. Mark my words. We are going to catch him."

Once Ness shook the reporters, he was able to do some real work. Even if this trip was mostly for show, there was no reason not to try to accomplish something while he was here. He wanted to search more thoroughly. Unfortunately, most of the residents were closemouthed — understandably so, since most of them were harassed by law enforcement officers on a regular basis. Even shabby homes like these were protected by the Fourth Amendment; he couldn't go in without permission or a warrant. And he couldn't force anyone to talk.

Thank goodness the official channels were not his only angle on the case.

Late in the afternoon, while his men were combing the area, Ness spoke to a man who said he was thirty but looked fifty. He'd been riding the rails since the Crash of '29 and it showed. Said his name was Jones, but Ness suspected it wasn't. He was hesitant to talk at first — and hard to understand, because he had lost most of his teeth — but once Ness charmed him out of his suspicions and road-learned reticence, he spoke more freely.

"I came in on one of the last trains into

town," he explained. "Haven't been any more. It's getting hard to get in or out."

"How's that?" Ness asked.

"Word's out on the hobo circuit. Stay away from Cleveland. Cleveland is where folks like us get their heads cut off. And no one's doing anything about it."

Ness suspected that probably would cut down on the desirability of a train stop or a free ride. It had certainly made a dent in tourism. "I know the trains are still coming into town."

"Trains, yeah. But no passengers."

"None?"

"None. Ask the railroad cops. Used to be a steady stream of bindle stiffs coming through here. No more. Nobody wants to be in Cleveland."

Even though hobo traffic was hardly desirable, Ness couldn't help being disturbed by this pronouncement. He was the safety director, after all. It was disappointing, after all the work he had done, to hear that Cleveland was considered too dangerous even for the lowest strata of society. "And you said no one was getting out?"

"Too many cops. Keeping too close an eye on everything. Ask 'em. There's twice as many cops around here as there used to be. They say they're looking out for this killer, and maybe that's so. But the end result is that a lotta folks like me are gettin' beat up and it's gettin' a lot harder to sneak a ride out of town."

"Did you ever consider taking a bus?"

"I could be wrong, mister, but I hear tell those buses require money. I haven't had a job in two years. And that one didn't amount to much."

"Have people been trying to leave town?"

"Are you kidding? You think anyone wants to be here right now? Bad enough to have a killer preying on the unfortunate. Hell of a lot worse when you can't get away from him, no matter what you do. They don't know which of us will be next. And it ain't good when people get scared, mister. When people get scared, they get dangerous. Do crazy things. Could be riots, violence, all kind of trouble. Just a matter of time. It's like a powder keg in there. And you know as well as I do — once the powder keg is lit, everything goes up in flames."

39

From the morning edition, February 24, 1937, Cleveland *Plain Dealer:*

". . . when fifty-five-year-old Robert Smith, cruising near the Lake Erie coast in his sailboat, spotted a mysterious object on the shore. Closer inspection revealed that it was a body part, a woman's torso, missing head and arms, that had washed up on the shore. There were no footprints nearby. Presumably the torso was tossed in at a different point and carried there by the tides.

"According to the police, the woman was approximately thirty years old, five feet six, and 120 pounds. She had light brown hair and, based upon the condition of her lungs, lived in the city. Detective Peter Merylo said the police had several leads they were pursuing, but given the repeated lack of results, it is hard to know whether to take such claims seriously. Merylo also claims he found a zigzagging trail of blood running from the shore to Lake Shore Boulevard. Merylo was following up reports of two suspicious men in an automobile parked on the Boulevard. This paper, however, has uncovered a witness who, hours before, watched a dog hit by a car limp all the way to the shore. It would seem, therefore, that the distinguished Detective Merylo is more likely to capture a dead dog than the barbarian plaguing our community.

"When questioned about these matters, Chief Matowitz insisted that although they still had not located the Torso Murderer, the police investigation has been so intense that over two dozen other serious criminals have been apprehended, as well as more than a dozen dangerously disturbed persons who were referred to mental institutions. While that may be of comfort to the police department, it gives no relief to the people of this city who wonder every night when it will be possible once more to walk the streets of the city without fear, without risk of becoming the next victim of this monstrous killer. Cleveland's shame has become a national story, holding the entire country in rapt fascination and horror, not only at the atrocities performed, but by the police incompetence and continued inability to catch a single killer. This paper formally calls for the police department to undertake the most thorough and exhaustive efforts to bring this maniac to justice.

"The office of Safety Director Eliot Ness was contacted before this story ran, but we were told that he was unavailable for comment . . ."

"You know I hate this sort of thing."

"You said you wanted to get out more."

"With you. With friends. Not with a thousand random people I don't know and don't care to know."

"Honey, I think you have a rather unpleasant attitude about this."

"I bet there will be lots of high-society swells. And reporters."

"Perhaps. Why do you think so?"

"Because otherwise, you wouldn't be here."

Ness gave his wife a long look. He hoped the driver wasn't listening, but how could he not? Didn't matter — he'd probably heard a lot worse in the past.

He and Edna had seen each other less and less since he rented the apartment downtown. He thought that was what she wanted, and it certainly made it easier for him at the end of a long night of work. There was no questioning, however, the fact that they had grown farther apart. Even if before all they ever did was fight. Now they had lost even that, and there seemed to be very little left in its stead.

"That was cheap."

"But true. You only bother with me when you want to be seen in public with a wife on your arm."

"That's baloney. It's just that it's a long way from our house to downtown."

"Don't I know it."

"If you're so bored, I would think you'd welcome a chance to get out."

"For the mayor's ball? Black ties and big shots and everyone wanting something and angling on how they're going to get it. Is that your idea of a good time? Because it is certainly not mine."

"The mayor wants to be reelected. We want him to be reelected, since he's the one who gave me my current job. I have to be here."

"Yes, I know." Edna sighed wearily. She turned slightly and adjusted his bow tie.

"And you do look splendid in your tuxedo. Like Gary Cooper in *Mr. Deeds Goes to Town.* You're a handsome man, Eliot."

"Thank you kindly."

"Just wish I saw more of you."

"I know you do. And as soon as we catch this killer —"

She held up her hand, stopping him cold. "Eliot, please. I'm not a fool. Just don't bother."

The driver pulled their car up to the curb outside the front door of the majestic Biltmore Hotel. A doorman opened the rear door and helped Edna out of the car.

Together, they made their way to the ballroom, admiring the elegant long, silky evening gowns that passed by.

"I feel so out of place here," Edna said under her breath.

"You shouldn't. You're the prettiest girl in the joint."

"Oh, I am not."

He touched her on the arm, still moving forward. "You are to me."

As they stepped through the ballroom doors, Ness didn't even need to pass the announcer his card. He was recognized immediately.

"Mr. and Mrs. Eliot Ness."

There was an immediate response: clapping and cheering and even a little squealing with excitement. Ness was pleased to realize that the killings had not totally eliminated all public appreciation of him and his work — at least not yet. They entered the cavernous ballroom, sumptuously appointed with marble floors, Doric columns, crystal chandeliers. A full band was playing a popular tune. Ness didn't get much chance to listen to the radio, but he thought it was "It's De-Lovely." He liked Cole Porter. His songs always had such clever lyrics. Edna preferred Irving Berlin.

Within minutes he and Edna were surrounded by people he didn't know. The mayor's assistant, Wes Lawrence. A lovely young heiress named Katy Conrad. Richard Turnbull, the owner of the largest slaughterhouse in the city.

"What was Capone really like?" Miss Conrad asked breathlessly. Ness sensed Edna thought she was standing entirely too close to him. "Are you really untouchable? I'm not."

More well-wishers and spectators swarmed around them.

"Why are you government boys so opposed to a drop of bourbon here and there?"

"Are you really leading a Boy Scout troop?"

"My husband says there must be three Eliot Nesses, identical triplets maybe, to get done all you get done. Is that true?"

"I'm telling you, these illustrated comic stories are going to be the next big thing. I could get you in on the ground floor."

"My uncle doesn't like you very much. He says The Harvard Club was the only place he could go to get away from his wife."

"That Shantytown is deplorable! When is the city going to do something about it?"

"Spiritualism is a true science now, you know. The existence of the other world has been proven. I could show you photographs."

"When are you going to catch that Torso Killer?"

The conversation, if you could call it that, ground to a halt. An oppressive silence suddenly filled their circle.

"I'm sorry," the woman mumbled, covering her mouth with a white-gloved hand. "Did I say something wrong? Do you prefer to call him the Mad Butcher like the papers do?"

Ness smiled slightly. "I think perhaps it's time to get my wife some punch." He gently carved a path through the crowd and tugged Edna forward . . . right into Congressman Sweeney.

"Where are you going, Ness? I'd like to hear you answer the young woman's question."

"I can assure you we're doing everything we possibly can."

"I'm not a reporter," Sweeney said, tugging at his vest. "So don't try to soft-soap me. This city expects results. You are the safety director, after all."

"And I have fulfilled all my duties as Safety Director and then some, Congressman." Ness glanced behind him, checking to see if anyone was listening. Naturally, they all were. "Have you seen the latest reports on labor racketeering? We've achieved some major convictions."

"Well and good, not that anyone really cares."

"Did you hear about my bribery investigations? That got the Torso Killer off the headlines for a few days."

"And now he's back again, isn't he? With a seventh victim — probably eighth, counting that unfortunate woman found in the lake before you became safety director. For that matter, there have probably been many others, perhaps dozens, that we know nothing about, because the body parts haven't yet washed ashore."

"You don't know that."

"I know this — the killings will continue until you do something to stop them. The city is terrified. I have a cousin who lives here, and he tells me he's so scared when he walks home at night it's driven him to drink! And let me tell you something else, just in case you're wondering — it won't be good enough to find this monster and charge him with tax evasion. The people want him dead!"

Ness knew he should just stay quiet, but he was finding that increasingly difficult these days. He was tired of being criticized because he couldn't do the impossible, when he was substantially improving this city on a daily basis. "Is that your opinion as a concerned citizen? Or as a Democratic congressman who would very much like to see a Democrat in the mayor's office?"

Sweeney arched an eyebrow. "Is there a difference?"

Edna intervened, stepping between them. "Gentlemen, we all want this killer caught. And we all know he will be in time. This isn't about politics, right, dear?"

Ness mumbled something under his breath.

"This is about public safety. And we all want that, regardless of what party we claim as our own."

"True enough," Sweeney acknowledged.

"Now if you'll excuse me, Congressman, my husband has promised me some punch. And after that, I'd like to see if the famed leader of the Untouchables still knows how to cut a rug."

The people surrounding them laughed. Edna took him by the arm and led him away.

As soon as they had some privacy, Ness whispered: "I didn't need to be rescued."

"Are you sure?"

"I can handle that blowhard."

"Maybe. Maybe not. You're good with the press, Eliot, because all they want is a nice picture and a nice story, and you're almost always good for both. But men like Sweeney won't be put off so easily. They have their own private agendas. There's no point attempting to reason with them because they have no intention of being reasonable. He wants Burton out of office, and since appointing you is the best thing Burton has done during his entire term, Sweeney would love nothing more than to see your star acquire some tarnish. The only chance he has of seeing that happen is to make as big a deal as possible out of these murders. Because he knows perfectly well that no matter what you do you may never catch the killer."

"Hey!"

"I know you're working hard, Eliot, both with the police and whatever secret efforts you've got rolling."

"How do you know about that?"

"I've been married to you a long time. But I can also see that this killer is probably never going to be caught until he makes a mistake. And there's no way of predicting how long that might take. Sweeney wants to exploit your helplessness to his own political advantage."

Ness gave his wife a long look. "You sure you don't like politics? Because I think maybe you're the one who ought to run for mayor."

She rolled her eyes. "A nightmarish thought. The fact that I can see things for what they are is exactly why I would never run for anything. And the fact that you can't is exactly why you might be tempted." She took his arm. "Enough of this. Now take me by the arm, Mr. Untouchable, and flash that goofy Jimmy Stewart smile of yours, and twirl me around the dance floor. Make my head spin. There might be something in it for you later."

His eyes lit up. "Gladly, my lady."

■ ■ ■ ■

They had barely finished the first waltz —
not Ness's best dance, the rhythm was too
tricky — when he felt a tap on his shoulder.

Mayor Burton was standing behind him.

"No," Ness said, "you may not cut in.
We're just getting started."

"I'm not looking for a dance, Eliot. I want
to talk."

Ness kept his grip on Edna's hand and
waist. "Can this wait till office hours?"

"I've called your office every day this week
and I still haven't gotten a reply."

"You know how busy I've been."

"Yes, I do, but I still need to talk to you."
He bowed his head slightly. "Would you
please excuse us, Mrs. Ness?"

Edna did not look at all happy about the
interruption. "I suppose we can't say no to
the mayor."

"Now that's an attitude I like. Wish my
own wife shared that view."

He pointed toward a room on the side of
the ballroom, a room Ness had noticed the
mayor passing in and out of throughout the
evening. It was a small alcove, more like a
large closet, stark by comparison with the
opulence outside. But Ness supposed it was

sufficient to provide the only thing Burton wanted at the moment: privacy.

Mayor Burton closed the door, then launched in. "I suppose you know Congressman Sweeney has been running you down all night."

"I exchanged a few words with him earlier."

"And had to be bailed out by your wife. At least according to him."

"That's preposterous."

"He's using this Torso Murderer to cut you down to size, Eliot, and by association, me."

"Why did you invite him here? You know he's a political opponent. I hear he has ties to President Roosevelt."

"He has ties to the newspapers, too, and that's a good deal more worrisome. Word is he pays for positive coverage. No way to prove it, of course. I tell you, Eliot — you want to investigate bribery, you should start with the newspapers."

"Unfortunately, I'm not sure taking money to write a story is even illegal."

"If not, it should be. Fraud on the public, that's what I say. Eliot — you've got to catch this murderer."

"We're doing everything possible, sir. I'm working closely with the police. They report to me every day. I also have some . . . private efforts under way. Undercover work. They've rattled a lot of cages."

"But they haven't caught the killer."

Ness threw up his hands. "No, all I've managed to do is reduce traffic fatalities from four hundred a year to less than forty. To clean up the police department. Break the back of the mob and the labor racketeers. Take the worst juvenile crime rate in the country and reduce it to nearly nothing. I've also rooted out extensive political bribery —"

"Which made you no friends in my circle, believe you me."

"Which is exactly why it needed to be done. By someone outside the political process. I have done my job, sir. I have made this city a better, safer place."

Burton laid his hands on Ness's shoulders. "And no one will remember a bit of that if you don't catch this killer."

"That's not fair."

"People are fickle, Eliot. They will turn on you in a heartbeat. You're too high-profile to fail. The press will hound you relentlessly. The public will never forgive you."

"I don't believe it."

Burton turned away. "If you haven't made any progress by the time the reelection campaign gets into full swing — I'll have to consider replacing you."

"What!"

"I'm sorry, Eliot, but I can't appear complacent. I have to be in motion, always taking action to address the public's concerns." He exhaled wearily. "If you can't do the job, I'll find someone who will."

"Are you threatening to fire me?"

"I won't have any choice."

"Over my dead body!" Ness stomped out of the room, slamming the door behind him. He grabbed Edna and, before another crowd had a chance to gather, led her out of the ballroom.

"Leaving so soon?" Edna asked, as he tugged her down the hotel hallway.

"Not soon enough," Ness growled.

Ness woke the next morning feeling rested but restless. The mayor's words still reverberated in his head. After all he had done for the city. All he had done for Mayor Burton.

He strode into the living room of the lake house, still wearing his pajamas and bathrobe. At least Edna had been friendly last night. She obviously wasn't too disappointed about leaving the party early, and he thought she was pleased that he came home with her.

The house seemed exceptionally tidy, even by Edna's standards. Why was that? There was nothing out on the kitchen cabinet, precious little in the living room. Had she just decided that if she had no visitors there was no reason to do anything?

He opened the nearest closet and found boxes packed from floor to ceiling. Boxes filled with personal belongings. As he opened a few and inspected the contents, he realized that it was all Edna's stuff, many of her favorite things, none of his.

Had they never been unpacked since they moved here?

Or was she packing now?

He closed the closet, suddenly concerned. As if he really needed one more thing to worry about.

It was then that he happened to glance at the front door, thinking about going out to get the paper. Mail had been pushed through the slot.

Was the mail delivered this early in the morning?

There wasn't much. Only one piece, actually. On closer inspection, he realized it was a postcard.

The front was just like the previous two he had received. On the back, in what was the same distinctive handwriting as before, someone had written:

FANCY FOOTWORK!

Ness felt a cold chill race down his spine. Then he noticed something even worse.

The postcard bore no stamp, no postmark. It had been hand delivered.

40

From the *Cleveland News,* June 7, 1937:

". . . and still the numbers of the headless dead multiply. The latest was discovered by a young Negro boy named Russell Lauer. Lauer was taking a shortcut home from the movies through Stone's Levee, a deserted field often used by area residents as a makeshift city dump. Beneath the second abutment of the Lorain-Carnegie Bridge, Lauer noticed a glittering object partly buried amidst the garbage. Upon closer inspection, the shiny attraction proved to be gold teeth protruding from a human skull. Subsequent investigation revealed a human skeleton, absent the arms and legs, in a burlap bag, as well as a wool cap, the sleeve of a woman's dress, and a severed piece of human scalp.

"Police at first expressed skepticism

regarding whether this corpse, at least a year old, was connected to the previous mutilation murders that have constituted the Mad Butcher's reign of terror over the city of Cleveland. Police Detective Peter Merylo argued that since there was no sign of trauma to the skull, it might be an unrelated death. Perhaps Merylo was anxious to prevent the Mad Butcher's victim count from growing larger, but all doubts were put to rest when the remainder of the skeleton was discovered and examined. Evidence of 'knife marks' and extensive 'hacking and cutting' were reported by the coroner's office.

"According to coroner, Dr. Arthur Pearce, this latest victim was a small Negro woman of approximately thirty years of age, perhaps five feet tall and weighing only a hundred pounds. Anyone who knows of a woman fitting this description who disappeared about a year ago should contact the offices of the *Cleveland News* immediately.

"It is the decided opinion of this newspaper that not only must this latest victim be considered part of the Butcher's death toll, but we must also count the first victim, the so-called Lady of the Lake, making the casualties of this murderous beast number nine, at least, with no end in sight. We once again call upon the Cleveland Police Department and the Office of the Safety Director to make all conceivable efforts to bring this killing spree to an end. We call upon the citizens of Cleveland to make their opinions known, both by contacting their elected officials now and voting accordingly when the new elections are held. The voice of the people is the only means we have . . ."

Chamberlin opened the inner door to the safety director's office and stepped inside.

"Sir, Detective Merylo has arrived . . . finally."

Ness pushed away the papers on his desk and rose to his feet. "Show him inside, please."

Merylo didn't wait to be asked. He appeared behind Chamberlin, sweating and breathing heavily. Chamberlin took a seat in the rear.

Ness narrowed his eyes. "You've grown a beard."

Merylo touched his chin. "Not against the rules."

"Not exactly the best image for the police department, either."

"My wife says it makes me look taller."

"You're late," Ness said, checking his watch.

"Sorry. I came as soon as I got your message."

"That was hours ago."

"I've been out in the field. Working."

"I'm glad to hear it. Does that mean you've finally caught this killer?"

Merylo's eyes narrowed. Ness always lorded it over him, always had a superior attitude. But he wasn't normally such an ass.

"No, but it means I've been sweating blood looking for him."

"I'm not interested in your sweat, Detective. I'm interested in an arrest. What have you been doing?"

"I found a man who believes the third victim might be his mother — a woman named Rose Wallace. Worked in a laundry, disappeared more than a year ago. Talked to her family and coworkers. Turns out, on the last day her whereabouts were known, she was seen in a car with a skinny, dark-haired white man. Other witnesses said she was in a car with three men. So I started looking for someone who might have some idea who these men were."

"And have you had any success?"

Merylo frowned. "Not so far."

"Sounds like you're hunting for a needle in a haystack to me. You have only the vaguest description to work with. You're not even sure the victim was Rose Wallace."

"I have to take the clues as I find them. And try to make them into something more."

"Which so far hasn't worked."

"It has in other cases."

"I don't care about your other cases. I want to know when you're going to bring me the killer!"

"My men and I are doing everything we possibly can."

"That's not good enough!" Ness pounded on his desk, then withdrew suddenly, as if startled by his own show of anger.

He collapsed into his desk chair. "Do you have any idea the kind of pressure I'm under? All anyone wants to know is when the Mad Butcher will be caught."

"For whatever it's worth," Merylo said quietly, "I don't think it is a butcher."

"And how would you know?"

Merylo's lips pressed tightly together. "Because I spent a week investigating every working slaughterhouse in the city. I've seen what they do and how they do it. I don't believe a butcher would have the degree of skill, or the knowledge of human anatomy, that this killer has."

"Then who do you think it is?"

Merylo titled his head to one side. "You remember Pearce's crime clinic?"

"Distinctly. They came up with nothing that wasn't already obvious."

Merylo disagreed. "They said the killer must have some anatomical and medical knowledge."

"Right, just like the papers. Possibly a medical student. Or a male nurse."

"That's what they said — because everyone in the clinic was a doctor, and they were too snobby to imagine that another doctor could be the killer. Pearce has the same attitude. But I've known some doctors that weren't so special in my time, particularly near the Run. Put a few of them behind bars."

"You think a physician is committing these atrocities?"

"I think there's a very good chance. And if you recall, Pearce's alienist thinks the killer lives in the Kingsbury Run area — otherwise he would attract too much attention when he visits."

"What's the point of all this?"

"How many doctors can there be living in the Kingsbury Run area? Not a whole lot, I'm thinking."

"So go find the few there are and talk to them."

"Why? You think anyone is going to admit they killed eight or nine people just because I show up? No, talking will never do the job. I need to catch someone in the act. Someone capturing a victim, kidnapping. Or I need to follow them home and discover evidence of mass slayings."

"All right. Do that."

"As a cop? Not possible."

The light slowly dawned in Ness's eyes. "That's why you've grown the beard. You want to go undercover."

"Why not? Those people are much more likely to talk to a fellow bum than a cop. Plus, made out like a vagrant, I might attract the killer's attention."

"Don't undercover operations have to be approved by Chief Matowitz?"

Merylo nodded. "He told me to ask you."

"It'll be dangerous."

"What isn't, on this job?"

"I couldn't bear the publicity if you were —"

"I'll take my gun. I can hide a thirty-eight under my tramp costume. No one will ever know."

"I don't want you to get killed."

"I know how to take care of myself."

"I don't know . . ."

"Do you want this creep caught or not?"

"You know I do."

"You said you wanted me to do anything that might help. I'm a lot more likely to figure out who this guy is if I can blend in with the vagrants and bums and everyone else living out near Kingsbury."

"I suppose that's true."

"Ness, let me do this. I'll find this guy."

"Sure. And while you're at it, why don't you locate Judge Crater and Amelia Earhart?"

"Come on. You chewed me out because I haven't caught the killer. Let me go find him."

Ness thought for a long time. Merylo wondered if he was really considering turning down the request, or just wanted to make a show of deliberation.

"All right, I'll authorize it. But only for a few days. Then you report in and tell me what you've got."

Merylo stretched out his hand. "Thank you. You won't regret this."

Ness took the hand but gave him a stern look. "Take care of yourself. I don't need any more bad publicity."

"Aw, the press hates me."

"Doesn't matter. If you get killed you'll

become a martyr. I can see the headlines now: COP KILLED ON NESS'S UNTOUCHABLE GOOSE CHASE."

Merylo grinned. "That won't happen."

"Good. Bring me home that killer."

Merylo gave him a tiny salute. "Yes, sir."

After Merylo left, Chamberlin took the chair in the center of the office. He and Ness spoke in hushed tones.

"Think I did the right thing?" Ness asked.

Chamberlin shrugged. "Who knows? At least now you'll have something to tell Burton when he makes his daily ranting phone call to check on the progress of the case."

"My thoughts exactly."

"And when it's over, you can tell the press about it. It's got just enough dash and romance to turn a favorable article or two. COP WALKS AMONG THE DOWNTRODDEN."

"That thought occurred to me also."

"And you need to be doing something you can . . . discuss with other people."

Ness raised an eyebrow. How much did Chamberlin know about the Unknowns? They worked closely together, but Ness had always kept that operation from him, or tried, anyway. Just in case there was trouble, he wanted Chamberlin to be clean. Not that the Unknowns had produced any more leads than anyone else so far. Despite the thousands of dollars Cleveland's businessmen had poured into the operation, so far they had produced no killer. Not even a promising lead.

"Think Merylo will find the Butcher?"

Chamberlin thought a moment before answering. "Honestly? At this point, I'm not sure I believe he'll ever be caught. If there's a way to do it, we don't seem to know what it is. It won't be by conventional police means, that much is certain. The important thing, from a political standpoint, is that you appear to be doing something, pushing forward. It's the politics of motion. Not results."

"I want this blemish off my record, Bob."

"I know you do, but —"

"Once this is out of the way, I can get back to what I was brought here to do. There's still a lot more work to be done with those labor racketeers. And I hear there's a new bunch of rumrunners gathering around the Cuyahoga, looking for a way into the city."

"I know that, but —"

"You think the Great Lakes Exposition was big news? I think there's a chance I can get the national Boy Scout Jamboree here next year. Wouldn't that be something to see? The best boys from all across the nation, right here in Cleveland."

"That would be swell, sir, but respectfully —"

He was interrupted by the pounding on the door. Without even waiting for a response, Ness's receptionist rushed in. Chamberlin couldn't think of a time when she hadn't waited — sometimes a good long while — for Ness to tell her to enter.

"Mr. Ness, there's a message for you." Her face was stricken, pale.

Ness and Chamberlin exchanged a glance. It was obvious what they were both thinking. "Not another one," Ness groaned.

She blinked. "Another — ? Oh, another victim? No."

"Thank goodness. Then what is it?"

She walked the message she was holding over to his desk. "It's from the county sheriff. The one who replaced Potts."

"O'Donnell? What does he want?"

"He says —" She swallowed hard, then started again. "He says he's caught the Torso Killer."

Both Ness and Chamberlin rose to their feet. *"What?"*

"That's what he says."

A thousand conflicting emotions raced through Ness's brain — hope, relief . . . and something else, as well. "How can he know? How can he be sure? He's probably just picked up some bum, hoping to get a little publicity and —"

"According to the sheriff," she said, handing Ness the message, "the man they've captured has confessed."

41

By the time Ness and Chamberlin arrived at the county sheriff's office, the press conference was already under way.

". . . and so my men began looking for links between the victims — the three that the Cleveland police have managed to identify, at least tentatively — looking for someone who might have known them and might have had some reason to kill them. This was no easy chore, but perseverance and hard work always pay off in the end, and this case . . ."

Ness made his way forward, trying to get close enough to see what was going on without attracting the attention of the reporters. He did not want to appear to be basking in reflected glory; in fact, in this instance, he'd just as soon not be noticed at all.

The county sheriff, Martin O'Donnell, stood behind the podium reading his report in a deep gruff voice. The fact that he mispronounced several words suggested to Ness that he'd gotten someone else to write it. He was a middleweight man in a beige uniform that almost blended into the podium, but his shock of white hair glimmered in the noonday sun like a halo.

Just behind him, six of the sheriff's men flanked a seated man who clearly was not a member of the sheriff's department. He looked dirty and tired. His hair was greasy and he sagged forward in the chair, almost limp. He hadn't shaved for days. Ness noticed that his shirt was torn and soaked with sweat. Perhaps even more telling, he was clutching the right side of his rib cage.

But the most noticeable attribute of the man was his stare — straight ahead, penetrating, but at the same time, strangely vacant. He reminded Ness of a hypnotist he had once seen on vaudeville. As creepy as his expression was, it was difficult to look away.

". . . and so I sent my men to a bar at the corner of East Twentieth and Central frequented by all three of the identified victims, as well as a horde of other prostitutes and pimps and petty criminals. One of my agents learned of a person named Frank who supposedly knew all three. In fact, he once lived with Florence Polillo. Expert investigative work soon led him to the man we now have in custody — Frank Dolezal."

O'Donnell gestured broadly, directing everyone's attention to the man seated behind him. The man — apparently Dolezal — took no notice. He continued to stare straight ahead with his spooky wide-eyed glare. Ness wondered if he ever blinked.

"The preliminary investigation into Mr. Dolezal revealed that he worked as a bricklayer — but previously worked in a slaughterhouse."

The reaction from the reporters was immediate. Pencils sailed across their notepads.

"Subsequent investigation revealed that he kept a stockpile of butcher knives in his home. We have obtained several reports from people indicating that he threatened them with the same knives. He lives in an apartment at 1908 Central, which as I'm sure you all know is very near where the remains of Flo Polillo were found, neatly wrapped up and placed in baskets. At this point, my men obtained a warrant and searched his apartment. What they found, gentlemen of the press, is nothing less than horrifying." He paused dramatically. "On his bathroom floor, and particularly in the bathtub, they discovered disturbing dark stains."

Ness had to give the man credit for at least one thing: He was spinning his yarn like a master storyteller.

"The conclusion seems inescapable. He knew the victims; he frequented the same bar. He had the weapons, the opportunity, and the violent nature. He killed these people in the bathtub, hacked them to bits, then washed away most of the evidence. But you don't have to rely on my reasoning, because after two days of intensive questioning by my officers, he confessed."

Once again, O'Donnell gestured toward Dolezal. "This man seated behind me has been the subject of the most intensive manhunt in Cleveland history." He paused looking straight out into the throng. "The Mad Butcher is Frank Dolezal."

No reaction from Dolezal himself. As soon as O'Donnell stopped talking, a dozen hands flew into the air. The sheriff recognized a reporter from the *Plain Dealer.*

"Is it common for the sheriff's office to be involved in local murder investigations?"

"No," O'Donnell said, providing the answer everyone attending already knew, "but extraordinary crimes call for extraordinary measures."

"Did you inform Chief Matowitz that you were investigating the murders?"

"No."

"Is it appropriate for the sheriff's office to independently supplement the city police's ongoing investigation?"

O'Donnell took a deep breath. "Under the circumstances, I thought they could use all the help they could get."

Broad grins spread through the throng of reporters. There was no need to explain what that meant.

"What I don't understand," another reporter said, "is how you were able to catch this man so quickly, when the Cleveland police have been investigating for more than a year, and they haven't even produced a viable suspect."

"You'll have to answer that one for yourselves," O'Donnell said. "Or perhaps you could ask our esteemed Safety Director, Mr. Eliot Ness." He pointed out into the audience.

All the reporters whirled around.

Great, Ness thought. Serves me right for coming here.

The reporters began to swarm.

"Mr. Ness!" someone shouted. "What do you think about the sheriff solving your case?"

Ness's brain raced. There were two ways he could handle this. He could tell them what he really thought, or . . .

"The sheriff is to be commended for his investigation," Ness said. "The leads he has uncovered will, of course, be followed up."

"But the man confessed!"

Ness nodded, smiling. "My department and I stand ready to make available to the sheriff any information or facilities that could be of assistance."

The reporter from the *Plain Dealer* scratched his head. "But the killer has already been caught."

Ness kept his expression steady and unresponsive. "I hope so."

"C'mon," one of the other reporters said. "Tell the truth. This has got to stick in your craw. You've been looking for this guy for so long — and now the sheriff swoops in and puts him behind bars."

"Doesn't matter who does it, or who gets the credit," Ness said firmly. "What matters is that the killer is put away."

"And preferably before the elections, right?" O'Donnell said, bringing the attention back around to himself. "Perhaps the next time our Reform mayor decides to go reforming, he should look a little closer to home."

He folded his script and tucked it inside his coat pocket. "Now if you'll excuse me, my friends, we're going to continue interrogating this murderer."

42

Well, this was disappointing.

Or perhaps he should be pleased. No one was close to him, that much was certain. They were busy putting away this poor washed-up idiot, oblivious to the real threat that lurked in their town.

They would learn their mistake, eventually. There was no way around it. How long could he go without pleasuring himself again?

But there was no denying . . . he didn't like the idea of someone else taking credit for his work.

There was only one thing to be done.

"Work? In one of them breweries?"

"Isn't that what you want?"

"I'll take any kinda work I can get."

"Family to support?"

"Not so much anymore. Once upon a time."

"I'm sorry."

"It's all right. Probably for the better. You a family man?"

"I was."

"Didn't work out?"

"You could say that. Shall we go?"

Later, back at the brewery, he encountered some . . . unexpected complications. If he had not had anesthesia, it would have been almost impossible, even granted his considerable strength. The Mad Butcher had received altogether too much publicity. People were on their guard. Even uneducated fools such as this one.

On the other hand, the lovely city officials said that the killer was in custody. What reason could there possibly be for apprehension?

At any rate, by the time the poor baboon awoke, he was trussed up and lying flat across the table.

"Hey, what's the big idea?"

"The idea is to prevent an interloper from taking credit for my achievements. Be still."

"What's with the axe?"

"You'll see."

"Don't do nothin' crazy now, mister. I can make you a lot of scratch."

"That explains why you're riding the rails and living in a trash heap."

"I'm just bidin' my time. I got a big score

comin'."

"Do tell."

"I'm talkin' big time. Major league. Enough to set you up for life."

"I'm already set. Thank goodness for the kindness of close relatives."

"Let me help you, mister."

"I will let you help me."

"Get me offa this table."

"I'm afraid that's not going to happen. Pleasant dreams."

He swung the axe.

But it was even more unsatisfying than the last time. How long could he continue repeating himself, never facing any real challenge?

He had thought the safety director might provide that challenge, but the man seemed woefully inadequate for the role. He had taunted Ness, but the man seemed impervious to every slap on the face.

How much more would he have to do to get a response out of the famed Treasury agent? He'd killed more people than Capone ever did. When would he get his due?

If it didn't come soon, as it should, he would be forced to take certain measures. One way or the other, he would command the safety director's attention. He had earned that. It would be his. No matter what he had to do.

43

Peter Merylo desperately wanted a bath.

Even a quick shower would be something. He looked grimy, felt greasy, and reeked like an outhouse. Maybe none of the people he encountered noticed. But Merylo did. Normally, he was a tidy, fastidious man. He didn't dress up fancy like Ness, but he didn't let himself go. Until now.

He'd been undercover for a week, his beard grown and his clothes torn and dirty, traveling all around the Kingsbury Run area, searching for clues, talking to anyone who would talk to him, which so far, was not as many as he would like. He had expected that. He knew vagrants were a suspicious lot, and with reason. He would have to hang around for a while, become one of the regulars, before anyone would tell him anything useful. That was fine. He was in this for the long haul.

This time of day, most of the transients

were either working, if they could find anything, or sleeping. He used the time to look around, at the people, the sorry excuses for homes, the abandoned buildings . . .

Just a few hundred yards from where the first headless corpses had been discovered, he passed through a long dark tunnel. Gave him the creeps. Sure, he had his .38 hidden securely under his hobo outfit. But that wouldn't do him much good in this pitch darkness; he wouldn't even know which way to point it.

He walked slowly and carefully forward, wondering if the Torso Killer had passed this way when he was delivering his little surprises. What if he had? Or worse, what if he were there now? What could Merylo possibly do about it if that maniac suddenly appeared in front of him and —

Merylo shook himself, breaking the train of thought. This was not productive. He needed to keep his mind on what he was doing.

In the distance, he detected a tiny pin-prick of light. He walked toward it, and as he did, the radius of the circle grew steadily larger.

Eventually, he emerged into the sunlight, very glad to be there. Off to the side, he spotted a row of repair shops tucked inside a side gully. All the shops appeared to be closed and boarded. How hard would it be for the killer to break into one of these shops and use it as a base of operations, a place to conduct his slaughter? It was close to where the identified victims lived, and close to where most of the torsos had been discovered.

The doors were unlocked. Inside, he saw tall stacks of scrap metal and tires and automobile parts. But no sign of life. Or death. Behind the first shop he found a deserted building. Small, but large enough for one man. Especially if he wasn't very social.

Merylo peered inside a window. He spotted empty food cans, a blanket, some torn and yellowing newspapers. But that was hardly telling. Given the huge number of transients in this area, this dump might seem like an ideal place for many to spend the night.

He peered through another window. There was a lightbulb dangling from the ceiling. It was on.

Someone had been here recently.

Merylo turned the knob. Unlocked.

Did he need a warrant? The place looked abandoned. At least, that's what he would tell the judge.

He stepped inside.

The room was almost entirely bare. The only furnishing was a small bench by the north window. He sat down on it and looked around.

There were dark stains on the floor. Not nearly enough to suggest that anyone had been killed here, much less decapitated. But still . . .

Was it possible the killer had brought the bodies here while he rested, or waited for an opportune moment to deposit them on the Run? A strong man could have gotten Andrassy's body from here to where it was found only a few hundred yards away.

If the killer had been here, he must've sat on this very bench. Or perhaps he placed the torsos on this bench while he waited for a chance to dispose of them.

Either way, Merylo didn't care to sit any longer.

He searched through the shop and the neighboring buildings but he found no signs that they had been used as a depository or a slaughterhouse.

Still no clues. And yet, he couldn't shake the feeling that he was onto something, that he was walking in the killer's tracks.

He spotted a crowd gathering about two hundred feet away, near the river. Time to stop playing policeman and to start acting like an unemployed bum. He'd decided not to tell people he'd ridden in on the rails, since he had been reliably informed that everyone knew about the torso murders all across the country, and consequently no one was stupid enough to get off the train here.

It looked like the usual assortment of society's refuse, the downtrodden and the riffraff, the crooks and the con artists, the sick and the suicidal. His many years on the force made it a cinch to tell who was who. Huddled around a barrel he saw prostitutes, marijuana dealers, numerous small-time crooks — and too many decent men having their spirit snuffed out by the Depression.

As he approached, he realized there was some sort of commotion. A middle-aged woman was lying on the ground. A man Merylo had never seen before knelt beside her. He was tall, medium weight, sturdy — and definitely not a vagrant. His suit was clean and untorn; in fact, it looked fairly new. He wore eyeglasses and had a salt-and-pepper mustache.

Merylo stepped closer so he could hear what was happening, trying not to attract attention.

"There now," the man said. "That should do it."

The woman looked dazed, disoriented. Upon closer inspection, he realized her right arm was in a sling.

"It's only sprained, not broken," the man said. He smiled reassuringly. "Just try not to use it for a few days. Should be fine."

The woman's hand went to her brow. "I — I don't know what happened to me."

"Passed out, from what these boys tell me."

"Why would I do that? I've never —"

"When was the last time you ate, Agnes?"

The woman averted her eyes. "It has been awhile."

"I thought as much. Look, you come by the Sailors' Home tonight around dinnertime. Mary cooks a wonderful pot roast on Thursday nights. I think there'll be enough to share with you."

"Thank you. Thank you so much."

The man looked up. "But that just goes for Agnes. I don't want to see the whole lot of you showing up."

"We're all hungry," one of the men said softly.

"You know where the missions are."

"There's never enough."

"I know that. I know." The man pushed to his feet. "Perhaps things will turn around soon. Remember what the President says.

The only thing we have to fear is fear itself."
The man tipped his hat and walked away.

Merylo couldn't help but notice that he
had a slight but noticeable limp. Looking
even more carefully, he realized that his
right leg was longer than his left.

What was it that alienist had said . . . ?

As the crowd began to disperse, Merylo
approached the oldest man in the group. In
his experience, the oldest were the most
likely to talk. Many of them had been on
the road a long time, even before the Crash.
As a result, they were less scared and suspicious. He appeared to be about sixty, although it was often hard to tell with these
transients. Life on the road aged a man
prematurely.

"That was really somethin'," Merylo said,
careful not to act too interested. "Never
seen anythin' like that."

The elderly man pursed his lips and blew
air through his teeth. "Aw, all he done was
put her arm in a sling. Didn't need to go to
medical school for that."

Merylo's ears pricked up. "That man was
a doctor?"

"I figure he must be. Everyone calls him
Doc."

"You've seen him before?"

"Sure. Comes through these parts every

now and again."

Merylo laughed a little, trying to sound like a bored man making idle conversation rather than an investigator pursuing a lead. "Doesn't look like he belongs in this neighborhood."

"He's not one of us. He just cuts through here on his way home. Not afraid to give a little help when he can, though, and that's more than I can say for most of the people in this city."

"You're tellin' me that fancy Dan has a joint of his own around here?"

"Not exactly a joint of his own. He's stayin' at the Sailors' Home."

Sailor? Merylo's skin began to tingle. "But ain't that a place for —"

"Yup. People with problems."

"And the doc — ?"

The man pantomimed taking a drink.

"He looked pretty sober to me."

"Guess he can go a long time. Then he flies off on a binge. We don't see him for days."

Merylo's eyes narrowed. Indeed.

"And then he shows up again, fit as a fiddle. Shame, really. Ought to be some way to help a person like that."

"Isn't that what the Home is supposed to do?"

"I suppose. Say — why you so interested in the doc?"

"No reason. Just passin' the time. Not like I got anything else to do."

"I hear that."

"You got any idea what the doc's name is? I might ask him to take a look at my bum shoulder, next time he comes through."

"I've heard folks call him Frank. Frank Sweeney."

44

Ness didn't wait to be announced. He marched into the office and laid his hat on the edge of the desk.

Sheriff O'Donnell had his feet propped up, reading the newspaper. He glanced over the top. "Did we have an appointment?"

"We do now."

"Well now, I have a very busy schedule and —"

"You can make time for me."

"Is that so?"

"Yes. I want to talk about your suspect."

"Now wait just one minute," O'Donnell said, his face still obscured by the newspaper. "Maybe you're used to telling those boys down at the city police which way to jump, but this is my office, I don't have to take orders from —"

Ness grabbed the paper and ripped it out of his hands. "Here are your choices, Sheriff. You can talk to me now, or I can call the newspapers and tell them what I know about your suspect. You choose."

The two men stared into each other's eyes for a long moment.

"Have it your way." Ness made an about-face and headed toward the door.

"Hold on," O'Donnell said, rising to his feet.

Ness stopped.

"Don't get so uppity and impatient. You want to talk, fine. Let's sit down and shoot the breeze."

Ness turned to face him. "I prefer to stand."

"What is it that's so all-fired important?"

"I think you know."

O'Donnell chuckled. "I know you're royally raked off because I caught that Torso Killer and you didn't."

"Yeah. Except you didn't actually catch the killer, did you? You just pummeled some poor loser till he gave you a confession."

O'Donnell leaned forward, pressing his fists against his desk. "That's a serious accusation, Mr. Ness."

"Murder is a serious charge. It shouldn't be leveled against someone unless there's evidence to support it."

"The man confessed!"

"Do you think I'm blind? Do you think I

couldn't see the bruises on his arms, his face? Do you think I didn't notice the way he was clutching his side? I sent a medic in yesterday to observe your prisoner, Sheriff. He thinks the man has a broken rib — maybe several."

"You had one of your men in my cell block? When was that?"

"I also understand he didn't get food, water, or rest for more than two days while you interrogated him."

"Who told you that?"

"Don't change the subject. How did your prisoner get so beat up?"

The sheriff made a clicking noise with his tongue. "Self-inflicted."

"Oh, please."

"It's true. The man's violent and self-destructive. Has tried to kill himself several times. I've got him on suicide watch. Two guards on him at all times."

"I've read the transcript of the confession," Ness said, ignoring him. "It won't wash. He's got the time of the Polillo murder wrong."

"He's a drunk. He forgets things."

"His description of the execution is wrong, too. And his knives aren't strong enough to bring off a decapitation. And if he left her clothes on Orange Avenue, why didn't the police find them?"

"Maybe they didn't look."

"I can assure you they did."

"There may be some minor inconsistencies, but that doesn't mean —"

"Even if I believed his confession wasn't coerced — and I don't — the only thing he confessed to is Flo Polillo's murder. Not the other eight."

"One is all we need to put him down."

"But the coroner says that the man who killed Flo Polillo also killed the others."

"All the more reason to put him down."

"But he couldn't have committed the other murders!"

"And how can you possibly know that?"

"Look at him, man. He's short, weak, emaciated. You think he could take Andrassy — a man a head taller than him who carried an ice pick?"

"You never know. Might've caught him by surprise."

"You think he could carry Andrassy's corpse to the bottom of Jackass Hill? That's a sixty-degree slope, if you didn't know. I doubt your man could walk it carrying nothing, much less carrying a corpse."

"This is all just sour grapes. You can't stand the fact that I beat you to the punch. You and all your high-powered men came up with nothing, while my investigators caught the killer."

"Except it wasn't actually your investigator, was it?"

That slowed him down a bit. "What are you babbling about now?"

"I'm talking about Lawrence J. Lyons, the private investigator. Who is most definitely not a member of your staff."

O'Donnell's forehead knitted. "How do you know Mr. Lyons?"

"I've known about him for months, ever since he started mucking about in this case. Merylo caught on to him right away. Told me all about it."

"Well, it doesn't matter. Your Detective Merylo didn't bring in the murderer."

"Detective Merylo didn't bring in Frank Dolezal because he isn't the murderer and couldn't possibly be the murderer. Merylo interviewed him twice and eliminated him as a suspect. I have the reports. The man might be a little loony, but he's no Torso Killer."

"Says you."

"Merylo talked to Lyons just last week and told him he was chasing the wrong man. That's why you went ahead and arrested him, isn't it? You figured we knew about your secret investigator and his work.

So you grabbed Dolezal before we beat *you* to the punch. Except of course we would never have arrested him. Because he didn't do it."

"My man says otherwise."

"What interests me is the fact that when Lyons thought he had a lead, he didn't bring it to the police department. He came to you."

O'Donnell hooked a thumb under his belt. "Could be he just had more faith that we'd be able to get the job done."

"Or it could have something to do with Ray Miller, the former mayor and Democratic crony."

"You're grasping at straws."

"I know Lyons went to Miller and told him what he knew. And Miller sent him to you — a Democrat. Because he didn't want the case cracked by the mayor or anyone associated with him."

"You're barking up the wrong tree, Ness."

"Tell me, Sheriff — you're a close friend of Congressman Sweeney, right? In fact, you're related by marriage."

"Is that a crime?"

"And Sweeney has been doing everything in his power to politicize these murders. To gain political capital by criticizing the Republican administration for not catching the killer. It would really spoil his plans if we did. So he sent Lyons to the only available Democrat in local law enforcement — the county sheriff."

"Balderdash."

"And you arrested the man and held a big press conference announcing that you'd caught the murderer, even though you had nothing on him other than a forced confession."

O'Donnell pounded his fist on his desk. "He knew Flo Polillo!"

"So what?"

"He had knives!"

"Who doesn't?"

"There are stains all over his bathtub!"

"Have you had those stains analyzed?" Ness gave him a sharp look. "Yes, I suspected you had. So have I."

"How did you get in there?"

"And you know what your dark stains turn out to be? Dirt. That's all. No blood. No bodily fluids. Common ordinary dirt."

"He still confessed."

"After you broke his rib cage."

O'Donnell tucked in his chin and stared into Ness's eyes. They glared at each other for a long moment. Then O'Donnell punched a button on the intercom box on his desk. "Send in Crawford."

"Yes, sir."

"You might like to know," Ness said, "that the American Civil Liberties Union is already investigating to determine whether you violated Dolezal's civil rights. The civil liberties committee of the American Bar Association is planning a similar investigation."

"Friends of yours?"

"Not at all. Just concerned citizens. People who don't want to see a two-bit political crony run roughshod over a man's constitutional rights. Even a man like Dolezal."

O'Donnell lurched forward. "Why can't you just leave it alone? The people want this thing to be over. It's better for everyone."

"Not if there's still a killer on the loose."

A moment later there was a knock on the door. A tall, burly uniformed officer stepped into the office. O'Donnell motioned him over. The two men talked in whispers for a few moments. Then the uniform left the room.

"Last-minute assignment?"

"Just asked him to prepare the prisoner. I assume you're going to want to talk to him."

"You're right about that."

"You know, Ness — Mayor Burton is going to lose the next election."

"That's always a possibility."

"And when he goes — you go with him."

"I've never had any trouble finding work."

"Until now. This could be your chance to join the winning team. If you'd just leave well enough alone."

"Don't think so."

"Give it another week and no one will remember who actually caught this guy. They'll just be glad it's over. And you can move on without this albatross hanging around your neck. No one will know the difference."

"Wrong. I'll know."

"And nothing will change your mind?"

"I'd like the suspect to take a polygraph."

O'Donnell sniffed. "Don't believe in them. They aren't reliable."

"I figured as much. May I see the prisoner now?"

O'Donnell's office door flew open, this time without the preliminary knock. "Sheriff!" It was his receptionist.

"Yes?"

"It's cell B-four. He did the Dutch! He's hung himself!"

Ness's voice dropped to a low whisper. "What have you done?"

"What have *I* done? Did you not hear the woman?" He turned to the receptionist. "Call the medics, Lily. Get them in there as soon as possible." O'Donnell rose. "If you'll excuse me, Mr. Ness, I have some business."

"I'm coming with you."

"I don't allow civilians —"

"I'm coming with you."

"County rules. Under no circumstances may —"

Ness looked at him levelly. "I'm coming with you. With or without the press."

O'Donnell frowned. "Suit yourself then. Hurry!"

45

Merylo cleaned up before visiting the Sandusky Soldiers' and Sailors' Home. He still wasn't planning to identify himself as a police officer. At the same time, he doubted he could persuade the proprietress to speak to a bum in an unkempt beard and filthy clothing.

He waited until he saw Doc leave the building, dressed in what appeared to be the same suit he had worn the day before. As soon as the man was out of sight, Merylo walked up the front steps. He knocked on the front door of the gabled two-story white house. Only a few moments later, a woman wearing a plain print dress opened the door.

"Are you Mary McGovern?"

"Yes. Can I help you?"

"Name's Peter Smith, ma'am. I work for the Board of Examiners."

She held the door only partly open between them, just enough to allow them to speak. "Who?"

"The Board of Examiners, ma'am." He paused. "The folks who are going to decide whether the good doctor will have his license to practice medicine reinstated."

"Oh dear. Oh dear me." She opened the door the rest of the way. "Please come in."

Mary showed Merylo into the front sitting room. He took a somewhat worn davenport while she took the armchair catercorner to it.

"I was afraid something like this might happen. I knew that he had lost his job, of course, but I had hoped he might find another one somewhere. Even in this awful Depression, people still need doctors, right?"

"That's right, ma'am. But we have to make sure those doctors can be trusted."

"Of course you do."

"Let me tell you first of all, Mrs. Mc-Govern, that this conversation will be held in the strictest confidence."

"Thank you."

"By the same token, I expect you to keep our little visit secret, too. You can't tell anyone — not even the doctor."

"Well, if you say so."

"We don't want to give him more to worry about without cause."

"Oh, no. Of course not."

Merylo pulled a notepad out of his jacket pocket, flipped to an empty page, and began to read. "The doctor was committed to this institution as a result of his alcoholism, is that correct, ma'am?"

"That's my understanding."

"Is your establishment subsidized by the state?"

"No, we're private."

"So the doctor is a wealthy man?"

"Actually, a relative is paying the costs. A wealthy cousin."

"Does the doctor have a job?"

"Not that I know of. He's been looking, but, well, I guess his colleagues at City Hospital have said some rather nasty things about him."

City Hospital? He worked at City Hospital?

The same place Edward Andrassy once worked.

"Do you know what they were saying?"

"I've heard that he came to work intoxicated on more than one occasion. And that he sometimes flew off the handle, which, bless my soul, I can't even believe. He's such a kind, gentle man. At least, when he hasn't been . . . you know."

"Of course."

"I even heard a rumor that he became violent and threatened a man in the hospital with a . . . a . . . oh, what do you call those little knives doctors use?"

"A scalpel, ma'am?"

"Yes. That's it exactly. A scalpel. But I can't imagine it. Perhaps the incident was exaggerated."

"Perhaps so."

"I'm sure he was just a little rocky. Men are sometimes, you know, when their home life is disrupted so dramatically."

"His home life?"

"You know about his wife, don't you?"

"I don't believe I do."

"Oh goodness. Then you need to. His wife divorced him. Just up and left."

"Poor man."

"Said the most awful things about him. Accused him of hideous things. Cruelty. Violence. Unnatural acts."

Merylo worked to maintain a straight face.

"Said he tried to . . . force himself on her. And not in the usual way. If you know what I mean."

"I think I do."

"But I just can't believe that. He's an educated man. You can tell that every time he speaks. So intelligent."

What was it the alienist had tried to tell them?

"It must've been hard on him, seeing his marriage break up like that. And she took the children away from him. Just about the same time he lost his job. Who knows what that might do to a person? He has no close family now. None at all. Had three brothers — every one of them is dead."

"Tragic."

"His only living relative is that cousin, and he's never once come around to visit." She lowered her voice to a whisper. "To tell you the truth, I think he may be a bit embarrassed. A man in his position probably doesn't want to be associated with a scandalous relative."

"No doubt. Can you help me understand the doctor's schedule?"

"How do you mean?"

"Well, my understanding was that he has been institutionalized here."

"Yes."

"And yet, he seems to be able to come and go as he pleases."

"It isn't a prison. We're here to help him, to whatever degree he'll let us. We have classes, get-togethers with everyone staying here. Times when everyone can share their troubles. Learn from one another. We've modeled our program after that new organization they started up in New York. You know the one. Alcoholics Anonymous."

"Does he attend these classes?"

"Sometimes." She hesitated. "Not that often."

"Is he still drinking?"

She looked down at her knitted hands. "Not here. But . . . he does disappear at times. Sometimes for more than a day."

"Where does he go?"

"I have no idea. I've asked, but he wouldn't tell me."

"You think he goes off to binge?"

"I hope not. But given his background . . ."

"Perhaps he goes to visit his cousin."

"Oh, I very much doubt that. Congressman Sweeney may be willing to foot the bill, but I don't think he would want his cousin dropping by his mansion."

Merylo's lips parted.

He rose to his feet. He had to get back to Ness. As soon as possible. "Thank you for your cooperation. And please remember what I said. Mum's the word. We don't want to jeopardize Dr. Sweeney's chances for reinstatement."

"No. For all his troubles, he really is a very kind man. So thoughtful."

"Well, I have to file my report. If you'll —"

Merylo was interrupted by an ear-splitting cry from outside the house.

"What in — ?"

Merylo jammed his notepad into his back pocket and raced out the front door. Standing not ten feet away, just beyond the picket fence, he spotted a woman, one hand pressed against her terror-stricken face.

As he approached, Merylo realized it was the same woman he had seen before, when he was masquerading as a vagrant, the one Dr. Sweeney had assisted. Her arm was still in a sling.

"What is it? What's wrong?"

The woman's hand trembled. She tried to speak, but couldn't force anything out. Finally, she just pointed.

Merylo whirled around. There was a dog on the sidewalk, a cocker spaniel.

He did not appear to be rabid. He wasn't growling or making threatening noises.

Perhaps because there was something in his mouth.

"You ladies go inside the house. Now!"

They obeyed. As soon as they were gone, Merylo slowly approached the canine.

"C'mon now, pooch. Let's see what you've got."

Good God — was it what he thought it was?

Merylo had never been good with dogs. Never cared for them much. He was more of a cat person, not that he would ever admit that to any of his fellow police officers.

He crouched down and held out his hand. "Come on, doggie. Come on. Give papa the bone. Hear me?"

The dog gave his head a little shake, then opened his mouth.

Part of a human leg dropped out of his jaws.

46

The speed and efficiency of the sheriff's medics impressed Ness — perhaps the only part of the office that did. In fewer than five minutes, they had arrived at cell B-4, lowered the body from the hook and administered oxygen, then insulin, in the hope of restarting his heart. But they were too late. Frank Dolezal was dead.

"Well," Sheriff O'Donnell said, sighing heavily, "that'll save the state the cost of killing him." He was surrounded by three of his uniformed officers.

Ness had remained silent and out of the way while the medics did their work, but now he could hold his tongue no longer. "I thought you said you had two men watching him at all times?"

The sheriff shrugged. "It was a fluke thing. Schuster left to escort some visitors downstairs. Then I called for Crawford. Apparently this man was just waiting for an opportunity. They were only gone a few moments."

Ness peered through the bars into the tiny cell. "I noticed the cell doors were unlocked."

"Dolezal was the only prisoner in this cell block. There was no reason to restrict him to the cell. The doors to the block were locked and bolted."

"But any one of your officers could've gotten in."

"But the point is, Dolezal couldn't get out."

"No, the point is, anyone who wanted to get to him, could."

"Just what are you saying?"

"I think you know." The medics had told Ness that Dolezal had been found dangling from a hook on the ceiling of his cell, hanging from a noose made from twisted rags. "Where did he get these rags?"

One of the uniforms, Crawford, stepped forward. "He said he was bored. Wanted something to do. So I gave him the rags so he could clean his cell."

"Is that right?"

"That's right."

Ness faced O'Donnell. "I thought you said he was on suicide watch."

"Yeah."

"So if he's on suicide watch, why would your men give him something he could easily turn into a makeshift rope and hang himself with? For that matter, why would you give him a cell with a hook in the ceiling?"

Crawford and O'Donnell exchanged a glance.

"Guess we never thought about that."

To their surprise, Ness withdrew a tape measure from his coat pocket and began measuring the cell.

"Now wait just a minute," O'Donnell said. "It's one thing to have you come look around but where do you get off —"

"Five feet seven," Ness said, cutting him off.

"Uhh . . . come again?"

"This hook in the ceiling. It's five feet seven inches off the ground."

"So?"

"So perhaps you can explain to me how a man who was five feet eight could hang himself from a hook that was only five feet seven inches off the floor."

Ness's inquiry was met with stony silence.

"I think perhaps it's time for you to leave, Mr. Ness."

"You won't get away with this, O'Donnell."

"The door is this way."

"I don't know why you thought you had to do this. I don't know if you and your squad of hooligans fancy yourselves some kind of avenging lynch mob, or if it's that you knew your case wouldn't hold up in court. Or a combination of both. But you won't get away with it."

"You're talking through your hat. You've got nothing. No one is going to care about how many inches high some hook is."

Ness smiled thinly. "Ever seen a man hanged before, Sheriff?"

"Haven't had the pleasure."

"I have." Ness crouched down beside the corpse. "Hanging leaves a very characteristic mark, because the back of the noose hangs higher than the front due to the upward pull of the rope. Makes a V-shaped scar." He pulled the sheet covering the corpse down slightly. "But as you can see, the bruising on Dolezal's neck circles the middle of his neck. There's no upward slant." Ness replaced the sheet. "He didn't hang. He was strangled."

O'Donnell squared himself directly in front of Ness. "You're asking for trouble, Mr. Safety Director."

"No, you asked for trouble," Ness replied, looking right back at him, not flinching an inch. O'Donnell's men moved in closer. Ness ignored them. "First, when you decided to mess around with my case. Second, when you decided to take a human life. And you will pay for that, Sheriff. I'll make sure of it."

"No one will believe you. They'll say you're just bitter because you didn't catch the killer. You'll look like a fool."

"Well, I've looked foolish before," Ness replied. "But I never killed anyone to cover up my own incompetence. Or political bias. That might be something you want to keep in mind." He placed his hat on his head and started toward the door. "Thank you for your trouble, gentlemen. I'll see myself out."

47

From the July 6, 1937, *Cleveland News:*

". . . while the National Guard was called in to restore order to the increasingly violent disturbances erupting from the ongoing dispute between the steel industry and the unions, the Torso Murderer struck again. Private Edgar M. Steinbrecher strolled out onto the West 3rd Street Bridge, attracted by a tugboat passing beneath, when he noticed a white object on the surface of the water. Upon closer examination, it proved to be the bottom half of a male torso, wrapped in newspaper, bobbing along in the Cuyahoga. Investigators subsequently discovered two forearms and the upper right arm. No one has managed to locate the head.

"According to the coroner's office, this tenth victim was killed about forty-eight hours before the body was discovered. He was approximately forty years old, five foot nine, and weighed around 150 pounds. The only distinguishing features on the parts recovered were two old scars on the right thumb and a cross-shaped scar on the left leg. Although fingerprints were taken from the right hand, no matches were found. Perhaps the most intriguing detail is that the torso was found with a woman's silk stocking, upon which forensic scientists discovered blond human hairs.

"The coroner's office also noticed that the killer's level of viciousness and savagery has escalated. The killer cut out the lower portion of the torso and re-moved all organs from the abdominal cavity. The chest was split open and the heart had been severed. There were also lacerations on the hand and diaphragm and more hesitation marks, suggesting either that the killer was becoming less careful or perhaps, that his weapon was growing dull. The coroner noted that this corpse showed evidence of what previously have been considered impos-sible — increased butchery by this rampaging murderer.

"Despite assurances from the sheriff's

office that the killing spree had come to an end, it seems the Mad Butcher continues his filthy work unabated. Worse, his wanton violence and thirst for blood has increased. Who knows what horrific acts might follow if the police and the safety director do not finally heed the voice of the people and devote their full and unrestrained energies to finding this mass murderer before he has another chance to . . ."

"David, you've got to give me something."

"I've got nothing to give."

"You got all those men. All that dough."

"And I've been using both to the fullest possible extent. But we still haven't found anything."

Ness slammed down the phone receiver. What a disappointment. He thought they had so much promise. But the Unknowns had become the Know-Nothings. Blast!

Chamberlin entered his office. "Any news?"

Ness folded the paper up and laid it neatly on the corner of his desk. "At least this puts the Frank Dolezal business to rest. The Torso Killer is still very much alive."

"What's happening with Sheriff O'Donnell?" Chamberlin asked.

"An inquest has been called."

"Think they'll nail him?"

"I doubt if they'll have the courage to bring formal charges against the county sheriff. But they can give him a few days of misery and bad headlines. He won't get another term of office."

"I don't think that's enough."

"Agreed. Did you hear about the National Association of Coroners convention?"

"Guess that one escaped my social calendar."

"Pearce made a big presentation about the torso killings. Hoped someone might think of something he hadn't, some new angle or something."

"Did they?"

"No. But the case got even more publicity — nationwide. Have you seen this?" He held up a slick magazine.

Chamberlin shook his head. "I'm more a Hemingway man, myself. Have you read *To Have and Have Not*?"

"Haven't had the time. This rag is called *Official Detective Stories*. And they're offering a five-thousand-dollar reward for information leading to the capture of the Torso Murderer — provided they get the exclusive story."

Chamberlin whistled. "Five thousand?

That's a lot of cabbage."

"No kidding. Almost as much as I make in a year."

"Think it'll help?"

"We're already getting fifty tips a day. And we chase down every single one of them, even the stupid ones. We've checked out a voodoo cult, numerous wife beaters, any number of doctors and undertakers. But nothing pans out."

"And your . . . private investigations?"

"They're spending plenty of money. But so far — zip."

"This killer must be the Invisible Man."

"I don't think so." Ness rubbed his jaw. "But I am beginning to think —"

He was interrupted by his office door flinging open without warning. It was Detective Merylo, with Ness's secretary hovering anxiously in the background. "Too busy to knock, Detective?"

"I've got something for you, Ness. Something big."

"A lead?"

"Better than that." Merylo leaned across his desk. "I think I've found your killer."

Merylo spent the next half hour telling Ness and Chamberlin everything he had learned, both undercover in Shantytown and at the

Sandusky Soldiers' and Sailors' Home. "I tried to figure out where the dog came from. Turns out he's a stray, but a lot of folks in Shantytown have seen him, particularly around those repair shops."

Ness nodded. "Interesting."

"It's more than interesting. It's perfect. Sweeney lives at the Home, very near where most of the bodies were found. It's also near the repair shop he could have used as a way station for transporting the corpses. He has medical knowledge. He looks strong. He disappears for long stretches of time."

"Long enough to capture someone and take them apart?"

"Exactly. He once worked at the same place as Andrassy. He's a drunk, so it's likely he goes to that sleazy bar that Flo Polillo and Rose Wallace frequented — also very near the Home. And I hate to admit it but —" He paused. "Do you remember what that alienist told us?"

Ness shrugged. "Sure."

"Well, Dr. Sweeney fits the description perfectly. He's smart, educated. Has access to money. Lived near the Run all his life, still does. White male, right age. Alcohol problem. Violent tendencies. Twisted sex preferences." Merylo leaned in closer. "He even has a physical deformity. A limp. One leg longer than the other."

"That's not so much."

"It's enough to make his childhood a misery, I'm betting."

"Lots of kids get teased when they're young," Ness said, his eyes wandering. "Doesn't make them criminals."

"Then factor in losing both parents at an early age. And three brothers. And then a divorce, and losing his license to practice. Small wonder he's messed up."

"Still, this doesn't prove anything."

Merylo reached inside his jacket pocket. "I checked him out with the VA. He was a soldier during The Great War and after. Eventually declared, and I quote, 'twenty-five percent disabled.'"

"Because of his leg?"

"No, they knew about that before he enlisted. They had him mostly doing hospital and desk work. Medical Corps. There must've been something else."

"Like what?"

Merylo gripped the edges of the desk. "Like he's a crazy killer, that's what!"

Ness leaned back in his chair. "I'll admit, there's some good circumstantial evidence in there. But hardly enough for an arrest. I'm not sure you've even got enough to bring him in for questioning."

"Have you been listening to me? The dog dropped a human leg! Practically in the man's front yard!"

"So what? We know the killer has been depositing bodies in the Run. The dog found a body part there. Doesn't prove anything."

Merylo clenched his teeth. "Take a look at this." He pulled more paper out of his coat pocket. "I got these at the county clerk's office. Sweeney's wife filed for divorce in 1934. According to her petition, her life had become a horror picture."

"Women always say stuff like that. It's the only way they can get the divorce."

"She says he started drinking much more heavily. Says he would become, and I quote, 'erratic and violent.' I'll just bet. Abusive to his wife and children. Says he hallucinated. Had weird delusions."

"Does it say what the delusions were about?"

"No, but I can guess. It's just like the alienist said. First he fantasizes about killing someone. And then, eventually, he starts doing it!"

"There's still no proof."

Merylo continued reading. "Says he showed up for work drunk, sometimes didn't show up at all. Says he would disappear for days without telling anyone where he was going."

"Probably on a bender. Sleeping it off in a ditch somewhere."

"Or trolling through Shantytown, looking for losers and hacking them to bits!"

"Merylo, get a grip . . ."

He continued reading. "The wife also filed a petition in probate stating that her husband was insane."

"She wasn't content with half the money. She wanted it all."

"As a result, he was committed to City Hospital — at the same time that Andrassy worked there. In the psychiatric ward."

"Coincidence."

"He got out a month later. But by that time he's lost his job and his license. The wife moves in with her sister, takes the kids with her. All in the same month."

"Tough month for the poor boozehound."

"Do you remember what the alienist said about how a combination of difficult events could cause the killer to break? To make the jump from fantasizing about murder to doing it? In the same month, this guy loses his wife, his family, and his job. His head was probably messed up from the start and he makes it worse with hooch. And get this — the next month, *the very next month,* according to the coroner, the Lady in the Lake, the first of the Torso Killer's victims, was murdered."

Merylo took a breath and waited patiently for a response. He got nothing. Ness stared straight ahead, apparently lost in thought.

"Do you not see how perfect it is? It all fits!"

From the back of the office, Chamberlin cleared his throat. "I think you're the one who doesn't see, Detective."

"I don't see what?" He was practically screaming. "I just gave you the killer. What's your problem?"

Chamberlin kept his voice on a calm, level plane. "Our problem, Detective, is that your suspect's last name is Sweeney."

"Who cares?"

"We have to," Ness said. "We have no choice. Congressman Sweeney has been criticizing me about not catching the killer. What's he going to do when I bring in his cousin as a suspect? He'll claim I'm retaliating against him."

"I don't care. I'm telling you — Frank Sweeney is the killer."

"But you can't prove it. And neither can I."

"Let me bring him in. Work on him for a few days."

"He'll ask for a lawyer."

"Tell him to take a flying —"

"We'll have to allow it. He'll be instructed to say nothing. We won't get anything. We'll have to release him. The press will have a field day."

"Maybe we can keep it quiet. Maybe —"

Ness shook his head. "If Congressman Sweeney weren't a Democrat, I might take the risk. But he is. Anything I do to his cousin, he'll say it was political."

"He's the one who's been trying to make it political. I told you, that's why he sent Lyons to the sheriff —"

"You and I know that. But the press doesn't and we can't prove it. If we bring in the cousin of a political opponent, everyone will think we're trying to get even. To do the same kind of shady political backstabbing they've been doing."

"The important thing is that we get this monster off the street and let the people of Cleveland stop being terrified."

"Yes, that was the county sheriff's argument. And it was good — till the next corpse turned up. Then he looked like a fool." Ness's eyes seemed to recede and darken. "I don't want to look like a fool. Like some kind of . . . big mess."

"Just let me bring him in!"

Ness and Chamberlin looked at each other. They were clearly in agreement. "No. Too risky. Burton wouldn't like it. Could impact his reelection. You can watch the man if you want. Look for more evidence. But you may not make contact. And under no circumstances will you interrogate him or bring him into custody. Do you understand?"

Merylo felt as if his head were smoldering. He leaned across Ness's desk, close enough to slap him. "You told me I could do whatever it took to catch this killer. You said you would support me. Right down the line."

"Well, the line stops at political suicide."

"You don't care about catching the killer. You're afraid you'll lose your job. Your driver. Your invitation to society parties."

"You're way out of line, Detective."

"I don't care. You're putting yourself before the people."

"Am I?" Ness's neck stiffened. He spoke in short, clipped words, increasing in volume with each sentence. "Where will the people be if I'm not in this office? What will happen to the traffic situation, huh? The Boys Clubs. Mobsters and labor racketeers. I've done a lot of good for this town and I'm not going to see it undone because I make a stupid mistake on this stupid case!"

Merylo grabbed his rumpled hat and headed toward the door. "I'm going over your head."

"There is no one over my head."

"Then I'm going to the press."

"And tip off Sweeney? You do that and you'll never catch him." Ness looked at him levelly. "Don't make me take you off this case, Detective."

"You wouldn't dare."

"I would. The press might see it as a positive development."

"Matowitz knows I'm the best detective he's got."

"Matowitz will go along with anything I want."

Merylo could feel the bile rising in his throat. Ness's words wouldn't sting so much — if he didn't know they were true.

"Look, Detective, you've been under a lot of stress. Go home. Spend some time with your wife. Have a drink or two. You'll see things differently in the morning."

"I don't think so."

"And then, if you want to continue tailing your suspect, you do that. From a discreet distance. Maybe eventually you'll get some real evidence, something that might justify the gigantic risk of bringing in the congressman's cousin. Something so telling that the press couldn't possibly criticize us for bringing him in." He paused. "But you don't have it yet. And we're not touching this man until you do."

Merylo opened the office door. "I will be back."

Ness nodded. "I'm counting on it."

48

Ness tiptoed quietly into the house. Once again, he was late. Probably he should've gone to the apartment. But he had told Edna he was coming home tonight. He felt as if they were making a little progress — had been ever since that party for the mayor. If only he didn't have to spend so much time on this torso case. And then there was a flare-up on the labor front. Then Burton summoned him in for an emergency strategy meeting. And . . .

And the next thing he knew, he was late. Exactly what Edna had been complaining about for so long. He'd done it again.

He poked his head through the bedroom door. She was asleep. Wearing her best, silken nightgown, too, he noticed.

Maybe he should give her a gentle nudge, see if she woke up. Or maybe that would lead to more embarrassment . . .

She was a lovely woman, Edna was. Ten-

419

der. Sweet. She looked beautiful lying there, her head on the pillow, her brown curls poking out from under the covers. Absolutely lovely . . .

But when he was on the job . . . on the chase . . . bursting through doors and catching thugs with their pants down . . . well, there was nothing like that. Nothing at all.

He gently closed the bedroom door. He'd see her in the morning. If she got up before he went to work. They'd have a chance to talk then, with any luck.

He returned to the living room and started to sit down on the sofa, but Edna's enormous purse was lying in the center, tipped over on one side. He picked it up . . .

Something fell out.

He started to reach for it — then realized it was a postcard.

His heart began to race. His legs felt wobbly. He sat down, breathed deeply, then took the card into his hands.

On the outside, it was just like all the others. A city view of beautiful Cleveland, taken before congestion and smog made it dark and sooty. It was addressed to *Eliot "Weak" Ness*. The message contained but a single word.

TOUCHABLE.

It bore no stamp or postmark.

It had been in Edna's purse.

Without even thinking about it, Ness picked up the phone and dialed.

"Merylo? Yes, I know what time it is. Listen to me. I've had a change of heart. I want you to bring in the doctor."

He waited while a groggy voice on the other end of the line tried to assimilate what it was hearing.

"Yes, I know what I'm saying. No, I haven't been drinking. Yes, I've had some thoughts about that, too. We'll rent a hotel room. Do the whole thing in secret. No one at the station needs to know about it. Just you and me and a couple of handpicked men I can trust to keep their yaps shut."

There was more rattling on the other end of the line, as Merylo ran through every objection Ness had made earlier in the day.

"Yes, well, I've had some thoughts about that, too. Didn't your lady at the Sailors' Home say he's been sober for a long time now? He's about due for a bender. Keep an eye on him. As soon as he's good and sloshed, grab him. Anyone questions us, we'll say he was drunk and disorderly. And once we have him in custody, we can ask him about anything we want."

49

Merylo had been told to wait until Dr. Sweeney was seriously intoxicated, but it was possible he had waited too long. He arrested the man for public drunkenness and, as directed, brought him through the back door and up the rear stairs to a private room in the Cleveland Hotel. But Sweeney was so far gone that they spent the first three days just waiting for him to dry out.

When he was finally sober — and desperate for a drink — the questioning began. Merylo wanted to do it, but the safety director had insisted on handling it himself. Merylo wasn't surprised. Even though he was the one who found the man, if there was going to be a confession, or even a slip leading to an arrest, Ness would want to be able to take credit for it.

Ness closed the drapes across the windows and made the room totally dark, all but for one light dangling low in the center of the room between the questioner and the questioned. Merylo and Zalewski and Chamberlin were allowed to watch, but they remained in the darkness.

Sweeney was handcuffed to his chair, but it was hard to imagine that he could be any threat. He wore several days' stubble and stinking wrinkled clothes. His mustache was in bad need of a trim. His glasses were bent and they rested crookedly on his face. His eyes were bloodshot and his face looked tired. It took a lot of imagination to envision this dissipated drunk as the sadistic murderer of ten people.

Ness stared across the room at Sweeney, his voice level, his expression even.

"Hello. My name is Eliot Ness."

"I'm all atwitter."

"You know who I am?"

"Doesn't everyone?"

"Do you understand why you're here?"

"I assume you must think I'm running hooch."

"No."

"Or you think I'm running the mob. Do you think I'm running the mob?"

"No."

"Isn't that what you do? Track down mobsters and make them pay their taxes?"

"Not this time."

"Then can I go home?"

Ness took a long deep breath. "Please state your name."

"Gaylord Sundheim."

"We know perfectly well that is not your name."

"Then why did you ask?"

"Is your name Francis Edward Sweeney?"

"I think you're better off with Gaylord Sundheim. Because if word gets out who I really am, you're going to be in serious trouble."

Ness ignored him. "And your friends call you Frank, right?"

"I'm not sure I have any friends."

"And you currently live at the Sandusky Soldiers' and Sailors' Home?"

"If you can call that living."

"And you've killed ten people and then mutilated and discarded their bodies."

A slow smile lifted the corners of Sweeney's mouth. "Don't be absurd. I'm a doctor."

"Exactly. Good with your hands. Good with a knife."

"Are you interrogating all the doctors in town?"

"No."

"Just the ones with relatives in the Democratic party?"

"Just the ones who worked with Edward Andrassy."

"Ah."

"Did you know Flo Polillo?"

"We had a few . . . encounters."

"And Rose Wallace?"

"A little skinny for my taste."

"And somehow, you all got involved in something. Something that went bad. So bad you had to kill everyone involved."

"Is that what you think? Or your police crony?"

"That's what I think. The detective thinks you like to have sex with victims and corpses."

"And you disagree?"

"I don't think a total madman could pull off what the Torso Killer has done and get away with it. The Mad Butcher may be a murderer, but he is also smart."

"And you don't think it's possible for a man to be smart *and* crazy?"

"I've visited lunatic asylums. That's not what I saw."

"Maybe the Torso Killer is something new. Something special."

"In my experience, every crook thinks he's something special. But they still get caught eventually."

"Exactly my point. You caught them. But

not the Mad Butcher. What's the difference?"

"Why don't you tell me?"

"I'm sure I don't know."

"We've taken your prints. We're running
tests on your clothes. We're going to search
your room at the Home. We have science on
our side."

"Oh, my. Well, if you have science, you'll
undoubtedly catch your killer. I'm surprised
you didn't catch him ten victims ago. Or
perhaps more."

"Have there been more? Some we haven't
discovered yet?"

His sickening smile intensified. "How
would I know?"

"Are you the Mad Butcher?"

"I told you already. I'm Gaylord Sundheim." He shrugged his shoulders and
grinned like the Cheshire cat.

Merylo wanted to hit him so badly he
could taste it.

After three hours of questioning, all of it
unproductive, Ness agreed to take a break.
Zalewski went out for sandwiches. Merylo
went downtown to visit a judge he knew,
told him discreetly what was happening, got
a warrant, and searched Dr. Sweeney's
room at the Sailors' Home with a man from

the forensics lab.

They found nothing. No knives, no traces of victim's clothing, no heads, no blood. Merylo assumed Sweeney didn't bring his victims back here, but he had hoped to at least find a bloodstained knife. No such luck.

He didn't know why Ness had changed his mind about interrogating Sweeney, but he did realize that Ness had climbed out on a very shaky branch and if the limb broke, Merylo would likely be the scapegoat. This suspect had no priors, no criminal record of any kind. He was related to a Democratic congressman and perhaps worst of all, he was a physician — someone investigators had repeatedly refused to believe could commit these crimes. If they didn't get something out of the interrogation, this could turn very bad, very quickly.

As soon as everyone returned to the hotel room, the questioning resumed.

"Am I correct in my belief," Ness asked, "that since you lost your job at the hospital, your cousin the congressman has been supporting you?"

"A man's got to eat."

"That's why most men work."

"I've had some problems."

"Are you talking about the booze? Or

something else?"

"I am rather fond of a drink. Every now and then." The suspect's eyes burned toward Ness's. "You've known the comfort that comes from a bottle yourself on occasion, haven't you?"

Ness's forehead creased. "Are you joking? Me?"

"The self-righteous often have the most to hide."

"Let's get this conversation back on track. Why is your cousin supporting you?"

"I lost my position. And my license. You know that."

"Why are you staying at the Sailors' Home?"

"I believe the thinking was that the good woman running the place might be able to help me."

"Was she?"

"No. Problem is, she wants to help me in a way that doesn't interest me. She's a very energetic woman for her age."

"Why don't you move?"

"A deal was brokered. I have to remain at the Home, at least for now. My dear cousin was able to avoid a great deal of trouble by telling the folks at the hospital that I had been institutionalized."

"But Detective Merylo tells me you're free

to leave whenever you please."

"Shhh!"

"And Mrs. McGovern says you sometimes disappear for days."

"A man's got to have some fun every now and then."

"So what do you do when you're having fun?"

"Haven't you ever wanted to cut loose, Mr. Ness?"

"Funny you should use the word 'cut.' "

"Nothing funny about it."

Ness pushed himself out of his chair and began pacing, wringing his hands. "You were fired by the hospital administrative staff."

"Busybodies."

"What did you do?"

"Didn't they tell you?"

"No. They said it was confidential. Involved doctor-patient confidences."

"How deliciously unhelpful of them."

Ness's lips thinned. His face flushed. Merylo thought he was be coming visibly frustrated and angry. "Why do I get the impression you're not taking this seriously?"

"Possibly because I'm not."

"You should. Do you understand why you're here?"

"Apparently you think I'm the Torso Murderer."

"I have a lot of evidence that tells me you're the Torso Murderer."

"Then I guess it must be so."

The room fell dead silent. Ness and Merylo exchanged an uncertain look.

Ness leaned in close. "Did you just confess?"

"All I did was agree with what you said. I'm sure you wouldn't mislead me. If you say you have evidence, you must have evidence."

"I do."

"May I see it?"

"No."

"Have I been charged?"

"Not yet."

"If you have so much evidence, why haven't I been charged?"

"That's really none of your business."

"Am I under arrest?"

"No."

"Well now, this is perplexing. All this evidence against me, but you haven't arrested me or even charged me. Does my cousin know I'm here?"

"No."

"When he finds out, this party will end. You'll be lucky to keep your job."

"Is that a threat?"

"I'm just saying. Maybe the smartest thing would be to call him now. Offer to turn me over to his custody. Apologize for the inconvenience."

"You really must be crazy."

"How will you explain keeping me prisoner when you're not prepared to proffer charges?"

"I like to take things slow and careful."

"Ah. Is it entirely legal to hold a man against his will for several days without charging him or arresting him?"

Ness did not reply. A phone rang. Chamberlin took the call. A few moments later, he turned on the tabletop radio, but kept it down low.

"This is all very strange," the suspect continued. "Perhaps I should have gone to law school rather than medical school. I think I'd like to retain a lawyer."

"You don't need a lawyer. You need to tell me the truth."

"I'm done talking to you. You're no fun."

Ness's face tensed up so much Merylo thought he might explode. "Have you been sending me those postcards?"

Merylo's lips parted. *What?*

"Why would I send you postcards? I haven't been on vacation."

"Did you?"

"Is sending postcards illegal?"

"Trying to interfere with an ongoing investigation is illegal. Threatening law enforcement personnel and their families is illegal."

"Did any of those postcards actually threaten you?"

Ness's eyes narrowed. "You did send them."

"And even if I did, would that prove I was the Torso Killer?"

"Why did you send them to me?"

"You might as well ask why someone would kill and dismember ten people."

"Okay, why?"

"I can't imagine."

"I know a doctor who thinks this has to do with a warped childhood. That you get some kind of . . . gratification out of kill-ing."

"How deliciously Freudian."

"Is it true?"

"I doubt it. Haven't the victims been of both sexes?"

"Yeah."

"Was there any sign of sexual activity?"

"No."

"Well then. It doesn't make much sense, does it?"

"Then why did you kill those people?" Ness barked. "What did they do to you?"

"You always act as if being killed is some sort of punishment, even though you know those people were the lowest of the low. Did it ever occur to you that the killer might have been doing them a favor?"

"How would killing anyone be doing them a favor?"

"What did they have to live for?"

"No one deserves to die. Especially not the way you do it."

"Some people are much too tied to the flesh."

"What are you talking about?"

"Pimps. Prostitutes. Con artists. Flesh peddlers. No chance of advancement or maturity."

"Is that why you're so obsessed with Kingsbury Run?"

"Man is the most dangerous game. And these are the killing fields."

"What are you talking about?"

"Many Eastern religions talk of achieving a higher plane. One must leave the flesh behind and become all spirit. Pure soul."

"And killing them accomplishes that?"

"Many African tribes perform blood rituals. Ceremonies. Sacrificial rites. To help troubled souls ascend."

"And the person performing the rite?"

For the first time, the suspect's eyes widened. The tiniest flicker of light shone within. "He becomes a god."

Ness didn't know what to say to that.

The silence was shattered by Chamberlin's voice. "Eliot?"

"Did you hear what he just —"

"I think you need to listen to this. On the radio."

"Are you kidding? He just —"

"It's Walter Winchell."

Chamberlin turned up the volume on the radio. The announcer spoke with a clipped dramatic urgency.

". . . the unsolved torso murders in Cleveland may result in the apprehension of someone connected to one of Cleveland's most outstanding citizens. This is what I've heard from a source inside the police department whose name I promised to withhold. A medical man with great skill is allegedly responsible for the gruesome crimes in which all the murdered were dismembered. My source tells me that Cleveland's famed safety director is currently interrogating the suspect in a secret hideaway far from the prying eyes of the city and its citizens. Attention, Cleveland, Ohio. This could mean that at any moment, a breakthrough . . ."

Ness turned to face his suspect.

He was smiling.

"That's it then," Sweeney said, with a voice both elated and eerily suggestive. "The party's over. Now it's time to pay the tab."

50

The knock on the hotel room door came less than an hour after the broadcast.

Ness opened the door. Chief Matowitz stood on the other side. Ness did not recognize the other man, but the briefcase and the three-piece suit with the carnation boutonniere gave him a clue.

"Sorry, Eliot," the chief mumbled. "Had no choice."

"This is a private interrogation," Ness began. "We can't be interrupted for —"

"My name is Carlton P. Danvers," the other man said, stepping forward. "I'm a lawyer. I represent the man you are keeping in there against his will."

"He hasn't spoken to a lawyer. He only just sobered up —"

"I was hired by his cousin and given a full retainer. It's perfectly legal."

"We're in the middle of an interrogation and —"

"No, this interrogation is over." Before Ness could stop him, Danvers pushed the door open. His eyebrow arched. "Hand-cuffs, Mr. Ness?"

"For his own safety. He went on an alcoholic binge. Spent three days shaking it off. Had the d.t.'s. We were afraid he might hurt himself."

"What do you take me for, a fool?" Danvers strode into the hotel room as if he had rented it himself. "Four men, barely any light, handcuffs. Did you train with the Bolsheviks?"

"We believe this man may be implicated in the torso murders."

"Indeed. And what hard evidence do you have?"

Ness stumbled a moment. "He knew some of the victims. He has medical expertise."

"And that's your proof?"

"You should hear what he's been saying."

"You're right, I should, but I didn't, because you kidnapped him and held him in violation of his constitutional rights. Did he confess?"

"In a manner of speaking."

"Didn't you tell me he was suffering from an alcoholic delirium?"

"He's over it. He's —"

"Is that your medical opinion, Mr. Ness?

When did you get your medical degree? This poor man looks to me as if he needs medical attention."

"He's fine."

"I'm taking him away. Now."

"Just a minute." Ness jumped in front of Danvers, blocking his way. "I'm not done with him."

"I told you already. This interrogation is over."

"I'll be the one who decides when it's over."

Danvers drew up his shoulders. "I think you're in quite enough trouble already, Mr. Ness. You have held this man a prisoner in clear violation of his constitutional and God-given rights."

"I'm the safety director. I was appointed by the mayor to —"

"Is this man under arrest?"

"Not at this time."

"Then I'm taking him."

Again, Ness blocked his way. "He's not going anywhere until I've had a chance to finish what I started."

"Mr. Ness, do you want me to get a warrant?"

Behind Danvers, Ness could see Chamberlin silently shaking his head no.

"Because if I apply for a warrant, that will

438

mean a hearing before a judge. At that hearing, I will have to describe the unconscionable conduct that I have witnessed being perpetrated on a poor man suffering from a disease and committed to a rehabilitative facility, practiced for days entirely against his will. I will not only get my warrant, you will likely be censured, if not forced to resign, removed from your post, etc. Is this something you want to read about in the morning papers, Mr. Ness?"

Ness's head was swimming. He'd been working much too long. Interrogating Sweeney, trying to make some sense out of what he was saying. Now this. He didn't know what to do.

"Let me answer for you, Eliot," Matowitz said, jumping in. "That is not what you want."

"I'll make that decision."

"No, you won't. Not this time. I'm the chief of police and this is still a police investigation. I don't want a lawsuit on my hands and I'm certain the mayor doesn't, either. Especially not when it involves Congressman Sweeney."

"Fine. Then I'll charge the man."

"With what?"

Ness's brain raced. "Drunk and disorderly."

Matowitz rolled his eyes. "Not tax evasion?" He turned his attention to Danvers. "You may take your client. Eliot, uncuff him."

"I'm telling you, Chief, he may be the killer."

"I told you to uncuff him, and I expect it to be done. Now!"

Ness removed the cuffs.

"There will be no more harassment or persecution of this man," Matowitz added. "You will leave him alone. Totally."

"Here is my business card, Mr. Ness," Danvers said, as he took Sweeney by the arm and led him out of the hotel room. "You will contact me if you want anything. You will have no contact with my client whatsoever unless I am present. If you wish to continue this conversation, you will schedule a mutually convenient appointment. Good day."

Just before they exited, Sweeney turned and . . .

Neither Ness nor Merylo knew how to describe the expression on the man's face. There was something in his eyes that hadn't been there before, something new and repulsive — and eerie. It wasn't exactly a smile, or a frown, or a sneer. It was more like a promise.

Chief Matowitz closed the door behind them.

"What do you think?" Ness said quietly, after they were gone.

"About what?" Merylo grunted.

"You think he's the killer?"

Merylo hesitated. "The only thing I'm sure about is this: You haven't heard the end of this business."

"I want Sweeney followed."

"I can't do that. You heard the chief."

"You work for me."

"I can't go against the chief. 'Sides, his cousin will keep him under wraps, at least for a while. You need to prepare for whatever else the congressman may do."

"Like what?"

"I don't know," Merylo said quietly. "But it won't be pretty."

51

From the August 16, 1938, *Cleveland News:*

". . . but so far all attempts to verify Mr. Winchell's story have been unavailing. Given the man's enormous reputation as a reporter, and the fact that he has a wider range of sources than any journalist in this country, this paper believes there must be some truth to the report. The safety director has refused to comment, other than to say that he is not prepared to make an arrest at this time.

"Congressman Sweeney was willing to talk with reporters. He said that this is simply more evidence of the safety director's unfitness to lead this investigation and his increasing desperation to preserve his overstated reputation. According to Sweeney, the safety director might well resort to desperate measures in order to close this investigation or to stifle the voices of critics such as himself. According to this elected official, Cleveland will never be safe until the investigation is put in the hands of more experienced and reliable . . ."

"I'm telling you, Eliot. It doesn't look good."

The Banker stood in Ness's office. He wouldn't sit. He paced. He was obviously nervous about being here, where he might be seen, during the daylight hours.

"We were following up a valid lead."

"I don't care. It stinks to high heaven."

"I can't help it that the suspect happens to be related to some political muckety-muck."

"That isn't the problem and you know it. The problem is that Sweeney has been an outspoken critic of you. Probably your most vocal opponent. And now you turn around and investigate his cousin."

"That had nothing to do with it."

"And the louder you say that, the more the press will suggest that it did. So will most of their readers."

"I don't believe that. I've always had a good relationship with the press."

"Oh, Eliot, how naïve can you possibly be?" The Banker pressed his hand against his forehead. "No one has a good relationship with the press. They'll be friendly if there's a story in it, sure. And they'll turn on you in a heartbeat, if there's a story in it. Their only allegiance is to the headline."

"I've made plenty of those for them."

"Which is exactly the problem. In a very real way, you've brought this on yourself."

Ness rose to his feet, his face uncomprehending. "What are you saying?"

"I'm saying this is your own fault. You courted the press. You used them to make your name, both in Chicago and here. You gave yourself a high profile. If you were less known, there would be no story. But when a shadow falls on the famed gangbuster, the press circle like vultures."

"I never courted the press. They always came to me."

"Let's not play word games, Eliot. I warned you a long time ago that you had no head for politics. And now politics are going to eat you alive."

"It's this blasted investigation that's eating me. I never wanted it. I tried to avoid it."

"Did you, Eliot? Did you really? Wasn't there even some small part of you that said, Hey, I nabbed Capone. I can bring in this murderer, too?"

"No."

"Did you envision the headlines? The accolades? NESS SAVES CITY FROM THE MAD BUTCHER. That had to be tempting."

"You're totally wrong."

"Maybe you aren't content with the Office of the Safety Director. Maybe you saw this as your ticket to greater things. Maybe you fancied a run for mayor."

"You're barking up the wrong tree."

"Doesn't matter. The important thing is that you drop this business with Sweeney's cousin."

"I've already released him. I don't even know where he is. His lawyer seems to have spirited him away."

"I think it would be best if you offered Congressman Sweeney a formal apology."

"What?"

"I'm not the only one who thinks so. I've talked to the others and they agree."

Ness fell back into his chair. "I don't believe it. You want me to apologize to that man? After everything he's done and said?"

"Doesn't have to be anything formal. Definitely don't put anything down on paper. Just call the man up. Scratch his ears a little bit. Might do more than just smooth over this current kerfuffle. Might work to your advantage in the long run." He paused.

"Especially if you have political ambitions."

"I will not apologize to that blowhard."

"Eliot." The Banker leaned against the edge of Ness's desk. "Maybe I need to make myself clearer. This is not merely a request. This is something we want you to do."

"Are you giving me an order?"

"We're asking for a favor. After all we've given you — our support, our money — it seems little enough to give us in return."

"I'm sorry. I won't do it. For all I know, Sweeney's cousin really is the killer."

The Banker sighed heavily, shaking his head. "Then I'm sorry, Eliot. If that's the way you're going to be about it — I'm afraid this is the end of the Unknowns. We're not going to continue to fund an operation that might prove . . . embarrassing."

"You're scared of Sweeney?"

"We're businessmen, Eliot. Businessmen during the hardest economic crisis this nation has ever faced. We can't afford to get on the wrong side of a congressman."

"I don't believe it."

"Doesn't look to me as if our money has accomplished much anyway. Your man is no closer to solving this case than you are. Nothing personal, Eliot — but I think you should have stayed at the Treasury Department."

"The mayor hired me to clean up this city."

"The mayor hired you because he thought he would get favorable coverage and it would fulfill his promise to be a Reform mayor. But he's been distancing himself, Eliot."

"What?"

"Surely you've noticed. If you'd brought in the killer, fine, he'd reclaim you as his own. But you haven't." He shook his head. "If I were you, I'd start looking for another job. Before it's a necessity."

"I got rid of the crooked cops, the labor racketeers. Brought juvenile crime down to nearly nothing. Reduced traffic fatalities to a tenth what they were. I have been a good safety director!"

"But that isn't the point, is it? When are you going to see that? You're only as good as your last success. And one mistake can erase everything."

Ness's fists clenched. "I have done all I could think of to solve this case."

"Maybe so." The Banker took his hat off the rack. "But as long as people keep on dying, that's not going to be enough."

The Banker left the office without saying another word.

Ness grabbed the phone, furious. The

Banker thought he could be fired, after all he'd done? Ridiculous. He'd been a huge plus to the mayor's administration. Accomplished more than all the previous safety directors combined. And he was still following up leads on the Torso Killer. It was only a matter of time . . .

The operator connected him with the mayor's office.

"Eliot Ness. I need to speak to the mayor. Immediately."

"Just a moment."

The line went silent. About a minute later, the female voice returned.

"I'm sorry, Mr. Ness. The mayor isn't able to speak with you right now."

"When will he be able to speak to me?"

"The mayor was unable to give me a time."

"Well, look at his calendar. When will he be free?"

There was a moment of hesitation. "I don't think he's ever going to be free . . . for you, Mr. Ness."

"What the heck does that mean?" Ness said, practically shouting into the phone.

She cleared her throat. "I believe it means that the mayor doesn't wish to speak to you."

"But I need to talk to him!"

"I'm afraid that won't be possible."

"Just tell him that I —"

The line disconnected in midsentence.

Ness threw the receiver down so hard it bounced against the cradle and flew off the side of his desk. What had happened? How had the world turned upside down so quickly? All he did was interrogate a man he thought might be the killer. What was wrong with these people?

He was breathing hard and fast, barely able to catch his breath, sweating profusely. What was happening? He'd stayed cool when the moonshiners were after him with their squirrel guns, but now he was getting palpitated by these bankers and politicians.

He glanced at his watch. It was past dinnertime.

Edna. Good grief — for a while there he'd thought their relationship was improving. But since Merylo brought him Sweeney . . .

How many days had it been since he'd spoken to her, much less come home? He couldn't even remember.

He should go see her, now. There was no point in staying here. He had nothing to do and any more work on this case might blow up in his face. He'd go home and see Edna and make up for all the time spent apart while he tried to make the city better for these ungrateful people. He'd call her right now and tell her he was heading home.

He placed the call. The phone rang. No answer.

He let it ring ten times. Still no answer.

Where could she possibly be this time of night? On a weekday. It didn't make any sense. Unless . . .

Unless she'd finally done it. Unless she'd had enough and gone and done it.

Without even having a conscious thought, he reached for the bottom desk drawer, pulled it open, and removed the flask.

He sipped at first. The warm liquid coated his throat. He could feel his respiration returning to normal. His breathing was back under control.

He heard Chamberlin approaching seconds before he opened the door. He barely had time to get the flask back in the drawer before he entered.

"Boss?" Chamberlin did a double take. "Are you all right, Eliot?"

"I'm fine. What's up. More bad news?"

"I'm afraid so."

"Am I fired?" he asked, licking his lips.

Chamberlin stared at him, puzzled. "Fired? No. I mean, not that I know of. Is there some reason — ?"

"Never mind. What is it?"

"It's . . . the Torso Murderer, sir."

"Don't tell me he killed another victim."

Chamberlin swallowed. "Two."

"Two?"

"At the same time, sir. Bodies found in Kingsbury, not far from Shantytown. Detective Merylo is already on the scene. Would you like to come?"

"Yes. Of course. I'll be right there. Just give me a minute."

"Of course, sir." Chamberlin closed the door.

Ness opened the bottom desk drawer and poured the entire flask down his throat. Then he grabbed his hat and coat and made his way out the door.

52

Ness stared down at the brown paper mess unearthed in the midst of the trash dump. His lips parted, dry, thick.

"He's getting worse," Ness said quietly. "Not better. Worse."

Merylo laid a hand on his shoulder. "You okay? You seem a little shaky."

"What human being wouldn't be after seeing . . . that?" Ness wiped his mouth with his sleeve. "Who found it?"

Merylo nodded to his assistant. Zalewski stepped forward. "Man named James Dawson. Scrap and junk dealer. Was sorting through all this, looking for something he could sell."

"Where did this trash come from, anyway? I don't remember a dump being here. They just got Lake Shore Drive finished."

"Most of this refuse was left behind by the Great Lakes Exposition. There were plans to cart it somewhere, but it never happened. Dawson was rooting around, looking for iron, and he saw flies buzzing around a pile of rocks. Looked a little closer and saw a coat sticking out. Moved a few rocks — and found this."

Ness peered down at the mound again. "He called the police?"

"Yes, but word leaked out. There was a crowd here before the police arrived. We've been trying to contain them, but the mob is growing by the minute."

Ness stared out at the teeming throng surrounding the crime scene. He had never seen so many people gathered in one place in Cleveland. According to Merylo, it was larger than the grotesque group of rubberneckers that watched while Victim 6 was pulled out of the lake. And they were angry. He could sense it. Restless. They shouted at the police. Waved fists. Called names. He could not placate them. If anything, Ness thought their anger increased when he emerged onto the scene.

They knew the Butcher had struck again, but they had no idea how horrific the spectacle truly was. And that was a good thing. Beneath the pile of rocks and several large pieces of concrete, a human torso had been wrapped in brown paper. Butcher's paper? Ness wondered. And if so, was that a clue — or the killer's sick idea of a joke? Beneath the torso they found another package, also wrapped in brown paper and held together by a rubber band. It contained the thighs. Five feet away, they found the head, and not far from that, in a brown cardboard box, the arms and lower legs. A thorough search of the dump produced yet another corpse, also dismembered, also wrapped up neatly and efficiently.

Ness looked away, hoping to never look again. "What can you tell me, Dr. Pearce?"

Pearce stepped forward, fingering his wire-rimmed glasses. Ness noticed that in addition to his white suit, he was wearing white buck shoes. Probably hadn't realized he'd be visiting a trash dump when he dressed this morning.

"Not much," Pearce answered, glancing over his shoulder at the mob. "Isn't there some way to cordon them off? They might contaminate the evidence." He lowered his voice. "Or find the next corpse. Before we do."

"We got here too late," Zalewski explained. "They were already all over the site. We pushed them back as far as we could with the available manpower."

"Get more men," Pearce said, then turned his attention back to Ness. "I think one of the torsos belongs to a woman, but these bodies are so badly decomposed I can't be sure about anything."

"How long have they been dead?"

"Months. Perhaps half a year. But I don't think they've been out here that long. They would be in worse shape than they are if they had."

"Then the killer has some place he stores bodies? Till he's ready for us to find them?"

"Seems likely. Maybe he still has some parts hidden away. It would explain why we've found so few heads."

"Why give us heads now?"

"You're asking for a logical explanation," Pearce said. "I doubt if there is one."

"Anything else?"

"The dismemberment appears to be much the same as the others. Head disarticulated at the level of the third intervertebral disk. Knife marks on the dorsum of the second and third cervical vertebrae."

"While they were alive?"

"Most likely. I'll need to run some tests."

"Is he still using that preservative?"

"It's possible. And that could throw off all my estimates about time of death. Until further testing."

"Anything else you can tell me?"

Pearce used his walking stick as a pointer.

"Apparently he reads."

Surrounding the gray bodily remains they had also found the usual assortment of tantalizing but ultimately unhelpful items: two burlap bags, a coat, a multicolored quilt, and the March 5 issue of *Collier's*.

"I want someone to read every word of that magazine," Ness said. "And then explain to me why the killer might have read it. Or left it behind."

Merylo grimaced. "I'll do it. But we won't find anything."

"Don't quit before the job is done."

"This killer is smart. And orderly. He wouldn't leave anything that might be helpful."

"Then why leave anything at all?"

"Because he's playing with us. Giving us the horselaugh. He gets kicks out of that, like the alienist told us." Merylo drew in his breath. "Because he knows we can't catch him."

Ness felt the words burrow into his brain. *Because he knows we can't catch him.* He *knows.*

Momentarily distracted from the evidence, Ness heard shouts coming from the all-too-close crowd.

"When are you going to catch this madman?"

"Why aren't you protecting us?"

"How many people are going to have to die before you do something?"

To the amazement of his colleagues, Ness turned toward the crowd, hands spread wide open. "We're doing everything we possibly can."

"You would've caught him long ago if he were killing people uptown!"

"No one cares about us!"

"He's making you look like a fool!"

Ness turned away. "Do you hear them, Merylo? Do you hear what they're saying?"

Merylo looked puzzled. "Who? The crowd?"

"They're laughing at us. Just like the killer is. Everyone is laughing at us."

"I don't hear anything. No point in listening to that mob."

"Get rid of them," Ness said, under his breath. "Disperse the crowd. Miles away."

"I'm not sure we have the right," Zalewski said. "This is public property."

"This is a crime scene. They're interfering with an official investigation."

"We'll need a lot more men."

"Then get them!" Ness snapped. "Get them now!"

Zalewski glanced at Merylo. Merylo nodded. "I'll get right on it, sir." He skittered away.

Ness approached Merylo, much too close, laying his hands on the man's shoulders. "We have to do something, Merylo. We have to catch this killer."

"We've been trying. We don't have anything. Our best suspect got away."

"We have to find someone else. We have to end this."

"I agree. But how? He owns this neighborhood. It's his own private hunting ground."

All at once, the words flashed through Ness's memory like a branding iron on flesh. *Man is the most dangerous game. And these are the killing fields.*

"That's it," Ness murmured under his breath. "That's the answer."

"What?" Merylo said, his face contorted. "What are you talking about?"

"He was giving us a clue."

"Are you feeling all right? I think maybe you need some rest. Get some shut-eye. You'll feel better in the morning."

Ness pushed away from him. "No. We have a busy night ahead, Detective."

"Doing what?"

"We need more men. Lots more. Forget about the crowd. Call everyone you know at the department. I'll call my people.

Maybe we can even get some loaners from the fire department."

"To do what?"

"It's simple, Merylo. Why didn't I see it before? If we can't catch the killer, we'll remove his prey."

"And how are we going to do that?"

"By taking Shantytown away from him."

"Are you kidding? Do you know how many people are living out there? They'll never agree to move."

Ness peered straight ahead, his eyes fixed and glassy. "We won't give them a choice."

53

Ness stood in the midst of the assembled officers and volunteers at the top of the Eagle Street ramp, just on the edge of Shantytown. It was a pitch-black night, but from their vantage point they could still see the sprawling hobo village stretching out in the distance. Ness had managed to assemble twenty-five detectives and uniformed police officers. Several firemen and a fire truck. They were armed with clubs, guns, flashlights, hammers. Ness was carrying an axe handle, the same implement he had used to break down the doors of speakeasies and hooch warehouses. They were all hanging on his every word, ready to implement his instructions on his command.

"McDonald. I want you to take your men to the hill at the junction of Commercial and Canal. Stop anyone trying to slip out the back way."

"Understood."

"Go." They did. "Marshall Granger?"

"Yes, sir."

"I want you to park your truck at the crest of the ramp. Shine an arc lamp down on Shantytown. I want to be able to see what we're doing. I want to see everything."

"Understood."

"Good. Do it."

He split the remaining men into groups, then divided Shantytown, giving each of them a piece. "I want everyone taken out for questioning, then removed. No one takes anything with them. I don't want any evidence disappearing."

"Yes, sir."

"Consider this a military operation. An attack behind enemy lines. We miss nothing."

"Yes, sir!" the men responded.

"And then," Ness said quietly, "we make sure they never come back."

Ness led his team down the ramp and into Shantytown. Almost no one was up and about this late at night. Ness was instantly assaulted by the pungent smell of cheap liquor, human waste, boiled chicken. It was like stomping through the sewer. He hated it, but he kept marching forward, scattering stray cats with almost every step, plunging deep into the twisted heap of cardboard boxes and canvas and corrugated metal.

Ness pounded the door of the first hovel he reached with his axe handle. "Police! Open up!"

There was no response, but Ness could hear movement inside.

"Open up! This is your last chance!"

Chamberlin laid a hand on his shoulder. "Boss, even if it's made out of metal, it's still a home. They have rights."

Ness shrugged him away. "He's a squatter, Bob. He's not supposed to be here."

"But —"

"We're coming in!"

Ness battered away at the flimsy metal door. It didn't take much to knock it down.

The men shone their flashlights inside. The squalor was shocking. Chicken bones on the ground, several days old. Almost a dozen empty booze bottles. It stank worse in here than it did outside.

In the rear, a grizzled old man cowered, trying to hide himself in blankets. "D-d-didn't . . . do anything!"

"You'll have to vacate immediately," Ness said.

"I'm . . . not goin' anywhere! I d-d-didn't do anything!"

"You're drunk. Drunk and disorderly. Haul him away, men!"

"No! This is my home!" Two of Ness's officers stepped forward and grabbed the man's arms. "I ain't done nothin' wrong!"

"We just want to talk to you."

"Let me get my things!"

"No.

"This is all I got! All I got in the world!"

"Don't make me arrest you. You're a vagrant, and pursuant to Municipal Code section —"

"I got a job! Down at the factory. But I'll lose it if they find out I've been arrested!"

"You're just being taken in for questioning. Now go!"

"I — I don't unnerstand. My stuff —"

"Believe me, this is for your own good."

"But I don't want to go!"

Ness nodded to his men. "Take him to the way station at the Lorain-Carnegie Bridge. There are trucks waiting to transport the vagrants to the Central Police Station for further questioning. Now!"

Ness stepped outside. All around, he could see his men in action. They were raiding each and every makeshift home, hauling the occupants out. Most of the men looked drunk or hungover, but there were also women and a few children. They were confused, disoriented. They didn't understand why they were being awakened in the middle of the night and herded together. Children cried for their toys and dolls, but they were allowed to take nothing. The land was alive with the thunderous tumult of swearing, pleading, crying, dogs barking, doors being battered down.

Shantytown had become hell on earth.

By three in the morning, every living occupant of Shantytown had been rousted out and herded like human cattle to the nearest way station. Everyone was questioned and fingerprinted. Officers from the Animal Protective League patrolled the now vacant grounds, rounding up stray animals, saving them from what was soon to come. Ness and his men made a final sweep, searching the hovels for stragglers and evidence. They found nothing of value, nothing that related to the torso murders.

When he was sure the area was completely vacated, Ness enlisted the aid of two complete companies of firemen led by Battalion Chief Charles Rees.

"Are you ready, Chief?" Ness asked.

Rees nodded. "At your order, sir."

"The word is given, Chief." Ness turned his eyes toward Shantytown. "Burn it. Burn it to the ground."

The firemen swept through what was left

of Shantytown pouring coal oil on the cardboard boxes, trash, personal property, everything. And when it had been thoroughly soaked, they set it on fire.

The blaze raced through Shantytown with a speed that amazed even Ness. What had only a few hours before been a teeming hobo village was now an inferno. Flames stretched to the sky; from a mile away people could feel the heat. The fire raged like an incinerator grown to the size of a city block, so intense that onlookers had to shield their eyes.

Now Shantytown really was hell on earth.

54

No more Shantytown? But it was so easy!

Perhaps that was the point. He had to admit he was intrigued. Finally, Eliot Ness had become interesting, For so long, he had been predictable. Just another policeman. And now this. How should he respond?

Nothing to do but to proceed with one's work.

But without Shantytown, where would he go to find his people? Perhaps it was time to move on . . .

But the business felt unfinished. Too much left undone. If he was leaving Cleveland, he needed to create some kind of climax worthy of the adventure. Some way to escalate the business, to bring it to a satisfying conclusion. The esteemed safety director had devoted so much time and energy to him. Wouldn't it be delightful if he could turn the tables? Man was the most dangerous game, after all.

He knew where Ness lived. He knew his wife was leaving him.

Endgame. That was what they called it back in the Chess Club. The time had come for the endgame.

The hunter and the hunted should meet. Face-to-face. What kind of conclusion would it be if he never had the satisfaction of looking into those eyes just at the moment when Ness realized how stupid he had been, how painfully ignorant, how utterly at sea?

Ness believed science could solve everything. But he had brought the safety director something science had no answer for.

Ness would never understand, would never realize how foolish he had been.

Till the day he died.

55

Ness slammed shut his bottom desk drawer the instant Chamberlin entered his office.

"Sir, have you seen the article in the *Press*?"

"Is it any different from the others?"

"Much the same. Except perhaps . . . stronger."

"We did the right thing, Bob. I don't care what the newshounds think."

Chamberlin gave him a long look.

"All right, maybe I care. But I won't be second-guessed. I'm the safety director. I have to do what's right for the people."

Chamberlin threw the paper onto Ness's desk. "I think perhaps you'd better read the editorial. Sir."

Ness grabbed the paper and sought out the article in question.

". . . dwellers are not thanking Mr. Ness for his concern about their remaining unidentified if their heads should be chopped off. Nor do they thank him for burning down the village. The net result of the director's raid seems to have been the wrecking of a few miserable huts and the confinement of the occupants. We can see no justification for the jailing of the jobless and penniless men and the wrecking of their miserable hovels without permitting them to collect their personal belongings and . . ."

Ness slapped the paper down on his desk. "Are these people blind? Do they not understand that we might have found evidence identifying the killer?"

"I wish we had," Chamberlin said. "We'd look a lot better."

"If we let people take anything, the killer would've taken everything."

"Some people think he did."

"That's ridiculous." Ness pushed himself out of the chair and began pacing. "If he'd been there, we'd have caught him. He just wasn't there."

"Which unfortunately makes some feel like we burned Shantytown for no good reason. Like we were being cruel to people in need."

"Cruel? Those folks can relocate to the

Wayfarer's Lodge. That's where they should have been in the first place. We can't have people camping out at Kingsbury Run. It's unsafe and unhealthy and perpetuates these murders."

"It still seems cruel to some — taking away from those who have little at all. Like instead of helping them, you're hurting them."

"Why would I do that?" Ness leaned against the windowsill and stared out at the city. "Have there been any more murders since we took away Shantytown?"

"It's only been a week."

"The answer is, no. No more murders."

"That we know of."

"No more murders because we took away the killer's hunting ground. Those vagrants the *Press* is so concerned about were easy pickings for the killer. Now he doesn't know what to do."

"For how long?"

Ness whirled on his assistant. "Are you questioning my judgment?"

Chamberlin thought a moment before answering. "Does it matter?"

Ness's eyes burned into Chamberlin's. "How long have you been against me?"

"I'm not against you."

"But you're attacking me over this Shantytown thing."

"I thought it was a bad idea at the time. I would've told you so. If you'd asked."

"Then I'm glad I didn't. I did the right thing." He paused. "I just didn't go far enough."

"What do you mean?"

"I took away the killer's victims. But that's not good enough for these people. They want more. They want the killer's blood."

"Are you feeling all right? You're talking a little —"

"Fine. I'll give it to them."

Chamberlin's eyes widened. "You know who the killer is?"

"I know how to find him. Flush him out. Should have done it a long time ago."

"Sir . . . I think maybe you need some rest."

"There's no time to rest, Bob. Not with this killer on the loose. All those people, telling me I hadn't done enough. They were right. I said I'd done everything I could, but the truth is, I'd done everything that was safe. Well, it's time to stop being safe."

"I don't like the sound of that much."

"How long have we been chasing this lunatic, Bob? How long? Too long. Round up some men."

"Sir, after this Shantytown fiasco, I don't

think anyone will be too eager . . ."

"I don't need your excuses, Bob. Just find me some men. I'll call Merylo and his assistant. They'll come."

"I'm not so sure. Merylo wasn't happy about —"

"He'll come. He works for me. He understands that it takes extraordinary measures to catch an extraordinary man. Then I'll round up some fire wardens."

"Fire wardens!" Chamberlin's eyes ballooned. "What are you planning now?"

"Don't go into a panic, Bob. I'm not going to burn anything."

"Then why?"

"Just get them, Bob. I'll meet you on East Fifty-fifth, by the Cuyahoga. We're going to find the Torso Murderer. I guarantee it."

The wind was cold coming off the river, but the officers assembled did not notice. They were much too engrossed in the words of the famous man delivering their detailed instructions. He had obviously given this plan much thought, worked out every detail. He split the twelve men into two groups and assigned each their territory. Together they would cover the entire area from East 55th to Prospect Avenue, one of the poorest districts in town, and most of the neighborhoods closest to Kingsbury Run. The two teams would saturate over ten square miles of territory.

"I want every house searched," Ness said, as he handed the leader of each group its map. "Every one. No exceptions."

"What if no one comes to the door?" Merylo asked.

Ness looked at him pointedly. "If you were the Torso Murderer, would you come to the door?"

"Point taken. But don't we need a warrant?"

"You do," Ness said succinctly. "But a fire warden does not."

Merylo's eyebrows rose.

"Pursuant to the Cleveland city charter, a fire warden is authorized to enter any home and conduct a routine fire inspection."

"But — you said we were going into every house."

"Have you looked at these shabby joints? Each of them is a potential fire trap."

Merylo smiled a little. "Understood."

"We know the killer must have some kind of . . . laboratory somewhere in this area. Someplace where he kills his victims without being detected. Someplace he can store body parts until he's ready to distribute them. No matter how good he is, after so

473

many murders, there must be discernable traces. Blood. Bone. Preservative chemicals."

"*Collier's* magazine," Merylo added.

"Whatever. There must be traces. I want you to find them."

"If he's here," Merylo said, "we'll find him."

"One last word," Ness said. "You're probably wondering why I'm only using twelve men. This will probably take you a week, at least. More men could get it done faster. But I don't want to attract attention. I don't want to tip off the killer before we get to his place. I don't want to read about this in the papers. I don't care whether the editorial writers think it's a good idea. It *is* a good idea." He paused. "So go find me that killer."

Merylo pounded on the door. "Police."

He waited. He knew that might conceivably give the occupant a chance to escape, maybe even to destroy evidence. But he also knew breaking down a door could potentially attract attention. So he waited. At least thirty seconds. Unless he heard sounds of rapid movement. After posting someone to cover the rear exit.

No one answered. He asked Zalewski to

take charge. Using only his shoulder, Zalewski had the warped and rickety front door open in fewer than ten seconds.

Slowly, cautiously, they entered, Merylo leading the way. Little light crept in through the window, leaving the house much too dark for Merylo's comfort. The front room — the only room — was barely furnished and filthy. The place stunk like an outdoor toilet. The walls were water-stained. He saw a huge rat skitter across the floor. It was barely a step up from the shacks in Shantytown, if that.

"Disgusting," he murmured under his breath.

In the far corner, a blanket moved. Someone was underneath it.

Brandishing a club, Merylo removed the blanket.

He did not find a person underneath. He found five. An entire family, filthy, dressed in rags, hiding. A man, a woman, and three children, none of them older than six. The man was blurry-eyed and malnourished. They all appeared underweight. Merylo realized that they all lived in this one room, all five of them. Dad was probably drinking his meals, and the others might not be eating at all.

Then he saw the cardboard box in the opposite corner and realized why the place stank so badly. There was no indoor toilet.

"Please don't take me away," the man said, holding out a feeble hand, wheezing as he spoke. "I ain't hurt no one. I'm lookin' for work. Honest. My wife takes in laundry."

Merylo was both touched and appalled by the pathetic spectacle and realized there was no way any resident of this hellhole was a killer. But it was indeed a firetrap.

"I heard what happened to all those people out at Shantytown. Please don't burn down our house. It may not be much, but it's all we've got. I may not be much of a provider, but I don't know what these kids would do without me. Don't break us up, mister. Don't take our stuff away. This is all we've got in the world."

So that was what he thought they were here for. No wonder he hadn't answered the door. Torching Shantytown was a mistake they would never be able to live down.

Merylo drew in his breath. "Sir, I'd like to introduce you to John Perkins. He's the local fire warden . . ."

56

Ness stumbled as he opened the front door. Fortunately, and to his surprise, Edna was there to help him.

"Eliot! Good heavens, Eliot, what's wrong with you?" She took him by the arm and led him to the sofa. "Have you been drinking?"

He looked at her through blurry eyes. "Does it show?"

"Eliot, tell me you didn't drive home. Did your driver bring you?"

Eliot shook his head in a wobbly fashion. "Don't have a driver anymore."

"Think what might have happened if you'd been stopped. The publicity!"

He fell back against the sofa, then pulled a newspaper out of his coat pocket, slurring as he spoke. "Could it be worse than this?"

"... but this reporter has learned that

Mr. Ness has conducted a systematic and probably illegal raid of the entire Kingsbury Run area using the pretense of fire inspections to violate the constitutional rights of our citizens. And the worst of the matter is, once again, his brash and borderline criminal actions have produced nothing of value. He is no closer to catching this killer than he was two years ago. The increasingly desperate actions of this alleged public servant evidence an erratic mind unable to deal with the task put before him. Although the mayor's office had no official comment, insiders have reported that Mayor Burton is seriously considering a replacement for the job of Safety Director. It is time for Mr. Ness to return to Chicago and leave Cleveland to those who are able . . ."

"Oh, Eliot," Edna said, covering her mouth. "That's horrible. How can they be so mean?"

"That's what they do," Ness said, staring at the ceiling. "Vultures. Living off the carcasses of other people's achievements."

"Perhaps you can call that reporter at the *Plain Dealer.* What was his name? He's always been sympathetic to you."

"I don't want anything to do with reporters."

"Well, you should sober up first."

"I'm not drunk." He pushed himself off
the sofa, but he tottered so much he almost
fell forward onto the coffee table. Edna
grabbed a hand to steady him, then helped
him back to the sofa.

"I know how this must have hurt you,
Eliot. You always took so much . . . pleasure
from the attention of the press."

"We found nothing," Eliot said, his voice
gravelly. "My men searched for more than a
week. Every single house in the area. And
they found nothing."

"Maybe the killer saw you coming."

"Or maybe he was never there. Doesn't
matter. I failed."

"Eliot, don't look at it that way. You've
done everything you possibly could."

She nestled his hand inside hers. His head
jerked, staring down at the two joined
hands.

"Thought you'd be gone. Thought you'd
left me."

Edna drew in her breath. "I went to visit
my mother, Eliot. We talked."

"But you came back."

The moment she hesitated before speaking seemed as if it lasted an eternity. "To

get my things." She placed her other hand on the side of his head, slowly turning it to face her. "But I am leaving you, Eliot."

He looked at her helplessly. "Why?"

"Don't bother arguing with me. I can't imagine that you really care, even in this sad state. You just don't want to acknowledge what a disaster this marriage has been. Or how little you've given to it. I don't blame you, Eliot. Honestly, I don't. But there's nothing in this life for me. I want more out of life. I want to feel like I'm really living. I want to be loved."

"You — promised —"

"Please don't start that." She released his hand and rose. "I would've left already, but I didn't think I'd see you tonight any more than I have the past week."

"The raids . . . busy . . ."

"Yes, I know. You're always busy. But not with me, Eliot. Never with me."

"I can do better. I can —"

"Please stop. You've made this promise a thousand times, and you never follow through. And do you know why? Because you don't really want to. Because you like your life apart from me much better than you like your life with me."

"Edna, no . . ."

"It's better this way, Eliot. Honest it is.

Better for both of us."

"At least . . . stay tonight."

She walked to the back room, retrieved her suitcase, and started toward the door. "No, I don't think so. Best that I leave immediately, since you've so kindly brought me the car. I'm taking it. I'll send for the rest of my things." She lingered by the door a moment. "Goodbye, Eliot. I hope you find someone who can give you whatever it is you need. What you never found with me. I really do."

And then she was gone.

Ness fell forward, tears streaming from his eyes. He grabbed the newspaper on the table and ripped it to shreds.

A postcard fell out from between the folds.

The front was a city view of Cleveland, just like all the others. It was addressed to *"Eliot Ridiculous-Ness."*

Ness screamed with rage. He flung himself against the mantel, knocking off the candlesticks and framed pictures. He screamed again, kicking the coffee table so hard it splintered. Then he fell down face first on the sofa, pounding it with his fists.

He remained there the rest of the night.

The message on the postcard was: GOTCHA.

And signed: YOUR PARANOIDAL-NEMESIS.

57

The mayor did not wait for Ness to open his office door.

"Eliot, what in the name of all that's holy is going on?"

Ness looked up at him slowly. "I don't know what you mean."

"I mean —" He stopped in midsentence, staring. "Eliot — have you been drinking?"

"Course not."

"You look horrible. You need a shave."

"I . . . had a rough night." He pushed himself to his feet and tried to stay steady.

"I don't doubt it. I read what those newspapers had to say. Vile stuff. After all you've done for the city. But the fact is, people are scared. They want this monster caught."

"So do I."

"But you haven't been able to bring him in. Mind you, I'm not saying it's your fault. But this is politics."

"I thought it was law enforcement."

"Either way, sometimes you have to toss the people a scapegoat. Cut off the feet to save the head."

"Am I the feet or the head?"

"I think you know the answer to that."

Ness took a few baby steps around his desk, stopping when he got to the mayor. He looked at him through bleary eyes. "You've been talking to Congressman Sweeney, haven't you?"

Mayor Burton harrumphed. "I'm not sure I'd call it talking. More like listening. He's very angry."

"I'm not surprised."

"First you pull that stunt with his cousin."

"Best suspect we ever had."

"Did you ever consider consulting me before you started grilling him?"

"You haven't been taking my calls."

"Then you go and torch Shantytown, again without consulting with me first. Then you pull these raids that you and I both know wouldn't survive judicial scrutiny. Even if you did find the killer we might not be able to convict him."

"I had all that covered."

"Maybe, maybe not. The point is, Sweeney is our political opponent, and you've been giving him the ammunition to destroy us like it was his birthday."

"My job is not political."

"Don't be infantile, Eliot. You've created a serious problem. I'm forced to make a serious response. Much as it pains me —"

"So I'm going to be the scapegoat?"

"You've brought this on yourself."

"I did everything you appointed me to do. And then some."

"Do you think I don't know that? But sometimes, everything is not enough. These people play hardball."

Ness flopped down in the easy chair, sitting sideways and twisting his legs over the arm. "You're afraid of Sweeney."

"That's right, Eliot. I am. And with good reason. I'd like to continue being mayor a while longer, and that man stands between me and what I want. Do you have any idea how powerful he is? How many people he has to do his bidding? How much money he has at his disposal?"

Ness pressed his fingers against his mouth, stifling a hiccup. "I didn't know congressmen made that much money."

"Congressmen? What's that got to do with it? He was born rich. The Sweeneys made their pile years ago, back before Prohibition."

"Mobsters?"

"No. Perfectly legit. Had a brewery on the

riverfront. Not far from where you and your men made your illegal raids."

Ness sat up, suddenly alert. "Near Kingsbury Run?"

"Not too far."

"What happened to it?"

"Closed it down when Prohibition came. Took their profits and invested them. Not in the stock market, lucky for them. In land. They're one of the biggest landlords in all of —"

"Do they still own the brewery?"

"Far as I know. I don't think they could sell it if they wanted to."

"And it's still closed down?"

"Absolutely. Boards on the windows."

"No one goes there? Large open place? Far from prying eyes?"

"I suppose."

"Drainage into the lake?"

"What on earth are you talking about?"

Ness was already halfway into his coat. "I'll be out of the office for a while."

"I'm not finished talking to you!"

"You can fire me tomorrow. Or I'll resign. Whatever you like. Doesn't matter."

"Eliot, you're not making sense. Come back here!"

"Sorry," Ness said, closing the door behind him. "I've got work to do."

58

It was well past dark by the time he finally located the old abandoned Sweeney brewery. Knowing that it was near Kingsbury and on the shore of the Cuyahoga still left a lot of territory to cover. Most of the buildings in this area were worn out or shut down. Still, Ness reminded himself, he was a trained investigator. Even if he wasn't in the best possible condition, some things worked instinctively. He tracked it down and confirmed that he was right with a quick phone call.

He considered calling for more officers, but talked himself out of it. It was clear now that there was a leak. Someone was feeding information to the press. Even after he dramatically purged the police department, there was still someone spitting out the skinny on his activities, his hotel room interrogation, the fire warden raids in the Kingsbury neighborhood. He couldn't take the risk of tipping off the killer — or feeding the press information about yet another failure.

He would go in alone.

He parked well away from the brewery and ran the distance. If he drove anywhere near the brewery itself, anyone inside would hear. It was ridiculously quiet out here, well away from the noise and smoke of the city. A perfect place for someone whose work required privacy.

Slowly he approached the building, careful to make his footfalls light. The gravel on the ground could easily make more noise than he wanted. The windows were all on the upper level and they were indeed boarded up. It was impossible to see inside at any angle, impossible even to tell whether there was a light burning.

On the side facing the river, he found a sliding door unlocked.

Slowly, he depressed the hammer and felt it release. He pushed the door along its runners, slowly, silently. The door did not squeak; it barely made any sound at all.

He entered a dark, cavernous room. The first thing he noticed was the tremendous stench, intense and almost overpowering. The second thing he noticed was that he could not see, not at all, not even an inch in front of himself, nothing. Thank heaven he'd thought to bring a flashlight. He shone it into the bleak darkness. Cavernous wasn't enough — the room was huge. Once, it had undoubtedly held all kinds of brewing devices, vats and casks and fermenting equipment. He felt disoriented, and it wasn't simply because of his inability to see anything that wasn't directly in front of his light. The darkness was so pervasive it took him more than a few moments to figure out what was wrong.

The floor was slanted.

Ness knew why. His experience chasing down rumrunners had given him more than a little information about how alcoholic beverages came to be. The floor was sloped to simplify drainage. He walked to the river side of the room and found what he expected — a removable iron grating covering a tunnel. The tunnel undoubtedly led to the river. A simple and efficient way for a brewer to dispose of waste by-products.

A simple and efficient way for a killer to get corpses into the river, without any possibility of being seen.

Enough space to do his twisted work. The privacy he required. A way to rinse away the evidence. And when he desired it, a way to dispose of his corpses. Perfect.

Ness knelt down and examined the sloped floor. He found something else with which his years in law enforcement had made him all too familiar. The dark stains were everywhere, and there were splatter patterns on the walls.

Blood. So much blood. More than a single body could possibly contain. More than a dozen bodies could contain. Even if the killer rinsed most of it into the river, the stains remained, seeping into the wooden-plank floor, leaving its indelible reminder of all the lives lost in this sick laboratory.

Ness followed the blood trail to the center of the room, where the stains were darkest and thickest. There were bits of . . . debris, for want of a better description. Everywhere. Human flesh. Chips of bone.

He hesitantly put a finger down in the center of the largest stain. The blood was still sticky. Fresh.

This was where they had been killed, all of them, perhaps more than he could imagine.

Where was the table? He stood, scanning the room with his light. Dr. Pearce had speculated that the killer pinned the victims down to some sort of chopping block before he decapitated them. But there was nothing in the room, no furniture of any kind, nothing but the smell of blood and rotting flesh and death.

Had the killer moved on? Found another place to operate?

Or had the building been rearranged? Had he changed his operation, found a more efficient or satisfying way to kill? Or perhaps, fixed up the place for company.

Ness's throat went dry. He needed a drink, any kind of drink. Was it too late to reconsider calling for assistance?

Somewhere farther inside the building, he heard movement.

The short hairs on the back of Ness's neck stood at attention.

There was a door on the opposite wall, one that undoubtedly led farther into the building. It was a regular door, with a knob, and clear space beneath.

No light was visible beneath the door.

Creeping forward as quietly as possible, Ness crossed the room. He took the doorknob in his hand and gently turned it to the right.

The door opened.

Ness stood behind the door, following standard Treasury agent procedure. Despite the apparent darkness, it was always possible there was someone in that room. He would not make a target of himself.

Nothing happened. But Ness heard the tiniest sound, so quiet it was almost not there at all. Muffled. Indistinct. Were there words? Was it just a humming noise? The wind whistling through a crack in a window?

A floorboard creaked.

Ness put away the flashlight and took his weapon out of its holster. He always preferred to avoid guns. Even when rousting mobsters and rumrunners, even though he was a crack shot, he almost never drew his weapon. Led to more trouble than good, he thought.

This time his gun was going into that room first.

Back against the door, he swung through the opening, his weapon at the ready. He looked left, looked right, saw nothing. The stygian darkness permeated this room just as it had the last. He could see nothing. But there was still that noise . . .

Slowly, cautiously, he put away the gun, reached for his flashlight, and shone it into the center of the room.

There was a body, a body bound and gagged. Another victim.

Wait — no. He detected movement, squirming. It was hard to see clearly, but that body was still alive. That was a living, breathing person, someone he might still be able to save.

He took three steps forward before he could see clearly enough to make the identification.

Edna!

Her eyes went wide as soon as she saw him. She rocked back and forth, straining against her restraints. Was she trying to tell him something?

"Sweetheart. My God, what happened?" He grabbed the gag in her mouth and pulled it down to her neck. "How did —"

"Look out!" Edna screamed, shattering the darkness and sending shivers down his spine. "Behind you!"

The blow struck him on the back of the head, hard, delivered by some kind of blunt instrument wielded by someone with enormous strength.

He dropped to the floor, his head aching, confused, disoriented. He rolled over onto his back, squirming.

He saw that hideous face again. Hovering over him. Smiling.

Frank Sweeney.

"I thought you'd never get here," he said, and then he swung the axe handle once again, and then for Ness the world became entirely black, and then it was nothing at all.

59

His head throbbed. That was all he was aware of at first, all he could be certain about.

The next thing he realized was that he could not move. He was pinned down, immobilized. He was sitting in a chair but tied up, his hands behind his back, his legs tied to the legs of the chair.

But he was alive. That was the part that surprised him most. How could he still be alive — and intact?

And what had happened to Edna?

He was still in the brewery, still in the stark expansive room he had first entered, the one with the sloped floor that led to the tunnel. The overhead lights were on now. And there was a table, a table painted with blood, soaked with the remnants of countless victims.

Apparently he was going to be the next. If he just tipped forward a little, tilted at a ninety-degree angle, he would be spread across that table, unable to move or run or resist, just like all the other victims before him. The killer could lop at his head at his leisure. At his pleasure.

Ness pulled at the ropes that held his hands, burning his wrists. It gave, just a little. That was something. Maybe if he kept working. Maybe if he ignored the pain and kept pulling at it . . .

"Hello again, Mr. Safety Director."

Frank Sweeney emerged from the darkness, still smiling, limping a little, carrying a chair in one hand and an enormous butcher knife in the other.

He placed the chair at the opposite end of the table and sat facing Ness, the knife spread across his lap. "Now this is an interesting role reversal, isn't it? I hope you slept well."

Ness found it hard to speak. His head was still cloudy, muddled. But one thought emerged clearly. "Where's Edna?"

"The tramp left you."

"I want to know what you've done with my wife."

"Do you really care? About the woman who betrayed you? Or are you just reciting the lines you think you're expected to say?"

"Tell me what you've done with my wife!"

"She's safe."

"Is she alive?"

"Does it matter? She's out of your life."

"I want to know what you've done with my wife!" Ness shouted, rattling his brain. "Answer me, Sweeney. Now!"

He smiled. "Call me Gaylord Sundheim."

Ness closed his eyes. The man was mad, that much was clear. He was everything the alienist had said he would be and then some. He was nothing like the criminals Ness had spent his adult life chasing. He was something different, something utterly unfathomable.

He was playing with Ness, like a cat might toy with a crippled mouse.

"All right then, Gaylord. What are you doing with my wife?"

"Helping you."

"How is kidnapping my wife helping me?"

"Well, you must admit, you weren't having much luck finding me. I thought perhaps we should up the ante. Give you some added incentive. I gather you were able to solve the code on the postcard?"

Ness looked at him blankly.

"No? You found this place some other way? What a clever man you are. Well, the important thing is that you got here."

"You wanted me to catch you?"

"I wanted you to come here."

"Why?"

"Well, you took away my usual source of material, didn't you? That was a naughty thing you did, Eliot. Burning Shantytown. Why did you have to do that? Was I really hurting anyone? Paring down the numbers of the bums and vagrants and crooks and whores? The dead and the dying." He laughed a little. "The most dangerous game. I've hunted rabbits that gave me more trouble."

"Perhaps it's time to go back to the rabbits."

"Perish the thought." He playfully flipped the knife back and forth. "Do you remember what I told you? Back when I was the one tied to the chair and you were the one playing all high-and-mighty?"

"As I recall, you said you thought killing people would make you a god. Doesn't look to me like it worked out for you."

"No, it didn't. And I was forced to ask myself — why? What was I doing wrong? And then it came to me. I'd been taking the easy way out. Selecting people of no importance, offering little resistance. Easy marks. I needed a challenge."

"And that would be?"

"Killing my greatest enemy. You."

Ness made no reply.

"I was getting a bit bored with the chase, to tell the truth. You were never going to catch me."

"I did catch you. Your lawyer took you away."

"Because you were being naughty. You broke the rules."

"I was doing what I had to do to put away an insane murderer." He paused. "And as it turned out, Merylo and I were right. You're the Mad Butcher."

"I suppose I am."

"Shouldn't you be at the Sailors' Home? It's after curfew."

"Funny thing about that. Mrs. McGovern is no stricter about attendance now than she was before. Even after my cousin gave her a stern lecture."

He glanced down at the knife in his lap. "This is my favorite. I have many. I keep all my knives and axes and things under the floorboards. You missed that, too."

"It was dark."

"You always have an excuse, don't you? Did you find the bodies?"

Ness felt his skin crawling.

"I guess that means no. There are many, you know. I haven't begun to share all the work I've done. I've just let a little bit of it trickle out at a time, just enough to keep you interested."

"I guess you like being in the papers, too."

He thought for a moment. "Yes, I suppose I do. It makes me feel . . . alive. Noticed. Like I really exist. I get quite a charge out of it. Is that what it does for you?"

"I don't know what you're talking about."

"Yes, I thought it was. You're not so much with the wife, so you look for your thrills elsewhere. You and Edna may not have had much, but you and the papers, now there was a love match. While it lasted. Did it hurt very much?"

"What?"

"When your lover broke up with you. When they turned on you."

"That was your fault."

"No. Yours. You just can't see it. It was inevitable. Fame is a harsh mistress, and Americans love to see their heroes fail. It's a national obsession."

"You're sick and twisted."

He sighed. "That's what my cousin keeps saying."

"Does your cousin know you're using his brewery as a slaughterhouse?"

"Well, we've never discussed it. But I have to wonder if he doesn't know, or at least suspect. When I look into his eyes, I see a bit of myself reflected in them. I wonder how he keeps it all inside. I can't. You know what I mean?"

"No, I don't."

"I see the same thing when I look into your eyes, Eliot. I see myself in you."

"You're insane."

"And your point is?"

"I'm nothing like you."

"You're wrong." All at once, Sweeney lurched forward, still holding the knife. He pushed the table out from between them and leaned in close to Ness. He began sniffing him.

"Yes, we're very alike, aren't we? We share the same infirmity."

"You're babbling."

"Horrible stuff, isn't it? Liquor. We were better off when you were keeping it off the streets. Too bad they repealed that law."

"I may take a drink now and then, but I'm nothing like you."

"Are you sure? You're still a young man, Mr. Ness. Best not to speak imprudently."

"We are nothing alike. Nothing!"

"Oh, you're wrong."

"Stop sniffing me!"

"But I like your smell. Very much. You smell like me!"

"I'm nothing like you! I'm not insane!"

"Yet."

"You're a madman rhapsodizing about the joy of killing people. I'm a college graduate. A man of science. Rationality."

"And I'm a doctor."

"Were."

"But science can only take you so far. And as for rationality . . ."

"I am nothing like you!" Ness bellowed.

"Temper, temper."

"You disgust me!"

"Now you're hurting my feelings."

"I'll hurt more than that!"

Pushing off from his bound feet, Ness sprang forward and sank his teeth deep into Sweeney's neck. Sweeney tried to pull away, but Ness dug in hard, clenching tightly. Blood seeped out, trickling through his lips. Sweeney screamed in pain; his cry reverberated through the large empty room.

Sweeney tried to raise his knife. Ness dug in even tighter, gnashing back and forth, swinging the man's neck, tearing the skin at each end.

While he held Sweeney tight, he managed to get his right hand free.

Ness bit in with all his strength. Sweeney screamed again and dropped the knife. Ness released Sweeney and grabbed the knife with his free hand. He thrust out with it, but Sweeney managed to step back just far enough, just in time. Ness whipped his hand behind his back and cut his other hand free. He turned back toward Sweeney —

Sweeney was gone.

Quickly, Ness bent down and cut his legs free. He stood. His legs ached and trembled but they still supported him.

"Where are you, Sweeney?" he shouted. "Where's Edna?"

From the next room he heard a piercing cry. A woman's voice. "No!"

Ness flung open the door and raced into the next room, still wielding the knife. Edna was on her knees in the center of the room, terrified, still tied up, but alive. Alive!

Sweeney was off to one side, tugging at the floorboards.

Ness had to make a quick decision. Sweeney first. He raced that direction.

The lights went out.

Suddenly, Ness was plunged into darkness.

"Sweeney! Talk to me. Tell how you're going to become —"

Sweeney sprung out of the darkness and dove at him, tackling him front and center and knocking him to the ground. Ness crumpled down, head first. The knife flew out of his hand and sailed across the room.

60

Ness did his best to recover, but he'd been shaky ever since he came to, and the fall knocked the wind out of him. He started to push himself up off the floor, but Sweeney fell on him again, punching him in the solar plexus. He fell back again, breathless. Sweeney's shoes battered his ribs.

How could he fight a man he couldn't see? He flailed his arms in the darkness, hoping to stop the next blow before it landed. He wasn't able to stop the kick, but he was able to grab the foot and hold on to it. He forcefully swung it to the side, causing Sweeney to lose his balance. He fell down, at last giving Ness a chance to get to his feet.

He hurt. All over, but especially in the abdomen. He had a hard time catching his breath. He was weak and he knew it. And Sweeney seemed to thrive on the darkness. Ness needed light.

He whirled around, trying to cover all

directions at once. "What's wrong, Sweeney? Scared of me?"

He was trying to bait the killer into talking, but of course, Sweeney was too smart for that. He had an advantage and he knew it. He would keep it.

A few moments later, Ness felt another blow on the side of his face. His eyes were beginning to adjust to the infinitely low lighting, but not fast enough. Another blow clipped him on the other side of the face. Ness swung out, trying to grab Sweeney's arm, but he missed.

He realized this was hopeless. He could not possibly win this fight. Sweeney would batter away at him until he fell. Then he would finish him off, on the table. And then —

Then a miracle occurred. The lights came on.

Out the corner of his eye, Ness saw Edna, still bound, pulling the cord that turned on the overhead light with her teeth.

He didn't have time to thank her. Sweeney was at his right, lunging. Ness managed to step away just in time. He stayed between Edna and Sweeney, not letting him get near his wife or the light cord.

"What are you going to do now, Mr. Safety Director?" Sweeney snarled. "Bite me again?"

"Whatever it takes." Ness faced him, bracing himself for the next attack.

"You can't win, you know." Ness could see the wound on his neck, still bleeding profusely. It was grotesque, as if he'd been mauled by a wild animal.

He could still taste Sweeney in his mouth. What had he said about the two of them? And how much they were alike?

He wiped his bloody spit away. "This is over, Sweeney. Give up."

"You must be joking. I'm much stronger than you. You know I am. I will take you apart and then I'll start on your wife. Then I'll flush you both down the river. You're weak, Ness. Weak."

He lunged, but this time, Ness did not step aside. He waited until Sweeney almost had him, then swiftly grabbed his extended hand, crouched down, and flipped Sweeney over his shoulder. Sweeney flew several feet, then crashed face first to the ground. He did not get up.

"You may be stronger and bigger," Ness said, heaving, wiping blood from his mouth. "But bigger isn't always better. Especially in jujitsu."

Ness stumbled over to Sweeney, knelt beside him, then flipped the man onto his back. His eyes fluttered open.

"You're under arrest, Sweeney. I'm taking you in."

Sweeney's nose was smashed and bloody. His eyes were red and his face was smeared with his own blood. And he smiled. "You can't do anything to me."

"I'm going to put you away forever, Sweeney. Or send you to the chair."

"But Mr. Safety Director . . . that's impossible." He spat out a tooth. "I've been certified insane, more than once. You can't incarcerate me. All you can do is have me locked up. Some sweet sunny bughouse. Like the Sailors' Home." The smile began to fade. "But I'll get out. And I'll find you. And Edna."

Ness glanced at his wife, still bound, breathing heavily, watching and listening to every word.

"I'll make sure that doesn't happen."

"How? With your vast political influence?" He began to laugh, coughing up blood with each chuckle. "There's nothing you can do. I'll kill you, Ness. And your wife. I'll cut you both up and there's nothing you can do to stop me!"

Just a few feet away, Ness saw Sweeney's knife, still lying on the floor. He dove for it . . .

He clutched it tightly in his hand.

"You have two choices, Mr. Safety Director. You can kill me. Or I kill you. Eventually."

Ness raised the knife high in the air. He pointed the knife toward Sweeney's throat.

"Do it, Ness. You know you want to. Do it!"

"I don't want to. But — my wife — I have to protect my wife!" His hand trembled in the air.

"You're just like me."

"I'm not!"

"You are. Kill me, Ness. Kill me now!"

The thick blade of the knife inched closer . . .

"Stop!"

Ness dropped the knife and jumped to his feet.

Six men entered the room. Led by Congressman Sweeney.

Mayor Burton was with him. Ness didn't know the other four men.

Ness staggered toward them. "Good news, Mayor. I've caught your Mad Butcher."

"Balderdash," Congressman Sweeney barked. "Thank God you told me what you told Ness, Mayor, so we could get here in time." Congressman Sweeney marched past Ness to his cousin. "Frank? Good Lord —

look at your neck! What happened?"

Sweeney's voice creaked. "He hurt me. He hurt me bad."

"Do you see what your safety director has done now?" the congressman bellowed. "I demand action, Harold. From the mayor's office. This is the worst case of police brutality I have seen in my entire career."

Ness pushed past him. "I'm telling you, Mayor, this is the Butcher. He attacked me. He kidnapped my wife. Look at her!" He walked over to Edna and began cutting her loose. He hugged her tightly. She was crying. He gently lowered her to the floor so she could rest.

"A likely story," the congressman scoffed. "You've simply continued the harassment you began at the Cleveland Hotel. I told you then there would be legal action if you continued your desperate persecution of my family."

"Your cousin is the Torso Murderer!"

"Prove it!"

Ness drew in his breath. "Search this place. Under the floorboards. You'll find bloodstained knives. Bodily remains."

"That proves nothing. Even if the killer operated here, that does not prove he was my cousin! Anyone could've gotten in here."

"He confessed to me!"

"Was that before or after you beat him to a bloody pulp?"

Ness turned back to the mayor. "Harold, listen to me. He's the killer. Ask Edna. She knows. We've got to arrest him. Put him behind bars."

"You're not doing anything to him," Congressman Sweeney said.

"If you think I'm going to let you —"

"Even if it were true, you couldn't charge my cousin. He's not of sound mind. The proper place for him is a mental institution. I will see that he gets the care he needs."

"That's not — !"

Mayor Burton laid a hand on Ness's chest. "Calm down, Eliot. He's right. If you try to do anything to his cousin it will only start a legal battle. We'll lose and you'll come out looking like the madman." He turned toward the congressman. "It has to be someplace real this time, Congressman. Not the Sailors' Home. Someplace with locks on the doors."

"Understood. I'll take him far away. I know a place in Dayton. Good doctors. Nurturing environment. But also . . . tight security."

"That should do."

"What are you thinking about?" Ness said, veins standing out in his neck. "This man killed a dozen people. At least!"

"I'm doing all that can be done, Eliot. Calm down and try to use some sense."

"He threatened my wife. Said he'd kill her. Said he'd cut her up!"

"Well, that won't be possible now."

"I won't stand for this."

"You have no choice. You work for me."

"Fire me. I'll go to the press."

Congressman Sweeney stepped in front of him. "Then I will also talk, Mr. Safety Director. I will tell what I saw tonight. You, behaving like a madman. A knife poised in the air, seconds away from murder."

"I wouldn't have killed him."

"That's not how it looked to me. I saw an attempted homicide, plus clear evidence of assault. You could go to jail for a very long time, Mr. Ness. And wouldn't that be an ironic end to your illustrious career?"

"No one would believe you."

"After the things you've done lately? Flagrant violations of the law. This is the next logical step in your slow sad decline. Everyone will believe it, Mr. Ness."

Ness fell silent, smoldering. He turned toward the mayor. "I can't believe you'd let him get away with this. You're the one who kept telling me the people needed the comfort of knowing we'd caught the killer."

"Obviously, at that time I didn't know who it was." Burton squeezed Ness's shoulder. "This is best for everyone, Eliot. You keep quiet. Stay out of jail. Frank gets locked up where he can't harm anyone. Once the killings stop, people will soon forget all about it. Everyone wins."

"The people should know the truth."

"War is coming, Ness. It's already raging in Europe. Soon people will have more important things to think about than some crazed killer in Cleveland. Now take your wife and get out of here."

Ness stared at him wordlessly. After all this time, all this work. Could it possibly end this way? He didn't know what to do, what to say.

His wife broke the silence. "Eliot, I want to go home."

He turned to face her. "Really?"

"Please. Take me home."

Slowly, limping slightly, Ness escorted her out of the abandoned brewery.

After he watched Ness's car pull away, Sweeney thanked the mayor for his assistance. "I think we may be able to work together after all," the congressman said, smiling. "Maybe even during your second term."

"I'd like that." Mayor Burton shook his hand, then departed.

After the mayor left, Congressman Sweeney helped his ailing cousin to his car. With the help of his four men, he poured coal oil throughout the abandoned brewery, lit four torches, and handed one to each man.

He pointed toward the brewery. "Light the fire, gentleman," he said, his eyes like stones. "Turn it to ashes. Every last trace of it."

61

Merylo, Zalewski, and Ness sat together at the counter of the diner just down the street from the Central Police Station. It was Merylo's favorite place; he came at least twice a week. Agreeable of Ness to meet him here, Merylo thought, so far from the office, on his turf. First time that had ever happened.

"Here's the thing, Peter," Ness said, as he polished off his club sandwich. "I'm closing down the investigation."

"What?" Merylo and Zalewski both looked at him bug-eyed. "Why?"

"What's the point? There haven't been any killings for a long time."

"That doesn't mean anything."

"Probably won't be any ever again."

"You don't know that."

Ness hesitated a moment. "At any rate, I can't afford to devote so many resources to one dead investigation, and neither can

Chief Matowitz."

"Have you talked to the mayor about this?"

"In fact, it was the mayor's idea. He wants to put this thing behind him."

Zalewski wiped his mouth with a paper napkin. "Should've known. Politics. Do a clean sweep before reelection time."

"Something like that."

"I'm just surprised — well, if you don't mind my saying so — I'm surprised you're going along with it, Mr. Ness."

Ness looked away. "No sense in beating a dead horse."

Zalewski looked down quietly. "No. I guess not."

"So what am I supposed to do now?" Merylo asked.

"What you always did. Investigate crimes. Current crimes. You'll go back to reporting to Chief Matowitz. Like it used to be. You'll be happier, I'd imagine."

"Maybe so."

"Here, let me get this." Ness grabbed the ticket and put a dollar fifty down on the counter. "That should cover it. Enjoyed lunch. Hope to see you boys again soon. And thanks for all your hard work."

They watched as the safety director left the diner.

"Can you believe that?" Zalewski asked.

"Yeah," Merylo replied, as he finished off his pastrami. "I can believe it. He's a politician now. Not a cop. He'll probably be running for mayor next."

"So, are you going to do what he says?"

"He's not my boss. Not anymore."

"You know what I mean. Are you going to stop investigating the torso murders?"

Merylo stared straight ahead, his eyes fixed on the image in the mirror behind the counter. "Never."

". . . so it's really a good thing. I can be more use to the country working for the government."

Chamberlin could not hide his surprise. "Back to the Treasury Department?"

"Not this time. The Army."

"You're enlisting?"

"No. They're creating a special post for me. Where I can be of the most service. You know — war is coming."

"That's what I hear."

"We're all going to have to contribute. Pull together. Help out any way we can."

"Of course. Maybe now you'll have more time to spend with the wife."

Ness did not answer at first. "Yeah."

"Well then." Chamberlin drew his tall

frame to attention. "Best of wishes, sir. The Army is lucky to have you."

"Thanks, Bob." He started for the door. "Oh, by the way. I wasn't going to say anything . . ."

"Yes?"

"But — I know."

"Pardon me?"

"I know, Bob. I know you were the leak."

"I can't imagine what you're talking about."

"You're the one who kept feeding information to Congressman Sweeney. And then he sent it to the press. When he wanted it publicized. The secret interrogation. The Kingsbury raids. It was you."

Chamberlin looked down at the floor. "I suppose there's no point in denying it?"

Ness shook his head.

"It was nothing personal, you know. But it was illegal — all of that. If we allow our public officials to violate the law, soon there will be no law. And a guy has to look out for himself. I liked working for you. But I could see you wouldn't be around forever, not the way you shook things up. I had to think ahead."

"You going to work for Sweeney now?"

"He offered me a position, if I ever needed one." He paused. "Think I might wait and see how the elections come out first."

"That's sensible. Good politics."

"Yeah."

Ness pressed his fedora down onto his head. "It's ironic, you know. I cleaned up the police department. The mob. The labor racketeers. But I forgot to clean up my own office." He opened the door.

"Mr. Ness?"

He paused. "Yes?"

"You never said — what are you going to do for the Army?"

Ness smiled a little. "I'm going to keep people safe, Bob. That's what I do."

EPILOGUE

February 16, 1957

Ness stared at the postcard clenched in his trembling hands.

PARANOIDAL-NEMESIS, it said, in shaky handwriting. And just above that: F. E. SWEENEY, M.D. He had pasted down an article about poison. It was postmarked DAYTON, OH.

How many of these had he received over the years? Ness wondered, as he ambled back to his armchair. More than he could count. They'd started in Cleveland and followed him his entire life. Every time he moved, the postcards still managed to find him. He had tried to keep it from his wives. His third and current wife, Betty, knew nothing about them, or about Frank Sweeney, or why he had been permanently institutionalized in a Dayton mental home. Where they kept him under lock and key. But apparently allowed him mail privileges.

Ness took a drink, and as the dark whiskey coated his throat and warmed his gut a flood of memories returned. He didn't miss Cleveland. The press had been hard enough on him when he supposedly failed to apprehend the Torso Murderer. But after the alleged hit-and-run incident — he'd been drinking — they savaged him. Oh, the irony. The great Prohibition agent caught drunk driving. It was just too marvelous for the press to resist. He spent the World War II years traveling from one place to the next, advising soldiers on the horrors of venereal disease.

After the war, he returned to Cleveland and someone got the crazy idea that he should run for mayor. Worse, Ness was crazy enough to listen. Harold Burton was gone and the Democratic incumbent ran him ragged. What did he know about politics? Small wonder he was trounced. When the reporters asked Ness about his opponent's time in office, he admitted the man had done a pretty good job. And of course, the campaign gave the press another opportunity to bring up the torso murders.

The torso murders. His great failure. It was enough to make a man sick.

He should never have gone along with that deal. Letting Sweeney go. Never should've agreed. But what choice did he have?

After the war, Ness decided to go into business. The watermark venture, insurance, others. None of it panned out. He had a head for law enforcement, not business. He lost all the money he invested and a lot more besides. And now he was stuck in Pennsylvania, dirt-poor, forced to sell his life story for three hundred dollars.

It wasn't enough, not for all he had done over the years. But they needed grocery money.

"What do you think was the problem in Cleveland?" Oscar Fraley asked. "Why couldn't they catch the guy?"

"I said I didn't want anything about that in the book."

"I know, I know. Indulge my curiosity."

Ness did not answer the question. "You heard anything about profiling?"

"Can't say that I have."

"I got some friends over at the FBI. I used to want to be in the FBI, did I tell you that? Wanted it more than anything in the world. Turns out J. Edgar Hoover was jealous of me. Yeah, I got it on the best authority. He was jealous of all the publicity I attracted. He liked being the only guy in law enforcement who got good press. That's why he shafted poor Melvin Purvis. That's why he never let me in. Even spread some nasty gossip about me."

"You're kidding."

"I'm not. But that's not my point. Nowadays the Feds got this new thing they call behavioral science. They're looking closely at these crazy cases, the people who go around killing, sometimes torturing and mutilating, for no apparent reason. Crazy, yeah, but crazy how? Turns out all these guys have stuff in common, and if you know what it is, it helps you track them down. Like what the alienists used to say, only a thousand times better, more detailed. Maybe someday might even make it possible to identify these kooks before they strike. At least that's what the Feds are hoping."

Fraley whistled. "Bet you wish you'd had that back in Cleveland."

Ness nodded. "Even after I got out of there, Merylo continued to investigate the case whenever he could. I wanted to tell him, but —"

"Tell him what?"

"Never mind." Ness took another drink, a long hard pull. "Look, I really don't want to talk about Cleveland."

"But it's such a big part of your life."

"Yeah, but not such a good part. No safety

director. No Torso Killer. No hit-and-run. No mayoral race. No Edna. Just write about Capone." He fell back into his chair, his eyes fogged. "Those were the good years. Write about Capone."

"If you say so."

"That's the story worth telling. The rest I just want to forget. Now if you'll excuse me, Oscar . . . I'd like to take a little nap. Before Bobby gets home."

Fraley put away his notes and collected his hat. "All right, Eliot. We'll do it your way. But are you sure? It really is a great story. And people are always intrigued by an unsolved mystery."

Ness closed his eyes, shutting out the pain. "Unsolved to you, maybe."

AUTHOR'S AFTERWORD

This novel is based on true events. In Cleveland in the 1930s, a serial killer murdered and mutilated at least twelve people, probably more. Eliot Ness, as Cleveland's safety director, worked on the case for more than two years. The Torso Murderer was never caught, at least not according to the official records. Although I have invented dialogue and in some cases telescoped events, all the scenes relating to the case involving Ness and Merylo, prior to the climactic scene at the brewery, really happened. Most of the newspaper and radio excerpts are extracted from or based upon actual passages from journalistic accounts of the time. For dramatic purposes, in a few cases, I moved events forward in time and conflated some characters. For instance, I have allowed Merylo and Zalewski to perform acts actually performed by other officers before Merylo was officially assigned to the case. Similarly, I have combined Ness's two assistants — the first of whom was required to resign following a scandal — into the single character Robert Chamberlin, and I combined the two coroners who worked on the case into the far more prominent of the two, Arthur Pearce.

Ness never recaptured his former glory. The so-called hit-and-run incident, following a night of drinking with Edna, tarnished his reputation even further, as proved perhaps by his pitiful showing in a subsequent mayoral race. His business ventures were all failures and when he met the writer Oscar Fraley he was desperate for money. The book Fraley produced, *The Untouchables,* was a success, and after it was adapted into a television series by Desilu Studios, Eliot Ness became a household name and an American folk hero. Ironically, the series was narrated by Walter Winchell, the same journalist who broke the story that Ness was interrogating a suspect with a medical background. Ness died in 1957, about a month before the book was released, due to a massive heart attack, possibly exacerbated by alcohol abuse.

Late in his life, during his conversations with Fraley and others, Ness claimed that he had a suspect that he believed was the

Torso Killer, but the suspect was well connected to a prominent politician who arranged for him to be committed permanently to a mental institution, thus escaping arrest. At the time and for many years thereafter, no one believed him. But when Ness's adopted son died of leukemia, his wife donated Eliot Ness's scrapbooks to the Western Reserve Historical Society. Among the fascinating things contained therein were postcards from someone threatening Ness with cryptic messages and bizarre jokes. One of the postcards bears a name: F. E. Sweeney, M.D.

More recently, John Hansen, a police officer fascinated by the torso murder case, began investigating it in his spare time. His efforts revealed that the cards were sent by Francis Edward Sweeney from a mental institution in Dayton, Ohio. Sweeney was a former doctor who had been in Cleveland at the time of the murders, had been repeatedly certified as dangerously insane, and whose cousin was Congressman Martin Sweeney. He was permanently institutionalized shortly after the last torso murder victim was discovered. Additionally, the diaries left behind by Peter Merylo reveal that Ness and others did in fact bring a suspect, under the pseudonym Gaylord

Sundheim, to a room at the Cleveland Hotel and interrogated him for more than a week. Merylo writes that the interviews were promising, but they were forced to release him because he was well connected.

Suddenly Eliot Ness's tall tale looked a lot more credible.

A book such as this one inevitably involves an enormous amount of research. I've made several visits to Cleveland and have had the pleasure of talking with many knowledgeable people, experts on the case, the period, and the man — including two people who actually knew Eliot Ness and were invaluable sources of information about him. I am greatly indebted to the archives of the Western Reserve Historical Society, the Cleveland Press Archives at Cleveland State University, and the *Plain Dealer* archive at the Cleveland Public Library. There are two nonfiction accounts of the torso murder case: *Torso,* by Steven Nickel and *In the Wake of the Butcher,* by James Jessen Badal. The most prominent biography of my lead character is *Eliot Ness: The Real Story,* by Paul W. Heimel. All three books were extremely useful to me as I researched and wrote this novel and I am indebted to the authors. I also want to thank John Hansen for his investigative work; writer Max Allan

Collins, one of the first researchers to understand the significance of the postcards; and Rebecca McFarland, librarian, historian, and trustee of the Cleveland Police Historical Society, for suggesting that the Torso Killer might well have operated out of one of Cleveland's many abandoned breweries.

As one of my characters says, America, and certainly the media, seem fascinated with watching heroes fail. Eliot Ness was a major force for justice in the early part of America's twentieth century, and he deserved a better end than he received. I hope this book might play some small part in helping him receive the attention and praise he deserves, even with respect to this: his least favorite investigation, that of America's first true serial killer. What we should remember is his tireless pursuit of a madman he simply did not have the tools to catch. I can perhaps be forgiven for forging an ending, consistent with the historical record, that still allows Eliot Ness to solve his last big case.

William Bernhardt

ABOUT THE AUTHOR

William Bernhardt is the author of many novels, including *Primary Justice, Murder One, Criminal Intent, Death Row, Hate Crime, Dark Eye, Strip Search, Capitol Murder, Capitol Threat,* and *Capitol Conspiracy.* He has twice won the Oklahoma Book Award for Best Fiction, and in 2000 he was presented the H. Louise Cobb Distinguished Author Award "in recognition of an outstanding body of work in which we understand ourselves and American society at large." A former trial attorney, Bernhardt has received several awards for his public service. He lives in Tulsa with his three children.

wb@williambernhardt.com
at www.williambernhardt.com